FOR YOU, THE READER...
A SPECIAL INVITATION

Come journey with us to the wildest frontiers of the heart...

Diamond Wildflower Romance

A breathtaking new line of searing romance novels

...where destiny meets desire in the untamed fury of the American West.

...where passionate men and women dare to embrace their boldest dreams.

...where the heated rapture of love runs free and wild as the wind!

"Look into my eyes, Firemaker. Would I lie to you?"

Carter had taken hold of Firemaker's arms to stop her flight from the hospital tent. He had never held her so tightly before. His hands were strong. Warm.

He stared fixedly into her eyes. "Do you understand what I just said?"

She did, for the most part.

But she also saw the look in Carter's eyes and felt the power of his touch. She wanted to tell him all that was in her heart, but until she had the words, there was perhaps no way to share this understanding, this deepest part of herself, with him.

Then suddenly Firemaker blushed a brilliant crimson. She felt the heat of her thoughts radiating from her throat and neck. She looked back at Carter and wished they might be alone. . . .

AUTUMN BLAZE

SAMANTHA HARTE

DIAMOND BOOKS, NEW YORK

If you purchased this book without a cover you should be aware that this book is stolen property. It was reported as "unsold and destroyed" to the publisher and neither the author nor the publisher has received any payment for this "stripped book."

This book is a Diamond original edition, and has never been previously published.

AUTUMN BLAZE

A Diamond Book / published by arrangement with the author

PRINTING HISTORY
Diamond edition / February 1993

All rights reserved.
Copyright © 1993 by Sandra Hart.
This book may not be reproduced in whole or in part,
by mimeograph or any other means, without permission.
For information address:
The Berkley Publishing Group,
200 Madison Avenue, New York, New York 10016.

ISBN: 1-55773-853-X

Diamond Books are published by The Berkley Publishing Group,
200 Madison Avenue, New York, New York 10016.
The name "DIAMOND" and its logo are trademarks
belonging to Charter Communications, Inc.

PRINTED IN THE UNITED STATES OF AMERICA

10 9 8 7 6 5 4 3 2 1

For Jane Jordan Browne.
Thank you
for never giving up.

The sky will change color.
The sun will grow dim.
A great rushing will fill all the corners of the earth.
From the east will come a man
With eyes warm as summer.
You will know him.
He will know you.
You will put your hand in his and walk for a time.
Clear will be the sky then,
Soft, the light of morning.
Great will be the love in you,
But deep will be your sadness,
For you will be in twilight,
And long will be the journey . . .
. . . home again.

—Medicine Woman's prophecy

AUTUMN BLAZE

PROLOGUE

*Ten miles south of West Creek Fork
Texas, 1851*

JANE HEARD WIND rush suddenly, softly, through the reaching arms of twelve cottonwoods scattered along the shell-rock bank of West Creek. Heart leaping, she straightened, her knuckles raw from rubbing Hugh's shirts against the scrubbing board.

She strained to hear her baby's cry in the shack behind her. "Mandie?" she called, her voice a husky drawl.

Only the wind replied, whispering like a worried friend. It hurried toward the shack's drooping porch, buffeting the lean-to kitchen's weather-stained tarp roof, disturbing wilted bluebonnets transplanted by the chicken shed.

To the north, scattered clouds hung motionless in a sweep of light blue sky. Jane listened for the approach of her husband's horse but heard only the whisper of hot wind across a vast sea of buffalo grass. Hugh was all right, she told herself.

Every day her husband went out for more hours than she cared to count, searching for mustangs, cottonwood for the corral fence, or quail for their supper. Sometimes he went into town.

Thinking of that, Jane shuddered. Always he came back, acting as if he'd been gone only a moment, offering a kiss and an indulgent grin as if that should make up for everything. Always he came back, smelling of whiskey.

Jane sucked thoughtfully on a scuffed knuckle. Her hands

looked old. Her back ached. She was angry again, and she didn't want to be. Frowning, she watched the ridge to the west that bounded their broad, rolling land. Good land for raising horses, Hugh claimed.

Jane wished her heart would slow. There was nothing to worry about. Their hound, January, looked dead, lying stretched out beneath the porch. 'Lassas and her two-month-old pups lay unperturbed in the shack's eastward shade. Two hens roosted in the exposed white roots of the cottonwood next to the still. The milch cow was standing by the dugout shed, ruminating.

Wind teased past the sun-bleached farm wagon. "He ain't fixed that cracked wheel yet, either," she muttered. "I wish to God I could go to town, too."

There was so much to do around the place. Every night Hugh promised to do all the work in the morning, first thing. He laid elaborate plans of how the place would look one day.

At first she'd listened. She loved him so. It was a comfort still just to watch how he held his mouth as he formed his words.

But that's all his dreams were, then and now. Words. Those convincing, pretty dreams of his teased her along, day after lonely day. They always talked of his dreams when the vast Texas landscape closed them into their shack's single room at night. If she mentioned anything practical, like him being with her during the day, he'd grow quiet. A space as broad as the Texas sky would open between them. He'd sigh.

He knew what she needed of him, but the more she needed it, the longer he stayed away. How long did it take to bring back a runaway horse, anyhow? she asked herself. Did he love the open range so much more than her? Or even his horses?

Shivering, she gathered her faded checked skirt covered with its stained muslin apron and started up the dusty incline toward the dirt dooryard. The ground felt hot beneath her bare feet. She pushed at her damp dark sleeves, stitched too narrow to roll back very far from her wrists.

Feeling as if she were suffocating, she pulled open two more buttons at the neckline of her snug bodice. The wind seemed as hot as a smothering quilt against her face, as insistent, unwelcome, and irritating as her thoughts.

She tore off her deep-brimmed sunbonnet and fanned herself with it. How was she to remain sweet-tempered and agreeable when she was always worried?

And if she complained . . . oh, then he'd look hurt. He'd give out with that sigh that meant he just didn't understand her. And she'd feel awful.

"I don't know where to God he goes," she cried, her tone strained. She threw the sunbonnet onto the crate by the doorway. "I wish to God he'd come back. I wasn't raised up to spend my life in this place all by myself, thinking I hear voices on the wind."

Looking around, she felt choked with disappointment. After two years on the place, the shack was still a sorry excuse for a house fashioned of vermin-ridden pine logs with the bark still on. The chimney leaned south. The roof leaked. She was glad her people back home in Kentucky couldn't see it.

Shielding her tired eyes against the afternoon glare, Jane loosed her sweat-damp hair—whitey-blond, Hugh liked to call it—letting the sweat dry. Almost ten hours since he rode off. Ten god-blessed hours.

"Your pa's coming back any minute now, darlin'," she called to the baby inside the shack.

To the south their land dipped and swelled like a great earthen skirt, as parched as Jane's throat, as lonely as her heart. West Creek Fork lay ten miles to the north, a windswept settlement with a one-room trading post, a few shacks, and a stone express office where the Butterfield Stage stopped on its long journey to Santa Fe and beyond.

The town might as well have been a hundred miles away for all the protection it afforded them.

Ten hours. Jane clutched at the oval gold locket hanging from a thin chain around her neck. Scarcely bigger than a robin's egg, it still looked shiny new. Soon Hugh would be back to open her bodice, button by button, and kiss the locket where it hung between her breasts. At least that hadn't changed.

She loved her square-jawed man. She wanted his big callused hands on her hips, his insistent lips on her mouth. For those brief moments when she had him that way, he belonged only to her.

Edging closer to the open doorway, Jane paused, listening again. The wind sighed as if weary of trying to gain her attention. Slipping inside, she pressed the plank door closed and threw the heavy iron bolt into place. Leaning against the door, she fought to slow her breathing.

If Hugh could see her, he'd gather her briefly into his arms and kiss away her terror. "You durn little fool," he might say.

The shack smelled of sun-warmed pine, gun oil, and savory rabbit stew simmering in the lean-to kitchen. It looked untidy with the morning's dishes and cutlery still in the bucket. Garden greens were going limp on the table.

Her grandmother's clock stood on the shelf, ticking, a reminder that somewhere there was a civilized world. It was ten of three.

Two years before, her ma had begged her not to go with Hugh, but Jane hadn't listened. She couldn't when passion ran hot in her veins for the cocky horse trader with his tales of Texas come to do business with her father. She would have followed Hugh Tamberlay anywhere.

"Ma!" Mandie chirped, struggling in her plump-legged awkwardness to climb from the cradle. She flashed a bright, two-toothed smile. "Ma!"

Mandie couldn't walk yet and was due for a fall if she

kept trying to get out of the cradle alone, Jane thought. Hugh had promised to make something bigger for her.

"Take care, darlin'," Jane murmured, shaking off her thoughts, giving her baby a forced smile.

The summer before, Mandie had taken eighteen unimaginable hours to arrive in the back room of the general store in West Creek Fork where Jane and Hugh had ridden in search of a midwife. She still marveled to think she hadn't gone home to Kentucky for the birth.

Forgetting the muffled wind outside, Jane lifted Mandie from the pine cradle and sank into the rocker. The child was already twenty pounds and plump as a goose. Amanda Tamberlay would someday be a startling beauty, tall like her pa, strong like Jane, with Hugh's searching gray-blue eyes and that whitey-blond hair that ran in Jane's family.

Mandie rooted for Jane's breast, her pink mouth moist and sensuous. Jane dreamed of stairstep boys and pink-cheeked girls in smocks, their voices filling the Texas silence with the security Jane had so recklessly left behind.

She thought of her pa, too crippled up from a fall to work. She thought of her ma, whose letters, written by Jane's literate younger sister, voiced too clearly her secretmost fears: *Caint you cum home two vzit? We worre 'bout them injuns out there.* Hugh hesitated reading those portions to her.

Rocking stiffly, Jane stroked Mandie's hair. "I dream of nights . . . in my lover's arms." Her mother's favorite ballad brought a lump to Jane's throat. "I may see him nevermore. He's gone away, 'cross fields so green, to wait beyond the shore."

Sunlight slanted through the oilcloth window. The air inside the shack looked like swirling gold. With the door closed, the temperature inside rose quickly, bringing a sheen of perspiration to Mandie's round cheeks.

Jane found herself listening again, her breath held high in her throat. Her heart started galloping, and her milk wouldn't come down. Scowling, Mandie suckled all the harder.

Leaning back, Jane tried to picture the sweet-pea vines growing by her ma's porch, and the fields, briars, and wooded country lanes of home. She thought of her ma's smile as she waved her last good-bye. Her eyes began burning.

Scowling as intently at the doorway as Mandie scowled at her reluctant breast, Jane stiffened her resolve. Hugh was all right. He was a straight shot, coolheaded and fearless. He'd be back any minute. He hadn't gone into town.

Abruptly she put Mandie back in the cradle. Wiping sweat from her neck with a corner of her apron, Jane buttoned her bodice. Not town. Not all night. Not again. At the window she squinted through the filmy oilcloth, hoping to see Hugh riding in.

Several dark shapes stood on the western horizon—riders on paint ponies with fourteen-foot lances. Long leather fringes fluttered from their thighs and heels. The wind paused, leaving Jane staring in silent stillness until her eyes went dry with disbelief.

Comanches.

Spinning from the window, Jane found she couldn't draw breath. This was such foolishness, she told herself, fists aching. There was nothing out there. *Nothing*.

The wind swooped against the shack, tearing at the tarp. It swept dust into devils that danced in swirling cones across the barren dooryard. This was a very bad attack of nerves, indeed, she thought, looking out again. There was nothing. . . .

Dark shapes hurdled toward the shack. Six, seven . . . ten.

For an endless moment Jane watched them. The bleached sky looked serene. The buffalo grass rippled in waves as if stroked by a giant, invisible hand. Blood began pounding in her ears, filling her with a hot, throbbing sensation that time had stopped and would never start up again.

The cradle tipped wildly from side to side. "Mama!"

"Where's your pa when I need him?" Jane screamed, wanting to hit something, and finally pounding her fists against her thighs. "Damn him. Damn him straight to hell!"

It was too late, and had been for some time. Whirling, counting herself already dead, Jane stared at the high-backed oak bedstead where she made love with Hugh, at the heirloom cherrywood rocker where she nursed Mandie. She stared at the two sorry-looking wobbly cottonwood stools Hugh had made where they sat together at supper each night.

Mandie pitched over the cradle's side onto the floor, her fall cushioned by the pink-and-yellow Jacob's-ladder quilt Jane's sister had pieced and scented with jasmine. Mandie's big gray-blue eyes filled with tears.

A faint thunder came from the west now, an ominous, unflagging approach of unshod ponies. Faint whoops made Jane think of lobo wolves.

The women of West Creek Fork had told her what to do.

Slowly, woodenly, Jane lifted Hugh's Hawken rifle from the mantel. Its striped maple stock looked beautiful, deadly. She couldn't hope to hold off ten Comanches. Even a man couldn't load and shoot a flintlock fast enough for that.

But if she fired at once, and loaded again quickly, she would have time for two shots, one for Mandie, one for herself.

Loading and priming, laying the charge in the pan, she drew back the rifle's stiff hammer and aimed the long heavy weapon at her child. She stood thus for five precious seconds, then ten. Fifteen.

Sweat broke out on her forehead and rolled into her eyes. As she pictured Mandie with blood in her whitey-blond hair, Jane's belly cramped. The pain spread to her heart, her lungs, her brain.

Knees buckling, Jane began to gasp. She couldn't do it. Hugh would come. Hugh had to come.

How many times had they talked of this, the women of West Creek Fork, talked as dispassionately as if killing children were as easy as wringing the necks of chickens. Jane had sat listening, shivering in the Texas heat, nodding, saying yes, she understood. She could do it if she ever had to. A quick death. The only way.

But what if by some impossible chance those riders were just in her imagination? What if Hugh returned to discover she had gone mad and shot Mandie for nothing?

Even if Comanches *were* thundering toward the shack, they might ride away again, satisfied with Hugh's seven Kentucky horses in the corral. Hugh was not there to tell her what to do.

Hesitation meant excruciating death. Jane tried to imagine her baby in the hands of savages, bloody and dying. She tried imagining unimaginable tortures inflicted upon herself, but nothing came to mind more horrifying than seeing her baby dead by her own hand.

Mandie crawled toward the rag rug covering the root cellar's trapdoor in the floor. Her plump fingers closed around the fringe. Jane's clenched jaw began aching. She laid the rifle on the table. There was no time to reconsider.

Plucking up Mandie and the quilt, and giving her baby a fierce hug, Jane kicked away the rug, exposing the two-foot-square trapdoor.

"I won't let them get you, darlin'," Jane whispered over a dry throat.

Fumbling to lift the thick iron ring lying in the chiseled recess, she wrenched up the heavy trapdoor. Losing her grip, she dropped it. The door crashed back down, almost on her toes.

With a savage grunt, Jane tore up the trapdoor and threw it back against the floor. Panting, she clambered one-handed

Autumn Blaze

down the narrow ladder; Mandie held her mother's hair with one hand and her bodice's neckline with the other.

Flinging Mandie across a heap of burlap bags filled with potatoes and grain, Jane burrowed a hiding place deep in the corner against the musty Texas earth. In front of her baby she pushed her trunk that contained Mandie's christening gown, her ma's wedding dress, and her most treasured family likenesses.

Nearly lost in the folds of the quilt, Mandie tried to work her way back into Jane's arms.

"Hold tight, baby girl," Jane whispered, worried that Mandie would be frightened once she was closed in the darkness. "Mama won't be long. Killin' Comanches can't be all that hard."

She couldn't seem to take her hands from her child's warm cheek. So precious, so small . . .

It took all her strength to straighten in the cramped space, to step back and turn away. Nothing on God's earth would ever look the same after this day, she thought. If something happened to her, how would anyone know who Mandie was? she wondered suddenly. Surely if Hugh was not there now, he was dead. He had better be.

Reaching beneath her sweat-soaked hair, Jane unlatched the locket and chain Hugh had given her on their wedding day. She rubbed a trembling thumb over the engraving on the back.

In the darkness she couldn't see the marks Hugh said meant, "To my beautiful bride Jane from Hugh Tamberlay, 1849. All my love and affection, always." She didn't care what it said now. He had brought her here, left her to this.

Breathing hard, Jane stared at the two tiny pictures inside the locket, of Hugh and herself painted by her mother in pokeberry ink. It was too dark to see their smiles. She didn't want to see them, to think of her mother or home or any of her dreams soon to be dead.

Placing the locket against Mandie's chest, Jane smiled.

"For luck, darlin'," she said. "We'll have stories to tell one day."

The locket slid into the folds of the quilt. Frantic, Jane tied the chain around Mandie's plump wrist. Mandie waved and gurgled. The locket thunked once against her forehead, causing her to pout.

"Shhh," Jane whispered, laughing softly, her throat thick. "No crying. You don't want them Comanches to hear—" Her voice broke. Lifting Mandie's tiny curled fist to her lips, Jane kissed each finger tasting of her own milk.

Turning away abruptly, squaring her shoulders, Jane climbed back up the ladder. Dropping the heavy trapdoor back into place, she was just covering it with the rag rug when the dooryard erupted with thundering hooves. Mandie's startled cry came up through the floor.

Comanches on horseback swooped past the window and galloped in circles around the shack. Already Hugh's freed horses were galloping wildly in every direction. 'Lassas and January were baying amid the fray.

Half-naked warriors leaped to the hard-packed ground, whooping triumphantly at their find. Their raw shouts sliced through Jane's pounding head.

Edging away from the rug, Jane never cast her eyes back toward it. She ignored the faint cries coming from below. Woodenly she lifted the rifle from the table. With chilling calm, she laid another charge of gunpowder in the pan, pulled back the hammer, and brought the long heavy iron to her shoulder. "Dad-blamed horse-hungry sons of bitches," she whispered, squinting along the sights.

The door slammed open. The latch hung from the splintered door frame like a broken arm. Golden eddies of dust swirled into the low room. Looking into a pair of black eyes accented with grainy red paint, Jane felt her heart harden to stone.

He had a face shaped like a gourd, with smooth, shoulder-length, bluntly cut black hair. Between his eyes was a deep worry crease. She aimed at it and squeezed the trigger.

The explosion flung her backward. The shack filled with the stench of gunpowder. Her shoulder ached from the rifle's recoil. As she struggled to sit up, nine warriors crowded through the doorway and stared at the mangled man she had killed at point-blank range. One let out a whoop of disbelief.

Without thinking, she leaped to her feet, grabbed the carving knife from the bucket of dirty cutlery, and lunged. The nearest warrior knocked her arm aside, but not before she sliced his chest. Bright red blood cascaded down his dusty coppery skin.

He frowned at the blood as if unable to believe she was resisting. She stared at it, too, confounded to think his blood was the same color as hers.

Stumbling back, she threw herself through the low doorway into the lean-to. Grabbing the pot of rabbit stew, she scrambled back, throwing a boiling arc of broth, meaty bones, and hot bits of vegetables at the advancing Comanches' faces.

"Git out of my house, damn you!"

Yelping like madmen, they swarmed toward her, filling her home with their musky odors of mud, sweat, bear grease, and buffalo dung. A blur of black-painted scowls loomed over her. One merciless hand gripped her upper arm. She glared into black eyes filled with alarm and anger as bright as her own. He said something guttural as he struck her down.

She fell hard.

The boards felt gritty against her cheek as she was dragged toward the doorway. She couldn't tell if she was resisting. She heard the clock begin chiming three, and then it, too, fell in a crash.

Out in the dooryard, the Comanches fell on her. She fought until her last sensation was of something hot moving along her hairline. Even then she was trying to drag herself back toward the shack to protect Mandie. It was in flames.

In time— a minute, an hour perhaps— darkness settled around Jane's shattered thoughts. She dreamed of Hugh as he had looked on their wedding day, with his easy stride and charmer's smile. He held out his hand. She remembered taking it, believing that with Hugh Tamberlay she would find everything she had ever wanted.

Briefly Jane realized she was lying near the corral, her bared breasts burning in the afternoon sun, her hands flexing, open, closed. Open, closed. Somewhere, Mandie was crying loudly.

Jane couldn't move. From behind her lashes the sky looked far, far away. A dark shape appeared briefly over her, held something high, silhouetted against the glare. Mandie's cries seemed nearer.

Then there was nothing but the tiny flame of Jane's anger, burning in the darkness.

NEW MEXICO TERRITORY

1871

ONE

The Sangre de Cristo Mountains

GRASPING THE EXPOSED root of a wind-twisted pine, Firemaker pulled herself atop the rocky escarpment. In the valley below, dawn mist lurked along the twisting creek. She sank to a boulder and tugged her tattered brown calico skirt over worn knee-high moccasins.

Closing her eyes, Firemaker allowed the night's disturbing dream to return. There had been a woman's face, so clear in the dream but gone now. Firemaker had smelled that compelling fragrance she couldn't name. She'd felt a caress as soft as love itself, and had known a sense of belonging and safety unlike anything she knew while awake.

Then darkness. Darkness.

Shaking herself, Firemaker forced her eyes open. It came to her so seldom now, the dream. It could mean nothing. She didn't want to know who or what she dreamed about . . . not really. Not anymore.

Wind murmured in the pines. From this vantage point the village below looked bleak and deserted. None of the women was up yet. Only a hint of smoke curled from the sooty tops of twenty-two ragged buffalo hide tepees. Piles of bones, baskets of yap root, sleeping liver-colored dogs, and debris of every kind littered the trampled spaces between each tepee.

Despite everything, Firemaker liked this grassy valley bounded by piney ridges. She wished they could stay, but the old men were talking of moving again, to the foothills where it was warmer. Unfortunately this new place was near the valley where the white men had built a fort five years before.

The war chief, Snakehorn, wanted to kill the soldiers there and burn their buildings. His younger brother, Walking Bear, wanted to go deep in the mountains where no one would disturb them. Unable to decide, the People, as they called themselves, did nothing.

Wiggling her big toe where it stuck through cracked, worn doeskin, Firemaker gave an aggravated sigh. Could they not see that each time they moved they grew more tired, more hungry, more desperate?

The People were dying, in body and in spirit. Few had strength left to resist the inevitable coming of the white man. Only Snakehorn, and those who followed him, went on fighting. He spent the lives of his warriors as cheaply as reservation Indians were said to gamble chits at agency stores.

Snakehorn intended no reservation for them. Believing his peyote visions, he continued to raid deep into the white man's Texas. He came back, not with horses, new blankets, or corn, but with fresh scalps. No woman dared ask him why the whites never retreated as he promised, or why so many Comanche husbands and sons died—two last time, three the time before.

Their village had become a place of widows, orphans, and old ones with grief-dulled eyes. Depression filled each woman with quarrelsome bitterness, each child with unspoken fear, the old people with apathy and despair. Even Four Toes didn't know what to do.

Four Toes had once been their most daring raider. Twenty summers before, he had come back to the People with seven of the tallest horses anyone had ever seen. He brought home a long iron thunder stick no one knew how to fire—a flintlock rifle. He brought two scarcely weaned liver-colored pups and her, Firemaker. He had enjoyed great honor in those days.

The People had called her Little White Hair then, but in time some came to believe she brought Four Toes and the People bad luck. Sickness came. The buffalo became harder to find. White men moved deeper and deeper into their lands.

Four Toes had always protected her. It wasn't seemly for a warrior to hold a child in such regard, especially a girl child, a *white* girl child who yearned to be a full-blooded Comanche son, but Four Toes had.

Lately, however, grumpy old Four Toes looked at her in the full bloom of her young womanhood and no longer saw the treasure he once ransomed for two hundred prime Mexican ponies. He saw in Firemaker an uncommon creature as tall as Comanche women were short, as lean-limbed and slim as his women were stocky, as quick-witted and fresh as all his people were dull and discouraged.

He saw in white Firemaker everything the Tall Horse Comanches could never be again. He hated her now, or so it seemed sometimes, she thought with a sigh.

"One day you'll leave me," Four Toes once shouted in anger.

"I'll stay with you until you die," she had vowed. At five summers, her resolve had been as firm as it was at twenty.

The day Firemaker entered the women's tepee to bleed for the first time, however, she had cried bitter tears. No more would the women allow her to braid his hair, bring his food, or hear his tales in twilight. To do that would have made her his wife, and he would have no more wives. All his wives had died. His heart was sore. The People wanted no more bad luck, and neither did he.

Firemaker had made herself a tepee next to her father's but no more could she pretend to be Four Toes' son, more proud than Snakehorn, more wise than Walking Bear. She had become a woman, destined by age-old custom to serve like a beast of burden and obey like a slave.

She would never forget when Four Toes told her she was white. She had been seven summers, tall, skinny, and stubborn. Her white mother fought well, he told her. Little White Hair's white blood had strong medicine.

When Four Toes presented her with a gold amulet he said had been tied to her when she was a baby to protect her from evil spirits, she had been greatly disturbed.

"You are more than a daughter, more than a son, to me," Four Toes had said. "I took you from the burning earth. You have become my heart. My spirit. My firemaker."

Bearing her new name, Firemaker had walked proudly after that. When she was fifteen summers, however, she realized that Four Toes had probably killed a white woman for her. She saw little honor in such a deed. She asked again about the story. Her doubt about the rightness of what Four Toes had done filled her with confusion and shame. He'd explained, but she was left feeling dissatisfied. That was when the dreams began.

Young braves had long since given up leaving horses for her. She wanted none of them. The women of the tribe still disliked her. Girls her own age conspired to exclude her, then and now.

Firemaker was born of the enemy, destined to be alone.

Pushing back waist-length blond hair, greased and twisted into braids in the Comanche fashion, Firemaker sighed. She could do nothing about the color of her hair, eyes, or skin. She supposed Walking Bear had no intention of offering horses for her. He had caught Snakehorn's murder-lust. She was better off alone.

Still, she dreamed of a mate with stature. She dreamed of great love and a family, but no man worthy of her walked among the slovenly campsites of the People's dwindling village. Snakehorn had led them all into death.

In the village below, Snakehorn's wife, She-Who-Weeps,

slipped from her tepee and went to the creek to fetch water for Four Toes, her father-in-law. Moments later she found Firemaker's buffalo horn filled with water lying beside Four Toes' tepee.

Not seeing Firemaker anywhere, She-Who-Weeps kicked the horn aside, replacing it with her own. She sauntered away as if proud of her petty deed.

Firemaker shook her head. From the scooped neckline of her worn red shirt, she pulled her timeworn oval of gold. The amulet had saved her from white man's measles, which decimated the People when she was eight. It kept her from dishonor when Apaches held her at ten. It would keep her strong all the days of her life, she thought, somewhat consoled.

How clever the whites must be to create something so small, with thin scrolling lines on the front and curious markings across the back. Inserting a fingernail along the side, Firemaker popped it open and frowned thoughtfully at the faces inside of a man and a woman. Had they loved her?

The wind rose suddenly, chilling her.

Looking up, Firemaker scanned the valley with keen eyes. Below, one of the hounds began baying. Several women emerged from tepees and stood as Firemaker was now standing, listening, sniffing the air, squinting as the sun climbed over the jagged eastern ridge.

Slipping and sliding, Firemaker started down the graveled slope. Far to the south she saw a smudge of dust, evidence of someone's approach on the narrow deer trail skirting the creek.

Before she could raise a cry of alarm, she saw the tiny speck of a rider break from the distant marsh grass. Heeling his horse to a gallop, the rider was followed by another and then another.

Firemaker watched in astonishment. She counted ten, twenty, twenty-five! There seemed no end to the blue-coated soldiers bolting from the trail at full attack speed.

"White men," Firemaker whispered in Comanche, terror flooding her body with energizing heat. "Horse soldiers."

She had never seen riders approach so fast, not even Apaches. She tried to think but her brain seemed empty. The faint call of the soldiers' battle horn sounded like the frantic braying of a mule. She wanted to laugh at them, but instead a strangled cry tore from her throat.

A braying reply came from across the valley.

Whirling, Firemaker saw another detachment of soldiers now approaching from the valley's northern outlet. Where would they run, the women, the children, the old ones?

The first shots sounded like distant pops. Shooting? They were *shooting* at women and children? Where was the honor in that?

Then a third detachment tumbled down a narrow pass on the far side of the valley where Firemaker sometimes climbed to sit on the broad rocks by a brook there.

So many soldiers. From three sides now they came, the hoofbeats like endless thunder. Riders plunged noisily across the twisting creek, bearing down on her village just as Four Toes had described attacks on Texas homesteaders.

Never had Firemaker considered the terror of a Comanche attack. Her white mother must have felt like this, she thought. Below, women were running in circles, gathering small children. Dim-eyed old ones bumbled a few steps, still befuddled with sleep.

Firemaker slid her skinning knife from the tall cuff of her right moccasin. With her attention riveted on the advancing soldiers, she scrambled down over the rocks. She would earn great honor today, she thought. With each touch of the enemy, with each daring coup, she'd prove herself a true warrior.

Four Toes stepped from his tepee and straightened with stiff-boned effort. As calmly as if he had been expecting an attack, he turned to face the soldiers. A rust-colored blanket about his shoulders slipped, revealing a copper-skinned chest scarred twenty years ago by a carving knife.

Sharp gravel tore into Firemaker's worn-out moccasins as she climbed down the last few feet to the grassy valley floor and started running. A bullet whizzed over her head. Another dug into the trampled grass beside her.

She threw herself to the ground. From the tops of her eyes she watched the riders gain the village. She felt the reverberations of a hundred hoofbeats pounding the ground. She smelled gunpowder and heard rifle reports thump through the air.

A woman nearby, Walks-with-a-Limp, clutched her chest, gave a cry as blood gushed between her fingers, and fell.

Horrified, Firemaker sprang to her feet, her knife held at her side, ready to strike. "This can't be!"

Riders thundered past her, their saddle gear clanking, firing at will. An old woman, Humming-Bird, fell like a dropped blanket. Shot through the neck.

Four Toes' best friend, Crooked-Stick, clutched his face, fell to his knees, and went limp onto his hands.

Shouting a command in English, an officer ordered the mounted soldiers to wheel for another assault. She turned to meet them.

Heeling his mount to a gallop, his pistol spitting bullets hither and thither with fiery flashes, one horse soldier started toward her.

She lunged at him. The horse swerved. Ten yards away, the blond soldier yanked his horse around in another prancing circle and stared at her in amazement. Baring his teeth, shouting something, he urged his horse to a gallop again. He was headed directly for her.

At the last minute the horse shied, veering to the side where it overran Small Eagle, a boy of four, standing beside the body of his mother.

"No!" Firemaker screamed.

Her knees buckled. Gulping back cries of disbelief, she fell on all fours. This couldn't be happening. She must be dreaming. This onslaught felt like the end of the world.

Willing herself to stand again, she saw the same murderous rider bearing down on her again. She lashed out with her knife, aiming for the horse's throat. She missed. Rearing, the horse pawed the air and threw his rider to the grass.

Without a second thought, Firemaker flung herself on the husky bluecoat's back. Her knife plunged into the sod only a breath from his sunburned ear. She heard his shout of surprise as he struck backward at her, catching her chin, knocking her head back.

When Firemaker could think again, she was face-first on the ground, the weight of the man's body on her back, his hand crushing the nape of her neck.

She couldn't breathe, for the grass and soil smashed against her nose. Her spine felt ready to snap. Her lungs were flat. She had lost the knife. Her wrist stung as if broken.

Thunderous horses plunging through the village began slowing. The shots ceased, leaving a wind-whispering valley hush broken only by wailing children. Desperate to fight, Firemaker tore at the bluecoat's side until she felt his blood wetting her fingernails. Yelping, he struck her head.

Dazed, she lay staring blankly across the grass at burning tepees. Comanche women gathered and huddled within a circle of tall, snorting horses. Panting blue-coated riders glared down at them, pistols at the ready.

So many bodies lay twisted and still in the grass. An outstretched hand, a tangle of bloodied black hair. . .

Soldiers waved smoking pistols, shouted orders, and turned about, looking annoyed. Her father stood clutching his blanket, head high, white tendrils of thin old hair streaming down his back. He used the long thunder stick to support himself.

Dismounting in front of Four Toes, two soldiers seized

the rifle and clubbed him with it. Four Toes dropped to his knees. Firemaker wanted to run to her father, but she had no strength left. In moments she expected to be dead.

Stealing a peek at the soldier astride her, Firemaker felt a hot wash of curiosity, fear, and rage flood her body. He had an alarming glaze to his pale blue eyes. His hair was almost as pale as hers. He was trying to kill her.

Feeling momentarily overwhelmed, Firemaker closed her eyes and concentrated on the pain in her neck, her back, her heart. Father, don't forget me when I'm dead, she prayed to Four Toes. She wanted to be standing next to him so they could go together to the next life. For the first time she wondered if she would go to the same place as the People.

Straddling the Comanche bitch's squirming body, twenty-five-year-old Sergeant Clay Burdette drove her mud-painted face deeper into the matted buffalo grass. If she smothered, or her slender neck snapped, no one would be the wiser.

No one was looking, he thought. He could do it. He could kill the bitch with his bare hands.

Her body stiffened. She struggled harder. Her fingers gouged his forearm as deeply as she had gouged his side. The harder she tore at his flesh, the deeper he pushed, deeper, deeper.

He was growing erect now, feeling power and pressure build in his groin. He was going to do it. He was going to—

"Hey!" Something hit his shoulder.

Clay Burdette went on squeezing, pushing.

She was tearing up fistfuls of grass, fighting for air.

He was going to do it. He was going to . . . He fumbled for the hem of her skirt. He felt the firm round flesh of her bare backside.

"Hey. Clay!"

The voice was close by his ear. Something hit his shoulder hard enough to break his concentration.

Clay started shaking.

"Hey, g'dammit. Don't you hear? The colonel wants 'em over there. What're you doin'? Take the necklace if you want it, but let her up. You're killin'—"

Clay's body screamed for release. He pushed. He strained. Necklace? He wanted satisfaction. He wanted the bitch dead. What damn fool had time to think of fuckin' Comanche quill-and-bead necklaces when he could be . . .

Losing the focus, Clay released his quarry and spun, lashing out. "Whaddaya want? Get away from me!"

Tom Mosie ducked and punched Clay's shoulder again. "You gone crazy?"

Disoriented, Clay ran a shaky hand over his sweat-drenched face. He felt suddenly cold.

Mosie's closely set cornflower-blue eyes bulged. His pimply cheeks looked an ungodly red. The skinny corporal's lips drew back over yellowed teeth. "Jesus, Clay, you looked like you were tryin' to rape her and kill her at the same time. Can't do neither. The fightin's over. There ain't a Comanche buck in the whole place. We've been shooting old women and little boys. I feel like shit."

Clay gave a disgusted sniff. His voice came out ragged. "Comanche hags are the best torturers on the face of this earth. They need killin'. Comanche bastards grow up to scalp softheaded fools like you. Get outta my way."

He *had* wanted to kill her, Clay thought. The idea had come over him the moment she lunged at his horse. In the heat of battle, he liked killing. To kill a woman . . . how often did he get a chance like that? Look at them legs.

Mosie straightened and looked nervously toward the troopers surrounding the ragged women and naked Comanche brats. He scratched his chest. "They look half-starved."

Autumn Blaze 25

Some old Comanche fart was speaking to their mangy-bearded scout, Timber McTigue.

Heart slowing, Clay glared back at the young woman lying blue-faced between his splayed legs. She was staring blankly in the direction of the crude skinning knife he'd knocked from her hand. Damn Mexicans, trading knives to Comanches. Oughta be shot. A tingle went through his body. Maybe he had killed her after all. She looked dead.

Her greasy blond hair lay tangled around her face. He was just comprehending the color when he thought of what Mosie had said about a necklace.

Goddamn, she was wearing a small locket on a leather thong. It looked like real gold.

Just as he was about to reach for it, her slender sun-browned arm lashed across the grass like a snake's tongue, grasping the skinning knife, and swung, catching Clay's cheek in a cool slice that left his jaw and throat bathed in sticky warmth.

"Look out!" Mosie yelped, gawking at Clay's split skin.

Clay caught Firemaker's wrist and bent it until the knife was pointed at her left eye. "Cut me, will ya, bitch. . . ."

Mosie seized his arm. "She's got blue eyes! Well, gray, anyway. Look. Look, goddammit!"

"Gimme that locket," Clay hissed, grabbing at her shirtfront while trying to twist the blade into her.

He was about to rip her shirt clean off to find that oval of gold when pain exploded in his groin.

Kicking like a wild mustang, she scrambled away. She had the knife still, and she was going after Mosie now.

"Here comes the lieutenant—" Mosie was saying as she lashed at his back. He whirled just in time, gave a cry, and swung, his fist connecting with her jaw.

She went down hard, gray-blue eyes closed, her outstretched arm stiff as a stick.

Coughing, Clay lay doubled around his privates. He

watched Mosie stomp on her wrist and jerk the crude knife from her fist.

"Wild little bitch!" Mosie said in a voice squeaky with fright.

White or not, Clay thought, she was going to be goddamned fuckin' sorry she'd ever cut his face. She'd be sorry she was ever born.

A lanky officer with pale hair and a sissy blond mustache approached and dismounted. The brass buttons on his coat front glittered in the morning sun.

"Gentlemen, the colonel requests all prisoners be brought to the middle of the village. Are you wounded, Sergeant Burdette?"

To keep from spitting on the West Point asshole's perfectly buffed black boots, Clay clamped his teeth together. "No . . . sir."

Deftly pocketing the skinning knife, Mosie interrupted. "Lieutenant, sir, look't this'n's hair. I think she's white, but she's mean as a wolverine bitch."

The young woman stirred. She opened eerie pale grayish-blue eyes that looked strange in her tanned, mud-smeared face. The three men stared as her gaze focused and moved from one to the other of them.

Blushing, the slim young officer extended his hand. Not a drop of blood smudged his dove-gray gauntlet. "Ma'am, are you all right? May I assist you to your feet?" He leaned over her. "Have you been a captive long?"

With a flash of white teeth and a throat-tearing growl, she lashed at him. Her reach fell short. She collapsed back in the grass, wincing, closing her eyes.

Leaping back, the lieutenant blinked and swallowed. "Pardon me."

Clay started to laugh, but his cheek oozed warm, thick blood into his mouth. He spat into the grass. "I say this bitch is some kinda goddamned Comanche albino, and I shoulda tore out her throat when I had the chance."

"That'll be enough, Sergeant," Lieutenant Graham said, trying to look stern.

Not by a damn sight, Clay thought, struggling to his feet. He hobbled away toward his horse. He'd have more than her necklace before he was done.

TWO

Fort Bradley
Maguey, New Mexico Territory

AT TEN O'CLOCK the parade ground felt as hot as ninety degrees. Colonel Jedediah Chiswell stepped from his cool stone office onto a freshly raked gravel walk. Tugging braid-trimmed cuffs over thick wrists, he strode angrily toward the corral at the northeast corner of the grounds where his Comanche prisoners were being held.

No walls confined the heathens, just a pine-rail fence. The fort itself had only a fieldstone wall surrounding the adobe buildings clustered on scrubby tableland. No man could approach or flee unseen for three miles on all sides.

Near the adjutant's office, Jed's buckskin-clad scout joined him. "Morning, Colonel. Hotter'n hell itself today, ain't it?" Timber McTigue claimed to have been a buffalo hunter once, and still smelled like one.

Ignoring McTigue, Jed took note of troopers loitering near the quartermaster's store. At his approach the men sprang to attention and saluted.

A trickle of sweat began to creep down Jed's temple. He hated New Mexico Territory. Back from the mountains less than twenty-four hours, and already he found disorder at every turning. "Exactly what happened with the Comanche prisoners last night?" he demanded of McTigue. "The morning report was incomplete."

"Some jackass was trying to get at the white woman."

Jed's jaw ached. Western recruits were the worst he'd

28

ever had the misfortune to command. Thieves and whoremongers, the lot of them.

Since marching the Comanche women and children from their burned village down the pass, that white captive had given his men nothing but grief. They'd tried to talk to her, but she spat on them. They'd tried to pry her from the savages, but she fought them as bitterly as any Comanche.

One woman was not worth this much trouble, Jed thought, certainly not one as acclimated to Indians as this one seemed to have become.

How would he explain this rabble to his commanding officer at Fort Kirby, he wondered, or his superiors in Washington? One lousy old man, fifteen ragged squaws of various ages, six dull-eyed girls, four dirty little boys, a suckling infant in a cradle board . . . Lord have mercy, he must've been insane to take them. The paperwork would be endless.

On McTigue's advice, Jed had written President Grant himself the week before, saying he'd found Snakehorn's village. He'd given his word that the war chief would not escape this time. When Washington found out not a single warrior had been in the camp when Jed ordered the attack, much less Snakehorn, he'd be a laughingstock.

"You fixin' to find her people and send her home, sir?" McTigue's sunburned cheeks rounded above his split beard.

Jed's lip curled. She was better off dead, he thought.

At the corral fence Jed indicated he wanted to speak with her. Two troopers cautiously ducked between the fence rails, revolvers drawn.

Seated apart from the rest, she sprang to her feet, wary and defiant. Jed shuttered. He'd never seen a white woman move like that.

Summoned, Sergeant Clay Burdette stepped forward, black sewing-thread stitches bristling along a slash from his cheekbone to his chin. He saluted and stood at attention, eyes glittering defensively.

"Burdette, you were seen among these Comanche prisoners last night." Jed pinned the handsome blond weasel with his most intimidating stare.

"Not me, sir. I was in the hospital tent all night."

Aware the man was lying, Jed asked, "Are those fresh scratches on your neck?"

"Musta been my razor, sir. Duller'n shit."

At Jed's command McTigue questioned the white Comanche. Her replies sounded angry. Abruptly McTigue drew the colonel aside. "Sir, I *told* you I seen Snakehorn. We got his tribe here. She calls herself Firemaker. She says he'll be comin' real soon. It sounds like she said 'vengeance' for something stolen. Keep these people a few extra days, sir, and Snakehorn'll walk right up to your office door."

Jed stiffened. "What do you mean, it 'sounds like' she said vengeance? Do you, or do you not, understand the Comanche language?"

McTigue shrugged. "It ain't always easy, sir. There's as many dialects as there are bands of these heathens."

Loath to trust the man again, Jed wondered if there was yet a hope of saving what was left of his reputation. Snakehorn's capture and transport to the reservation would dishearten Indians from all tribes across the southwestern theater. Jed would be promoted and transferred back east. His wife, Olivia, *might* remember how to smile.

Grinding his teeth, Jed started back toward his office. He'd have to—

Behind him the white Comanche gave a shout and scrambled between the fence rails. A starburst of surprise flooded Jed's chest as her body slammed against his back. She circled his shoulders with grimy arms and gouged at his eyes.

"Get her off me!" Jed yelled. With all his strength he seized her arms and twisted her body to the ground.

Three troopers fell on her. Immobilizing her, they held

her spread-eagle at his feet. Her clothes were dirty, her knees scabbed and bloody. She glared at him as if he were the devil himself, babbling what he knew instinctively were curses.

Jed staggered back, panting, revolted. "What the hell is she saying, McTigue?" His voice betrayed emotional disarray. He swept the assembly with a scathing look that silenced all titters.

"She keeps pointing to Burdette, sir."

Shuddering, Jed dusted his cuffs. "Corporal Mosie, fetch a washerwoman to clean this . . . this female. She stinks of bear grease. Then I want her kept in the stockade until I can think what to do with her. Burdette, come with me. I have a few questions for you."

At dawn Firemaker could scarcely believe she'd survived a whole night in the stockade. She was so tired she couldn't think. What was she going to do?

Wailing inside, but showing no outward sign of it, she paced three steps from the flat iron bars along the north wall of the cell to the solid stone wall on the opposite side. She refused to admit how afraid she was.

The suffocating building had no windows, only a few auger holes near the rafters for ventilation. The floor was cold, hard-packed dirt. The walls were so thick, she could scarcely hear the anxious murmurs of the women in the corral outside.

Separated from Four Toes, she had no way of knowing what he was thinking and no hope of helping him. Since the attack, and coming down from the mountains, Four Toes had not spoken to her. He hadn't allowed anyone to dress the gash in his temple. He seemed too stunned to comprehend this final devastation of the People.

He might die without her, she thought. She dropped to her haunches to keen softly in her throat. Four Toes might think she wanted to be with these white men, and that was not true. She felt nothing for them. Nothing. Not even curiosity.

Stroking her bare throat where the gold amulet had been torn away in the darkness of the corral the night before, she wondered how she would survive now without it.

She was trapped. There were eight cells in the stockade. Eleven men had slept in them the night before. Thankfully they were outside now, working. She was alone, free to wonder what spirits she had offended to find such terrible bad luck.

The door leading to the dayroom where the guard sat at a desk opened. Heart leaping, Firemaker pressed herself into the cell's farthest corner. After a lengthy pause, a short white woman with fawn-brown hair peeped in. She smiled hesitantly.

Clutching a huge black box or package to her bosom— Firemaker wasn't sure what the object was—the short young woman stepped into the cell block. "Hello. Good morning."

Firemaker gave no sign she had heard or understood, but she did. This was her first glimpse of a white woman. She couldn't help but steal peeks at her.

Smiling, the plump, pretty thing put her hand protectively over her rounded belly and whispered something over her shoulder. She was seven or eight months with child, Firemaker concluded.

A taller, thinner woman in a fancy sky-blue dress stepped in. This woman's hair was dark brown and strangely curled. She regarded the cramped cell block with disgust and began fanning herself with thin white fingers. As she glanced at Firemaker her face whitened. "God's nightgown, would y'all *look* at her!"

Olivia Chiswell couldn't take her eyes from the unkempt, ragged excuse for a white female squatting in the cell's corner. "If that was me, Mary, I'd rather be dead. Don't get so close to those bars. You heard what they said she does."

"All women bite if teeth are the only weapons they

have," Mary Graham whispered. "She is *not* trying to eat anyone. Mercy. The troopers act more frightened of her than if she were a Comanche warrior."

Olivia stared at the white Comanche's ragged shirt and dingy gathered brown skirt. The creature was wearing a fringed rawhide belt trimmed with a scruffy gray squirrel's tail. Some kind of fringed skin bag decorated with the paws of some hapless mountain cat dangled next to it.

The white Comanche had bulky, badly stitched moccasins that went to her knees, fringed along the sides and at each heel. They were cracked and nearly worn through.

It was her mane of long greasy blond hair that most offended Olivia's sensibilities. "How can she stand herself?"

Mary Graham forced a cheerful smile. "If we're patient, Livvie, she'll realize we want to help."

Maybe you want to, Olivia thought, giving her neighbor a sniff of disgust. The little fool. What use was helping this creature? It was highly unlikely Jed would notice or care if she tried to do her so-called Christian duty. All he cared about was capturing that Comanche, the one called Snakehide, or whatever. Jed was so caught up in his obsession he hadn't turned to her in weeks. Olivia scarcely considered herself second to a Comanche war chief.

Damn Jed for bringing her to Fort Bradley, Olivia thought, squirming as her snug bodice dampened under her arms. Damn New Mexico Territory for being such a blazing pest hole, and Goddamn the United States Army straight to hell for making it necessary that she marry a Yankee in the first place simply because that was all that had been left to her after the war.

"I feel dirty just bein' in the same buildin' with her," Olivia muttered, resisting scratching her forearms as she cast sidelong glances at the glowering white Comanche.

Mary cautioned her. "Anyone who survives captivity must be very courageous, Livvie."

Olivia tossed her curls. "How she survived is only too apparent, sugar. She should have killed herself rather than —well, all I can say is, Jed should have had her drowned instead of thrown in the creek. She wouldn't let them touch her with soap. If she gets the chance, she'll slit our throats. Y'all wait and see."

"Hush, Livvie!" Mary opened her Bible. "Good af-ter-noon, Firemaker." She was using the scout's absurd English translation of the white comanche's name. "I am called Ma-ry. This is O-li-vi-a. Blessed are the poor in spirit; for theirs is the kingdom of heaven."

This was too much, Olivia thought, hating anyone and anything drawing the focus from herself. Watching Firemaker's feral gray-blue eyes, Olivia plucked nervously at her throat where her new necklace hung. Y'all are doin' so well, sugar, I think I'll just take a little stroll."

Edging toward the door, Olivia wondered if Clay Burdette was at the powder magazine yet, indolently smoking in the shade. Naughty boy. Did he think this locket entitled him to a kiss? Well, it didn't. It never would, but he didn't have to know that. She couldn't abide those stitches along his cheek. He was ugly now. But he was quite a diversion. She couldn't seem to resist that hungry glint in his eye.

Shouting, the white Comanche sprang to her feet. Mary gave a squeal and fell back from her place near the bars. Firemaker's sun-browned arm reached between them. She waved frantically.

"What did I say?" Mary gasped, holding her throat.

Olivia jerked Mary toward the door. "Jed should have her in the sweatbox! Just *imagine* what a Comanche buck must be like." Her blood tingled to consider such a thing.

The dayroom sergeant swaggered in. "What the hell's the fuss in here, ladies?"

Olivia pushed at his belly. "Get out of the way. Let us out of here."

Trying to get around the grinning man, Olivia lifted her

eyes and saw her tall, uniform-clad husband silhouetted in the sunlit stockade doorway. Her heart froze. Automatically she laid her hand over the exposed locket hanging around her neck.

"What are *you* doing here?" Jed asked, stepping into the dayroom.

She couldn't think. "Mary . . . needed my . . . help."

"Colonel," Mary interrupted, her eyes bright. "Firemaker seems to want Livvie's necklace. Why, do you suppose?"

The necklace? Stiffening, Olivia tried to comprehend *how* Mary Graham could conclude such a thing. "My . . ." This was too much. She would have to swoon.

Jed stepped closer. "Let me see it, dear."

Knees weak, Olivia grabbed the doorjamb for support. "This ol' thing?" She curved her lips up. Would he suspect? Would he guess . . . ?

"If we give it to her, she might be more willing to communicate with us." To the sergeant Jed said, "Get McTigue over here right away."

Saluting half-heartedly, the man lumbered out. *He* suspected, Olivia thought sickly.

"Livvie," Jed said, waiting impatiently as if she were an errant schoolgirl, "Let me *see* it. I'll get you another."

Wishing she'd never set *eyes* on that cracker Clay Burdette, or listened to his lewd insinuations because she was so bored, or accepted his trashy little trinket as a lark, Olivia tore the chain from around her neck. "Here then. Give her anything she wants."

The moth-eaten scout swaggered in, smelling of chili and onions. "Got a wild hair, Colonel?"

After only a brief, scathing pause, Jed explained.

Nodding, and then listening to Firemaker's shouts, McTigue gave a startled laugh. "By damn, sir, she says Miz Chiswell's doodad *belongs* to her. Somebody stole it offa her the other night. Remember, she was jabbering about something when she jumped you. She called it a charm. I didn't know what the hell she was talking about. It's from her white parents, she says. Where'd *you* get it, Miz Chiswell?''

Olivia's stomach rolled over. Backing away, she choked out,"*Hers*?"

Clay had given her a locket *stolen* from that . . . It could only mean he had. . .

Olivia couldn't swoon. Too many glistening globs of tobacco-stained spittle littered the hard-packed dirt floor at her hem.

Firemaker shook the bars and demanded in English, "Walk! Hand!" She shook her dirty open palm at Olivia.

Jed frowned at the locket. "This looks twenty years old, Livvie. I've never seen it before. Where *did* you get it?"

Dabbing sweat from her upper lip, Olivia rolled her eyes back and sagged against Mary's shoulder. "This place is too close."

Purpling, Jed hissed, "Get outside then," and exited without a backward glance at her.

Mary stared after him. "I've never seen Jed so rude," she whispered, steadying Olivia. She looked ready to swoon herself.

"I have," Olivia snapped.

Hurrying after her husband, Olivia found him polishing the locket on his sleeve and squinting at the worn engraving.

"'To . . . my . . . bride from . . . Hugh Tamberlay,'" he read. His lips thinned. To the sergeant on duty he barked, "Sound assembly." He turned saber-sharp eyes on Olivia. "Either *you* stole this from our white Comanche the other night, or someone else did . . . and gave it to you."

Wearing her most wide-eyed expression of innocence, Livvie gazed up at her husband, "W-what a thing to suggest, sugar."

Several minutes later Firemaker was dragged from the

Autumn Blaze 37

stockade by two badly scratched troopers. The moment she was outside, she broke free and lunged into the assembled ranks. She leaped on Sergeant Clay Burdette. Chaos erupted around her with laughter and shouts of alarm.

Olivia twisted away. First the heathen, then her? It couldn't be borne. She'd ruin the weasel. Would Jed strike her? Olivia was wondering, oblivious to the ensuing commotion. He probably wouldn't do anything, and with that thought she was suddenly so furious she started to stalk away.

Jed caught her arm. His fingers cut deep. "*Him?*"

"And why not?" she hissed. "If you would spare me a little of your precious attention, offer me a scrap of affection, a wife's *due*, such things wouldn't happen."

Four men dragged Firemaker back into the stockade, a task not unlike stuffing a wolverine into a box. Olivia wished she could express her rage like that.

Wiping a bloodied nose, Clay was brought before the colonel. "Sir, I—I, uh, *sold* that locket to Livvie."

Groaning at the humiliating use of her familiar name, Olivia snapped, "*Missus* Chiswell to you, trooper. That's right, sugar. He *said* it was an heirloom, the thief."

Jed's expression looked carved in stone. "*Private* Burdette will forfeit six weeks' pay—"

"Aw, Colonel!"

Ignoring them both, Olivia sidled away, swinging her skirts. She didn't hear Mary's whispered questions as they started for officers' row.

As Clay was dragged, swearing protests, into the stockade Olivia was certain that by suppertime she'd know exactly how to handle Jed. At least she now had his attention.

Firemaker sprawled face-first onto the cell's dirt floor. How foolish to think the guards had been about to let her go, she thought, her knees burning. She listened as they locked the heavy iron door behind her.

They put the man who had strangled her during the attack on her village, and had later robbed her in the corral the first night, into the opposite cell. Bur-dette, she thought. Lowly Coyote-brain Bur-dette.

"Goddamn sonovabitch," Burdette was yelling as they locked him in. "What'd I do? What'd I do?"

The guard snickered. "Ain't too wise diddlin' the colonel's wife, son."

Firemaker crawled back to the corner and cast Burdette a bitter glance.

He whirled. "What're *you* lookin' at, bitch?" He made a circle with the thumb and first finger of his left hand. With the other hand he stuck a finger in and out of the hole. "I ain't done with you. Not by a damn sight."

Appalled, she gave him her back.

"Hey, Comanche whore. I'm talkin' to you. I've had enough trouble outta you. I'm goin' to make you hurt more than any murderin', scalpin' Comanche bastard ever did. Goin' to make you know what it means to be had by a *white* man."

Focusing on the dirt, she shut out the biting words she didn't know but instinctively understood.

"You and them heathen bitches outside ain't never goin' to see that reservation. We're goin' to starve every one of you. Some night we'll gut them, and you, like you been guttin' our settlers all these years. We're goin' to carve off your best parts and roast 'em for supper. I'm going to wear black and *yellow* Comanche hair from my belt."

Firemaker turned, her eyes slits, her upper lip lifted as if smelling rancid flesh. She gave the white man a look of unflinching hate, filled her mouth with spittle, and spat.

"Goin' to get you good!" he shouted, throwing himself against the bars. "Goin' to tear you in two, and you're goin' to love every minute of it."

THREE

Machesney Ranch, Texas

AT THE RAIL fence, Carter Machesney tipped his Stetson low. He watched Oakley lose his grip and fall backward from the gyrating mustang. Wincing as the boy hit hard, Carter sighed. He was going to have to call that mare Dolores, Spanish for "sorrow."

Miguel, Hollis, and Joe tumbled from their seats along the fence to distract the wild mare while Oakley hobbled out of the way of her flailing hooves.

"Good job," Carter called to the boy. "You all right?"

Oakley nodded.

While the mare bucked and twisted in circles, Carter ducked between the rails. Stepping into the corral, he took a deep relaxing breath. He waved back his concerned ranch hands.

Every time he had to do this he thought of his pa, crossing a corral to face an animal capable of maiming or killing him. Carter couldn't remember how old he had been the first time he watched his pa break a horse. But he thought of him now and wished he was near.

Carter's ma had hoped for grander things than horse training for him, and had seen to it he went to Washington College. Carter had done all right there, but he hadn't been born for books. He belonged on a horse, atop a rocky escarpment, or leaping into a deep, cool swimming hole.

To be taming wild mustangs in Texas was to be a

half-broke youth again, strong, fearless, and a bit crazy. For just a while Carter didn't have to be pushing thirty, gimpy-legged and living like a hermit in the middle of the prairie, far from all he once knew and loved.

He had no intention of breaking the mare's spirit. She and he would come to an understanding. She would soon make a fine saddle horse. He'd sell her to someone with a gentle hand and a gentleman's appreciation of quality.

"Come on, now, girl. I won't hurt you," he crooned, inching closer.

She wheeled and regarded him with flaming eyes. Snorting and pawing up dirt, she twitched as he approached. When he caught the rope bridle, she reared up. He let the rope slip through his hand, controlling her as she tried to shake free.

The moment his hand touched the side of her long sleek neck, she quivered. He could smell her terror. And he understood. "It's not so bad," Carter whispered, stroking the mare's flank, looking up into her bulging eyes with calm confidence.

Slowly she stopped tugging to be away.

Soon he was stroking her legs, talking softly of the new life she'd have with all the hay and oats she could want, and a clean dry stall each night on a fine ranch somewhere.

He spent more than a half hour touching the mare all over, crooning and coaxing, until finally he was in the saddle, hunched over her neck, holding her, reassuring her as if she were a child.

"There now, girl. Let's walk around. There, there. It'll be a fine life for you. No more standing in the rain."

Two hours later Carter dismounted Dolores at the corral gate, patted her velvety nose, and watched Oakley lead her into the barn. The boys knew to treat Carter's newly broke horses as if they were newborn babes. Any man who didn't was immediately fired. Horses from Machesney Ranch were known to be the best saddle animals in Texas.

Carter limped to the trough, massaging his thigh where the old minié-ball wound still pained him, and doused his head with a hatful of cool water. At the sound of an approaching rider, Carter squinted into the late-afternoon glare.

Ranger Captain Heck Clanahan ambled in from the road and swung down from his huge horse. His round spectacles glinted gold with sunlight. "Carter, by damn, every time I see you, you look worse'n hell. Whyn't you get yourself a good Mex wife? You need meat on your bones."

Carter's accent sounded mellow compared with Heck's Texas twang. "Too busy to look." He seized Heck's meaty paw and pumped it.

"Busy, shit. If you don't watch out, you'll turn into a geezer like me."

Carter laughed. "You're the best in Texas, the ladies tell me. How's a man to compete with that?"

Heck guffawed and took off his hat, revealing squashed white hair. He sobered quickly. It was obvious he'd come on business.

Carter indicated his campsite, a lean-to beneath a clutch of cottonwoods next to the creek. "How about a touch of sipping whiskey?"

They repaired to camp stools in the lengthening shade.

"Remember me talking about that som'bitch Comanche bastard Snakehorn?" Heck knocked back his first taste and sighed. "He's been riding all over this state goin' on five years. Worst damned peckerhead lunatic we've ever seen. Army can't touch the Tall Horse Comanches." Heck belched and groaned. "How about a bit more of that?"

Carter handed over the bottle.

"Seems some jackassed colonel in New Mexico Territory attacked a few Comanche squaws and papooses couple days back. Thought one of 'em looked like Snakehorn, likely. Snakehorn's got pox scars all over his face, and them squaws is coyote ugly."

Carter chuckled. "Coyote ugly" was Heck's favorite description for a woman so homely a coyote would rather chew off his own leg than be caught in a trap near her.

"This damn-fool colonel ain't willing to admit he made a mistake. He's wrote to his superior at Fort Kirby saying he's holding the Comanche survivors prisoner until Snakehorn comes for 'em. He's counting on an attack, and some of them officers at Fort Bradley got wives and children livin' there." Heck shook his head. Then he tossed Carter a locket. "Have a gander at that."

Carter rubbed his thumb over the nearly illegible engraving on the back. "Tamberlay. What's this got to do with anything?"

Heck opened a rumpled piece of official correspondence from the commander at Fort Kirby. "There's a white woman among them Comanche squaws. Colonel Chiswell took that locket off her." He handed Carter the letter. "Sent it to us for identification."

Carter only glanced at the letter.

"The army tries to return captives," Heck went on, "but our ambitious colonel thinks she's Snakehorn's woman, so he won't let her go. General Simpson sent reinforcements, but like the letter says, the general's asking the help of the Texas Rangers. Can you beat that? Seein' as how I relish besting the army, and you like a challenge, I volunteered you for the job."

Carter's brow tightened. "To do what?"

"Find out what this white woman knows, and then escort her back to her family . . . if she wants to go."

"Go to Fort Bradley? You know my feelings on Yankees."

"Mine, too, son, but the war's been over a lot of years. Think on it this way. There's this poor woman being held by Yankee peckerheads. If they think she's been laying with an Injun, imagine how they're treatin' her. Not a gentleman among 'em. If she knows where Snakehorn is, and is willin' to tell, fine. If she don't, she ought to be let go. You can leave anytime. Tomorrow's fine."

"Tomorrow—" Carter coughed with surprise. "You want me to just ride out there and start questioning her?"

Heck cocked his head and grinned. "I'd finesse her a bit first."

Carter squinted back. "Taking her back to her family is of secondary importance to getting information about Snakehorn, right?"

Heck concentrated on pouring another drink. "Snakehorn's killed a lot of folks. He needs stoppin'."

Carter stood, his emotions beginning to smolder. "I understand that, but if I get involved, I'll be thinking of this woman's welfare. I know how Yankees get what they want from prisoners."

Heck stood, too, his belly protruding arrogantly, his six feet and five inches making Carter feel short at six two. "Do what you have to do, son, but report what you find to me first. Hold up your right hand there. Do you solemnly swear . . .

He'd be damned if he'd ride across west Texas to New Mexico Territory to tell some poor white woman, half out of her wits after being a Comanche captive for God knows how long, that he was taking her home to her family without knowing if she'd be welcomed back by them.

Trying to relax tensed muscles, Carter sat in the warehouse at Fort Kirby, reading through piles of old letters stored there. There were hundreds of them, letters written in spidery hands with homemade ink, detailing horror stories that made his heart ache. He hoped to find the white Comanche's identity among them.

His gut churning to be under a Yankee roof again, Carter felt memories of his own horror story lurking, of the snowbound prisoner-of-war camp in Illinois where he'd spent the last year of the war. He could almost taste the maggoty food and smell the stench of dying men all around.

Carter knew what some folks thought of former war prisoners, too. Those women in the Yankee hospital where he'd recovered from malnutrition and dysentery had looked at him as if he were beneath their contempt. Some might think a white Comanche woman lower than a whore, too, he thought. This woman at Fort Bradley was lucky to be alive. She needed someone on her side. She needed him. It was just possible he needed her, to give his life direction and purpose for a time.

Opening a cracked leather pouch lying at the bottom of the next crate, Carter slapped it against his open palm. At last! There were a dozen letters, painstakingly printed as if by a child, to every fort in Texas. They were from a woman named Jane Tamberlay.

He read off the dates, 1862, 1861 . . . 1855, 1854, 1853. *Have you seen my little gurl . . . ?* Each letter was printed in pencil on brown wrapping paper. *I got to git her bakk.*

Amanda Tamberlay, taken by Comanches, age one, in 1851.

Leaning back, Carter wiped his brow. Twenty years?

Also missing from the Tamberlay ranch had been seven Kentucky quarter horses, a gold locket, a Hawken flintlock, and two hound pups.

Carter pulled the worn locket from his breast pocket and stared at it. *To my bride from Hugh Tamberlay.* He wasn't going to New Mexico Territory to return a woman to her husband. He was going to find a twenty-one-year-old girl, raised heathen. His skin began to feel tight.

Surrounded by trunks, crates, and swirling eddies of dust, Carter pictured a burning homestead, a woman lying half-dead in the sun, and Comanche warriors riding off with some horses and a baby. He tried to imagine that baby grown . . . and couldn't.

Tucking the letter-filled pouch inside his shirt, he fled the warehouse for the clean dry air outside. She won't even remember being white, he thought, believing now that she needed him all the more.

West Creek Fork, Texas

Carter walked his blue roan Lonesome into a dusty four-street town along the old Butterfield Stage route to Santa Fe. The day was windy and overcast, promising a storm.

At the county courthouse he'd located the Tamberlay homestead on the original county plat. Ten miles back, he found the broad, rolling place abandoned, the remains of corrals and some charred weathered rafters of a one-room shack long buried in buffalo grass. Not a ghost stirred as he rode past.

West Creek Fork was lined with false-fronted, sun-scorched stores. At a redolent livery displaying the signboard TAMBERLAY & KEENER, Carter dismounted. He was grateful Jane Tamberlay's old letters had made his search this easy.

A middle-aged man emerged from the livery barn's shadowed doorway. Carter's small-rowled spurs chinged in the dust as he approached the man. "Hugh Tamberlay?"

"Ed Keener. Tamberlay don't come around no more. I run the place now."

Shaking hands, Carter made small talk and then asked, "Does Mrs. Tamberlay still live around here?"

The liveryman spat a long stream of tobacco juice onto a nearby prickly-pear cactus. "What's a stranger want with her?"

"I bring good news, I hope. Where'd you say the Tamberlay house was?" He flicked the man a gold eagle.

Pocketing the twenty-dollar gold piece, the liveryman sucked his teeth. "I didn't."

But Carter saw the direction of the man's glance.

Unbuckling his gun belt and looping it over his saddle, Carter left Lonesome to a nose bag of oats and started up the street. He made the hill without his thigh aching too much.

The wind-whipped Tamberlay house faced away from town. Opening the paint-bare picket gate, Carter crossed the yard and paused at the porch's sagging steps.

The thought of going inside made him break out in a sweat. As he knocked, a lace-edged white curtain twitched in the parlor window.

A young woman came to the door. About eighteen, she had light blond hair tied back, accentuating plain features. A pincushion was tied to her wrist. She held a quilting needle between tight, pale lips. Around the needle she said, "What."

"Afternoon, miss. I'm Carter Machesney with the Texas Rangers. I'm looking for Jane Tamberlay." He swept off his Stetson and gave a slight bow.

She began closing the door. "Ma don't see strangers."

"Excuse me, but I won't keep her long." His opinion of the Tamberlays began to plunge.

A woman's husky voice called from the rear of the house. "Corinna, who is he? What's he want?"

Corinna Tamberlay gave Carter a withering look. Leaving the door standing open, she hurried down the hall. Returning a moment later, she bit out, "Ma will see you. I can't offer refreshment."

"Thanks all the same."

The hall's sand-scoured plank floor seemed to tilt as Carter stepped inside. As he entered the cramped parlor, the drapes drawn against the afternoon heat, the spinning in Carter's head subsided. He drew a ragged breath.

Horsehair chairs, a divan and tables overloaded with whatnots lined the walls. Heavy picture frames tilted on wires from the cornice molding. Everything was covered with prairie grit. In the far corner stood a black parlor piano.

Several tintypes and fading daguerreotype photographs in homemade frames stood in ranks upon its top.

A woman scarcely in her forties entered from a rear door. She clutched a partially stitched quilt block. "Leave us, Corinna."

Crimson, Corinna Tamberlay yanked the pocket doors together.

As Jane Tamberlay approached, her right foot dragging, Carter matched stares with her. Her yellow hairpiece swept low over her forehead, almost covering her left eye. The natural hair in her bun was the palest blond he had ever seen.

Her twisted left cheek drew toward her brow, giving her a winking, humorless expression. She lifted her face aggressively. "What do you want?"

Every speech Carter had rehearsed along the way fled his mind. "Ma'am," he said with exquisite care, "I have startling news. You might want to sit down."

"I'll stand. What is it?"

"I don't know how to tell you this without upsetting you, but you look strong, so I'll just say it. I may know where your daughter is, your daughter Amanda."

Several seconds passed. Her expression softened. She began to sag. "You've seen Mandie? She's . . . alive?"

He hastened to assist the woman to the divan. Crouching before her, he withdrew the locket from his breast pocket. Years had etched a thousand fine scratches all over it. Teeth marks indented one edge where someone had bitten in to see if it was real gold.

She took the locket, but her hands began shaking so badly she had to drop them and the locket to her lap. "It was almost new," she whispered, her bottom lip quivering. "I—I can read them words now. They was just chicken scratches before. 'To my bride . . . ' Why, it don't say my name like Hugh said it did. It don't say 'love and affection always.'" Her mouth hardened.

After a pause Carter said softly, "A white woman has been found among some Comanches in New Mexico Territory. It might not be your daughter. Twenty years is an awfully long time out west. But she had this locket. If she's your daughter, I'll bring her home . . . if she wants to come, and . . . if you want her back."

Without hesitation Jane said, "I want her." Trembling, she opened the locket. Her brows tilted. She shut her eyes, and Carter watched her lashes go wet.

Straightening, Carter swallowed a suddenly thick lump in his throat. "Ma'am, you'll excuse me, I hope, for not staying, but I'm starting for New Mexico Territory tonight. If this woman isn't you daughter, I'm worried about getting your hopes up."

Jane's voice came out strong. "It's Mandie. I know it." She nodded to herself. "I always knew she was alive somewhere. Hugh looked for her, but he said all the little girls rescued from the Indians were too old to be her. We tried to go on, but when the war came, Hugh wouldn't look no more. He said Mandie had to be dead. Even if she survived, he said she'd become Comanche."

"I won't force her to come if she refuses," Carter said.

After a moment Jane Tamberlay pushed back her hairpiece, exposing a patch of scarred, hairless scalp the size of a greenback-dollar bill. Another jagged scar made by a tomahawk stood out just above her left ear. It was edged with a dozen darning-needle stitch marks.

She held her mouth in a peculiar slant. Her hand was trembling. "Comanches don't take the whole scalp, Mr. Machesney, just a strip. I won't make Mandie stay if she don't have no feelin' for me after all this time, but . . ." Her voice broke. "I got to see her once before I die. It's all that's kept me goin'."

Carter pried the locket from her fingers. "I'll be giving this back to her. What can you tell me about your daughter?"

Jane indicated the pictures on the piano top and struggled to stand. "Her eyes were blue. Light gray blue. She had my whitey-blond hair."

In a partially burned wedding picture, Carter spotted an attractive man standing alongside Jane. There was another likeness of Jane holding a newborn wearing a long white dress.

Without a word Jane handed the second picture to Carter. "Wait," she said, and Carter didn't move while she dragged out of the parlor, down the hall, up the stairs, and back again. He felt compelled to help her, as if he were sending out a rescue party for himself when he was a prisoner of war.

Offering a yellowing, tissue-wrapped package, Jane whispered, "Mandie's christening gown. My best things survived the fire. They was in a trunk in the cellar. They didn't open it. Good-bye, Mr. Machesney. Godspeed."

At the parlor door, Carter said, "As soon as I've seen her, I'll send a telegraph message. You'll have to be patient, Mrs. Tamberlay. If I'm to bring your daughter back, she'll have a lot to learn."

As if trying to imagine her daughter grown and no different from a born Comanche, Jane looked puzzled.

"It could take weeks to . . ." Carter couldn't bring himself to use the word "tame" in front of this woman. "I'll see myself out, ma'am."

She didn't speak as he left.

Outside the sky looked dark and forbidding suddenly. Carter was surprised to find himself exhausted. Corinna was waiting at the picket gate. When he reached her, she seized his coat sleeve.

"I confess to eavesdropping, Mr. Machesney. I think you're dead wrong about all this. Pa told me Comanches never take sucking infants captive. They killed Mandie. Twenty years ago."

Carter could see how frightened the girl was. "Miss Tamberlay . . ."

Not letting him finish, she glared at the package. "If my sister survived, she's not my sister now. I want Ma to live out the remainder of her days in peace. The doctor says she has less than a year. Let her forget."

"I understand how you feel—"

"No, you don't. I can't say this without sounding ugly, but I don't want my sister to come back. Every family for miles has buried someone mutilated by Comanche savages. West Creek Fork won't ever accept her. I won't. Mandie's haunted my life. I hate her!" Dashing tears from her cheeks, Corinna twisted away. "Go away and don't come back. I'm warnin' you."

FOUR

Fort Bradley stood at the edge of the Apache range of the Sangre de Cristo Mountains. The land thereabouts was riotous with yellow and lavender wildflowers. Piñon pines, scrub oak, and juniper dotted the low foothills rising west of Red Creek.

A crumbling adobe saloon and a string of shack-style chippie cribs lined the sun-drenched freight road leading away from the sutler's store by the fort's gate. South lay the sleepy village of Maguey.

In the afternoon heat the fort looked like a mirage, a rough patch of civilization in a sea of grass. To the west rose the rugged battlements of bluish mountains. Only freighter wagon trains passed by on their way to Sante Fe fifty miles away.

Hot and dirty after five days on the trail, and with his canteen empty of its last bitter drop of water, Carter urged Lonesome the final mile. He dreaded consorting with men whose blue uniforms would set his teeth on edge, but it wasn't the first or last time he'd set aside his own feelings to help someone.

At the gate he hailed the guard, marveling to think this collection of pale pink rock, raw pine, and rosy-colored adobe buildings protected by only a few adobe walls and rail fences could be called a fort.

A middle-aged corporal approached and saluted as Carter

dismounted. "We just got word this mornin' you was comin', Captain Machesney. Our colonel's out with a patrol three days now. He don't know about all this." He indicated about fifty peaked canvas tents in the middle of the parade ground, housing the recently arrived reinforcements from Fort Kirby.

To the left was officers' row, to the right two long barracks sporting sagging porches. To the south were stables, a wagon mechanic's yard, and a storehouse. North stood a formidable stone stockade adjoining the guardhouse. Around the perimeter were gardens and corrals.

Downwind, on the eastward bank of the creek, was a collection of packing-crate shacks, lean-tos, and dugouts housing laundresses and officers' servants, wives of black troopers. There were dogs asleep in the shade and small ragged children chasing chickens.

"The colonel's goin' to find it mighty interestin' to have a Texas Ranger underfoot when he gets back," the corporal said, winking as he escorted Carter to his quarters, a cramped, spare room in the barracks. The thick adobe walls smelled of Yankees.

"What're the chances of a bath?" Carter asked, not wanting to meet Amanda Tamberlay smelling of the trail.

"Only bathin' tub belongs to the colonel's wife. Want to borrow it?" The corporal winked, showing several gaps in his teeth.

Carter plucked a bar of lye soap from his saddlebags. "I'll use the creek, thanks all the same."

Stripped to the waist, Carter soaped from hair to belly and then sat idly scrubbing his socks in the icy creek running behind the farthest garden. In the twilight, he frowned at the shallow stone-lined irrigation trenches, mulling over the best way to approach Miss Tamberlay, poor thing.

When he heard the whispering approach of footsteps, Carter's right hand settled lightly on his pistol.

Autumn Blaze 53

"Why, Captain Machesney, I do declare, when Corporal Henny mentioned y'all had arrived and were washin' up in the creek like a common trooper, I said to myself, Olivia Chiswell, you must make our guest from Texas more welcome than that. Please do excuse me for disturbing you, sir."

Surprised to hear a simpering southern accent so far from home, Carter twisted around from his seat on the rocky bank. He looked up into the saucy brown eyes of a beautiful brunette standing behind him. "Excuse me if I don't get up, ma'am. I'm indisposed."

The woman's face took on a calculating pink flush. She tipped her head to the side and gave him a dazzling smile. "I declare, I can't tell you what a pleasure it is to have a new face at Fort Bradley. I'm Olivia Chiswell." Her eyes went over his naked back like eager hands. "Colonel Chiswell's wife."

"The pleasure is all mine, ma'am."

She stepped closer. "Y'all are invited to dinner at my husband's quarters this evenin', and every evenin' you're not otherwise occupied. And y'all needn't soap your clothes in that crude fashion. We have laundresses."

"Too late in the day to trouble them," Carter said, wondering if the woman greeted all fort visitors so charmingly. "Where will I find the white Comanche, ma'am? Is she staying with you?"

"Mercy, no. She's in the stockade where she belongs. *Must* I call you Captain, or will Carter do?" Not waiting for a reply, Mrs. Chiswell waltzed away, swinging her skirts. "Bye now."

Carter chuckled. A bored southern belle among Yankees? "Do I know how to find trouble or what?" he muttered, wringing out his socks.

It was dark by the time Carter approached the squat stone stockade, his hair combed and his jaw stinging from a hasty shave in the dimming light of his quarters.

Stepping across the scuffed stone threshold, his loathing of being indoors firmly under control, Carter introduced himself to the soldier on duty behind the desk. He stated the purpose of his visit.

"Well, well, well, Captain. You want to see the bitch, it's your funeral." The man took the lantern and ushered Carter through a stout plank door into a dry, cool cell block. The rank odor of unwashed men was stagnated inside.

In the first cell sat a husky, sandy-haired trooper, scratching his chest. Blinded by the lantern light and failing to recognize Carter as a stranger, the trooper made a vulgar hand motion toward the cell opposite his. "Needs it bad," he whispered. "Gimme just five minutes with her. Five minutes."

Seething, Carter forced his attention toward the shadowed corner cell. At first he thought a mountain lion was pacing inside.

The sergeant lifted the lantern. Yellow light washed across a rag-clad woman who dropped to a defensive crouch in the corner the moment she was illuminated.

Forgetting his anger and the suffocating closeness of the low-ceilinged building, Carter stared until his eyes ached. Twenty years, he thought in wonderment. Twenty god-blessed years with the Tall Horse Comanches.

Amanda Tamberlay might as well *be* a Comanche, he thought, except that her long hair, grimy with bear grease, was unmistakably blond. Though her face was still partially painted with reddish-pink mud, her bone structure was definitely the same as Jane's.

It was her. It had to be.

About to let out a whoop of triumph, Carter noticed the bruise along her jaw and rope burns around her wrists. He could almost taste her terror. "Why is she in here?" he demanded in a low voice thick with anger.

The sergeant scratched his ear. "She's crazy wild. Can't you see that? Ain't no use tryin' to talk to her. She don't talk

English no more. They musta tortured the brains outta her. It'd be a kindness to shoot her in the head."

Through clenched teeth, Carter whispered, "I want her released."

The sergeant looked at Carter as if he'd lost his senses. Leaving the lantern, he turned away. "Hell, Captain. You'll have to talk to the colonel about that. I ain't riskin' my stripes."

"I intend to do just that," Carter muttered as he approached the white Comanche's cell. "Mandie, my name is Carter Machesney. I've been to see your mother in Texas. She wants you to come home."

She didn't move.

Behind Carter, the sandy-haired prisoner muttered, "Jesus H. Christ, where you from, reb? Stupidville?" He plucked at the black thread stitches bristling along his cheek. "She done *this* to me, friend. Get a little closer so she can do the same to you."

"Your name, trooper?" Carter asked, his attention still focused on the white Comanche's fear-intense, pale gray-blue eyes.

"I'm Clay Burdette, you g'damned reb traitor. I know that bitch better'n anybody. She's Snakehorn's whore. A killer."

Carter took the locket from his shirt pocket. Holding it between thumb and index finger, he tapped the iron bars with it. The unfamiliar sound made the white Comanche stir.

Seeing the glint of gold from the corner of her eye, she leaped to her feet.

Carter's blood surged.

With her beautiful eyes narrowed and murderously cold, she looked like a savage, but her delicate, sun-browned face was still that of a young white woman. What had they been doing to her, the Comanches, the soldiers? Carter wondered.

He stopped tapping and stuck his hand between the bars. The locket lay in his open palm.

"Don't do that," Clay warned from behind. "She'll tear your arm off."

She was taller than Corinna. Her body was lean and strong, her breasts firmly rounded, pressing against a faded red overblouse that she must have worn for years. Feeling her eyes moving over him, Carter wondered what she saw—and why he cared.

"Does anybody know her Comanche name?"

None of the watching prisoners answered.

With two slim, dirty fingers she plucked the locket from his palm. He resisted grasping her wrist just to feel her skin. Slipping a grimy fingernail into the groove along the side, she popped it open. At the sight of the blurred painted faces inside, her brows tilted.

Quickly she placed the locket back on Carter's palm, her fingers brushing his like feathery flames. Regarding him with eerie, pale, suddenly expressionless eyes, she returned to her corner.

"Don't you want it?" Carter was baffled.

How could she respond? he asked himself. She didn't understand. She probably expected to be tricked and further mistreated.

Dropping the locket back into his shirt pocket, Carter stood several moments, staring blankly at Burdette's stitched face. What now? He was too tense to sleep. Though it'd be a relief to get out from under this roof, he took a seat on the hard-packed floor beside her cell. He massaged the dull ache in his thigh. From the corner of his eye, he watched her tuck her skirt tightly around her long, sleek legs.

Pulling his jackknife from his pants pocket and the chunk of mesquite wood he'd been whittling since he'd left Texas, Carter wondered when the best time would be to show her the picture of herself as a baby.

As thin shavings fell to the dirt around his boots, Carter continued to watch from the corner of his eyes. The young woman never moved. He couldn't tell if she was watching him or not. He couldn't remember the last time he'd felt as self-conscious in the presence of a woman, or the last time the curve of a woman's hip had been quite so distracting.

Then he shook himself. There would be none of that kind of thinking. He, of all people, must show her respect. But his heart was drumming, and there was a part of him responding to her in a way he could never have predicted.

After an hour Carter snapped the knife closed, put it and the wood back in his trouser pocket, and let his head loll back against the bars. Soft words, slow confident movements, food, a gentle touch . . . Would this wild woman ever let him touch her? As a friend, he sternly reminded himself.

A bath, clean clothes, a soft bed . . . "Remember me, my darlin', for I've been gone so long. . . . " Carter hummed softly until his thoughts grew dim.

Waking abruptly, Carter felt unsure where he was or how long he had been dozing. Hearing snores, he was almost in a panic, wondering what had awakened him. The place reminded him of the prisoner-of-war camp. He felt like he was back—

Something warm clamped hard against his throat.

His heart exploded with surprise. "Hey," he croaked, grabbing a slim, muscular forearm coming from between the bars behind his head. "Hey!"

Crushing his windpipe and voice box with all her strength, the white Comanche held Carter in a death grip. His boots scuffled against the dirt floor, rousing the sleeping prisoners. They began caterwauling at the sight of him pinned against the bars by a woman.

Clay rolled over and regarded Carter. "Well, g'damn, Captain, you got her right where you want her."

The guard staggered in, yawning and waggling his pistol. His face split with a grin, too. "Don't say I didn't warn—"

Gesturing for time, Carter mouthed, "Wait," and tried to relax.

He could have easily tore her arm away, but he didn't want to hurt her. If she really wanted to kill him, she could have slit his throat with the jackknife in his pocket. He was convinced she *didn't* want to kill him. Wondering what she did want, he resisted stroking her arm in an attempt to calm her.

As a ringing began in Carter's ears, he forced himself to stop struggling. Her dirty little hand slid ever so slowly around his left shoulder. As if memorizing the feel of his shirt and the swell of his chest muscles, she reached into his breast pocket. His nipples tightened.

Muttering something that sent a prickling of arousal through his veins, she retrieved the locket and abruptly released Carter with a grunt of triumph.

The prisoners roared with laughter. Carter scarcely heard them as he fell forward, clutching his aching throat, pretending great pain.

"The fool fell asleep within her reach," Clay hawed to the guard. "Good job, reb. The colonel couldn'ta done better."

Carter struggled to his feet. She was stronger than she looked.

"Your name is Amanda Tamberlay," he said in a strained voice. "Mandie. Man-*dee*."

With a toss of her wild greasy hair, she pointed in the direction of the corral outside. Speaking a gruff Comanche word, she stalked to the bars. He resisted shrinking back. Jamming her arm between them, she shook her fist at Burdette.

"Whore *dog*," she snarled.

Word for word, she repeated all the man had said since she'd been under guard. To hear such filth pouring from her beautiful soft mouth raised the hair on Carter's neck. She was incredible!

With a sniff of dismissal, she withdrew then and curled back into her corner, the locket to her lips.

Carter could scarcely contain his astonishment. "With recall like that, Burdette, she could testify at your next court-martial."

Still undone by the white Comanche's savage display, Carter pushed his way outside the stockade. Had she known what she was saying? Gulping in fresh air, he found his thoughts whirling, his body drenched with sweat. His thigh ached something fierce.

Faint music drifted on the night air. Someone in one of the officers' houses was playing "The Battle Cry of Freedom" on a piano badly in need of tuning. He remembered when that song had first taken on a new meaning for him. It was a Yankee song declaring there should be no more slavery. He'd been twenty feet down in a stone well, freezing his ass off, feeling like a slave himself, realizing the Yankees were right.

The smell of wood smoke, coming from the tent encampment in the center of the parade ground, was strong in the tart air. Somebody there was trying to play "Oh, Susanna!" on a sore fiddle. That was a song less painful to his soul.

Hungry, craving more sleep and relief from the suffocating gloom of the cell block, Carter nevertheless couldn't take another step away from the stockade.

Burdette had apparently been terrorizing Mandie Tamberlay with threats of gang rape, torture, and mutilation. She might be strong and fierce, but she was no match for a man Burdette's size, or any of the men here.

Swinging back into the dayroom, Carter demanded of the sergeant, "Is there nowhere else to keep that woman? Supposing I take her into my custody. I'll . . . I'll keep her in my quarters, in irons if necessary."

The sergeant snorted. "Shit, Captain, ain't a one of us wouldn't give two months' pay to have her chained up somewhere priv—"

Carter bent into the smirking face. "I'm here to see Miss Tamberlay safely home to her *mother*. She is not an animal. She's a human being, deserving of your respect. Should you or anyone else forget that, I'll consider it a personal affront. I would not hesitate to make that completely clear to each and every one of you men, one at a time, of course."

The guard spat, missing the spittoon on the floor beside his desk. "She ain't *nothin'*, sir, animal or otherwise, so long as she acts like she done so far."

Storming out, Carter thundered into his quarters, got the blanket from his cot, and grabbed his bedroll from the floor in the corner. Fifteen minutes later he returned to the stockade with a speckled plate from the mess hall heaped with cold Mexican beans and a scorched tortilla.

For privacy, he tied the blanket across the bars of her cell. She never gave him a glance. Hunkering down alongside the blanket, Carter whispered then, "Are you hungry? The beans aren't half-bad." He stuck a fingerful into his mouth. Grimacing, he shrugged and grinned. "Maybe they are at that."

For all he could tell, she was made of stone.

Able to reach only half an arm's length through the closely set flat bars, Carter offered the tortilla. "Try it, please."

Behind him, a stripling lieutenant edged in from the dayroom. "Captain . . . Machesney, is it? I wasn't informed you were here until just now." Stroking his sparse blond mustache, the lieutenant avoided looking at the prisoners scowling at him from the cells with open disrespect. "I'm Lieutenant Matthew Graham."

Dropping the tortilla, Carter stood and shook the man's clammy hand. "Would you kindly authorize this woman's release this evening, Lieutenant? There's no need to keep her under protective guard now that I'm here."

Lieutenant Graham's eyes bulged. "I don't have the authority to do that, sir."

Carter reined his increasing impatience. "No? Then I'll be staying the night right here on the floor. She hasn't been safe in this stockade."

"She attacked the colonel, sir. I can't let you stay here. It's against regulations."

Those almighty regulations, Carter thought, seething. "I won't help any of these men escape, Lieutenant, I can assure you."

Chewing the inside of his cheek, the lieutenant finally mumbled, "All right, but I'll have to discuss this with the colonel as soon as he gets back. He won't like it."

"Obliged," Carter said sarcastically. "Very much obliged."

Firemaker held her trembling body as still as possible. Who was this man? He wasn't a horse soldier; his clothes weren't the same. Though he had washed—she could smell the soap—and cut the whiskers from his jaw—his face was nicked in several places—he still smelled of horse. He had traveled some distance to see her.

He had said the white word "mother." She remembered this word from somewhere. Could he know of her white mother? She thought the woman long dead.

Why hadn't she killed this man Carter when she had the chance? she wondered. She had wanted to, but his calm unnerved her. The tortilla lay where he had dropped it. Her stomach rumbled, but she wouldn't let herself move toward it yet.

He was still awake, shifting this way and that, trying to get comfortable on the dirt floor against the stone wall, out of her reach this time. More than once he glanced about the dismal cell block and then closed his eyes as if his thoughts gave him no rest.

At length he slumped to the side. His lips looked soft as he slept. The bone structure of his face was less pronounced than a Comanche's, but by any race's standards, he was terribly attractive. His skin was reddened by the sun, his arms covered with a fascinating mat of reddish-blond hair. She marveled at the shape of his jaw, so strong, so compelling.

Convinced at last that he was sleeping, listening to the even rhythm of his breathing, Firemaker edged toward the tortilla. Wondering if the man would awaken and seize her arm, she stuffed the tortilla in her mouth and quickly backed away, chewing with silent care, giving thanks for the blanket he had put up. What a relief it would be the next morning not to see the whore dog fondling his erection, gesturing toward his mouth, and then shaking his fist as if he had someone by the hair.

What did *this* white man have in store for her? she wondered.

Men were taskmasters, captors, owners, Firemaker reminded herself. To most men, women were like horses, to be traded, bought, sold, or given as gifts. She must not let herself hope this white stranger was any different. No matter how well a man might regard her, even as her father, Four Toes, had once regarded her when she was a child, this man or any other could do what he pleased with her.

Let this man return her amulet, she thought, shaking off her softhearted gratitude to him. Let him give her food. Let him understand her need for solitude. She would not trust him. He was a man, and white. Twice her enemy.

With a breathy snort, the man woke. As if lost, he searched the darkness with deep brown eyes. He might be a man, and white, but he was different. She sensed it. She edged back. She didn't trust herself.

He straightened. The discomfort of his position on the

floor was evident in his face. Why was he putting himself to this trouble on her account? she wondered. Did he expect gold or horses for her? If her white mother still lived, was the woman paying for her return, now, after all this time?

Or was this man lying? Would he free her from the horse soldiers' stockade only to sell her to the Apaches or Mexicans as Snakehorn had once done?

Don't weaken, Firemaker warned herself. You're nothing to this man but a weapon, a tool, or a plaything. Be strong. Be safe. Be alone.

The cell block grew stuffy in the night, but Carter woke to dawn's gray light feeling chilled. Looking up at the bare pine rafters, feeling the press of the stone walls against his back, he let his dream linger.

He felt engulfed by something he couldn't see and couldn't name. Was he dreaming of battle again or the well? He felt as if he'd been sleeping against the slick, damp stones piled twenty feet over his head again, stones that had looked as if they might cave in at any moment, to bury him alive.

As if back in prison, Carter could almost picture the oaken bucket they had lowered his food in each day, swinging next to his shoulder, a fat gray rat nibbling contentedly within.

A sickening ache began to spread through his thigh. The wound felt burning fresh again. He'd almost lost his leg, and now he started shaking as if with that old fever. He'd been dying breath by breath in that well, thought by thought, moment by moment, for eight seemingly endless months.

Yet the war had ended. Carter's captivity had ended. His body had healed, and he had eventually gone home. All he had to show for those bloody, irrevocable, shattering, sobering years of civil war was a scarred, aching thigh and a spinning head whenever he came under a roof.

The well hadn't made him fear enclosed spaces, Carter

knew. The well had opened to the rain and sun, direct access to the God of his boyhood. He had learned to pray again in that well, and to survive.

The rats hadn't made him afraid, Carter thought. He didn't fear rats. It hadn't been the hunger that carved at him until he emerged at the close of the war looking like an adolescent.

It hadn't been the leg irons chafing his ankles raw, nor the beatings, laughter, or neglect. It hadn't been the sucking mud beneath his hindquarters, or even his sorely tempered arrogance.

If not those things, what made him dream like this, six years after the fact? Carter wondered. He was in New Mexico Territory now, free to go outside whenever he chose. He was a prisoner no more.

Glancing at the white Comanche, Carter wondered how she could sleep with these men watching her, taunting her. He couldn't tell if she was sleeping now or not. He had presumed she was savage because she was raised Comanche, but what did he know of Comanche women? Anyone might attack as she had if she found herself among those who had murdered half her family.

Half his family was gone, too. He had returned home to Virginia after the war to a poorly set grave marker in the family plot instead of the father he had so longed to see again, to talk to, to throw his arms around.

Was her grief as sharp as his? Would it last as long?

There had been no grave markers for his two younger brothers, whiskerless lads when they joined up two years after Carter. They were now buried somewhere in Georgia. To Carter, Ned and Jason would never be truly dead. They would always be romping in the meadow, a poignant memory aching in his heart as painfully as his thigh.

How did this poor woman feel, knowing those left of her people were living in a horse corral now, soon to be marched to a reservation in the Oklahoma Indian Territory, their lives to be irrevocably changed? Some of those killed during the attack on her village had probably rotted where they fell, untended.

How could she bear it? How could she ever accept him, a white man, as a friend to whom she might be willing to reveal information?

Carter thought of his little sister, Mary, her face once a shining mirror of innocence. He'd left her a girl with pink cheeks and curls, and returned after the war to find a woman as callous as a cracker's wife. She'd married a man down from Pennsylvania, wounded at Gettysburg, a Yankee. She'd saved his life. Eric had been measuring what was left of the Machesney acres in tobacco when Carter left.

War had carved its ugly signature into all Carter had fought to preserve. Even his sweetheart, Sarajane, had changed. Without her party frocks, big house, and blooded horses to give her chin that saucy tilt, she'd become a clinging, whining child he couldn't abide.

"But, Carter, why *can't* we get married?" she'd asked again and again those first days he was back. "I can't go on like this. You promised. You did, you know."

One week of Sarajane, one week of watching Mary work alongside Eric in the fields, one week beneath that leaking old roof without his father, and Carter had left for Texas. He tried to explain in a painfully inadequate letter to his sister that Virginia had changed too much. He no longer belonged there. But if he didn't belong home, where did he belong?

Carter hadn't yet been able to explain to Sarajane that he would never marry her. Of one thing he was certain: He needed a woman to talk to, to help him, a woman who could think and fight, if need be. How could he tell Sarajane she could never hope to measure up to his changed needs?

At nineteen, Carter had ridden away from Murphysboro, Virginia, and into battle as a cocksure yearling. He'd galloped back and forth from Louisiana into Texas for horses, an invincible Confederate blade.

Late one afternoon on his way to help Major Twyford, a blue-belly had come out of the woods, taken Carter's horse, and put a pistol to his head.

"You're coming with us up the Mississippi a piece, reb."

A year later Carter had ridden away from the Yankee prisoner-of-war camp in Illinois to a private hospital on a hayrack, a changed man.

How could he tell Sarajane he'd proven not to be the young god she'd once worshiped? He needed love and understanding now, not adoration and demands. He wanted to feel a woman's love in his gut, in his soul, not dragging from his elbow like deadweight.

In his dream, Carter had seen his father riding closer, closer, but never arriving, always elusive. "Pa," Carter had called to him. "Pa!"

A boy again, Carter had run as fast as he could through the tall grass of their Virginia farm. The grass had grown taller, and so thick Carter couldn't move. He'd been trapped, swallowed, left behind. As he fell Sarajane appeared and bent over him, weeping softly, pulling at him to hold her, kiss her. She clung to him, smothering him, crushing him, burying him.

What sort of peyote did this white man smoke to bring him such dreams? Firemaker wondered, watching Carter's tortured sleep on the far side of the bars.

From across the parade ground, the abrupt notes of morning call roused the troopers in the barracks, the Comanche captives in the corral, and the prisoners in the stockade.

Within the cells, the men rose with their usual profane grumblings. Firemaker pretended sleep while each man pulled on a stiff wool uniform coat and cracked boots. They stood like sheep at the cell doors, waiting to be let out.

Brushing himself off, Carter climbed to his feet, too. The guard plodded in, unlocked all doors except Firemaker's, and laced a chain through each leg iron as the eleven prisoners filed out.

Firemaker felt Carter watching her. Now that the prisoners were gone for the day, would he have her door unlocked? She remembered where he kept that folding knife. She could easily get it from him and felt more than ready to use it against him.

Carter, however, tiptoed soundlessly out of the cell block, closing the dayroom door behind him as if trying not to disturb her sleep. Firemaker didn't know what to think. Suddenly tears welled behind her closed lids. She couldn't stanch them.

If her white mother still lived, she thought, why had she taken this long to look for her? What could they mean to each other now?

Firemaker wanted to hate all whites and fight them. She wanted to be with Four Toes, awaiting whatever fate the soldiers planned. She wanted to die defending the only life and family she had ever known. She didn't want to think about a white mother far away, or of this stranger called Carter who would mean nothing to her, ever, no matter how strong, tall, and kind he seemed to be.

FIVE

SEATED AT A greasy plank table in the mess hall about an hour later, Carter forced down another gulp of bitter coffee. He was so tired from sleeping on the stockade floor all night that he couldn't think. How did one teach English? he wondered.

"Mornin', Captain. Mind if I sit here? The name's Tom Mosie." A pimply-faced corporal set a slopping tin plate on the table and sank to the bench. He smelled ripe in the blue wool. Glancing over his shoulder at four loutish troopers sniggering nearby, Mosie whispered, "I heard you was sleepin' in the cell block last night."

Wondering what he and his cronies wanted to know, Carter regarded the smirking, yellow-toothed young blue-belly.

"Word is you come to take the heathen white woman away. To a sideshow?" Mosie chuckled, shaking his head. "Or a Mexican sportin' house? Cleaned up some, she'd bring a good price."

Carter picked a coffee ground from the tip of his tongue. There had been a time when he wouldn't have found it so prudent to let a remark like that pass.

Mosie's expression turned sly. "Me 'n my friends thought could be you'd deal us in some night when you're . . . *sleepin'* in the stockade."

Surveying the mess hall crowded with men in blue uniforms, Carter let the pause lengthen. Then he pushed his tin plate aside. "I'd best be checking on my horse."

68

Autumn Blaze   69

Mosie detained him. "When the colonel's washerwoman tried to scrub her up a bit, back a few days ago, I helped hold her down." With his tongue between his lips, Mosie nodded. "Keeps a man awake at night, thinkin' bout that. You look kinda tired, Captain. Wore you out, did she?"

"How can I help you?" Carter asked, eyes narrowed.

"Interestin' you should ask. Our friend Burdette's in the stockade on account of that white Comanche bitch. Did you know that? Now, everybody knows she stole that locket offa somebody. Probably scalped 'em to get it, too. Burdette had as much right to it as anybody." Mosie leaned closer. "He gave it to Miz Chiswell, you know. She's that kind. Gives all the men that look of hers. You ask me, Clay Burdette ain't in the stockade on accounta he stole somethin' offa no white Comanche slut. No, sir. He's in there 'cause the colonel's covering up for his wife."

Carter sat back down. So that's how it all started, Carter thought. "Burdette had the locket and gave it to Mrs. Chiswell?"

Mosie grinned and went on to explain.

Rolling her eyes toward Firemaker, Leota lumbered into the suffocating cell block. "Fartin'est bunch of white fools I ever did smell," she muttered. "Place stinks worse'n a pigsty. Don't know how you stomach it, honey, though I 'spose anybody'd put bear grease in her hair ain't got no nose. You ain't catching me tryin' to wash you no more, neither. You be learning manners first. Got to understand who yer friends is."

Leota left a chunk of dry sourdough and some hardtack on the dirt floor beside Firemaker's bars. Then the washerwoman stood a moment, shaking her dark curly head. This situation reminded her of her sister back in Alabama, just before the white mens used her to death.

Rubbing her bruised rib where she had been kicked when washing Firemaker by the creek back that first day, Leota went out. Didn't make no never mind if Miss Firemaker got manners or not, she thought. Didn't make no difference if she was white or Comanche, black, yaller, or green. Firemaker wouldn't never be free. She was female, and in this world that was a life sentence.

Sweating in his cramped quarters that afternoon, Carter struggled to compose an adequate telegraph message to Jane Tamberlay in Texas.

Looking at the leather packet stuffed with her painstakingly printed old letters, he tried to imagine how the woman must feel now that the wait for her daughter was over. What could he say to help her bear a few more weeks or months of waiting?

Carter was nearly out of paper when he gave up and went out to the stables to check on Lonesome. He found him grazing in one of the corrals.

He was stroking his horse's flank when a boy of eight ran up to him. The boy was wearing his mother's approximation of a Yankee uniform. "Hey, sir."

"Hey, yourself, son," Carter said, smiling.

"Them's Comanche Injuns in the corral. I'm a-gunna scalp me one."

"Scalp women and children? How come?" Carter crouched to the boy's eye level.

"That's what Injuns do. No good dirty som-bisshes." The boy dashed away toward three waiting friends. "Pow! Pow!"

The boys made for the corral where the Comanches were huddled. Whooping and making gunfire noises, they galloped as close as they dared before the sweating guard shooed them away.

An infant began wailing, softly, plaintively.

Across the parade ground, a freight wagon rolled beneath the crossed pine trunks serving as the fort gate. Down by the river, black washerwomen hung long gray drawers on lines slung between twisted cottonwoods. Around them children ran and squabbled.

The wind was strong, smelling of sagebrush, as crisp and clean in Carter's lungs as icy water. The word "savage" seemed to apply to folks on either side of the fence, he thought, ruefully.

Returning to his quarters, Carter wrote quickly. *Dear Mrs. Tamberlay. I have arrived at Fort Bradley. It is different from what I expected. The white Comanche woman seems in good health. She has blond hair and blue eyes. I'm pretty certain she is your daughter. She needs clothes and cleaning up. It will take time to teach her English. Keep the faith. I'll write again in a few weeks. Yours cordially, Carter Machesney.*

No use saying too much, Carter thought, deciding to send the letter by mail packet. Frowning at the daguerreotype of Jane and baby Mandie standing on his desk, he hoped somehow to give Mandie Tamberlay enough information about her new life that she could decide for herself, eventually, who and what she wanted to be.

Firemaker heard Carter whistling as he approached the stockade later that afternoon. In spite of her resolve to remain unaffected by him, her heart lifted.

Entering the hot, silent cell block, Carter smiled and called, "Remember me?" His voice was full and strong, warming her desolate heart.

Though she turned away, she was glad he was back, and waited breathlessly to see what he would do now.

Tucking the blanket out of the way, he peeked in at her. "It's hot as hell in here. I'm trying to get you out, but I'm not having much luck. You've got everybody spooked."

She couldn't follow his words.

"They tell me the scout spotted signs of Snakehorn again a few days back, so the colonel's led a patrol in pursuit. If you ask me, what with those reinforcements out there, Snakehorn's miles away by now."

Firemaker recognized the white translation of her Comanche brother's name. If Snakehorn was near, she thought, she needed to be with Four Toes immediately. Snakehorn wouldn't fail to rescue his father, wife, and son. Even though she was only his white sister, she didn't want to be left behind.

"Do you remember anything of your white mother?" Carter asked, dropping to the floor and getting comfortable. He massaged his thigh more out of habit than need.

Repeating the whore dog's words the night before had been a mistake, Firemaker realized. Carter was speaking to her now as if she understood everything he said.

When she failed to respond, Carter pointed to her and then himself. "Carter? Carter." When he pointed back to her, he looked at her questioningly as if wanting to hear her name.

She didn't bother with her Comanche name. He wouldn't know what it meant. But she supposed she shouldn't be too difficult. This man was likely her only hope of getting free of the stockade. She'd have to risk talking to him. How to translate her name into white words, she wondered.

"Fire," she whispered, cupping her hands and blowing.

His smile broadened. "Yes, fire . . . That's it?" he asked, eyes locked with hers. "That's all? Fire?"

Her heart was leaping at the shine in his eyes. She had never seen eyes so brown, so warm on her, as if she was fascinating and marvelous. Never had she seen a mouth curve into a more beguiling smile. She found herself wanting to touch the curve with her fingertip to see if his lips were as soft and sensitive as they looked.

"Your name is fire?" he asked.

Firemaker could have repeated everything he had said so far, but the words were only sounds. She didn't know what most of them meant. She remembered little of the white words she'd learned from captive white women being held by the Apaches ten years before.

"Car-ter," she repeated softly, wondering if his name had a meaning. "Fire . . ." She blew into her cupped hands again.

"That's right. My name's Carter. You made the fires?"

She made large gestures. "Fire," she said as if the forest were burning. Then she cupped an imaginary coal in her hands and dropped it with a startled look. "Fire!" She showed him her hands. Her palms were smooth and white with old scars.

He looked alarmed, then frustrated. "Campfire? That's not a very agreeable name for someone as beautiful as you. How did your palms get burned?"

She drew a pine tree in the dirt.

"Pine tree? Burning Pine Tree is your name?" He laughed suddenly. "This is crazy. It's easier to talk to my horse."

Carter stayed with her all afternoon, leaning against the wall, talking to amuse himself. Sometimes he gazed thoughtfully, silently, into the distance of his memories. Sometimes he smiled, and her heart warmed.

Whenever he looked at her, his expression became earnest. Though she couldn't determine what he was talking about, Firemaker was surprised by the number of white words she did remember and understand. It was just difficult to concentrate. It was difficult because of him.

She couldn't seem to stop watching him. His hair was the color of earth, soft and brown and shining, curling against his neck like small caresses. Whites didn't grease their hair as Comanches did, and she wondered why. How did they keep vermin away?

What did he think of her, she wondered, so different from the women of his world? What might her hair look like without grease, lit by the sun? She felt unsettled to contemplate trying to look white.

When Mary Graham arrived an hour later, the plump young woman stumbled and gasped to find a man on the floor at her feet. "Mercy, sir, I almost stepped on you. Howdo," she said, turning scarlet.

Carter stood and greeted her.

"Livvie told me you had arrived, Mr. Machesney. What

a relief to think someone is here to help this poor woman. I'm Mary Graham, the self-appointed schoolmarm, Sunday-school teacher, and all 'round do-gooder at Fort Bradley." She smiled prettily. "I believe you've met my husband, Lieutenant Graham."

"Yes, ma'am. I have a sister named Mary."

"Well," she said, "I'm honored."

When Carter realized Mary was pregnant, he hastened to fetch her the stool from the dayroom. Watching him smile solicitously as he helped the bulging matron sit, Firemaker felt an absurd flash of jealousy.

"I've been reading to Firemaker these past few afternoons," Mary said, opening her Bible.

"Firemaker? Is *that* her name?" Carter laughed. "My abilities with sign language would amuse you."

"It's the scout's translation. He wants us to believe the Comanche language is very complex. I think he's stringing the army along with lies, but I suppose that's none of my business. As for Firemaker, I think she remembers more English than she lets on. When McTigue and the colonel return, you'll have a much easier time communicating with her."

"In the meantime, will you help me teach her English?" Carter asked.

"She can't have forgotten as much as all that."

Carter explained.

Firemaker glared when Mary's expression turned to wonder.

"Twenty years? Oh, my Lord, I had no idea. The poor thing. Everyone is saying the most appalling things about her, you know. The officers' wives. Our cooking girls. Even the children. Why, if they knew how long she'd been a captive, they'd realize she had no choice. She probably thinks she *is* Comanche."

"It'll be our job to tell them about her," Carter put in.

"Indeed. She's not a traitor. My husband told me Firemaker was nearly strangled to death during the attack on her village. Some of the troopers here don't even try to be any better than they should be."

"It's not much of a life," Carter agreed.

"I felt so awful for her, I just had to do something to help. No one else seems to care what happens to her. None of those Comanche people should have been killed. Mattie said they didn't even resist. All the Comanche men were away. Did you know that? I'm as sympathetic to our unfortunate settlers as any, but that attack was a slaughter."

Carter was watching Firemaker. She ignored him.

"I know the troopers can't help their ignorance," Mary went on. "Most can't read or write. Their lives were difficult in the States, and their lives are just as difficult here. Colonel Chiswell relishes the most upsetting punishments."

"Bucking and gagging?" Carter asked.

Nodding, she blushed. "They can be quite uncivilized on payday. The morning after, a dozen or more can be seen spread-eagled on the ground, slowly baking in the sun. The vicious cycle of abuse and brutality is perpetuated by unfeeling commanding officers who condone such cruelty in the name of discipline. My husband will never be like that."

Carter regarded her. "I hope not."

"I mustn't go on like this. It's seditious." Mary forced away her scowl. "I find you a surprisingly easy man to talk to, Mr. Machesney. I hope you'll be able to join us for dinner *this* evening. We missed you last night. I'm sure you'd have no trouble whatsoever charming Livvie into a more agreeable temper than she's been in lately."

"Ma'am?"

"Livvie had her girl, Leota, make dried apple pie for your welcome, and chicken and dumplings according to her family recipe. We waited until past nine. Since I'm expecting, Livvie's had Leota coming over to do my chores, too. It's rather generous of her but a lot of extra work."

"Now that you mention it, I do remember Mrs. Chiswell inviting me. I owe her an apology."

"I would assure you of Livvie's forgiveness," Mary said teasingly, "but I can't say for sure that she'll forgive, at least not until she's made you squirm awhile. Ordinarily Livvie Chiswell would have little to do with a common preacher's daughter like me. But we're all forced to make sacrifices. From your accent, I've concluded you're from the south, too."

"Yes, ma'am. Virginia."

"Well, I won't hold that against you, if you forgive me for being from Albany."

Did all white women act this foolishly in the presence of white men? Firemaker wondered, disgusted by the display of childish flirting. Comanche women never talked with men like that. It was all done in private.

Tightening her grip around her scabbed knees, Firemaker resolved that Carter could smile at anyone he liked. She did *not* care. She certainly would never act like that.

"We owned twelve slaves, all fine horsemen," Carter was saying. "Before the war, that was the way of things. To realize we were wrong, that our slaves had rights . . ."

"Prison camp apparently made quite an impact on you," Mary said. "The war, I fear, changed us all. I lost three cousins. My father, though he was too old to fight, was on hand to lend comfort to the soldiers. He was a preaching man. The war ruined his health. I would be there with him today were it not for my duty to my beloved Matthew. When Mattie survived the war, I vowed I would follow him anywhere. We all fought for and sacrificed a great deal, Mr. Machesney, and the war goes on still, in mean and small ways. I think it always will."

She opened the Bible and began reading. "Blessed are the peacemakers. . . ."

"The U.S. Army can spare a few blankets for children," Carter barked to the quartermaster, his smile as false as his cordial tone, "regardless of their skin color."

Autumn Blaze 77

The sergeant had just opened his mouth to reply when they were interrupted by a breathless redheaded corporal pushing into the quartermaster's store.

"The colonel's rider has arrived, sir. The patrol's an hour out. Colonel Chiswell will be tired, but I'll tell him you want to see him."

Nodding his thanks, Carter turned back to the scowling sergeant. "And canvas to make lean-tos . . ."

"I ain't givin' nothin' to them Comanche bitches or their whelps," the sergeant shouted. "Two of 'em snuck down to Suds Alley last night, kilt a dog, and boiled it. Filthy, thievin' savages." The sergeant spat on Carter's boot. "They can starve, freeze, and die."

An hour later, his gut still churning with fury, Carter waited outside the colonel's office. He remembered being hungry enough to eat rats. A dog would have been a feast for a Yankee prisoner of war. Only the knowledge that Confederates had starved just as many prisoners of war kept Carter's temper in check.

He hunched deeper into his coat as a chilling wind ripped across the valley floor. Thunder rumbled in the foothills.

A message to Oakley would have four of his best horses en route to New Mexico Territory by morning, Carter thought. After their sale, he'd be able to buy whatever was necessary to feed and clothe the Comanche prisoners from the sutler's store. The U.S. Army be damned.

Across the parade ground, a straggling line of bedraggled troopers rode dripping into the fort and dismounted upon command. The chuck wagon rolled on through the mud toward the mechanic's yard. The pack mules looked as exhausted as the rain-soaked men just down from the canyon.

A gaunt officer with a rigid military bearing dismounted his weary gray pacer. Overhead, the clouds dropped a fresh torrent as the colonel started toward the office, his walk painfully stiff and bow-legged.

The red-haired corporal detained him, whispered something, and gestured toward the encampment and an approaching major out from Fort Kirby. The officers exchanged curt greetings, and then the colonel shot Carter an evil glance as he drew near.

Storming past Carter, who was taking refuge from the rain under the roof overhang, Colonel Chiswell thudded through his office and disappeared into a back room. "Have a seat," he called.

Ready to blast the colonel with his lengthy list of complaints and demands, Carter stepped inside. He was instantly distracted by a long rifle displayed on the wall behind the colonel's desk.

Moments later Colonel Jedediah Chiswell emerged, hastily scrubbed and wearing a clean blue uniform coat. His boots were tracking mud everywhere.

As if every bone in his body were broken, the man lowered himself into the chair behind his desk. He fixed Carter with bloodshot eyes. His lips were moist. The biting odor of alcohol was fresh on his breath as he snapped, "You've been sent here to *help* question the white Comanche about Snakehorn? *What,* may I ask, have you learned?"

"Not much so far. She scarcely speaks English."

"Are you telling me *you* don't speak Comanche? Then why the hell were *you* sent? This is a military fort soon to be attacked by hundreds of Comanche warriors bent on scalping my men, raping their wives, and murdering innocent children."

"No, sir, I don't speak Comanche."

"I don't have time to play nanny to a civilian from Texas or anywhere else. Somehow Snakehorn escaped the attack on his village and eluded a weeklong pursuit patrol. My backside is on the line in Washington for that, Machesney, a fact only too evident by the presence of reinforcements from Fort Kirby which I did *not* request. All the more reason for me to expect answers from that woman. If you can't get them—"

Lieutenant Graham knocked and entered without permission. Realizing his mistake, the young man snapped to attention. Rain dripped from the tip of his nose. "Excuse me, sir."

"Get those Comanches ready to march to the reservation tomorrow morning. Machesney hasn't gotten a thing out of the white woman. Tell McTigue to stay sober until we're done with her tonight. I should've questioned her personally before—"

Carter stood. "I didn't come all this way to—"

The colonel reared so abruptly his chair overturned. Planting trembling fists in the middle of several reports, he hissed, "I don't give a mule's ass what you did or did not come here for, Machesney. If you have nothing to report, you're relieved. I don't tolerate incompetence."

Carter took a step closer. "I *didn't* ride all the way from Texas at the request of your superior at Fort Kirby to beat information from a woman. Sir. I'll find out what she knows in my own way, in my own time. I suggest you release Miss Tamberlay into my custody at once."

Rage stained the colonel's sweat-sheened cheeks. "While Lieutenant Graham marches the Comanche prisoners to the reservation, *Mister* Machesney, Snakehorn's whore will be staying here, under arrest. Snakehorn has one week to show himself. If he doesn't, I'll send out another patrol. And another and another until he's brought to justice. In any case, that white woman will be transported back to the States to stand trial."

Carter wondered if the man's mind had snapped. "For *what*?"

"The attempted murder of a United States Army officer. I want that filthy creature in the New York State Women's Asylum in a locked ward."

Carter hadn't seen such pompous irrationality since the

war. He kept his tone silky. "I wonder how Miss Tamberlay's attorney will plead."

The colonel's eyes tightened. "Attorney?"

"I've heard Miss Tamberlay was nearly strangled by one of your troopers. She has been robbed, beaten, and probably raped. By imprisoning her with the rest of your surprisingly numerous miscreants, considering the size of this fort, you've subjected her to constant verbal abuse as well."

The colonel's eyes darted to the lieutenant, who was trying to look invisible. "*Verbal* abuse? Does anyone give a damn about that?"

"When you're not attacking undefended villages, Colonel, perhaps your sole purpose is to abuse women—black, white, Comanche. It doesn't seem to matter to you."

The colonel looked ready to erupt.

"And while we're on the subject of theft, Colonel, where did you get that Hawken?" Carter indicated the rifle on the wall behind the desk. "That's a striped maple stock. Back in my quarters, sir, I have letters written by Miss Tamberlay's mother, describing items taken from the Tamberlay ranch the day Miss Tamberlay was captured by Comanches . . . *twenty years ago*. Spoils of war, sir?"

It was rather pleasing to see the colonel becoming apoplectic.

"She has . . . family?" the man croaked.

"The woman you are holding in your guardhouse is Amanda Tamberlay, taken from her parents' Texas homestead at the age of one year. That she survived twenty years with the Tall Horse Comanches will be of intense interest to thousands back east. After I gain her trust, and she tells me whatever she chooses about her life with the Comanches—*and* about the war chief Snakehorn—I'll take her back to her white family. Perhaps she'll go on to *college* in New York State. She may become famous."

The colonel measured his words with unexpected care. "I am the authority here, Mr. Machesney, and by virtue of that authority I outnumber you two hundred to one. Plus reinforcements. If you hamper my efforts to protect the United States' interests in this theater, you may find *yourself* in my stockade. In such an event, I cannot say *when* I would find time to order your escort back east for your trial . . . for treason."

"No need to threaten me, Colonel," Carter said, his eyes never wavering from Chiswell's face. "Given a reasonable amount of time, all purposes can be served."

The colonel's rage cooled. "A week."

"A month, Colonel, after which time you'll release Miss Tamberlay into my custody or on her own recognizance. Until then, I'm sleeping in the stockade next to her cell, with my pistol."

"A week, Machesney. We might not be alive a month from now. I can't guarantee your safety, or hers, so long as Comanches are running rampant in the foothills."

Carter drew a deep breath. An army patrol had galloped around northeastern New Mexico Territory for a week without sighting a single Indian, but the colonel still saw Snakehorn behind every bush. Or perhaps the man was warning Carter that he was making himself a target.

"Given time," Carter said, "Miss Tamberlay will be wearing a corset and button shoes, taking to the ways of white women so naturally we'll both wish she was Comanche again."

The colonel failed to see Carter's humor.

Carter exited before he could make any further rash promises. Conjuring a vision of Firemaker in petticoats and curls, Carter paused outside. It was raining in sheets.

The colonel's hushed words slammed through the closed door. "What's been going on while I was away, Graham? I thought I could trust you. I should have *you* thrown in the stockade with Snakehorn's whore. Let her scratch *your* eyes out. Your father will hear about this, I can assure you. Get out of my sight. You're the most useless man at this fort."

SIX

IT WAS DUSK. To Carter, McTigue looked more like an unkempt bear than a scout. They had just spent a maddening hour trying to get Firemaker to talk, to no avail.

"Are you sure you won't join us down at the First National?" McTigue asked, grinning up at Carter. "The women ain't much to look at, but the whiskey's good."

Carter patted the shaggy man's shoulder. "Thanks, but Mrs. Chiswell is expecting me. You've been a lot of help."

"I'll be around tomorrow to help you talk to Miss Firemaker again. She'll be two-steppin' with you sooner than you can say fuck the U.S. Army."

Chuckling, Carter watched the buckskin-clad scout waddle toward several mounted off-duty troopers waiting with his mule, Charlotte, at the fort's gate. Down the road, the yellow lamplight of the First National Saloon beckoned. Momentarily he reconsidered. Drunken Yankee blue-bellies were preferable to one simpering belle with devilment on her mind. And her asshole of a husband.

After their meeting that afternoon, Carter had no desire to eat at the colonel's table, but he felt a certain obligation to Mary Graham. As he approached the colonel's quarters he heard a sad piano rendition of "Lorena" that put him in mind of home.

Admitted at his first knock, Carter found Mary Graham at the piano. She blushed prettily when he nodded hello. Her fingers stumbled over several notes of the song before she regained her composure.

"Welcome, Mr. Machesney," Olivia Chiswell purred, slipping to his side and giving him a provocative smile. "Y'all have met my husband, I believe, and the Grahams."

Carter made his way inside, forcing himself to ignore the increasing ringing in his head.

Beside Mary stood her gangling lieutenant husband, Matthew, blond mustache and all, holding a fiddle beneath his chin, bow poised to play.

"Don't stop on my account," Carter said as the parlor walls seemed to close in.

As Matthew began playing it was obvious he was no soldier.

The colonel sat near the window, watching shadows dance between the tents on the parade ground. His eyes looked dead. On the table beside him stood a half-empty whiskey decanter.

"Ah, yes. Carter Machesney," the colonel murmured, draining his tumbler of amber liquid. "Champion of women."

For twenty minutes Olivia orchestrated the small talk while the colonel drank and Leota laid the table.

During supper, Carter noted that Mary looked tired. Matthew never spoke, not even when Carter asked how early his departure for the reservation would be, come morning.

"Mattie's not goin' anywhere, is he, sugar?" Olivia said, fixing her husband with a stern eye.

"I've reconsidered the hazards of travel at this time," the colonel said, his eyes half-closed. "The march has been postponed . . . due to rain."

Carter was surprised—and relieved—to hear that. Then he supposed that Matt Graham couldn't be spared on a long march so near his wife's confinement.

Soon the colonel's slurred recounts of his recent "campaign'' into the foothills left no doubt in Carter's mind that he was a habitual drunkard and unreliable. Carter began to worry about Firemaker's future safety at this man's command.

"If you ladies will forgive me," Carter said when the clock struck nine, "I must withdraw. The evening has been most entertaining."

"But, Mr. Machesney, Mary wants to play for us again," Olivia said with a pout, jumping up and grabbing his arm. She rubbed against his side. "I'd hoped we might sing . . . and dance awhile."

Mary looked too exhausted to protest. "Do join us in a song before you go, Carter."

At the piano, as Carter began singing, Olivia pressed close. She gazed up into his face. "You're an *accomplished* tenor, *Carter*. You must join us tomorrow mornin'. Mary leads the Sunday meetin'. I won't take no for an answer."

Crouched outside the Chiswells' parlor window, Tom Mosie watched the rebel ranger at the piano. Ducking down again, the corporal took a long pull on the battered tin flask hidden inside his uniform coat. No sense giving it all to Clay.

Bolting across the parade ground then, Mosie slipped inside the stockade. "All clear. Reb won't be nosin' around here for at least an hour."

The guard lowered the lantern's flame. Taking the keys, they crept into the dark cell block.

"Clay, wake up," Mosie hissed, kicking the bars of Clay Burdette's cell.

Burdette sprang to his feet and seized his cell door. "It's about time." He grabbed the flask Mosie stuck between the bars. By the time the guard had unlocked his door, Burdette had drained it. "Lemme at her," he growled.

Firemaker came awake, instantly wary and apprehensive.

"Hurry," she heard a man whisper amid the jingling of keys and feet scuffling the dirt floor.

Dim lantern light outlined the whore-dog Clay Burdette as he swaggered through the open doorway of his cell toward hers.

Heart hammering, Firemaker watched the guard unlock the rest of the cells. The freed prisoners swarmed into the aisle behind Burdette. Grinning, he pulled her door open. "You ain't never goin' to forget this night, bitch."

Unable to press herself any more tightly into the corner, Firemaker gouged two fistfuls of dirt from the floor.

His trousers unbuttoned and displaying his weapon in all its swollen glory, Burdette stepped into her cell and reached for her. "Come on, now. I know you want it. Easy now. Easy."

Surely he could feel the heat of her hate, Firemaker thought, waiting until the man was crouched with both hands on her ankles. She thought of nothing but the space between his eyes.

As he started pulling her legs apart, his eyes riveted on her thighs where her skirt was riding up, she aimed her heel. Just as he dipped his head for a better look, she kicked, catching him sharply on the left cheek when he flinched.

With a grunt he fell back, stunned.

Yelling, the troopers swarmed in, grabbing at her over Burdette's limp body. She flung both handfuls of dirt into their eyes.

"Quiet! Quiet!" someone hissed.

Momentarily the hands tearing at her clothes withdrew. Then someone's full weight fell on her. Something clamped around her throat. She couldn't make a sound.

They were only breasts, Firemaker thought, feeling fingers bruising her tender flesh. It was only a body. He would never reach her heart.

Her legs were painfully forced apart. She felt fumbling fingers groping. Then the cell-block door slammed against the wall. She opened her eyes to glaring yellow lantern light swooping across the pale pink stone walls. Four twisted faces, leering down at her, turned in surprise.

Burdette was atop her. His stitched cheek grazed her lips. Automatically she bit down, catching one of the black thread stubs between her teeth. She tasted blood when he twisted away, tearing the wound open. He let out a howl. Releasing her throat, he slapped the side of her head.

Feverishly Clay went on rutting against her, trying to gain entry with a suddenly flaccid penis. "Damn. G'damn. Damn you, bitch, to hell!"

Seizing the nearest man blocking Firemaker's cell door, Carter flung him backward into the aisle. "Get out!" he snarled, hauling another man and another from her cell.

Firemaker had never seen a more welcome sight than Carter's broad shoulders filling her doorway. Burdette was still trying to revive his erection.

Carter seized him by the hair and dragged him back. "You goddamned animal. You're not worth the dirt you sleep on." With one good punch, he rendered Burdette half-senseless.

Firemaker gave Carter no opportunity to do what was hers to do. Lunging for the appendage shrinking back into Burdette's trousers, she left claw marks across the trooper's hairy belly when she tried to grab him.

Carter yelled and knocked her aside. "No," he yelled, pushing Firemaker back. "No!"

She paid him no heed. On hands and knees, she scrambled after Burdette to show him what happened to a man who wanted to hold a Comanche woman's head in his lap.

Giving a shriek of alarm, Burdette scrambled to his feet, arms flailing like a dervish.

"No! Now, Mandie . . . Firemaker, no!" Carter seized her arms and flung her to the floor. "You can't keep doing this. Let me handle him."

Burdette flung himself out of the cell. "Look at her,

Machesney. She's dying for it. Just help me hold her. You can be next."

Carter lunged out the door and slammed it with a resounding clang. Whirling on Burdette, he hissed, "I've shot lesser men than you for lesser crimes. I come from a Virginia horse farm. I know what to do with your kind."

Staggering back into his cell, Burdette fell back onto his cot to examine the bleeding scratches on his belly. Blood trickled from his torn cheek. Already his eye was blackening. "I'm goin' to kill her good, Machesney. You can't be everywhere at once."

Angrily Carter motioned for the gawking guard to lock the man's cell.

Shrugging an apology to his friend Burdette, Mosie crept out and fled.

Covering her legs, Firemaker pressed herself back into the corner. She couldn't stop trembling. She wanted to shriek with rage. The taste of Burdette's blood was still in her mouth. With a vengeance, she spat it out.

For several minutes Carter stood glaring at every prisoner in the cell block. "You call yourselves men," he muttered, massaging his sore knuckles. Then he detained the guard as the man started edging toward the door. "Lock me in with her for the rest of the night," he said, entering Firemaker's cell. Taking out his jackknife, he placed it on the hard-packed dirt floor between her and himself. "If I'm dead come morning, you men can do whatever you like with her. If I'm alive, I won't report this to the colonel. And you'll leave her alone."

Someone snickered. "Right, reb. We trust ya."

Burdette shook the bars. "She's Snakehorn's whore. I'm goin' to skin her alive."

Carter jerked the cell door closed. "You're a coward of the lowest order, Burdette. You couldn't skin a dead cat to anyone's satisfaction, and you couldn't do a she-goat justice."

Someone else snickered in agreement. "Seen him try."

Jerking off his torn frock coat, Carter dropped to the floor in the corner of the cell opposite Firemaker. He slammed his coat into the shape of a pillow and tried to get comfortable against the stone wall.

Firemaker's heart began hammering harder. No bars separated them now. She shut her eyes, unsure how she should fight this man when he approached.

"You sure about this, reb?" the guard asked, peering between the bars.

When Carter didn't reply, the guard locked the door, picked up the lantern, and went out, closing the door to the dayroom. "Sleep tight, sir."

At once the darkness felt suffocating, even to Firemaker. She could smell Carter sitting so near. She could hear him breathing deeply, as if trying to relax.

"We'll be listening," someone whispered.

Chuckles rumbled in the darkness.

Firemaker wished she was anywhere but in the cell with Carter. If she let down her guard even for a moment, he might reach across those few inches between them and melt the last shreds of her strength. She was tired, so very tired of fighting. Part of her wished he *would* reach for her. Part of her wished she could just walk away with him and forget everything.

She waited and waited, rigid, afraid, exhausted. Why wasn't he reaching? she wondered after an hour. Of all the men, why didn't *he* want her?

She was shaking now. If he did touch her, she would be forced to lash out. She might batter him with her fists. She might . . . she might surrender. Her entire body began to melt at the thought.

She watched him watch her until his eyes drooped and his chin fell onto his chest. Don't sleep, she thought, feeling abandoned. How could *he* sleep? Was his heart not pounding for her? Was she nothing to him but a foundling to be returned to her mother?

She mustn't let herself feel this, she admonished herself. She mustn't need him. She mustn't feel a scrap of gratitude toward him. She must hate him, resist him, fight him until she was dead. She could not, would not, want him.

At dawn the bugler sounded morning call. Firemaker was still watching Carter, fighting the sensation of protection he afforded her.

Carter woke, groaning. "If this doesn't cure me, it'll kill me," he said, casting a look of disgust toward the rafters. Pushing back sweat-soaked hair, he sighed and met Firemaker's weary gaze. "Good morning. I'm sorry about last night. I hope you understand now that I'm your friend."

The waking prisoners gawked at him.

Getting up, Carter stretched, flexing his chest, working the tight muscles in his back, reaching his long arms to the rafters that he seemed to despise. He scratched his hair and shook out his hands to massage his thigh.

Then he took the jackknife from the dirt and offered it to her. "You've proven a very important point, Firemaker. I'm glad you didn't kill me while I slept. I would've had to haunt you." He grinned. "Take this. I can't be here every minute. I have the colonel to contend with. If you have to, use it. If you kill one of these fools, you won't be any worse off."

She was so stiff she could scarcely reach to take his knife. Her fingers brushed his and thrilled to the warmth of his touch. His eyes were dark, circled with fatigue, his soft dark hair disheveled, his jaw rugged with stubble. No man had ever looked so good, she thought.

Something new and strange moved deep within her. It was like a softening, a tingling of awareness, that compelled her to be close to him, to touch him, to taste him. With a shudder of terror, Firemaker closed her eyes. She didn't hate him.

"Friend?" he asked.

"F-frienn-d," she whispered, telling herself she was lying.

She must be. She did not want to feel what she was feeling for this white man. The knife felt small, cool, and comforting in her hand. She should kill him. Now.

She felt his hands close on her shoulders. She didn't even think to resist. He eased her back into the corner and then paused, crouched before her. Tentatively she opened her eyes to his sober examination of her scrapes and bruises. When he cupped her cheek, she drew in a tight, ragged breath. His palm felt so warm, so delicious. She wanted to press herself against him, but she couldn't move. She didn't dare.

"You'll be all right," he whispered, sliding his warm palm down her arm to cover her fists.

She felt small and safe suddenly, immeasurably grateful that for whatever reason he had come into her life.

"Try to get some sleep."

She wondered what he was saying. He looked straight into her soul. It was as if she had always known him, and always would. But she could say nothing. She could let nothing show on her face. He could never know what he was making her feel.

"Guard?" Carter called as she slipped the knife into her knee-high moccasin unseen. "I've got duties to attend to, if you don't mind."

In moments Carter was gone, leaving Firemaker's cell devoid of all comfort. The prisoners were taken out. She was left to fall into an uneasy sleep, where she dreamed of the woman's face, the unknown fragrance, and the darkness.

Then she dreamed of Carter Machesney's dark brown eyes, his deep caressing voice, and his warmth. She woke to the suffocating midmorning heat of her cell, a fully aroused woman.

SEVEN

As Jane held Carter Machesney's unopened letter in trembling hands, twenty years seemed like only a few weeks. She had been hanging laundry that day. Chickens had been roosting in the cottonwoods. Her fingers were scarred now where she burned them lifting the cook pot from the fire in the lean-to kitchen.

Jane couldn't remember the actual attack. It was only when she saw her reflection in a pot, or at the window, that any of that long-ago summer day seemed real. She kept no mirrors in her house.

If ever she felt that sorrow, or that rage, or that grief closing in, all she had to think about was getting her baby back, and everything associated with that day evaporated. Believing Mandie was alive out there somewhere had kept Jane alive so that she might live to see this day. She thanked God.

Standing behind Jane in the hallway, Corinna snapped, "Just read the letter, Ma." Her voice was wretched with reproach.

Poor child, Jane thought, unable to console her. She closed the front door to the boy who delivered their mail each day. This moment was hers, she thought, anticipated for twenty years. She didn't want to share it with anyone. "I'd like to be alone," Jane said softly.

"No, Ma. Read it. I want to know."

"But you don't—"

"I *do* care, Ma. And I've written to Pa. I've asked him to come." A note of triumph crept into Corinna's voice. "He'll want to know, too."

Something erupted inside Jane, exploding from her heart and mind with such force she was startled by its strength. "I don't want him here. Because of him I lost my baby. I would've gone after her myself, but I was too stoved up. I should've made him keep looking."

"He *tried* to find her, Ma. I remember how many times he shouted that he had. What more could he have done?"

Jane's eyes narrowed. "He damn well could've brought her back." Dragging her weak leg, she started for the kitchen.

"The attack wasn't his fault, Ma. Why do you blame him? Losing Mandie wasn't his fault, either. Where was he to look? The west is a big place."

"If he'd been with me that day, she never would have been taken. He could have fought them off, or we all would have been killed. He had no right gallivanting all over creation after one damn horse, leavin'—" Jane stopped herself. She knew where he'd been. She'd always known.

Corinna clutched at her hair. "I wish you had died that day. I wish I'd never been born."

How many times had she herself wished the same thing, Jane thought, limping around the quilting frame to the backdoor. "Dying would've been easy, that's sure," she said, more to herself than to Corinna, "but God wanted me alive so folks could stare and whisper. I don't know what I did to deserve that. I don't know what you did to deserve me for a ma, but we're stuck with each other, Corinna." She threw open the door and stumbled down to the stone step, almost falling.

"Careful, Ma," Corinna grumbled.

"Folks think I should've killed Mandie and myself,

rather than risk being taken. Damn fools." Jane sank down to the step and clutched the unopened letter like a prayer.

Corinna's tone reflected an effort to be reasonable. "Will you try to be nice when Pa comes? Maybe he can go to New Mexico Territory now. He'll know if there's any truth to that man's story. I don't trust that ranger. It's no use getting in a lather if it's not her. Pa would know what to do."

Trembling, Jane said flatly, "It *is* her, and if Hugh Tamberlay shows his face here again, I'll shoot him. Don't you understand the kind of man he is?"

Jane held back the words that would shatter Corinna's innocence about her pa, but she almost wanted to shatter her daughter in order to hurt Hugh through her. Instead she clutched the unopened letter all the harder. "Run along now."

"Is it that he's divorcing you?" Corinna cried. "He's not divorcing you because of your scars. It's you, Ma! You're not with us. Part of you has always been out there somewhere with Mandie."

"That's right," Jane snapped. "If it was you out there, you wouldn't want me to forget."

"That's just it, Ma. I'm *here,* and I *am* forgotten."

Jane knew Corinna was right, but she couldn't help herself. "I suppose your pa's so much better."

"At least he cares."

"Then where is he? Where was he when I needed him? Where was he when you were born? Where was he when Andy took sick? I'll tell you where he was—in town, in the saloon, in an upstairs room. Every time."

"Stop it!"

"Every god-blessed time I needed him, or you did, he had his—"

Shame and heartache as piercing as a tomahawk blade flared deep inside her, but Jane quickly dispelled it with an anesthetizing memory of Mandie trying to climb from the cradle that terrible day twenty years before.

"Ma, come back. Look at me. *Look at me!*"

Corinna grabbed the letter from Jane's grasp, wadded it, and threw it back into the kitchen, dangerously close to the cook stove. "Look at *me!*"

With a cry Jane clawed past Corinna and sprawled headlong into the kitchen, flattening herself on the floor with the letter crushed beneath her chest. "Get *out* of here."

With a sob Corinna fled.

Gathering her wits, Jane sat up and tore the letter open. She spread the single neatly penned page on the floor. With her good eye, she painstakingly made out each blurry word.

When she was done, she wept.

Her baby girl . . . in New Mexico Territory . . . needing a dress and a bath.

An hour later when Corinna ventured back, she thought her ma had died on the floor by the cookstove.

Jane was sleeping.

For the first time since his arrival at Fort Bradley, Carter was properly scrubbed, combed, and curried, wearing his best collar and go-to-meeting trousers. His frock coat was rumpled and his boots scarred, but he would do.

Services were to begin in Mary Graham's front yard at ten-thirty. He had two hours to sit with Firemaker. He had hardly been able to shave for thinking about her.

Taking Jane's letters, the wrapped christening gown, and the daguerreotype picture, he set out. The morning was clear and dry. He could think of nothing else he would rather be doing than sitting in that musty stockade, sweating and claustrophobic, with the most fascinating woman west of the Mississippi.

In honor of Sunday, the prisoners weren't working. They sat in their suffocating cells playing poker, trading stories better suited to a Saturday night. They scarcely acknowledged Carter when he arrived.

Her usual stony self, Firemaker ignored Carter's greeting,

too, when he came in. He brought the stool from the dayroom and settled onto it.

"Your white mother wrote these letters years ago, Firemaker, hoping to find you," Carter began, opening each and pointing to the crudely printed words.

"'Dear Sir, I am lookin for my baby girl what got took by Comanche injuns two years back. I don't think shes kilt. If somebody could go look fer her, I will pay one good horse. . . .'"

Carter paused, wondering if Firemaker understood the concept of a letter. Regardless, he read each one through, and then sat awhile, watching her.

Gradually he became aware of the silence in the cell block. Each prisoner sat, wearing surprisingly thoughtful frowns. Jane Tamberlay's inelegant letters had touched them. He hoped they were thoroughly ashamed of their actions of the night before.

"Firemaker," Carter said at length, "come over here. Come here." He tapped the bars and waved the picture. "Look at this. This is you. On the back your mother has written, 'Amanda Jane Tamberlay, age four weeks, West Creek Fork, Texas, 1850.' This is you, Firemaker. *You.*"

He pointed to her, and then to the picture.

As glad as she was to have Carter back since his brief absence after their long night locked in the cell together, Firemaker was unsure what he wanted now. The papers he held belonged to her white mother—of that she was fairly certain.

Then Firemaker saw the small square of paper he held out. She could see the tiny likeness of a woman in a dark dress holding a baby in a long white dress. Her heart began to trip. She had heard talk of the white man's mysterious photographs.

As if stalking prey, Firemaker rose. Moving close to the barred wall, she stood a long moment marveling at paper that could take on the likenesses of people. She moved close enough for her arm to touch his knuckles. She almost wished she could lean against him.

Carter let her take the picture and withdraw her hand. It was burned along one edge, but the faces were still clear enough to make out. The woman's hair was pale, combed to one side and flowing over her shoulder like a waterfall. The baby was small, wearing a peculiar white dress. Her sparse hair was whitey blond.

Carter tapped the picture. "You," he whispered, pointing to the baby and then to her. "Little Firemaker." He made a rocking motion with his arms together. "Baby."

How did the white men *do* this? she wondered, frightened to think of their powerful medicine with mere paper. What *more* could they do that she couldn't begin to imagine?

Carefully Carter tore into the yellowed paper package. He unfolded the long white dress, scorched and torn.

Recognizing it as the same dress as in the picture, Firemaker yanked it between the iron bars, snagging it and watching it tear nearly in half.

"Ah!" she cried in anguish.

Holding the dress to her chest, she couldn't imagine herself small enough to fit into it. How did the whites make such thin fabric with tiny stitches looking like flowers and vines? How did they make the thunder sticks that killed from far away, and these stone houses that didn't fall down? How did they make the ticking thing Carter occasionally glanced at in his small pocket? And the little knife that folded up? They must be wizards.

Or were they the evil spirits she and the People had feared and somehow offended?

She felt dizzy. Closing her eyes, she sensed that mysterious, unsettling dream lurking on the edge of her memory. The caress, the darkness, the woman's face, the fragrance . . .

Smothering her face in the soft, musty-smelling fabric, Firemaker felt images swirl in her mind. The woman's face began to grow more distinct. Quickly she peeked at the picture. A word came from the depths of her memory, a word and a voice like a child's erupting from her throat.

"Mama!" she blurted. "Ma-ma!"

Looking thunderstruck, Carter leaned closer, his expression intense. "You remember!" He reached through the bars and touched her hand. "You remember!"

"Ma-ma!" she cried, feeling a joyous blend of recognition and heartache combined into the one white word that truly had meaning for her.

She felt unsettled to hear herself speak as if she were a child again. Suddenly she was afraid. She no longer knew herself. Her white blood was taking over. The sun's mark was fading from her forearms. The bear grease had been partially rinsed from her hair. The protective mud was gone from her cheeks. Merely by sitting in the white men's stockade, she was becoming like them.

Staggering back, away from his touch, she fought tears already soaking her cheeks. "Mama," she said softly, shutting out everything but the warmth of that long-forgotten word surrounding her. "Mama." Until that moment she hadn't known how deep her sense of loss cut into her heart. She felt so alone she almost wished herself dead.

She didn't acknowledge Carter's soft questions. After a long while she became aware that he had left. She went on holding the dress against her face while staring over the lacy hem at the picture, memorizing the woman and the baby. *Mama! Mama! Mama!*

Outside, in the hazy morning sunlight, Carter gulped in great lungfuls of thin air. He had to fight a stinging sensation in his throat.

What must she be thinking? he wondered, wandering across the crowded parade ground like one lost. His thigh seemed worse. Would he ever be able to communicate with her fully? Talking with any woman was difficult enough without these seemingly insurmountable barriers. Touching her was definitely unwise.

Then he laughed. He let his eyes brim. What did any of that matter? Jane Tamberlay and her daughter Mandie would soon be together again. That's what was important. If only he could forget about the war chief Snakehorn. He had so much to report to Heck Clanahan and hadn't yet put a word to paper. Perhaps writing would ease his thoughts.

At that moment, in a small room behind the enlisted men's barracks, Timber McTigue was gouging another fingerful of Gold of Olympus pomade from a little black tin in his palm. He slathered it into his graying hair. Brushing it with an old currycomb, he hummed with anticipation.

He smoothed his bushy brows, picked his teeth, and poked a few unruly hairs back into his nostrils. Then he drained the brown jug beside his cot. The firewater cut a hot path down his gullet and turned to a warm pool of courage in his belly.

Slicked and polished, he looked rightly pretty, he thought, parting his beard in the center of his chin. He smoothed the long coarse whiskers into two pointy bunches down over his blue cambric shirtfront and gave his brown suspenders a snap.

With a wink at himself, he stepped out into the brisk southwesterly wind. It was Sunday, and he was going a-courting.

Over in Miz Graham's front yard everybody was joyfully shivering while bringing in the sheaves. Machesney, in his long black frock coat, towered over the officers in blue standing beside their prim little missuses. A few troopers had joined the group, but they stayed to the side opposite the washerwomen and their families.

That was as good a place as any for Machesney, Timber thought, polishing the pocket mirror he'd bought at the sutler's the night before. It was worrisome to discover another man as interested in Firemaker as he. No time to lose.

Teetering into the stockade's dayroom, Timber gave the sergeant behind the desk an elaborate salute. "How's it draggin', trooper?" His tongue felt as thick as a certain other portion of his anatomy.

The guard's eyebrows went up. "Weddin' or funeral, McTigue?"

"I come to see our white Comanche," Timber said grandly, chin out, whiskers at the alert.

The guard grinned. "Funeral, then. She's been babblin' to herself all mornin'. They was at her half the night last night, or so they claim. The Texas Ranger, too. He slept right in the cell afterward. No lie! I let him out myself, at dawn."

"Sonuvabitch!" McTigue cried, steadying himself on the corner of the desk. "Turn my back, and the whelp ups and does me in. And to think I thought him a gen'leman."

Moments later Timber faced Firemaker, his face in a pout.

She looked up quickly. Her expression of anticipation fell as abruptly as his enthusiasm for this fruitless venture. He'd never been good with the ladies, not even the hired ones. What had made him think he would be any better with this savage?

She was nothing more than a slut anyway, he thought, kicking the bars. "You're in a heap of trouble with the colonel, Firemaker, my dear. I been askin' around, and there ain't no family waitin' for you in Texas, leastwise no family that'd take to somebody what's been with Comanches like you surely been. If you take up with me, though, we can go off somewhere into the mountains. It'd be a life you're used to. I wouldn't let nobody abuse you."

Firemaker's puzzled expression made Timber wonder if his Comanche was as bad as the colonel sometimes suspected.

"Carter says he knows my white mother. Did I misunderstand?" she asked in Comanche.

Hellfire and damnation, McTigue thought. "Carter, is it? That jaybird is just tryin' to find out what you know."

Outside the voices singing hymns faltered. An eerie keening had begun in the northeastern corner of the fort. After a moment it was all anyone could hear.

Firemaker sprang to her feet. "The mourning cry," she whispered in Comanche. "Someone has died."

Timber noticed the white fabric Firemaker was holding. It looked like a dirty old baby dress. She held a daguerreotype likeness, too, of a blond woman and a child.

"Lookee here," he said, holding the mirror between the bars while hoping to take those things from her. "I brung this for you." He repeated himself in Comanche. It was hard, looking at her, to remember she understood little English.

She was pacing. "I must be out."

Coming up short, she caught sight of the mirror and snatched it up.

"Ah!" she cried, dropping the dress and photograph and gaping at the mirror. "My white mother!"

"That's you you're lookin' at, you dumb little shit," Timber muttered. "It's a mirror."

She flung the mirror to the dirt. It cracked in half. Her face twisted with surprise. "No!" she cried softly, glancing at Timber as if he'd cursed it. Retrieving the two pieces, she now saw twin images of herself. "Ah!" she yelped in disbelief.

What a damn fool idea, Timber thought, storming out. Females was all alike. Give 'em a present and they got uppity. Machesney could have her.

Everyone who had been gathered in Miz Graham's yard was now standing around like ignorant posts, excepting Machesney, who was loping across the parade ground toward the corral where the Comanche women were taking on something fierce.

Somebody *had* died, Timber thought with a sinking heart. He wondered if there was any gold left in California, or Colorado, or Wyoming. Or hell.

Following Machesney, Colonel Chiswell looked his usual self, his face a blister of anger. By the time Timber reached them, the Comanche women were keening like harpies in a nightmare.

"What the hell's going on?" Timber muttered, realizing at once he'd used the wrong tone. Whiskey for breakfast was not a good idea.

"I'm expecting *you* to enlighten us," the colonel hissed, curving his mouth into a facsimile of a smile. "Have you been at the jug already? *No* intoxicants on Sunday."

"Just followin' example," Timber muttered, "sir."

Before Timber could formulate a diplomatic way to placate the purpling colonel *and* ask the mourning Comanche women why they were carrying on so, the colonel ordered four troopers into the corral with sidearms drawn.

"Aw, now, Colonel, that ain't a good idea—"

"What can they do to us, McTigue? Attack? If that noise doesn't stop, I'll shoot them all myself and have done with it."

It's called a hangover, Timber thought, his well-oiled patience giving way.

"Colonel, you're the goddamnedest fool I ever met up with. I'd sooner lance a boil on my backside than go on dealin' with you another day. Fifteen dollars a month ain't enough to put up with your bellyaching. It ain't *near* enough for my hair."

The colonel leveled acid eyes on Timber. "What are you saying?"

"I reckon I'm making myself clear. I ain't stayin' to watch you start your own private war."

"Is that a fact?"

"Yes, sir. If you let more captives die, not only will Snakehorn roast your innards and hold a picnic supper for all his warriors watching us from them foothills, but the U.S. Army's goin' to fricassee what's left of your bones and serve 'em in Washington come Christmas. On toast."

Machesney edged between the two men. "Gentlemen, can either of you tell me what's happened?"

Timber stepped back. "Son, in case you weren't listening, I jes' retired."

Machesney caught his sleeve. "I need you to help me talk with Firemaker."

"From what-all I heard, sonny, you communicated with her right nicely all last night. Jes' remember, the first time you turn your back, that little lady will show you amazing feats with her skinning knife."

Within the corral came a scuffle. The four guards broke for the fence but came up short, as reluctant to face the scowling colonel as stay inside with the keening Comanche women.

"Sir, the littlest one's died," the tallest guard blurted. "They won't let us take the body. It's still laced up in its cradle board. It's mother's gone plum crazy."

Timber's gut knotted. "There'll be hell to pay now, Colonel."

Carter was still clutching McTigue's sleeve. "Colonel, this is your opportunity to show these Comanche women how they'll be treated on the reservation. It might do you well to show respect for the dead child . . . and give them supplies. Later they might persuade Snakehorn to surrender. There's no telling the good that might result from fair treatment today. Isn't that right, McTigue?"

"No tellin' at all, Colonel," Timber muttered sarcastically. "Comanches is known for their forgivin' nature. They surely are."

The colonel seemed amazingly suggestible suddenly. "What's your plan, Machesney?"

"Perhaps Firemaker could take the baby from them and help us bury it in the cemetery."

"As long as they're quiet," Jed Chiswell remarked, "you can hang it from the flagstaff for all I care."

EIGHT

FROM THE CORRAL, Four Toes noticed a detail forming on the far side of the stockade. Moving slowly as if in pain, Firemaker emerged from the stone building, flanked by four guards. Wearing leg irons around her ankles, she could only make small steps. Her hands were locked before her in shackles. Her breasts looked as plump as melons beneath her shirt.

Holding her head high, she strained for her first glimpse of the Comanche captives. It had been so long since Four Toes had seen his white daughter that he had feared the soldiers had killed her.

He saw anguish in her twisted brow, her tortured eyes, in the pinched muscles around her mouth. She was reining her temper as he had never before seen her do, and suddenly he felt able to stand and meet her courage with the remnants of his own.

The mourning women fell silent. They knew why Firemaker was coming; she would take the baby's body away. Four Toes knew it was necessary. The women did, too, but they did not greet her with gladness. And Firemaker didn't look surprised.

Watching Firemaker's halting progress, Four Toes thought of her first awkward steps across his tepee so many years before. Some had laughed because she walked so late, but Four Toes' wife believed Firemaker had known great shock. She had nearly died on the ride from Texas and didn't adjust well to their Comanche food. For a time her development had halted.

Children, Four Toes knew now, were not puppies or horses to be taken or traded. This girl child he had plucked from the white man's cellar had been his finest treasure, but he could see that she belonged to him no more.

He had no regrets about taking her. He would do it all over again, but with age came the knowledge that all things carried a price. The price for bringing Firemaker to his grieving wife twenty years before had been giving her up the day of the horse soldiers' attack on their village.

Firemaker stood at the rail of the corral now, the sun's dark color less pronounced on her cheeks, her hair tangled, her clothes stained. Four Toes' heart hurt, but he met her red-rimmed eyes squarely.

When she twisted away from the sight of the women and naked children huddled together behind him, every bluecoat within three feet raised a weapon.

"What have you done to deserve this?" Four Toes asked Firemaker in Comanche.

"I don't know," she answered softly.

"Then let yourself see this, Firemaker. This is all that's left of us. Little Cloud has died. We will speak his name no more."

Four Toes watched as Firemaker forced herself to look from Morning-Sky to Laughs-at-Birds and all the rest. If the band had survived undisturbed, Four Toes thought, Firemaker would have made a great medicine woman one day.

"I am powerless," he said, saddened to think how he had avoided Firemaker in the past few years, and how little comfort he had offered her on the march down the pass. "You must lend these women your strength now. Look how the horse soldiers guard you. They don't guard me. You are the one with great medicine."

She shook her head.

The white man who had been bringing them food at night interrupted with a question in English. Four Toes watched a softening in his white daughter's countenance when she looked up at the man. He found her expression of trust most interesting. She looked at the stranger as if she could expect his help. Then as quickly as her vulnerability became evident, she masked it.

Four Toes had no time to ponder what the stranger might mean to Firemaker. "We're starving," was all he said.

Firemaker turned wounded eyes on the guards. "Eat! Eating! More eat!" She was speaking English. After her rescue from the Apaches, she had sworn to Four Toes she would never say white words again.

Now to Four Toes she cried, "They won't let me out of the stone house. What can I do?"

"Forget your anger, my daughter," Four Toes said in Comanche, "until the time comes to remember it."

He watched her struggle with her rage and grief. He saw victory in the gradual settling of her shoulders.

"Are they planning to take you to your white mother?" Four Toes asked.

Firemaker shook off his question. "Where is Snakehorn? Why hasn't he come for us?"

The stranger interrupted again. Firemaker cast him an impatient glance. "Wait," she said in Comanche. "Eating!" she snapped in English, pointing to the Comanche women.

Someone gave a command to hurry the proceedings along. Suddenly Four Toes knew why he had been compelled to take a seemingly worthless white infant from a burning homestead twenty years before. She was destined to save the People.

"Daughter," he said softly.

He remembered the feel of her little body in his hand that day when he held her high over the white woman's ravished body and shouted, "No white man shall ever penetrate so deep into my lands as I have into yours."

Four Toes had no shame for his youthful boast. No Comanche could have known then of the coming changes. Perhaps life was in the warmth of flesh, not in the possession of lands or horses. For his lands were gone. His horses were dead. The whites had not only penetrated into Comancheria and driven the People headlong into war with the Apaches, but they had conquered. All Four Toes had left now was his spirit grafted onto Firemaker's heart.

He found himself saying, "Don't forget me."

She shook her head. "I want to fight with you, die with you!"

"That's not the way for you, Firemaker. You aren't a warrior. You never have been, and you must not continue to try to be. Forget the flames of your anger. Use the ways of women. Use the coals. You are the Firemaker, not the fire."

He saw that she understood, suddenly, the name he had given her so many years before. She was the spark, the heat. He nodded a little, his honor restored. She truly was his heart. And where *was* Snakehorn? he wondered. Was his dreamer of an eldest son at long last dead?

Would Four Toes have to watch these women and children die, too, one by one? Good warriors died young, he reminded himself. It was easiest that way. The spirits had elected to keep him alive to watch this shame. Four Toes felt suddenly weary.

He hobbled to the far corner of the corral and took the dead baby in its cradle board from One-Basket's arms. "We cannot bury the child here," he said to her. "Firemaker was once one of us. She was always your friend. She'll make certain your child meets the spirit world well prepared even if it must be from the white man's holy ground."

As the keening resumed, Four Toes carried the cradle board to the fence rail. He looked into the colonel's skittish eyes, saying with his silence that horse soldiers who starved infants had no honor, no manhood.

Then he looked at his daughter, bound in chains. How proud he was. How sad.

Realizing Firemaker couldn't take the cradle board from the old man while she was bound, the colonel ordered the leg irons and shackles removed. The surrounding troopers edged back, watching her every move as she was freed.

The man in the long black coat and string tie edged closer, lending a kind of comfort to Firemaker but one she scarcely noticed. Four Toes noticed, and his guilt eased. She would be all right with this man.

Firemaker's eyes fell for the first time on the face of Little Cloud peeping from its swaddling of gray-and-white rabbit fur. Four Toes watched his daughter's expression go blank. Her countenance hardened. She would not cry.

The sadness in Four Toes spread until he felt weak. With the passing of the baby went the leadership of the tribe. His life was done. He felt ashamed to be living it still.

Firemaker fought the welling of pain in her heart. She blinked. She thought of her smarting wrists and stinging ankles. She couldn't allow herself the luxury of grief. She wouldn't allow tears.

She was bound to honor her father. In the past few moments he had bestowed upon her his greatest gift, his respect. She had worked all her life toward that. She couldn't let him down now.

Lifting her eyes to Carter's, she pointed toward the stockade. "Mama."

"What?" Carter said, searching her face. "What do you need? The picture? Why?" He shook his head, his brow furrowing. "Not the gown. Oh, the gown. Of course."

Cautioning everyone to wait, Carter started back for the guardhouse. As he broke into a long-legged lope Firemaker turned back to her father. She felt responsibility for the survival of these remaining women and children settle onto her shoulders like a great black mountain. Never had she dreamed her father held her in such regard. Perhaps he hadn't until this very moment.

"I'm afraid," she whispered in Comanche.

"I'll always be in your heart, daughter. When I die, I will come to live in your thoughts. You have made the white man fear you. Now you must make them trust you."

Behind her, Carter's footsteps came quickly back. When he reached her side, she felt stronger. Once again he offered the fragile old baby dress with the long embroidered skirt.

She took it. She understood suddenly how her mother must have felt so long ago, placing her in the cellar with the amulet, facing a Comanche attack alone. The small gold oval had never been meant as a luck charm, as Four Toes thought. It had been a token of a mother's love. One-Basket had no such token to give Little Cloud. Firemaker had only the dress.

With one swift jerk, Firemaker tore the christening skirt open and held it spread before her like a shroud. Four Toes pressed the cradle board onto the yellowed folds. She closed the lacy edges over the sleep-filled face with the dark lashes fanned on the cheeks.

She drew the board close, amazed at the grief in her heart. "No more hunger. No more sorrow," she crooned in her throat. She knew what to do.

One of the women came forward with a scrap of dried meat. Another hastened to offer a small bladder of water. One of the older boys offered a stick shaped like an arrow.

"Thank you," Firemaker whispered. "With these things, he'll do well in the next life."

"This way," Carter said.

Though she didn't understand Carter's words, she knew he was guiding her.

She felt his hand close on her left shoulder, cautious, warm, strong. His touch was life-giving. She drew a deep, cleansing breath. She could do this. She could carry this mountain.

The watching troopers fell away before her, creating a path that led to a small fenced plot lost in the tall grasses and wild flowers growing on the far side of one of the gardens. The white men's sun-bleached crosses and weathered wooden markers stood haphazardly among a number of rock-covered mounds.

One of the troopers began digging in the gravel, but Carter stopped him and took the spade to dig the grave himself. Firemaker stepped in his way. She shook her head and indicated Carter must hold the cradle board while she dug the grave.

Looking into his gentle, pained eyes, Firemaker felt herself give way inside. Like an earthen dam softened by too much rain, she felt Carter's warmth and his concern flowing into her, soothing her, calming her, strengthening her. She could not help herself. She trusted him.

Then painstakingly she dug the grave with her bare hands, facing it east as was the Comanche custom. When Carter gave her the body once again, he closed his hands over hers. His palms were dry, his skin warm, his fingertips trembling slightly.

Tenderly she laid the cradle board in the grave along with the provisions for the baby's trip into the next life. She wanted to leave her locket, but the locket held no meaning for this child. She must return it to Jane White Mother.

As Firemaker scooped the warm, dry earth over the embroidered lawn, she felt a stabbing ache in her heart. She could not grieve and carry the mountain, too, so she shut out the pain. She shed no tears.

When she was done, Firemaker raised her voice in mourning, letting her constricted throat pour wailing notes across the sun-drenched Sunday morning. The Comanche women's voices joined with hers, accompanied by the uncomfortable shuffling of soldiers' feet as counterpoint. Everyone in Mary Graham's front yard remained silent.

In time Carter pulled Firemaker to her feet. She didn't feel his touch any longer. She was grieving only with her voice. In her heart she was searching for a way to lead the women and children, and her father, home to the mountains. She would do whatever was necessary to accomplish that.

Holding her head high, Firemaker walked from the cemetery back to the stockade. The soldiers followed, but she paid them no heed. She stepped across the threshold and went into the cell block unassisted.

On the floor in her cell lay the picture of her white mother and the broken mirror. Firemaker understood why Timber had offered it to her, and also why he had gone away angry. He was like most men. He wanted to possess her. For that reason she had spurned him.

She longed for a strong, tall horse of a man to help her, to walk beside her—a man like the one called Carter—to give her the freedom she needed to be herself.

"Mama," she whispered in Comanche, "I feel your heart crying in me. I may not live to see you. I have these People to protect."

Carter was watching her, unable to understand the soft Comanche words, which he mistook for a prayer.

"I'm sorry, Firemaker," he said, his voice thick. "I knew the baby was failing, but I couldn't get anyone to authorize better rations. I should've ridden to Santa Fe for tinned milk myself."

She didn't understand. She didn't need to. She could see that Carter was in anguish over the baby's death. And he was there to help her. How sorry she was that she would probably be driven to betray him.

She knew now that she wanted Carter. She wanted to share herself with him. She wanted to know him, and for him to know her.

But she had to remain aloof. Though his presence was a

comfort, she couldn't let him see what she was really feeling. He stood so tall, so strong, and so kind that she let herself smile just a little. She would pretend. Her heart shivered at the sight of him. He was her friend. She could not be his.

Crossing the cell, Firemaker presented herself at the bars. She looked up into Carter's face and began reciting every white word she could think of that she understood. "Good book, morning, night, sun, star, head, hair, eyes, teeth. Eat, eating, horse, blessed, walk, hand."

She clutched the oval of gold hanging around her neck and stood looking up at Carter with a question in her eyes.

"Locket," he said, gaping in astonishment.

"Lo-ket," she repeated.

He looked at her so long she feared she wouldn't be able to keep her heart from sabotaging what she suspected she would eventually be forced to do.

"Blessed are the meek. . . ."

He clutched the bars separating them. "Oh, Firemaker."

She touched his fingers, so rugged, so strong, and nodded. How good it would feel if he could hold her. She wondered if he would want to. By the look in his eyes, she suspected he might. Her heart hurt all the more.

"More . . ." She touched her mouth, trying to indicate talking. "Carter. Firemaker. Mary. Lo-ket. Ma-ma." She tried to think. Her throat tightened. She fought tears. "Baby." She pointed to the broken mirror on the floor at her feet.

"Mirror," he said. "Broken mirror." He pretended to break something over his knee. "Broken."

"Bro-ken," she said. Oh, yes, she felt broken.

The silence fell long between them. But it was a full silence, heavy with words that needed no voice. Carter was there to help her. She was ready for him.

Looking pale and overwrought, Mary stepped in from the dayroom. "Matthew forbid me to come, but I came anyway," she said breathlessly. "Is Firemaker all right? Livvie says my baby'll be marked if I keep associating with Firemaker, but I . . ."

Whatever Mary had been about to say was forgotten as Firemaker repeated more white words.

Mary stopped and stared, her face spreading into a smile. "Listen to her!"

Behind her, Matthew Graham edged in. "Mary, please. You should lie down."

"She's ready to learn," Mary said, her eyes glistening with tears. "Seeing the captives must have frightened her to death. She must realize her fate if she doesn't join us."

"I wonder," Carter said, looking deeply into Firemaker's eyes. "I wonder."

Firemaker let him look all he liked. He would never see what truly lay in her heart, a Comanche spirit.

"We must begin right now," Mary said, turning to her husband . . . and swooning directly into his arms.

Momentarily forgotten as Carter and the lieutenant carried Mary out, Firemaker worried about the one white woman who had so far shown her such kindness. This was not a good time for Mary to fall ill, Firemaker thought. Yet there was no time to lose. There was so much to learn.

A while later Carter returned with Mary's Bible, and the lessons in English began.

"Blessed are the poor in spirit. . . ." he read, and Firemaker listened with all her heart.

NINE

STANDING IN THE doorway, Corinna squinted into the saloon's murky gloom. The moment she recognized the silhouette of her pa, leaning against a post near the bar, her heart skipped.

She could understand why her ma had married a man like him and had followed him so far from her family. He cut the finest figure Corinna had ever seen. Her heart bled with love for him.

He turned from a gaudy woman he'd been talking to, his smile suggestive. Spying Corinna, thin and severely dressed, squinting in at him from the glaring sunlight beyond the swinging doors, Hugh Tamberlay edged away.

A different sort of smile stretched his lips. For an instant Corinna thought the smile looked false. As soon as she thought so, she corrected herself. Her pa was just embarrassed to be caught in a saloon at that hour. He was not sorry to see her.

"Baby girl," Hugh drawled, stepping into daylight less than kind to his fifty-three years. His skin looked sallow, his eyes glassy and expressionless. "Look at you, all grown up into a fine young woman."

"Papa," Corinna whispered, hardly able to speak for the knot of happiness in her throat. "Papa!" She gave him a hug.

"What're you doin', writin' to saloons to find me, girl?" He steered her along the boardwalk. "That ain't right."

"Ma always says that's where I'll find you if I care to look."

"A man does business where he can," Hugh said, his tone reproachful.

"Why must you stay away so long, Papa?" she asked, although she understood perfectly why he did. Her ma kept him away. "I'm so lonesome without you."

He just shook his head as if her concerns were those of a tired child. "Tell me what's wrong. Is your ma ailin'?"

"I—I'll tell you when we get home. I don't want to talk about it here." She cast a worried look up the street at some women watching from the general store.

"Now, baby girl, I won't be seein' your ma anymore."

"But Ma and me have had words, and she's actin' . . . peculiar."

Hugh looked as if he wanted to be on his way. If he decided to go, nothing would stop him. Corinna decided she had better tell him everything.

As she explained about the ranger, Hugh paused at the cross street and looked sternly down at her. She whispered, "He had the locket, Pa."

She saw not a flicker of reaction in her pa's eyes, but at once she felt tension emanating from him just as she could feel tension in her ma when the woman was ruminating about Mandie.

Hugh took out a lucifer match and snapped it with his long thumbnail. He lit a thin brown cheroot. "An engraved locket," he said with no inflection in his voice.

"Yes, the one Ma's always carrying on about. But it didn't say all she remembered. Pa, you told me Mandie was dead! *He* says she's out in New Mexico Territory, alive!"

Corinna hated the whine creeping into her voice. When her pa said nothing, she began to panic. "He's bringing her back here!"

"Mandie." Hugh spoke the name softly.

"Yes, Mandie. God-blessed Mandie, with dirty hair

and . . . and wild ways. Papa, what are we goin' to do? She can't come back. I've been livin' with a half-crazy woman all my life. I can't have a Comanche sister, too. I'll never catch a decent beau. Let me come away with you."

"Now, baby girl, I'm on the road just as much as ever. It's in my blood." He looked so distracted Corinna wanted to pummel him.

Hugh pulled at his jaw. "I suppose I'd best see your ma after all. Run along and warn her. But this is the last time, Corinna. I swear it."

What could he say to Jane to end all this? Hugh wondered, watching Corinna dart for home. She kept looking back over her shoulder, taking little skipping steps like she used to when she was small.

His baby girl all grown up, his *other* baby girl . . .

Hugh rubbed the back of his aching neck. Turning away, he squinted into the clear morning sun. Goddammit, the business with Mandie just wouldn't rest.

He supposed he didn't really have to speak to Jane. He could just ride out of town. Lord knows he'd ridden away from her enough times in the past.

Jane was probably hysterical. She'd want him to go get Mandie, and that was impossible. There was no Mandie left to get. Never had been. Their Mandie was dead.

God only knew what was in New Mexico Territory. A heathen. A whore. What did it matter? Thank God Jane was too crippled up to ride any farther than church. If she could have, she would have gone in search of Mandie herself. Years ago.

He'd had a bellyful of her obsession, he thought. He'd thought by the tone of Corinna's letter that Jane was dying. He'd hoped she was. He slammed back into the saloon. What kept her going?

What more was he expected to do? He'd given up his ranch. He'd bought the house for her in town. He'd endured the stares, the whispers, the speculation. Corinna and Andy had been proof Jane hadn't been raped; he wouldn't have bedded her if she had, or so he told everyone.

But she had been raped, nine times, and Hugh had known it. He'd drunk himself nearly to death to bed her, knowing that, but he'd done it. He'd given her back her reputation. She repaid him with obsession.

Hugh slumped against the bar. "Leave the bottle," he said.

How had Mandie come to be so haunting? he wondered. She'd been an ordinary child. What had the Comanches wanted with her? How could he have found her?

He might have spent the rest of his life wandering around the west, and what was the point of that? There was no Mandie after that terrible day. He'd written her off in the blink of an eye. There was no Mandie now.

Everything might have been all right if Andy hadn't died, Hugh thought, probing the still-painful abscess in his heart that was his dead son. Hugh might have gone on with Jane, but with the passing of that boy because of Jane's indifference and neglect, Hugh had given up trying.

As Hugh drank, the years fell away. He remembered back to the early days of the war. He'd still been with Jane then, at the house. Andy was gone. Corinna was always hiding in one gloomy corner or another.

He'd stopped sleeping with Jane. She was like a corpse in his arms. His thoughts had turned to Maylene and all the others who managed to remain sweet and agreeable no matter how long he stayed away.

When it looked as though the Confederate army would draft him, Hugh left West Creek Fork, saying he was going to enlist. He went west instead. But not to find Mandie.

Even so, he'd made the occasional effort to ask after white captives. Why not? There had been no hope, not a sliver. Yet one night at a faro table, a shaggy gizzard licker of a mountain man took him aside.

"I heard you call yourself Tamberlay. Got me something back at my place, bought off an Injun trader last spring. It's all engraved and fancy. Real gold. Might be you'd want to see it."

"My business is horses, friend," Hugh had said. He had turned away, an uneasy churning in his belly.

"The piece might have your name on it."

Sick with anticipation, Hugh had followed the old geezer to his digs. He had watched with growing horror as the man produced Jane's locket. The very one.

Hugh knew that piece of gold better then he knew his wife's face. Before Jane, he'd given it to Annie. Before Annie, Martha. Had it not been lost, he would've given it to Maylene. She couldn't read either.

By that time, Mandie had been missing ten years. For nearly as long, Hugh had felt free of shame. To see the locket again, scratched and bitten up, made Hugh sick at his stomach. He'd felt bound to erase *anything* capable of bringing back the harrowing images burned into his memory.

Trading his horses for the locket, Hugh had hired a guide to take him into the Apache mountains. With every mile he had wondered why he was going after Mandie after so long. He had told himself he was doing it for Jane, but that had been another lie.

He'd done it for himself, to cleanse the wound of his shame. He couldn't get the sight of Jane out of his mind, her face black with blood, her scalp raw, her gashed temple stitched together by Ed Keener's wife with a darning needle.

He didn't want to remember, clear as crystal, the day Jane was rocking on the Keeners' porch afterward, watching the western horizon. At the stroke of three she'd leaped to her feet. "Find Mandie," she'd said to him in a voice he hadn't recognized and never wanted to hear again. *"Bring her back."*

He'd used up a good six months, trading across Texas,

New Mexico Territory, and Colorado before returning to Jane with threadbare lies that he couldn't find their baby daughter. He hadn't wanted Mandie back, not after a year, or three, or ten.

The child was dead to him, as dead as he was to his pa, the man who'd thrown a thirteen-year-old boy from a farm wagon at the county line. "Git yer ass off my place and don't never show yer face 'round here agin."

To this day, Hugh didn't know why his pa had done that. He didn't care. He'd gone back and shot the man a year later. His ma never asked why.

Half blind with whiskey, Hugh hunched over the bar now, the thoughts still thick in his head. Folks had assured him Jane would be all right after Corinna was born, but she sat in the porch rocker as if no babe wailed in the nursery. Ellie Keener would've raised both Tamberlay children if she hadn't taken sick with fever and died that year.

Hugh drained the bottle before him. He smoothed his shaking hands on the damp bar. If Jane hadn't been rocking, watching the western horizon, if he hadn't been in town that night Andy took sick with fever, too . . .

He couldn't tell if the whiskey was going into his mouth or down his shirtfront. All Hugh Tamberlay could see was his four-year-old son lying still in his bed. Superimposed on that memory was his wife, her breasts bare, her hands flexing, open, closed. Open. Closed. And one-year-old Mandie, smiling with two bottom teeth. Gone.

That summer of 1862, Hugh had ridden into the Apache mountains determined to find the Indians who had traded Jane's locket to the mountain man. The ghosts of his children, living and dead, had followed him every mile.

"These here Apaches collect white captives," his guide had explained. "They sell 'em to the Mexicans for horses. The Mexicans, they use 'em in bordellos. The women last two years, three at best. You want one cheap?"

Hugh hadn't answered. He'd just sat before the campfire and oiled his gun.

Deep in the high country, the guide offered gifts to a passel of half-naked Apache savages in order to get a glimpse of eight white captives, ranging in age from ten to eighteen, filthy as beggars.

Hugh had recognized Mandie at once, rawboned and gangly like Jane's younger sister, the one who could write. Mandie had been homely as a new calf.

Dressed in a ragged calico smock, her filthy whitey-blond hair had streamed past her shoulders in shaggy tangles. Never had Hugh felt more shame. It was on his account she looked like that.

He hadn't paused to think. He drew and fired at her, so shaken he missed by several feet. The Apaches flattened him to the stony ground. They took everything, his clothes, his boots, his gold. And the pistol. All he had left was the locket in his shaking hand. Fearing for his life, he'd held it out to the shaggy-haired little girl who ran up to him.

She spat on him. The Apaches let her drop little coals from the campfire onto his hairy belly. Each one had burned black little craters into his skin. She'd been forced to do it bare-handed. The Apaches had laughed. He couldn't forget her blistering gray-blue eyes as she did what her captors commanded. He'd always wondered if she knew who he was.

Then she'd thrown a handful of coals into the dry timber surrounding the Apache camp. Flames flared into the pines as she snatched the locket from his palm and fled into the rocks.

Only the trader's glib tongue had saved Hugh's life. Hugh still wasn't sure how they'd gotten away. He'd fainted. They had beat him nearly to death. He was taken to Maylene's. For two years, he refused to return to Texas. Later he told Jane he'd been wounded at Two Rivers, fighting under the Confederate flag.

* * *

From the porch, Corinna saw her pa staggering up the road.

Letting himself in, Hugh found Jane in the kitchen, bent over the quilting frame, squinting with her better eye, poking the needle straight up and straight down through the layers of fabric.

"I'm back," Hugh said, his tongue thick.

Corinna crept up behind her papa and gave both her parents an imploring smile. "Say hello to him, Ma. Be nice."

"There's something you and me got to talk over," Hugh said, shrugging off Corinna's touch. "Baby girl here tells me there's news of Mandie, but I got to tell you, woman, that child died. Somebody's pullin' your leg."

Jane accidentally jabbed the needle into her finger. She gave a little yelp and jerked away, dripping a bright spot of red onto the quilt square.

They were going to quarrel, Corinna thought, fleeing up the back stairs to her room. With the door half-closed, she listened to the voices rising below, rising as the pain of years and years of disappointments fueled their words. She couldn't remember how to pray.

Then the words quieted. Corinna's hope flared. She crept back to the landing and listened.

"Now, Jane." Hugh sounded alarmed. "Whoa . . ."

Corinna slipped down several more steps and peeked around the stairwell wall. From the folds of her apron, her mother had drawn a pistol.

"Ma, no!" Corinna tumbled into the kitchen.

"I ain't listenin' another day to his lies." The shot that followed resounded like thunder.

Corinna gave a shriek and clutched at her hair. She dropped to the floor, screaming. She couldn't bear to look.

Unhurt, Hugh wrestled the pistol from Jane's grip and knocked her angrily to the floor. Leaning over Corinna, he slapped her. "Shut up, baby girl! Mandie's dead. The Comanches killed her. Shootin' me ain't goin' to change that. I ought to have you both locked up."

"Pa," Corinna whimpered. "Please."

Jane snatched at his pant leg. "I lived with you long enough. I can tell you're lying."

Fighting her flailing arms, Hugh gathered Jane up from the floor and carried her awkwardly into the parlor, where he flung her on the divan. "You ain't worth this nonsense, you durn fool. Mandie ain't in New Mexico Territory. She can't be," he said, his tone tight with frustration.

Her pa sounded scared, Corinna thought, her tears drying. Could her ma be right? Was Mandie really out there?

"Pa?" Corinna said carefully.

"Why'd you lie about what was engraved on the locket?" Jane asked him, her voice suddenly low and soft.

His face turned red. "I don't have to listen to no more of this. Baby girl, I don't want you staying here with your ma no more. I'll see about a place for you in town."

Corinna's heart shivered to a stop. "I want to be with you, Pa!"

He shook his head.

"Don't you want me?" Corinna cried.

Jane struggled to her feet. "I don't know why I'm trying to kill you, Hugh Tamberlay. You ain't worth killing. You know my girl's out there. You've known all along, and you don't care. But you care for your pleasures and you care about your boys."

Hugh took a step closer. "Think about what you're saying, woman."

Jane smiled sadly, shaking her head. "I don't know what I've been doing, coverin' up for the likes of you all these years. Corinna, I'm truly sorry to be hurtin' you like this, but if you can't abide me anymore, you got a pa with a decent house big enough for you and his other family, too. Just ask him. Go with him. I won't hold it against you."

Corinna found herself standing on the porch, looking at the open gate and the prairie beyond. She didn't know how she got there. It couldn't be true. Another family . . .

The words were in her mind now, words she'd held at bay since her pa came to her graduation two years before and stayed only long enough to strike a deal for some horses in Fort Worth. He didn't love her.

"Baby girl?" Her papa's voice sounded worried.

"I'm not your baby girl anymore, Pa," Corinna said, a part of her wanting him to protest, wanting him to snatch her up and shake her for saying such a thing.

She wanted him to assure her she'd always be his baby girl, but he remained silent.

After a moment his voice came out as silky as always. "You do have a way of makin' a mess of things, Jane," he said softly. "I should've shot you when I found you."

Jerking as if her pa had just struck her, Corinna whirled and stared at him as he stood stooped in the open doorway.

"Why didn't you?" Jane asked, her voice as free of reproach as Corinna had ever heard it.

If Hugh Tamberlay didn't love her ma, Corinna thought, and didn't pity her after all that had happened, and in spite of all that had happened, did he live in the same feeling world that Corinna knew existed in the depths of her loneliness?

"I couldn't split your head with an ax, Jane. All I had was my pistol. I had no way of knowing if those Comanches had more than bows and arrows."

"Jesus, Pa."

"She brought this out of me, baby girl, carrying on like a crazy woman."

"No, Pa," Corinna said, her tone suddenly as harsh as his. "Nobody can bring something like that out of a person unless it's already there. You're trying to hurt Ma because she's told your secret. The sorry fact is, Pa, I've known for years. About the ranchers' daughters, about the whores at the saloon. I've defended you to every person in town. Now I understand why folks feel sorry for me. It's not on account of Ma. It's on account of you. Go away. I'm sorry I ever bothered you with all this. Go back to . . . to whoever, and forget about me."

Corinna stepped down from the porch and crossed the yard to the gate.

"Where are you goin'?" Her ma's voice sounded worried.

"I'll be back, Ma," Corinna said absently, pushing through the gate.

The smell of slates and chalk brought back poignant memories for Corinna as she stood in the schoolroom doorway across town. It was late in the day. Classes had just been dismissed.

"Corinna Tamberlay! What a surprise to see you after so long. Have you reconsidered my suggestion?" Tying on her sunbonnet, Mrs. Edgerly emerged from the cloakroom. Her happy expression fell. "You look like you've been crying, child."

Corinna brushed absently at her damp cheeks. "I can't remember where New Mexico Territory is."

Mrs. Edgerly drew down a map hanging from a roller over the chalkboard. "T'other side of Texas, honey. Apache lands."

"And Comanche."

The woman's face took on an expression that suggested she suddenly understood Corinna's odd behavior. "Is your ma having another bad spell?"

"They've found my . . . sister."

As the words came out the hollowness inside Corinna began to overflow with grief. She looked at her old schoolmistress and began openly sobbing in a way that meant she was either terrified or exhausted.

Sinking into a snug chair attached to one of the small

Autumn Blaze 125

desks, Corinna stared at names carved in the soft yellow pine. She wondered if she could go all the way to New Mexico Territory. She wondered if she would kill Mandie or bring her home.

TEN

BLOCKING THE DOORWAY, Olivia glared up at her husband. "Do y'all have any idea what Mary asked of me this mornin'?" When Jed didn't venture a guess, Olivia jerked his sleeve like a petulant child. "She wants to borrow a dress . . . for that heathen female to wear. Can you feature that? One of *my* dresses on that filthy creature. Jed, y'all aren't releasin' her soon, are you?"

Jed's eyes never quite reached hers, which maddened Olivia.

"My orders are to give the 'creature' they refer to as Miss Tamberlay the freedom of the fort as soon as I am convinced she is trustworthy. I *don't* want her to become a political issue, Olivia. Now if you would be so kind, I have duties to attend."

"But Mary's talkin' as if *that creature* is goin' to stay at her house. That's next door, Jed. You mustn't allow it. Release her if you must, but send her on her way."

"Mary has mentioned the idea to me," Jed said, his lips thinning. "I would gladly send Miss Tamberlay on her way to the farthest corners of the earth, but she has certain military value. Besides, Olivia, she needs a woman's assistance to become socially tolerable. Personally I can't see that teaching a savage to pretend good behavior has any relevance, but from the first this situation has gotten away from me. We might have avoided all these problems. . . ." For a second he looked pointedly at her. "Since we could not, we must comply. May I go now, pet?"

"Jed," she whined, "you don't understand."

"Give her a dress if you wish, Olivia. If not, you can always beg off by telling Mary you have none to spare. Surviving on a colonel's pay is such a trial, especially out here."

Livvie clutched her throat. "I would never—"

Grinning without amusement, Jed slipped past her. "I thought not." He paused on the walk. "If it's any comfort, dear, I've ordered bars installed on the Grahams' quarters."

"You've already decided, then? Why didn't you say so? Has she *met* the requirements you've been harpin' on to Carter?"

"Harping? Who's side are you on? Moot point. You're never on mine. If you want to know, I hadn't decided until just now, but it's high time I plucked this thorn from my foot. You *will* school Miss Tamberlay in your particular brand of southern hospitality, I trust. There's a good wife."

"Let your light so shine before men, that they may see your good works, and glorify your Father which is in heaven." The words were as difficult to pronounce as they were to understand, Firemaker thought.

Finished with Mary's lesson for the day, Firemaker placed the great black book on the blanketed floor beside where she sat cross-legged in her cell. Her hands were trembling.

For every step forward that she took on her journey to become white, she felt another piece of her Comanche self falling away. Her resolve to control her feelings about the changes she knew she must make seemed to be crumbling, not only when reading the white man's confusing holy words, but particularly today as she strained to hear the colonel's approach.

"You're doing so well," Mary said, beaming, her pale hands clasped over her expanding belly. "I know he's going to let you out today."

"Thank you," Firemaker said, understanding enough, but unsure how to reply.

"Isn't she just amazing?" Mary asked of Carter when he returned from the dayroom.

"I don't see that he's coming yet," Carter said, his brow furrowed, his expression tense. "He's still at the gate, talking with McTigue. I wonder what yarns the old coot is spinning this time."

"I had thought McTigue gone for good, but we mustn't worry," Mary said, gingerly patting Carter's arm. "Whatever brought him back after only a week can have nothing to do with Jed letting Firemaker out of here today."

Carter's glance was anything but reassuring. "It likely has everything to do with Firemaker and her hopes for freedom."

Firemaker studied her paling hands, scrubbed raw and so like Mary's now. They had attempted to comb her hair, too, but Mary had insisted it would take a good washing to get it completely in order. That was a task for later, she said.

Today, Firemaker thought, Colonel Chiswell would sit in judgment of her. That was the first step. True freedom would also come later. Firemaker felt angry, hiding her feelings beneath the fragile veneer of Carter and Mary's daily instructions, while waiting to do what must be done . . . later.

"Yes, she is remarkable," Carter said in reply to Mary's earlier comment. He looked into Firemaker's eyes, warming her with his smile. He seemed able to speak directly to her heart.

Strangely, Firemaker felt as shy as a girl.

"Oh, I think I hear him now," Mary said, standing from the stool and smoothing her dress. "I can still scarcely believe we convinced him to review Firemaker after only three weeks. When you brought it up last night, I never thought he'd agree so readily. It's difficult to know what he's thinking sometimes."

"Considering his condition, I wasn't surprised at all that he felt cooperative," Carter said softly. "It was my only hope. Colonel Chiswell doesn't think. He reacts."

Mary cast Carter a reproachful look. "He's under a great deal of strain."

"As are we all," Carter said, his expression growing guarded.

When the colonel entered the cell block, Firemaker wanted to slink into the corner as she had done in the beginning. The colonel's coat was so clean, his hair so tidy, his boots gleaming. If she hadn't known him to be a fool, she would have been far more afraid.

Instead she stood proudly, head high, heart hammering.

"Good m-morning . . . Colonel Chis-well," Firemaker said, speaking the white words as carefully as she had been taught. "Thank you . . . for come—coming to"—she thought of Mary pointing to her eyes—"see me."

She attempted to form her lips into what Mary described as a "polite and ladylike" smile. And she dipped her knees in an awkward curtsy that she had been told was an act of respect done by women when being presented to men.

The colonel was supposed to acknowledge her with a slight bow. He just took her apart with his eyes.

"May I read . . . to you, sir?"

Colonel Chiswell's expression darkened. He turned his caustic gaze on Carter. "It's all well and good to teach a parrot to memorize a few sounds and tricks. . . ."

Mary's eager smile wilted. "Jed, ask whatever you like

of Firemaker. I've never known anyone to learn a language so quickly, not even when I was away at school. She's no trained animal, Jed. I'm deeply wounded you would suggest that I have been using my time and energy to pull any sort of wool over your eyes." Visibly shaking with emotion, Mary had to sit back down.

"That's just the point, Mary. You're in an advanced state of pregnancy, and yet you insist upon spending hours here. You have no vested interest in this woman. You belong in bed. If I was your husband . . ."

"You promised," she said, flushed and panting. "Last night you *promised* to unlock her door and let us stroll around the parade ground this afternoon and *prove* to you that she is ready to be treated in a decent and humane manner. She will not attack you, Jed, if that's what you're afraid of. She won't attempt to escape. She is ready to be welcomed back into the white world, and . . . and . . ."

Discomfited, the colonel made a nervous motion with his hand. "Don't get worked up, Mary. Olivia would never let me hear the end of it. I have no intention of going back on any promise I may have made to you last evening or any other time. Perhaps my mind was elsewhere."

It was all Firemaker could do to contain her galloping emotions. Holding herself rigid, waiting with exquisite control, she watched the colonel's gaze cross hers ever so briefly, as if he was afraid to look directly into her eyes. He found it far easier to rake her from her shaggy mane to tattered hem.

He glanced at Carter. "What about Snakehorn?"

Firemaker interrupted and searched her memory for the lesson on family. "Snakehorn. My . . . brother. No come . . . fort."

"Brother? He's her . . . This isn't what McTigue's been saying."

Mary fanned herself with her fingers. "Mr. McTigue has a way of embellishing the truth, Jed, or altering it, in case you hadn't already noticed."

Firemaker touched her forehead with her fingertips, trying to make a pained expression. "Worry. Dead. Fort Brad-ley, big. Comanche warriors . . ." She pointed in the direction of the mountains. "Gone. Days. Many days."

The colonel looked anguished. "Snakehorn dead? McTigue's not saying that, either."

Carter shrugged. Producing the map he had been using during his geography lessons in the past few days, Carter spread it before Firemaker and the colonel.

"Show him," Carter said.

Firemaker pointed toward the right. "U-nite States of 'merica." In the center, she pointed and said, "Texas. White mo-ther."

Her memory proved excellent for such as this, but she was uncertain if Texas really could be a week's ride across, even on a string of good horses. She found it impossible to believe the East Coast of the white man's country was many, many more days' hard ride beyond that. The world could not be that big.

She was baffled by the concept of an ocean and imagined a large lake. That there were continents of white, brown, black, and yellow-skinned peoples confounded her all the more.

The colonel jabbed at the nearby mountains represented by inked peaks bisecting New Mexico Territory at the continental divide.

"*Where* have the Comanche warriors gone? Does she know landmarks, Machesney? I need facts."

"We're working on that. I might actually have to take her riding to get an idea of the areas she knows."

The colonel's eyes widened. "You really think—" He shook his head. "Never mind. At this point your audacity shouldn't surprise me. Mary, you're too kind to offer Firemaker the use of your spare room. It seems Matt is as eager to assist in this effort as you."

"Yes, he is," Mary said, brightening.

"Very well, no need to take time walking about and causing a disruption. You have my permission to . . . entertain *Miss Tamberlay* as your . . . uh, houseguest. I've ordered bars on all your windows. I trust you understand. And there must be a guard posted at each door day and night. Under no circumstances shall Miss Tamberlay move about the grounds unescorted. *And* I expect a daily report . . . from the lieutenant."

"Why, Jed, I hadn't dared hope. Forgive my impatience."

"You're free to reconsider, Mary. As your time draws nearer, if she becomes difficult . . ."

Carter stepped forward. "Firemaker and I will be gone from Fort Bradley long before Mary delivers. And Firemaker knows that being difficult serves no purpose."

The colonel regarded Carter. "When, and *if*, Miss Tamberlay leaves the fort is for me to decide. Don't forget that. She is a valuable source of information. And regarding Snakehorn, Machesney, your presence is required in my office immediately."

The colonel's eyes darted at once to Firemaker, as if expecting to see a change in her comportment. Seeing nothing he could use against her, he returned his attention to Carter.

Firemaker's heart was hammering. Snakehorn must be near!

"McTigue has returned, as you probably know, and has news which I believe concerns us all. Mary will take over Miss Tamberlay's care now. You must step aside, Machesney. Remarks around the fort of a suggestive nature must cease immediately. There was a certain amount of logic to your presence here in the stockade these past weeks, but now you will confine yourself to your quarters when you aren't officially engaged in Miss Tamberlay's instruction. Or charming the ladies in my wife's parlor."

Firemaker watched Carter's eyes narrow, but he reined his temper, too.

"Are you up to this alone, Mary?" Carter asked, looking as if his elation had been dampened by the colonel's dismissal.

"Of course, Carter. Jed, if you'll be so kind as to help me up." Mary extended her hand.

The colonel assisted her to her feet. Taking the keys from the guard, he unlocked Firemaker's cell door. Firemaker felt the sweet breath of freedom flood her lungs as she stepped through the doorway.

Looking disappointed that he couldn't go with her, Carter nevertheless grinned and clasped her hands in a hearty handshake. "I'll be around to see you, later."

She wondered if and when they might find some time to be alone together.

Then he was gone, accompanying the colonel back to his office.

A guard fell in beside Firemaker as she emerged into the blinding morning sunlight outside the stockade. He nodded briefly to Mary and snapped to attention, his carbine clutched in trembling hands. He had *red* hair!

"Ma'am."

Blushing and looking somewhat unprepared for her newfound responsibility, Mary indicated the direction of her quarters on officers' row. "This way, Firemaker."

Stiffly the three began a self-conscious course across the parade ground.

"Livvie has been most gracious to send over a dress for you to wear," Mary said, peering demurely at the stares following them from every direction. "I'd gladly share my clothes, but I'm shorter than you, and you're a good deal slimmer than I am these days." Clutching her shawl tightly around her broad self, Mary giggled. Her progress was markedly slowing.

Firemaker had forgotten how many days had passed since she had felt the friendly heat of the sun on her face. It seemed brighter than she remembered. Her eyes hurt, as much from the glare as the tears of joy she wouldn't allow.

The bite of gravel through her worn moccasins felt sharp. The air smelled so fresh she almost felt light-headed. If only she could run and jump and dance with the happiness swelling in her heart.

Then her eyes fell on the corral beyond, and her purpose in all this sank like a crushing weight back onto her shoulders. The People looked like slaves.

Troopers, lounging in the shade of long narrow adobe buildings, stopped talking, chewing, and pitching pebbles to leer as Firemaker passed. Their eyes felt like the hands of the prisoners who had stolen into her cell so many nights ago.

Across the way, white women in calico and sunbonnets, with children in tow, edged back toward squat adobe houses. For weeks these same women had lived feeling little apprehension with full-blooded Comanche women and children in an open corral, but now that Firemaker walked free without chains, their worst fears came alive on their faces.

There, but for the grace of God, they might be walking in Comanche clothes, with Comanche memories, experiences, and knowledge, eyes keen, hair matted and filthy from weeks in a cell. God alone knew what had been transpiring in that stockade all this time, their expressions all said. Firemaker could almost read their thoughts as easily as Mary's holy book.

There was little movement in the corral where canvas

lean-tos now sheltered the Comanche women. Several of the children, now wearing castoffs offered by the washerwomen who had precious little to spare, stood watching Firemaker as if she was a stranger to them. And soon she would be, in calico of her own.

Curls of smoke rose from small campfires, but the Comanche women visible remained turned away, oblivious or perhaps indifferent to Firemaker's efforts on their behalf.

Firemaker's sense of triumph wilted. This was, indeed, only a first step. Next would come the hardest part of her charade. She must allow Mary to wash away the remnants of her Comanche self. She must put on the clothes of the woman Olivia. This would be a severe personal affront, for Olivia was the last white woman Firemaker wanted to look like. She would just as soon dress as an Apache or Mexican whore.

"Here we are," Mary said, slowing at her dooryard where the row of pink rocks parted, indicating a path leading to the entrance.

The house was small and low, with two windows deeply set into the rose-colored adobe. A half barrel of transplanted yellow wildflowers stood beside the door. In the open doorway stood Leota, her usual dark-faced scowl almost welcoming. She was holding an armload of snowy white towels.

"I'll start the tub water to heatin', Miz Mary," Leota called.

"No hurry," Mary said, smiling reassuringly at Firemaker. "She needs to adjust to all this. I know, because I'm trying to imagine how you feel, Firemaker. How would I feel if I was about to enter a Comanche tepee for the first time and put on your clothes and learn to act exactly like you, perhaps for the rest of my life? It would feel very peculiar indeed. I understand, and I'm here to help all I can."

Suddenly Firemaker was afraid. To act white forever?

"Come in. You're welcome in my home. It's all right. I'll show you around, and if you're not ready to bathe, I won't rush you. But I do ask that you try to get used to our ways. I've put my best sheets on your bed. I want you to like being a white woman. It's a chore scrubbing sheets, so your feet must be clean when you're sleeping. Come in now. I'll show you what I'm making for the baby."

Pausing at the doorway, Mary took a deep breath. "All the excitement," she said, paling, allowing Leota to grab her elbow and guide her firmly to a small hide-bottomed chair inside.

"You should be in bed," Leota remarked under her breath.

"I'll be all right," Mary whispered.

Firemaker stood on the threshold, squinting into the cool shadows of the first white man's house she had ever seen. White people built everything on the square. The room was like a box with those two deeply set windows in front, a stone fireplace in the corner, and two closed doors.

Two chairs with fringed red cushions were facing the unlit fireplace with a simple pine-branch table in between. Leota placed Mary's Bible there. Against one wall was a big black piece of furniture with a bench before it.

"This here's the lieutenant and Miz Mary's room," Leota said, throwing open a door to the right.

From where she stood rooted to the floor, Firemaker couldn't see much of the interior of the room except a white expanse of fabric covering something that might have been a low, round-edged table.

At the rear door, Leota said, "Cookin' room's back here. Your little room's off that. Want me to show her, Miz Mary?"

"Not just yet," Mary said as intrusive hammering sounded in the rear of the house. "Ask if they'll be long."

Leota went through the rear door.

Mary rose and waddled toward the chairs in front of the fireplace.

"Join me here, Firemaker," she said. "We'll rest and talk while the workmen finish. I want the house closed up tight when we start your transformation. No peeping fools to frighten you. Are you afraid?" She made a worried face and put a fist to her chest. "Afraid?"

Firemaker knew she couldn't disguise her true feelings from Mary, and so she nodded just a bit. "Small afraid," she said, glancing back at the red-haired guard left standing outside the door.

"You may close the door, Corporal Johnson," Mary called.

He saluted and obeyed, and Firemaker was greatly relieved.

Looking at the ceiling supported with pine beams similar to those in the stockade, to the walls mysteriously smooth and creamy pale, decorated at intervals with pictures like the one Carter had brought from her white mother, Firemaker crept soundlessly into the parlor.

Going from photograph to photograph, she made her way around the room, pausing to study the faces in the pictures, to gaze at the tables and the glass-chimneyed lamps upon them, the white crocheted doilies beneath them, the black iron wick trimmer with its twisted handle, the box of lucifer matches, the tiny carving of a bear done in mesquite wood that Firemaker recognized as Carter's.

A flare of jealousy made her snatch up the tiny whittled figurine and examine it with great care.

"You may have that if you like," Mary said. "Come and sit. Leota will bring us lemonade and ginger cookies. My mother sent the lemons. I was saving them for a special occasion. I do think this qualifies as one. Mother's worried I'll develop scurvy. She's convinced I'm starving and about to be murdered in my bed by—'' Mary cleared her throat, her cheeks flaming. "I feel quite safe, actually," she continued. "The walls of this house are stout. The guards patrol to all hours. Mattie takes excellent care of me. Leota believes herself to be an experienced midwife. I'm in good hands. The Lord is with me."

She smiled, but Firemaker heard the strain in her voice. Her hostess was fading quickly.

Approaching the chair, Firemaker tried to set herself into it without knocking it over. It was surprisingly comfortable to have her bottom and back supported, with her legs bent and feet upon the floor. She could easily jump up and flee if necessary.

Clasping her hands in her lap as Mary was doing, she held her knees together and briefly wondered what it would feel like to be a white woman, living in such a house, carrying a baby in her belly and loving a man.

It was a fantasy very unlike those of her girlhood, when she imagined herself keeping a tepee, carrying the wood for the fire, and scraping buffalo hides while waiting for a black-haired man with reddish skin to come home from a Texas raid. If the buffalo were being slaughtered, and the Comanches were marched to a reservation in some unknown place called the Oklahoma Territory, what sort of future could she imagine from that?

"By this evening when Carter sees you, he won't recognize you," Mary was saying. "You'll scarcely recognize yourself. I know this isn't going to be easy for you, but you've made a wise choice. I believe your heart is with the Comanches in the corral. You're to be commended for your loyalty to them, but ever since . . . Well, we know how you must feel. Carter and I have talked it over. We know how afraid you must be. You will do far more good for those you care about as a white woman than you would at their side as a Comanche woman."

Firemaker understood almost everything Mary said, and for the most part Mary was correct in her assumptions. Firemaker had chosen to become white for the express reason of helping the Comanche women and children in the corral. If she had been required to take on the ways of an Apache, however, she would have been equally intent.

"I have only one favor to ask of you, Firemaker." Mary's voice deepened. She was approaching a serious subject.

"Favor," Firemaker said.

"I need you to do something for me," Mary explained. "Please don't run away. Please don't take anything unless you ask for it first."

"Say . . . thank you."

Mary's sober expression lessened. "Yes, and say thank you. I think you know what I mean. Folks believe Indians to be thieves. It falls upon you to prove them wrong. You must not touch anything without permission. I do not mean to insult your integrity."

"Integ—"

Mary shook off any hope of defining that four-bit word. "I will be teaching these things to my own child in time," Mary said in a trembling voice. "It's not that I don't trust you."

"Trust. I know this. No run. No . . . touch. Sit-sitting . . . chair. Friend."

"Yes, dear. We're friends. You'll forgive me, I hope, when I tell you things that will surely insult you. To be honest, I scarcely know how to teach you to bathe and wash your hair."

Leota arrived with a mended white porcelain pitcher of lemonade on a wooden tray. Around the pitcher were twelve small cookies. "Jes' tell her what she needs to know, Miz Mary. Ain't no genteel way to do it."

Gazing up at Leota's stern face, Firemaker couldn't determine if the black woman liked her or not, but to Firemaker Leota was more like a Comanche woman, gruff and to the point. She was glad the washerwoman was there. White women were always surrounded by an aura of fear, tension, and self-consciousness that made them painful to be near.

Firemaker knew then she had already become more white than she realized. She felt afraid, tense, and excrutiatingly self-conscious. The transformation had already begun.

ELEVEN

THE COOKING ROOM had one small window overlooking the creek running through the fort. New iron bars blocked most of the light coming in.

Mary made certain the closed calico curtains gave no one outside even a sliver of a peek at the proceedings within.

Firemaker stood staring at what Mary called the bathing tub. Made of heavy-gauge tin, it was low and gray, half as long as a man, with a plugged hole sticking out the bottom edge connecting to a hose that Leota snaked out the backdoor.

Several kettles of heated water stood nearby. Every available bucket in the fort was also filled with creek water. Out back, Leota had yet another kettle on an open fire, heating yet more water. Firemaker's first bath appeared to be a major undertaking.

With the front door barred to all visitors, heaps of towels on the table, and Firemaker's change of clothes lying neatly folded over the back of a chair, Mary finally looked satisfied.

"All right," she said with an anxious smile. "I can help you, or you can do it all yourself. Perhaps you'd like to get in the tub first. When you're ready, I can help with your hair."

Firemaker frowned at the half-filled tub. "In?" she said, hoping she'd chosen the correct word.

Mary nodded. "Take off your clothes and get into the tub. Here's the soap, for scrubbing . . . all over . . . everywhere." She made washing motions against her forearms and then laid the oval of white Milk of the Nile toilet soap on the table. "But don't use this soap on your hair. This is the hair-washing paste." She indicated a tin of shampoo. "I'd like to help. Your hair is so long."

After an awkward moment Mary left the cooking room and closed the door. Firemaker's first thought was to flee through the backdoor, but she knew a guard was posted there, and really there was no getting around this chore. They wanted her to be white, and so she was going to pretend to be white.

Removing her shirt and skirt, she stood completely naked a full minute, unsure what to do with her things. The locket hanging from the thong around her neck began to feel cold. Finally she dropped her clothes in a heap and laid her locket on top of them.

She walked around the tub twice before stepping one foot into the warm water. In the parlor she could hear Mary and Leota talking softly.

Standing upright in the tub, finally, with the warm water about her ankles, Firemaker took the bar of soap and began rubbing it on her arms. This was a very cumbersome way to bathe, she thought, wishing for a creek and a handful of sand.

Tapping lightly at the door, Mary called, "Are you doing all right?"

Firemaker was unsure of the meaning of Mary's question. She was even less sure how to ask for assistance.

"Here," she said at length. "Wash, water, soap, bathing tub, cooking room, hair." Repeating the words associated with this mysterious procedure didn't help much.

Mary peeked in. "Oh, Firemaker." Mary stifled a giggle. "You may sit down in the water. Sit. Down."

Feeling the heat of embarrassment creep over her face,

Autumn Blaze 143

Firemaker gingerly lowered herself to a squat in the water. The warmth on her buttocks was disconcerting, and her nipples went erect. She crossed her arms against her chest.

Mary crept in. Leota marched in after her, a no-nonsense expression on her face.

"Like as not, she's been nekkid before, Miz Graham," Leota said, plucking a small cloth from the stack of linens. "Mind if I help?" she said to Firemaker. "Sit, girl. All the way in the water now. Ain't goin' to hurt you none." She swished her fingers in the water. "Gone tepid already."

As Firemaker sank to her bottom in the tub Leota deftly poured a kettle of steaming water in, flooding renewed warmth all around Firemaker's body. She couldn't think of anything that had ever felt quite so delicious.

Leota soaped the cloth and scrubbed Firemaker's left arm until the skin tingled. Never flinching, Firemaker wondered if bathing was always meant to be this painful.

Working at her as if she were currying a horse, Leota covered Firemaker's extremities, and then with brows raised offered the cloth and nodded. "You does the rest."

While Leota went outside to check on the last kettle, Firemaker scrubbed until not an inch of her body didn't sting. When she stepped from the tub, they wrapped her in towels and scrubbed her dry. She throbbed from her forehead to the soles of her feet.

"Now for the hard part," Mary said, indicating Firemaker was to bend over the tub and wet her hair.

They used up the entire tin of hair-washing paste, scrubbing and rinsing Firemaker's hair four times. They used all the heated water, and the cold water, and every towel.

Firemaker scrubbed her teeth with a small narrow brush dipped in Dr. Hill's Hygienic Tooth Polishing Soap, which tasted oddly sweet and salty at the same time. She gritted her teeth as they scrubbed her fingernails until they were white.

And then came the combing out of her long wet hair. It was well past noon by the time they had worked out every tangle.

They showed her how the long white underdrawers went on over each leg, and how the crotch unbuttoned for convenience. They let her examine the intricate stitching on her chemise before pulling it over her head.

Then came the size-twenty-two corset, with boning all around and laces crisscrossing up the back.

"She ain't never been laced, Miz Mary," Leota said, tugging and frowning at the results. "Her shape's gone natural. I expect her waist is almost twenty-six, at least. She ain't goin' to fit Miz Chiswell's day dress."

With her eyes popping, chest crushed, and breathing constricted, Firemaker was able to infer from Leota's tone that Olivia Chiswell's dress would be too small for her. Some indefinable female vanity impelled her to fit that dress regardless of the discomfort involved. After all, if she were to dress up as a buffalo, wouldn't she have to wear an equally absurd disguise?

She squeezed her hands into her sides to show there was far more room for cinching. In another fifteen minutes, she was measuring twenty-four inches, as small as her "natural" bone structure would allow. Leota went for her sewing box. Olivia's dress would have to be let out an inch.

Unable to sit, Firemaker stood at the backdoor while Mary brushed and rebrushed her hair into the afternoon breeze. Taller, Leota finished the brushing on top, and they all stopped for tea and corn bread at one o'clock. Firemaker could scarcely swallow a bite.

When at last Firemaker put on Olivia Chiswell's dress, a simple blue sateen with full skirt and snug bodice, and felt her legs encased in cotton stockings held up with garters, she could not imagine how she must look.

She couldn't even begin to find words, white or Comanche, to describe how trussed, crushed, bound up, and altered she felt. An overwhelming sense of pity came over her for the females of the white race. Surely this was the reason they were forever in a bad temper, or fainting, if Olivia and Mary were sufficient example.

"Now," Mary said, taking Firemaker's hand. "In a moment I'll show you your room. You simply must come and look at yourself in the pier glass. It's in my bedroom. I had it shipped all the way from St. Louis between two feather beds. You won't believe your eyes."

At first Firemaker was distracted by the bedroom with its heavy furniture and the broad expanse of bed covered with the white coverlet she had at first mistaken for a low table. The room was small and cramped with the wardrobe and dresser side by side on the far wall.

Mary indicated an oval thing in the far corner, held by a wooden frame and reflecting one of the bed's posters and the wall behind the bedstead.

Waddling forward, Mary tipped the pier glass so that it reflected the ceiling, then the rag rug, and finally a tall, slim young woman in a long, full-skirted blue dress.

The young white woman stood frowning, looking about herself, her hair streaming smooth and pale from a center part down over her square shoulders to her waist. She stood awkwardly, as if unable to draw sufficient breath, or understand anything around her.

She kept looking away from the reflection in the pier glass almost as if she felt lost. Then she looked behind herself as if thinking there was someone behind her. Leota was there, and she nodded back at the pier glass.

"It's you, honey. I cain't get over your hair. What do you think, Miz Mary? Shall I boil up the lemon rinds? They might do her skin, too."

"Oh, yes, Leota," Mary said, beaming. "Come closer, Firemaker. Are you terribly upset with us for changing you so?"

Again Firemaker looked over her shoulder. No blond-haired white woman stood behind her, or beside her, or anywhere in the room. Blinking, she squinted suspiciously at the pier glass and toyed with the possibility that . . .

Her heart skipped a beat. *The reflection was her!*

Marching right up to the glass, Firemaker leaned in so close to her face that she reared back again with a cry of alarm. The glass was smooth and cold. How could they know this was the largest mirror she had ever seen, and in it was a reflection of her white self and her white mother combined?

Her heart beat so wildly that she began to feel ill. Her hair! Her hair! Her face was so pale, her body now that queer shape. Her hair! Her *hair!*

By far she was the most pleased with her hair. Her hands trembled as she gathered up two handfuls of the flowing pale silk and smashed it against her nose. It smelled of spring.

"Ha!" she cried, tears stinging her eyes. She was lost.

Firemaker was lost, in disguise, and as confused as ever in her life, but her hair was a treasure.

Leaning close, she examined her eyes. No wonder she was such a marvel among her people. They were so pale. She was so used to living with dark-haired people with dark eyes. Her mental image of herself was like that.

To see herself, to touch her hand to the cold smooth glass and know it was her hand . . . She felt confounded by the truth of her appearance.

She *was* white.

TWELVE

"I'M TELLIN' YOU, Colonel, Snakehorn's watchin' us this very minute."

To Carter it looked as if the colonel really didn't care. He was weary of McTigue's claims.

Leaning against the colonel's office doorjamb, Carter folded his arms. "You have proof, McTigue?"

The old scout whirled. "Yer damn right I do. Tracks of at least a hundred warriors, and from different tribes, too. Ain't no mistakin' it. He's close. Go see fer yerself."

Colonel Chiswell regarded McTigue with disdain. "Our Miss Tamberlay thinks Snakehorn's dead. I was beginning to suspect so myself. It's been six weeks since—"

"You think I'd come back here if I wasn't sure of myself?" McTigue cried. "I got a bellyful of this place and I'm . . ." His voice trailed off at the colonel's darkening expression.

"If Snakehorn is watching us, he must see very well from a great distance because my guards report no sightings," the colonel said. "Nevertheless I'll ready another patrol."

"I'm talkin' about up that canyon yonder," McTigue snapped. "Ain't a Comanche dumb enough to stroll around this here valley, what with a bunch of jumpy troopers itchin' for hair."

Convinced McTigue and the colonel could debate facts

all the day long and never come to a head, Carter moved to leave.

The colonel's eyes hardened to flint. "Machesney, if you or your famous Miss Tamberlay have been holding anything back, you'll regret it. Taking her riding is out of the question."

"Then how am I to learn what she knows of the area?"

The colonel smacked the map on the wall. "Facts, gentlemen!"

McTigue tapped the line indicating the mountains accessed by the canyon nearest the fort. "Here's a fact for ya, Colonel. Camps badly made. Poorly disguised when abandoned. These warriors are travelin' without their womenfolk, who do this sort of thing for 'em. *We* got their women. They need 'em back, and it's time they got 'em. Winter's comin', and *they're* comin'. I feel it in my gut."

Carter interrupted. "McTigue obviously has more information than Firemaker or myself. Wouldn't it be wise for me to remove Firemaker from the fort altogether?"

Carter could see he wouldn't be budging the colonel on that point.

"She's still under guard. She'll stay under guard, under my command, until I decide differently. Give it up, Machesney. Miss Tamberlay stays at the fort until Snakehorn is in my stockade, and she is of no further use to me."

"Then may I have your permission to do some scouting on my own, to confirm McTigue's claims? Having one scout in part-time *retirement* isn't my idea of getting the job done." It was a reckless idea.

The colonel looked about to deny Carter when his eyes narrowed. "Very well."

Carter gave the colonel a conciliatory nod and exited the office, hoping McTigue really was the fool he'd made himself out to be so far. The colonel probably hoped Carter would be killed while he was gone, and Carter was already regretting his words. He didn't have the faintest notion what he'd do if he did encounter signs of Comanches. Run like hell, most likely.

Ten minutes later Carter was riding Lonesome west from the fort along the river, heading for the canyon. It was that or camp on Mary Graham's doorstep waiting for an audience with the scrubbed and altered Firemaker, whom he had left that morning on the threshold of Colonel Chiswell's stockade. He was altogether too impatient to see her again, and such feelings disturbed him.

Twenty miles away, Snakehorn's feelings were as black and as putrid as his right foot. Lying on a matted buffalo robe salvaged from his burned village, eating peyote to ease the pain and to bring back the dream visions growing more elusive by the day, Snakehorn listened to his brother Walking Bear calming the men at a small campfire fifty yards away.

Thirteen Tall Horse Comanche warriors remained. They'd been joined by a few Comanches from other bands, idle, intractable men who came along only for the sport of it. If they didn't taste blood soon, those men would be gone.

Signaling to all that he wanted to be left alone, Snakehorn retreated more deeply beneath the partially burned blanket covering his head. As war chief he was losing his hold and beginning not to care. This life was as frustrating and futile as the next promised to be.

Though he couldn't see the white man's fort from where he lay, and feared he might die before rescuing his family, Snakehorn could feel the white man's nearness like the advancing throb of poison spreading upward from his wound.

There was nothing to be done for him now. The last raid had caught him bearing down on a fierce white man bound to shoot him. That white man was hairless now, but his bullet had shattered Snakehorn's ankle.

Snakehorn could no longer walk and could scarcely ride.

He would make no more war. He'd reached this dismal camp on a travois dragged behind a lame mare. They'd just finished eating the last of the mare. Now there was talk of cutting off Snakehorn's leg. So far Snakehorn had refused to enter the next life without it. To him the matter was settled.

A runner appeared from the rocks and came to him. "A lone white man rides the canyon today," Kills Otters said in Comanche. "He looks for signs."

"Let him look. I don't want the soldiers coming yet. If we kill this foolish white man, they'll look for him. I'm not ready. I need to dream."

Kills Otters scowled. "You've been our greatest warrior, Snakehorn. When I was a boy, I looked up to you. I've always wanted to be like you. But you must go away now and die so we can kill the white men who attacked our village. We can't keep watch over you and get the women back, too."

It was a bold statement for one so young. Snakehorn respected the lad's courage. Certainly his words echoed Snakehorn's own dreary thoughts, but Snakehorn shook his head.

"When Red Leg and his warriors come, you will tie me to my horse. I will die with honor." Snakehorn's mind began to wander. He took up another button of peyote. "I will dream now."

Walking Bear approached and crouched before Snakehorn. "Kills Otters forgets we must watch for the supply trains and take what we need first. What good are our women and children to us if we cannot feed them through the winter?"

Kills Otters looked away.

Snakehorn rolled onto his side. "Listen to my brother," he said to the lad, feeling impotent to think Walking Bear should have to intercede on his behalf. In moments he was gone to the place of dreams.

The two frowning warriors stepped back. "It's a bad

spirit in his foot," Kills Otters whispered. "Snakehorn's medicine has died."

Nodding, Walking Bear looked deeply concerned. "We should take him to the pit. He might renew his medicine there."

Five miles up the canyon, Carter dismounted and settled himself into a comfortable position against a rock, facing the canyon, his rifle inches away. He'd seen enough, considering he didn't know what he was looking for in the way of signs. What he had really wanted was solitude.

Taking a pencil and paper from his pocket, leaning to see that Lonesome was safely grazing by the juniper he was tied to, he licked the lead and wrote to his sister. *Dear Mary, I am thinking of the letter you wrote to me last spring and hope you are doing fine. I am helping the Rangers in New Mexico Territory to bring in a Comanche calling himself Snakehorn. His band had a white woman since she was an infant, so she thinks just like an Indian. Soon I will be taking her back to Texas and her ma. I am teaching her to talk English. She has a lot of courage and makes me think how it must have been for you while I was away at the war. I am sorry I left so suddenly after coming home. It wasn't anything you did. I hope you will understand and forgive. How is Eric's tobacco crop coming along? I miss the old days and you and Pa, and I can't get it through my head that the boys are dead. Seems like you all are there waiting for me to come back from college. I don't know when . . .*

He paused, listening to the letter paper rustle in the wind, checking the horse again, feeling the itch of uneasiness creep up the back of his neck. There was no use asking himself why he was at Fort Bradley or why he was staying when he was accomplishing so little in regard to finding Snakehorn. He was staying on because of Firemaker; it was suddenly that clear.

. . . I will see you again, but know that I love you. You are all that is left . . .

Startled by a sudden swell of emotion in his throat, Carter swallowed hard and pinched the bridge of his nose. Until that moment he hadn't allowed himself to put those thoughts into words.

His sister was all that remained of his life before the war. He'd gone off from her as if she meant nothing to him. What must she think? And should he ever return to her, what would she think of a woman like Firemaker?

An equally startling wash of surprise flooded Carter's body. What kind of a thought was that? His sister and Firemaker would never meet. Firemaker had a life waiting for her in Texas. She had given little indication that she was inclined toward him. He always knew when a woman was interested.

He chuckled nervously and shook his head at himself. Firemaker was no ordinary woman. He couldn't hope to measure her motives or moods the way he had done with other women. Perhaps that was why he'd become increasingly disconcerted by Firemaker. Her every word was a surprise, her every expression a tantalizing mystery.

"Well, goddamn," he muttered, glancing at Lonesome, who pricked up her ears at the sound of his voice. "I'm soft on her."

He continued . . . *of my youth. To be away is like pretending it hasn't all changed. Take care, sister, and I'll be back when you least expect it. Your brother, Carter Machesney.*

After folding that letter, Carter took a second sheet and wrote briefly to Heck Clanahan that he'd learned little of Snakehorn so far. About all he could say was that Fort Bradley was commanded by a pompous fool.

After spending five minutes puzzling out the spelling of "pompous," Carter rubbed out the word, replacing it with "jackass." Heck would know the meaning of that, spelled correctly or not.

His next letter began, *Dear Jane, Firemaker got let out of the stockade today. The colonel is a careful man and he was afraid she would try to run back to the . . .*

Tearing that up, he began again, *Dear Jane, Firemaker is taking to white ways and learning to talk English. It must be hard on you to wait so long to see her, but I will be bringing her home to you perhaps in a few more weeks. I will not fail to write and let you know when we will be arriving. Firemaker is a smart woman. You will be proud of her. Yours sincerely, Carter Machesney.*

His duties done, he forced his shoulders to loosen, wishing he had his pa to talk to. For a moment he felt overwhelmed by the enormity of trying to assimilate Firemaker to white ways. He wanted to believe she'd seen a hopeless future with the Comanches after that baby died. He wanted to believe that was why she'd been so cooperative since, but his gut told him there was a banked fire behind those gray-blue eyes of hers.

Those Comanche women might resign themselves to a cattlelike existence in the fort corral, begging trinkets off the guards, staring dull-eyed at him when he delivered blankets or food, but Firemaker was only partly like them.

She had spirit. She was no mustang brought in from the range to be tamed for some lame job or some insensible future husband. She was a Thoroughbred, lost for a time, back now, and ready to be groomed for that very future he had witlessly spun to the colonel in the heat of his imaginative anger.

Until now Carter's purpose had been to free Firemaker from the stockade. That accomplished, he should now steer her toward the fame and fortune that could one day be hers. Was she capable of that much change? More importantly, was he the one to groom her for it? The only thing he really wanted was to feel her eyes on him, frank, clear, and curious.

Such thoughts troubled Carter, for he found it difficult to realize that while he knew little of the inner workings of Firemaker's mind, he felt as if she could see directly into his.

That brought to mind a matter he'd been avoiding, and now there were no more excuses to be had. He took another sheet of paper and wrote, *Dear Sarajane, I hope this letter finds you well and happy. I won't ask forgiveness for leaving you without a word of explanation. I don't deserve it, but I would like to say that I regret my long absence from you during the war and my failure to abide by our unspoken promise to marry when I was finally able to return. It is my sincere hope that you have found another man more deserving of your affections. Surely you must believe my leaving was not your fault. Call me changed by war, or whatever comes to mind. But know that when I was young, you were my treasure, and I shall never forget you.*

He frowned at the words, part truth, part not. He knew they would never erase Sarajane's hurt and disappointment, but he felt certain he could not explain in truthful words that which would only wound her.

He would take the blame because any change had been his fault. Sarajane hadn't changed. That was the surprising thing, to think he might have married her and never known there could be more to love than what they had felt.

That he could conceive now that there was more, a love for homeland going beyond the love of life, a love of mankind that went beyond all he'd been taught by his father, a love for family that meant accepting that which could not be changed, a love for a woman so strange, so savage he might never hope . . .

Overwarm suddenly, Carter sprang from the ground, startling Lonesome, and dropped the pencil. He forced his mind blank, and stretched the tension from his back. Then he grabbed up the pencil to scrawl a hasty conclusion . . . *There is nothing left to say except that you mustn't think to wait for me. I won't be back. I release you from any thoughts you might have had about my possible return. I alone bear the sorrow of our parting, knowing I failed you. My most sincere hopes for your happiness in the future. Fondly, Carter Machesney.*

The apology was inadequate, Carter told himself as he folded the letter, but it would have to do. He sighed, feeling no release into guilt-free freedom as he had anticipated.

And then he smiled, for a girl like Sarajane was likely married by now and expecting. She would never have given Carter the satisfaction of pining for him. He was almost tempted to tear up the letter and save himself the humiliation.

Still, as a gentleman, he could bear her wrath. To have stayed and married her, making himself miserable, and eventually making her miserable, would have been a far worse insult.

Feeling suddenly cleansed, Carter dusted off his trousers. Having had no intention of seeking any further signs of Snakehorn, he mounted Lonesome and wandered upstream. He tried to imagine Firemaker with a clean face.

Though it was growing late, and he had a good hour's ride back, he rode on. Was he doing all he could for Firemaker, or was he dragging his hind end like the good ol' colonel, stumbling his way through an assignment well beyond his capabilities simply because it was the easier course?

Olivia Chiswell's hall was as crowded as she'd ever seen it. That was exactly how she wanted it except that she was galled to be forced to include the rawboned sergeants and their uncouth wives just to make sure the room was filled.

To make the point that she was such a charming, sought-after hostess, however, Olivia had to abide them.

She wanted *everyone* to know hers was the best home at the fort, that she gave the best parties, and that they were particularly fortunate to be invited here.

She swished her expensive skirts and tossed her perfectly arranged curls. Her smile was neatly applied as she strolled across the room, where she could see and hear everything that went on in her domain. When Lieutenant Graham arrived, she hurried forward and caught his arm.

"Why, sugar, where's your darlin' little wife? She's not ill, I hope. I could have told y'all that havin' a houseguest at this time was unwise. Especially one of that sort."

"Mary's fine," Matt said, looking a bit more assertive than usual.

Olivia found that intriguing.

"In fact," he added, "I haven't seen her this happy in months. She's been lonely at Fort Bradley. I never should have let her join me here. She belongs back east with her pa. She's in her element helping Firemaker. She would have been delighted to come tonight, Mrs. Chiswell, but she didn't want to leave Firemaker alone her first night out of the stockade."

That was the very purpose of this collection of guests, Olivia thought peevishly, to distract everyone from the release of that loathsome creature.

"I shouldn't want that creature left to her own devices in my quarters, either," Olivia muttered, fanning herself. "I suppose Mr. Machesney is there, teaching lessons or some such."

How could a cultured gentleman like that Virginia-born Texan spend so much time with a heathen? Olivia wondered. Her own company was so much more enjoyable. Certainly she was always available, and perhaps that was the problem. She had not played Carter correctly.

"We haven't seen Carter all day," Matt said. "He went out earlier and isn't back."

"Out? Where . . . ? Why?" Olivia's heart began to patter with alarm.

"I can't really say, ma'am. To do some scouting, I think. I'm sure the colonel would be able to explain better than I. I wasn't there when he and Carter talked with McTigue."

A nearby sergeant interrupted. "What's McTigue claiming now, Lieutenant? If there ain't been an attack by them Comanches by now, there ain't going to be one. All this talk about herding the women and children into the powder magazine come battle time is bunk. I ain't ordering my Alice to blow herself up. Them Comanches ain't taking no prisoners so long as I got breath."

Olivia's eyes popped. "Blow ourselves . . ." Her eyes darted to Matt's disgruntled expression. "*I* would rather be dead than turn out like . . . Oh, Mattie, sugar, this is nonsense! There aren't any Comanches out there. I wouldn't believe a word McTigue said if it was written in blood. We're safe here. Well, I mean, I think we would be if *she* wasn't right next door. If there's a Comanche to worry about, it's the one who scratched my husband's face."

Olivia looked about at the gaping expressions of her guests and realized her outburst had silenced everyone. They were all staring at her.

"Goodness," she said, wanting to fall down somewhere so she could think. "Mr. Machesney's not back? Why should he go scoutin'? He's got no experience doin' that. He's a horseman. Why isn't anyone concerned about him? It's almost dusk. He could be . . ."

Speculative murmurs erupted throughout the room. It was a dreadful topic of conversation, but preferable to having everyone discussing her, Olivia thought.

"My party's in ruin. Play somethin' for us, do, Mattie, while I get my wits about me. Imagine the problems if Mr. Machesney comes back scalped and murdered. Who then would give a tinker's damn about your houseguest, hmm? Mary'd be stuck with her. And you. You ought to see *Miss*

Tamberlay on her way back to Texas, or wherever it is she belongs, immediately. I won't sleep a wink tonight, knowin' she's lyin' there plottin' the murder of every one of us. Isn't Mary comin' at all? I need her.'' Olivia's voice had risen to a petulent whine. She indicated her crowded hall. "I invited everyone just to please her. This was her suggestion, you know. Little abolitionist."

"There are no freed slaves here," Matt said, looking at her with a most irritating pointedness.

"Well, y'all know what I mean. She thinks we shouldn't segregate the . . . the . . . What is the word for those who insist on mixing the classes? There must be a word for it. I invited everyone, and now she's not here. How was I to know our white Comanche would be released today and cause such an annoying stir? Lock her into your guest room, if necessary, but do fetch Mary for me. My parties are nothin' without her at the piano and you at the fiddle, of course. You can tell her I said so. She probably wanted to spoil things for me. Look how bored everyone is." Olivia paused a moment and clutched Mattie's sleeve all the harder. "You do intend to bar her door at night, don't you? I just couldn't bear it if y'all were murdered tonight. I just won't tolerate such a thing."

The voices nearby had gone silent again.

Olivia prattled on. "And if she doesn't choose to slit your throat *this* night, there are worse things. They have no morals, you know. Comanches have a dozen wives, and you saw those children runnin' naked in the corral. Mattie, did you think this charitable act through? She might try to . . . to seduce *you*!" Could a man be raped? Olivia wondered distractedly, glancing at Lieutenant Graham's scrawny frame.

Matt's face flamed. Someone snickered.

Olivia patted her throat. "Why, while we're standin' here, worryin' ourselves to death, God alone knows what that creature has taken into her head to do to Mary in hopes of escape."

Finally, Olivia thought, watching Mattie's eyes bulge as his imagination conjured visions of his wife slain while he conversed with the colonel's wife next door at a party. Olivia pushed him backward out the door into the lavender dusk.

"Bar that creature's door and bring Mary here, where she'll be safe, at least for a while," Olivia ordered.

THIRTEEN

MARY CAST HER eyes toward the door to the spare room and hugged her husband's arm. "We *can't* leave Firemaker alone her first night free of the stockade."

"But there are two guards," he put in lamely.

"I don't mean that. It's rude to abandon her to all this strangeness. She's doing beautifully, but there's a limit to the changes one person can tolerate in a day. Did Livvie insist?"

His mouth tightened. "You know how she is."

"And I suppose Jed was there, too, giving you that look you hate so." Mary balled her fists. "They surely do try my patience! Has Jed actually written your father? No, and I doubt he will. He is full of empty threats and broken promises, a sore disappointment to us all. There, I've spoken my true thoughts, and I feel better for it."

"I am tired of catering to him, too, and her," Matt said in a rare moment of bravado. "I've been glad for Leota's help, but it's made us both beholden. If we do go there tonight, Livvie will only upset you. I have half a mind to resign my commission and take you home."

Mary felt her knees weaken. Quit the army? She dared not listen to her secretmost dreams spoken aloud by her darling. "I know you don't mean that, Mattie. Besides it's too late. I can't travel now."

"I do mean it. I just lack the courage. If I'm not a soldier, as all the men in my family have been, then what would I do with myself? Play my fiddle on street corners?'' He shook himself. "In any case, this is all a sham."

Wondering if Firemaker was listening, Mary peeked over her shoulder at the guestroom door. She pulled Matt into the parlor. "What is, darling?"

"This party of Livvie's. Everyone's there, even enlisted men and their wives. We know what Livvie thinks of them. It was an act of desperation. She's trying to distract us from what we're doing here with Firemaker. I don't know why Livvie feels so afraid. If Carter was back, he'd silence her."

Mary's heart leaped. "What do you mean, if Carter were back? Where has he gone?"

Matt explained. "If I'd known Carter was thinking of going out alone," he went on, "I'd have advised against it. I think Jed let him go in hopes that . . ." His voice trailed off.

Mary's hand stole to her expanded belly. She felt ill. "Is . . . that war chief . . . so very near as all that?" There was something alarming about the look in her husband's eyes.

"I would give anything to get you safely away, Mary. No, I don't think Snakehorn is near." Matt's tone was unconvincing.

"Well, I'm not leaving Firemaker, and I suppose we can't be rude to Livvie. I see only one alternative."

Mary thrilled to see the spark that came into Mattie's eyes. "It would be worth taking Firemaker just to see Livvie's face," he said.

Nodding, Mary stiffened her spine. "Firemaker is about to come out."

Alone in Mary Graham's spare room, Firemaker sat perched on a chair that tipped forward and backward every time she moved. Now that she was trussed up like a white woman, she didn't know what to do with herself.

The room was four times the size of the stockade cell, cool and shadowed with smooth stucco walls, a thing they called a bed, a blanket chest, and a washstand. There was no window.

On the washstand stood a white tin basin and a black ironwork candlestick that had a burning stick in it called a candle. It gave off a tall, steady gold flame on the top. Amazed, Firemaker fixed her eyes on it. Such small medicine for the task ahead, she thought, beginning to hum.

Mary tapped at the door and crept in. She looked flushed. "It's a lot to ask of you so soon after your release from the stockade, Firemaker," she said, wringing her hands, "but we've been invited to the colonel's quarters this evening. Livvie gets bored and likes to have us there to play and sing. If we make an appearance, I think it'll be safe to leave before you get too tired. Will you come with us?"

Firemaker puzzled over the words but could find little meaning in so many strange new ones. "Go?" she said, understanding that much.

"Go to the colonel's quarters. I'll play the piano. Matt will play his fiddle. We'll sing. It might even be fun."

Unsure just what Mary was proposing, Firemaker stood, letting the rocking chair tip wildly behind her. For now she would think of herself as their slave. She would do whatever seemed expected of her. "Piano. Fiddle. Singing."

Mary looked perplexed. "But you can't go in your stocking feet, and my shoes will be too small. I think you'll have to wear your moccasins for tonight. Oh, my. There'll be such talk, but I suppose they won't show too much if you walk carefully."

"Walk," Firemaker said.

In moments she had her familiar old moccasins on over her knitted kersey stockings held up with garters, but felt only a fraction more comfortable, laced as tightly as she was. They joined Matt waiting in the parlor.

Seeing Firemaker for the first time since her transformation, Matt gave her a once-over that Mary couldn't fail to notice. Firemaker watched his eyes and wondered, suddenly, if she would be safe in this white man's house at night.

"Take his elbow, like this," Mary said, showing Firemaker how to accompany the trembling lieutenant through the doorway.

Firemaker felt the man flinch as she grasped his elbow and brushed his arm. Ah, so she wasn't as attractive as she had supposed she might be in her white clothes. She was just as frightening as always. That was acceptable. Yet, strangely, she felt angry and hostile. She cast Lieutenant Matthew Graham a dark sidelong look.

His ears turned red.

Lifting her chin then, Firemaker let Mary's husband lead her out the door into the gathering darkness.

The posted guard outside looked astonished as Firemaker emerged wearing the blue dress, her blond hair falling to her waist like corn silk. His raking gaze left her feeling insulted. Eyes narrowed with warning, she made sure the young red-haired corporal realized that this change was only skin deep.

The freckle-faced lad stepped back, saluting sharply. "Good evening, sir. Ma'am. Uh . . . Miss Tamberlay."

"My wife, Corporal," Lieutenant Graham grumbled, indicating unaccompanied Mary lagging behind, smiling with satisfaction at Firemaker's composure.

The guard offered Mary his arm, and they all strolled along the flagstone walk to the quarters next door. The night was clear, growing cold enough to smell of the coming winter.

"Wait here," Matt ordered at the colonel's door, accepting the corporal's salute again. "Your relief should be along soon."

Yellow light streamed from the wood-framed windows set deep in the rosy pink adobe, which still radiated heat from the day's sun. A loud hubbub of voices became louder as the lieutenant pressed the front door open, allowing Mary to precede them into Olivia Chiswell's hall.

Oh, so this was the reason Mary was acting so nervous, Firemaker thought, her stomach tightening. She heard the high singsong voice of the colonel's wife calling hello as she spied Mary at the door.

It would be a kind of test, Firemaker thought, the white woman's version of running the gauntlet. She stiffened her spine. Her face went immobile as she fixed the appropriate expression in place.

As Lieutenant Graham guided her inside she felt instantly overwhelmed. She couldn't remember what to do or say. What was she doing, joining these people when she scarcely understood their language? Her strongest impulse was to run and never stop until a bullet found her back.

The moment Firemaker appeared, the room fell silent. Every head turned. Firemaker couldn't slow her hammering heart or prevent a hot flush of self-consciousness from staining her cheeks. All she could do was look back at everyone and marvel that with only her pale gray-blue eyes she could make each person in the room shrink back.

So many white female faces. So many bearded, mustachioed soldiers who, only weeks ago, would have cheerfully run her through with a saber, or raped her.

So many blue and brown eyes going from her face and hair down past her corseted body to the dirty, worn toes of her moccasins peeping from beneath the hem.

Firemaker watched the faces mirror astonishment, horror, curiosity, contempt. So much fear. So much disgust. The women edged back, leaning close to whisper to their husbands. The men just gaped until pulled sharply back by their indignant wives.

Olivia Chiswell in all her silk finery halted in her tracks, her mouth half-open, her expression quickly changing from one of exaggerated delight at Mary's arrival to pure horror at the guest at Mary's side. Olivia's attempt to cover her shock left a dozen emotions contorting her features all at once, until at last her eyes fell on Mary's rebellious little smirk.

The silence spreading across the hall throbbed with tension. Everyone waited for the colonel's wife to welcome or eject her newest guest. Olivia didn't move. She couldn't. Her trembling hand stole to her lips as if to bring them together forcibly.

"Oh, dear," Mary murmured with a backward glance at Matt. "She does look upset, doesn't she?" Attempting to fill the strained silence, Mary said loudly, "How kind of you to insist we come, Livvie. Firemaker feels truly welcome."

The silence seemed to expand.

Mary turned to draw Firemaker deeper into the room. "May I present to you all, Miss Amanda Tamberlay of Texas. I believe she would still like for us to call her by her given Comanche name of Firemaker. Her story of survival among the savages has inspired me. I imagine it inspires us all to gratitude for our own health and well being . . . and should serve to remind us of our Christian obligations to charity, mercy, and understanding."

Firemaker had never heard Mary sound quite so strong. Her admiration for her hostess grew.

All eyes turned back to Olivia Chiswell, who for the first time in her twenty-six years looked as if she really was going to swoon.

Abandoning Firemaker to stand next to Matt, her hands clutching the sides of her skirt, her mouth going dry, Mary hastened toward Olivia. She tucked her hand in the crook of Olivia's elbow and guided her to the nearest chair.

Olivia found enough composure to jerk free of Mary's solicitous touch.

Firemaker looked around the colonel's quarters. The place was far more richly done up than the lieutenant's. They had a piano, too, and furniture covered with fabrics she longed to examine.

There were pictures on the walls, glowing glass-domed lamps, odd things on the tables, and a patterned something upon the floor that was as thick and plush as a buffalo robe, but colored, smooth, and flat.

Matt saw her intent scrutiny and whispered, "Carpet."

It was nice to know the white word, Firemaker thought, heaving a sigh. What mystified her about all these strange white-man things was that not one came from an animal. Everything the white man possessed seemed to have been altered to a strange and amazing texture, color, or shape. There was not a feather or scrap of leather or bit of fur in sight. Even *she* was changed.

When the colonel entered the room from the rear, Firemaker forgot her baffling thoughts and met his eyes. She resented needing his approval, for as the fort's chief he had dominion over her. He was, she realized in a moment of startling clarity, much like Snakehorn. He was bound by his quest for honor in battle.

Glancing only briefly at his wife's stricken expression, Colonel Chiswell at last gave Firemaker his full attention and silent, blank-eyed perusal.

Firemaker couldn't guess at his reaction. Not a flicker of emotion showed on his face. That was to be expected of a war chief. Certainly the trappings of a female's appearance should have no interest for him.

Abruptly, without a word, Colonel Chiswell plunged across the room and was gone out the front door. That seemed logical. Firemaker was not being presented to him

Autumn Blaze

as a wife, so his opinion didn't matter. He likely had none. Yet he possessed the authority to free her, and because of that, Firemaker hoped he was at least satisfied that she was behaving like a properly subdued savage.

It was left to Mary and her husband to breathe life back into the rigid statues of blue-coated men and frumpy pale women huddled against the walls of the colonel's crowded hall.

Firemaker couldn't have felt more exposed had they brought her there naked, but a gauntlet wasn't meant to be pleasant, she reminded herself. It was a test of courage.

She accepted their stares. When nothing worse than a few scathing, disgusted looks occurred, Firemaker's discomfiture withered to contempt. It took little effort to withstand their surreptitious, fearful glances. They were like frightened rabbits.

Matt took up his fiddle and began playing something more haunting than a mother's lullaby. Firemaker's attention was immediately distracted. Her heart shivered to a stop. Her head began to spin.

She recognized the melody! How could that be? she wondered, moving soundlessly toward the piano where Mary seated herself upon the round fringed stool.

Everyone around Firemaker fell away, watching how she moved.

Firemaker hadn't seen Mary's husband play his strangely shaped box before, and although she'd heard strains of his haunting music on the night wind, she hadn't known what the sound came from.

As Mattie tried to play Firemaker placed her fingertips on the fiddle's body. The notes of the melody sounded strained and off even to Firemaker.

With titters emerging all around, Mary whispered, "Begin again, dear. Try to ignore her."

Firemaker edged back, feeling the tension in the room flow with her every movement. With all her heart, she wanted to whirl and growl and startle them all, but she dared not indulge such a whim. Every man in the room was armed.

Mary began touching the black and white keys. As the notes rang out, filling the room, Firemaker felt she was drifting into the air, caught somewhere among this strange new world, her old world among the Comanches, and that dreamworld of sounds, smells, and tastes she had never been able to name.

Mary began singing. "I dream of nights in my lover's arms. I may see him nevermore. He's gone away 'cross fields so green, to wait beyond the shore."

Although part of her wanted to be away immediately to digest these confounded emotions, Firemaker heard the white words from her dream song and now knew that they were real, that they were part of a white song from her past.

For the first time, learning English had true meaning for Firemaker. She understood the words. Becoming white, if only for a while, would enable her to unravel the mystery of her dreams.

She had to stay at the fort awhile longer, she told herself. She had to survive this uncomfortable, foolish disguise. Somehow she would find a way to free the captives.

Then, if the spirits were pleased with her efforts, she might be allowed to live long enough to meet her white mother, for with this white woman was the solace Firemaker sought.

Outside in the darkness, half of Fort Bradley's troopers were knotted in the stable yard by the big gate facing the avenue to the parade ground. They were watching something in the direction of officers' row.

With the wind whipping at his hat, Carter dismounted Lonesome, wondering if there was a fight among the reinforcements.

Strolling to the gate, he saw the colonel's quarters lit up like Christmas night. Even from that distance he could hear the fiddle and piano music lilting on the cold night air.

"Quite a party tonight," he said to no one in particular.

The troopers parted, regarded him, and muttered words too low for him to understand.

Surprised how sore he was after the day's ride into the canyon, Carter concluded that come hell or high water he would have to be on his way soon. He couldn't go soft while waiting for Jed Chiswell to take action one way or the other.

He'd been too long away from Lonesome and his work, Carter thought. He wondered if he'd ever get back to his ranch and his broncs. It was surprising how little thought he'd given to his work since meeting Firemaker.

Still puzzled to think the Comanches who had surely been watching him that afternoon had let him leave the canyon alive, Carter started across the parade ground. He hoped Mary would forgive such a late call, but he had to know how Firemaker had fared her first day out of the stockade.

He wondered if Firemaker had kept her temper as they bathed her. He wondered if she could tolerate a white woman's dress. His pulse quickened as he thought of seeing her now with no bars between them.

He still wasn't sure if his growing feelings for her were proper or appropriate. All he knew was that his step felt lighter. His heart was skipping as fast as a boy's, and his palms were damp.

Laughing, he approached the Graham quarters but found no guard posted at the door. The windows were dark. Had Firemaker been taken back to the . . .

Carter's alarm changed to disbelief as he noted a trooper guarding the colonel's front door. The piano music seemed particularly lively that evening. Mary was outdoing herself.

Surely they wouldn't have taken Firemaker there, not her first night out.

Forgetting he was covered with dust and sweat from his forehead to his boots, and forgetting that his hair was matted into the shape of his hat, Carter marched to the colonel's door. He noticed the colonel himself standing outside some distance to the north in the dark, gazing away at nothing apparently.

Carter decided against calling out to the man. He was in no mood to give report on what he hadn't found up the canyon. He was in no mood to spar with the man's pickled intellect, either.

Feeling restless and jittery, Carter pushed his way into the brightly lit, crowded hall. Some of the women nearby who caught a whiff of him edged back. He overheard a whispered, "Stinking rebel . . ."

He gave each lady his most beguiling smile and courtly bow. "And a very good evening to you, ladies."

It was a curious assembly of commissioned and noncommissioned officers present, Carter thought, briefly noting the difference between the badly constructed calico finery of the sergeants' wives and the expertly fitted though gaudy yellow silk Olivia was wearing.

She sat on a chair, her posture deplorable.

He expected her usual greeting, but when she didn't move, he noticed her pallid cheeks and distracted expression. When Olivia finally did notice him, she gave no sign she even recognized him. It was the first time Carter had ever seen the colonel's wife truly at a loss.

Red-cheeked Mary was at the piano. Matt was at her side, sawing on his fiddle with more gusto than usual. There was a tall blond woman at the far side of the piano, her attention rapt on Mary's fingerwork upon the keys.

Carter didn't recognize the woman. She didn't look like any of the officers' wives, or any of the noncommissioned officers' wives, and certainly she wasn't one of the washerwomen up from Suds Alley. He wondered if a stagecoach with travelers had arrived while he was away. He had never seen a woman her age wearing her hair down, and such hair. . . .

Then he felt the touch of her pale blue-gray eyes as she looked up and caught sight of him across the room. She didn't look away. She looked into him and seared his soul.

His heart began to drum. His body washed with fire. A primitive tension blossomed in his belly and spread downward, leaving him poised on the threshold of the colonel's quarters, gaping like a schoolboy.

Carter couldn't believe his first thought, that her hair, her eyes . . . It couldn't be, but it had to be Firemaker. She was not a Comanche albino, or a lioness. She was a beautiful, incredible woman.

Her skin tone was darker than the other women in the room, and her stance was rigid with schooled propriety. Her hair, long and pale, flowed down her shoulders and back, and hung in long silken tendrils over her accentuated breasts beneath that tight blue bodice. She was dazzling. He wanted to sweep her into his arms and devour her.

That had to be one of Olivia's day dresses kept for working in the garden, he thought. It was just shabby enough to suit Olivia's need to insult Firemaker, yet on Firemaker the dress looked perfect.

Firemaker's waist was obviously cinched. Carter was startled to realize how familiar her natural womanly shape was to him. It was all he could do to keep from whooping with delight at the sight of her.

She gave off a feeling of energy very similar to a wild horse newly corraled. There was a spark in her eye and a lift to her brow that showed unmistakable defiance. She might be scrubbed and cinched and rigidly schooled, but the spirit within her was still the snapping flame of his Firemaker.

His Firemaker.

The thought stunned him. It was an altogether inappropriate attitude to take. He knew that now, looking at her and knowing it was his job to get information from her . . . and then to take her home. But his heart, soul, and body were telling him this was the most extraordinary woman he would ever have the honor to meet. If he had been another kind of man . . .

Reeling, he plunged across the hall, a schoolboyish grin on his smudged face. "Hello!" he called out, turning every head, silencing every hissing whisper.

Even if he hadn't known her, he would have thought her the most beautiful woman he'd ever seen. Appropriate or not, he was smitten. He could no longer think.

She was taller than average, her frame strong and slim. She didn't smile her hello but looked directly into his eyes, showing she was pleased, and relieved, to see him. She trusted him. He was sure of it.

Her shoulders lowered and straightened. The upward tilt of her chin increased, giving him a thrill. There was the tiniest flutter of her hands as she tried to decide if she was supposed to curtsy or shake his hand.

"Firemaker," Carter whispered, thinking this lovely woman before him was capable of perfect savagery if she so chose. He remembered the first time she throttled him from behind the bars of her cell, and he wanted to roar with laughter. He had tamed her. She was magnificent.

And yet he knew she was not so changed as they all wished and hoped she was. Beneath the blue dress and her diligently memorized propriety, she was still possessed of a Comanche memory and a Comanche past. A few weeks couldn't erase her thoughts, her values, her beliefs.

His elation cooled. He bowed. She dipped her knees ever so slightly. He wanted to kiss her. Dear heaven, he wanted to know her in every way before letting her go. "Hello, Firemaker," he said thickly. "How are you?"

In the wide searching openness of her eyes, he saw how trying this appearance among the men and women of the

Autumn Blaze

fort was for her. She said nothing. Had she forgotten all her white words?

"Hello," he said again, wondering when he'd ever be able to tear his eyes away. "What is she doing here, Mary?" he whispered, when Mary left off playing.

"Livvie insisted I come," Mary said, her fingers stumbling over the notes of another song. "I wouldn't leave Firemaker alone. Do you think we might go now? Livvie looks positively peaked, and I can't stop myself from playing long enough to know if Firemaker is managing the stares."

"She's fine," Carter said, his heart swelling with emotion for the strong courageous young woman before him. "She's fine. When will she not do what she must to survive?"

Matt let the fiddle fall to his side. He was frowning at Mary, his concern for her own ability to cope evident in his stormy eyes.

Carter offered his elbow to Firemaker, who took it in her trembling hand as if she'd been doing it all her life. The warmth of her touch spread through him like wildfire. How would it feel to . . .

He shook himself. "Ladies, gentlemen," he said, "I believe it's time for Miss Tamberlay to retire. It's been a long, trying day for her. Mrs. Chiswell, thank you for welcoming Firemaker into your home tonight."

Olivia lifted her gaze to Carter. The malice he saw there should not have surprised him. Firemaker was merely leaving one savage world for another, he thought darkly as he drew her closer to his side.

The knowing looks that passed between the officers and their wives cut a ragged edge into Carter's shrinking elation. The joy left his eyes. He raked the room, saying with his silence that he expected little better of Yankee louts and their females.

"Good evening, then," he drawled.

With a gallant sweep of his arm, he indicated the door. Firemaker preceded him out of it. No southern gentleman could have made a grander exit.

Mary brought her playing to an end. Silence settled around them all once again, echoing on as Carter and Firemaker went out into the darkness to the click of the guard's heels at the door.

Inside came the rustling thud of Olivia Chiswell's body, dropping in a heap the moment she attempted to stand.

In the wind-whipped darkness outside Colonel Chiswell's quarters, Firemaker couldn't see Carter's face all that well, but she smelled the fragrance of clean mountain air on his clothes. And there was the familiar smell of horse and man sweat about him as well, not to mention leather and dust.

"Horse. Mountain," she said in a husky tone, too undone by his nearness to formulate more advanced white sentences.

"Yes, I went riding up the canyon today," Carter filled in for her, his tone softening, indicating he was pleased with her. "I found a good place to rest. I wrote letters to your mother and my sister." He smiled down at her. " And to an old friend."

Behind them, Mary and Matthew emerged from the Chiswells' quarters. "She's perfectly all right, Mattie," Mary was saying, her tone sharp with hurt and anger. "I don't for a moment believe she really fainted. Take me home."

"We should have known better," Matt whispered.

"Yes, we should have, but I'm not sorry. I'm not angry with you, darling. I'm just . . . furious about everything. Oh, Firemaker," she added as she came near. "You were grand. I couldn't be prouder."

Firemaker nodded, concerned to see Mary so upset on her account.

"And Carter," Mary added, "we're *very* relieved to see

you safely back. What do you think of our Firemaker now?"

Carter's eyes shone with wonderment. "What I want to know is, what does Firemaker think of herself?"

"Indeed," Mary said.

Questions were still sometimes difficult to decipher, Firemaker thought, impatient with her slowness to learn. "Think of self?" Firemaker repeated. "Of." The little words that had no object or action to go with them were the hardest to understand and use.

Carter and Mary posed the question to her in several different ways, defining unfamiliar contexts as they went until Mary was giggling and shivering. Carter grinned like a fool. Firemaker began to understand what they wanted to know. They wanted the truth of her feelings. She couldn't give them that.

"You'll catch your death," Matt said at length, urging Mary on toward their own quarters.

"Well, all right. I am awfully tired suddenly."

Matt led Mary inside, and though she didn't want to retire before she had heard Firemaker's reply, Mary deferred to her husband's loving insistence.

"You can tell me how you feel when you come in, Firemaker. Well, Mattie," Mary cried with vexation at his reproving expression, "she can't sleep in her stays. I'll have to unlace her. I'm not disturbing Leota at this hour."

Matt blushed. The door closed.

Carter's eyes wandered over Firemaker's altered figure in a disconcerting manner. The wind was teasing her pale, fine hair in swirls of light-catching silk around her head.

Firemaker was enormously relieved to hear she wasn't expected to wear her torturous costume all the time. She smiled.

With the guard at his station beside the door, Carter drew Firemaker a few feet away, where the light flaring in the Grahams' windows didn't reach.

"Well?" he said, eyes glowing, lips turned up so deliciously.

What did she think of herself? She felt like a warrior, wearing the hollowed skull and hairy hide of a buffalo, running with the herd and hoping to drive as many over a cliff as possible. It was an old form of hunting.

What could she tell Carter? Very little, she thought sadly. She longed to be truthful with him, but even if she had the words, she couldn't risk trusting him. The black mountain of responsibility she carried was far too heavy to forget.

To Carter she presented a placid expression and clear eyes. She pressed at the sides of her waist and made a pained grunt. Chuckling, Carter filled in the words.

She repeated, "My corset is very tight. Tight. Tight-tight." She made a sickened face, and Carter laughed.

"Your corset is so tight you feel sick."

She loved the way his lips opened and curved when he laughed. "You feel sick," she repeated. "No, no. Fire-maker feel sick. *I* feel sick. I, self, me, mine, my." So many words for the self, she thought. She tapped her chest and made an exaggerated breathing noise.

"You can't get your breath."

"Get?" She despaired. "White words very many bad thinking. Self dress Mrs. Chiswell very sick." She made the sick face again and brushed at the skirt in disgust. She mimicked Olivia Chiswell's aghast expression, assuming Carter would be disappointed in her for not feeling gratitude for the gown, but found to her surprise that he laughed all the harder.

"I doubt you'll ever be friends with Mrs. Chiswell. If my sister was wearing the gown of someone who didn't like her . . . " He shook his head. "I'm sorry, Firemaker. If I'd realized you'd be free this quickly, I'd have been better prepared."

"Pre—"

He shook his head. "Perhaps we can order something

new for you from the sutler. The problem is, it'll take weeks to arrive. I'd like to be gone by then. Can you stand to wear the dress awhile? A day, a week? A month?"

She puzzled some of the words. He spoke so fast. He thought because she could mimic words that she understood them all.

He repeated himself in different ways.

She was able to reply, "Wear dress . . ." and shrugged. "Firemaker wear dress, yes. Going to white mother day week, no. Hungry. More eating. People." She pointed toward the corral, which she couldn't see from Mary's quarters. She pinched her forehead. "Sick think of People."

"Worry? You're worried about them?"

She nodded. "Four Toes, old man, father . . ." She dragged at her cheeks. "Sick heart. Sick worry think. Bad think. Bad sick old bones. Cemetery, no." She shook her head. "White man dead ground, no."

Out of respect for the dead, she couldn't let herself say Little Cloud's name aloud in order to convey how little that poor child had taken into the next world, so she said, "Four Toes no horse, no food, no buffalo dress, no thunder stick rifle Hawken." She pointed, trying to find words for the concept of the next life and the things her father would need there.

"You don't need to worry about those people," Carter said. "I'm using my own funds to outfit them. They're eating well. Are you afraid the old man, your father Four Toes, is dying?"

"Die, day, week, holy mountains, ride, walk, going big. Going very worry no horse, food." She hung her head, trying to convey the concept of shame. She wasn't sure white men felt shame for anything, least of all a lack of material necessities in the next life.

At length she abandoned trying to tell Carter her true thoughts, since it would only reveal that she was thinking of her Comanche family more than of her white mother.

"You're having trouble with the white words tonight," Carter said as her silence grew long. "That's all right. I understand." His tone was deep, making her think he did understand, at least on a level beneath words.

"Trouble think—thinking. Tight. White women bad thinking tight dress. No shoe." She pulled up her skirt's hem, revealing a scandalously generous glimpse of her white ruffled petticoat and the battered old moccasins on her feet. "Big feet. Mary small feet."

Carter smiled at her. "I'm proud of you, Firemaker, for trying so hard. We'll find some shoes for you soon. You'll probably be sorry when we do. Now that you're free of the stockade, it's only a matter of time before we leave for Texas." He looked as if he was fishing. She decided to play along.

"White mother twenty summers worry, cry? Crying?"

They had talked only a little of her mother while she was trying to learn English quickly in the stockade.

"Big worry Firemaker dead baby?" she asked.

"Yes, I'm sure your white mother Jane worried. But she always hoped you would be found alive. You're very important to her."

Firemaker frowned at him. "Hope. Worry. Impor-tant. Crying. Jane White Mother. What—what . . . Firemaker having white-man father?"

Carter's brief hesitation before answering was noted.

"Yes, you have a white father, too. He buys and sells horses, so I'm told. He rides from town to town to do his work. I stay at my ranch. He doesn't live with your white mother now."

She puzzled over that. "White mother fighting Four Toes warrior of having horse? Many horse. Hundred horse. Horses," she corrected herself. "Many horses . . . big warrior. Kill white man Texas, having horses. Jane White Mother not dead after Firemaker baby get to Four Toes Comanches?"

"Your mother was crippled," he said. The pinch of Carter's brows concerned her.

She flapped her hands a bit to indicate he must elaborate.

He made a motion across the top of his head.

She felt a warm rush of horror flood her body as she imagined a scalped white woman.

Carter made a hitting motion against his temple, and then pressed the skin alongside his face up so that his eye was distorted and his mouth stretched up in a kind of frozen smile.

She looked away. She hadn't expected this. Four Toes had not killed her white mother when he stole her and the horses, the thunder stick, and the dogs. He'd scalped her mother, hit her, probably raped her. He'd never told her that. Where was the honor? Was her white mother as much an enemy as a white man? Had she fought that well?

Firemaker frowned into the darkness. There were moments when she wondered if there was an answer to this question of who should live on the lands of the west, red or white men. To wonder was to become confused, angry, and discouraged, for it seemed both were wanting and often unworthy.

Scowling in the direction of the corral where Four Toes slept beneath a canvas lean-to, Firemaker had an intense longing to sit a long while and talk with Carter. But she needed so many more white words.

Perhaps Four Toes had once been enough of a coward to scalp a lone white woman, but sometime between then and now he had come to have enough regard for a white woman's daughter that he entrusted the future of the People to her.

Four Toes was, perhaps, a very forward-thinking man after all. Firemaker might know that a woman was as worthy as a man, but it was rather out of the ordinary for a Comanche warrior to think so.

Her disgust erased, Firemaker raised her face to Carter,

thinking that if her white mother was "crippled," it was a badge of strength and courage. She wanted all the more to see her mother, and feared she never would.

"And Firemaker?" Carter said with caution in his voice. "You have a sister."

FOURTEEN

FIVE HUNDRED MILES away, Corinna Tamberlay strained to see Ed Keener's buckboard wagon approaching on the rutted road from town. As he came into sight Jane Tamberlay struggled to her feet from her resting place on the front porch step.

"There's no need for you to go to the depot with me, Ma," Corinna snapped. "It'll just make you sick, and besides, it's going to rain."

"Ain't so stoved up I can't see you off," Jane said, retying her bonnet ribbons. "Unless you changed your mind."

"No, Ma."

Ed came up the walk and tipped his hat. His face was all seams and furrows, his skin tanned and leathery. He smelled faintly of the livery but looked as if he'd stopped by the barber on his way up.

"Afternoon, Janie, Corinna. Not much of a start for a long journey." He squinted at the darkening sky. "I been instructed by half the town to ask you to forget this fool notion, Corinna. New Mexico Territory's too dang far for an unchaperoned young lady to travel all by herself."

Corinna glowered at him.

"In that case, I'm offering this pistol." He produced one from his coat pocket.

Jane shivered, watching her daughter take the pistol

without a moment's hesitation. Corinna tucked it into her reticule, her expression blank.

Jane had hoped Corinna, white-faced and on the verge of tears, would turn tail and scurry back to her room by now, but by the looks of things, the girl was going through with her plans. Jane intended to make the departure as difficult as possible.

Ed followed Corinna out to the buckboard and handed her up to the spring seat. Then he came back to the porch and squinted up at Jane from the bottom of the steps.

"I don't need to remind you how your head will feel after you've bounced along in that buckboard a minute or two. Say your good-byes here, Janie, and save yourself the aggravation. I'll come back after I've seen Corinna safely off. I'll cook us a beefsteak."

Ignoring Ed's reasonable tone, Jane made her way down the steps unassisted and scraped her way to the gate. *She* should be going west, Jane thought, not Corinna.

Gently Ed caught Jane's arm. "There now, dear. Don't be angry with me. I'm only thinking of your welfare."

Jane didn't believe anyone cared how she felt. "I'm not angry, Ed. I'm scared out of the half a mind I got left."

He took great pains helping her onto the seat beside Corinna. When he climbed up and took the lines, Jane felt snug between her daughter and her former husband's former partner. Ed Keener was a decent man.

"How's business since Hugh sold out to you?" Jane asked, attempting light conversation.

Ed's puzzled expression told Jane the question worried him because it brought Hugh to mind. Jane knew Ed's opinion of Hugh Tamberlay was not good.

Ed clicked his tongue. The buckboard lurched forward, dipping directly into a pothole. The mules turned a tight circle over a dozen grassy hillocks and headed back toward town. Jane's head began to reel.

"Business is good, Janie, now that I can run things my

way. Hugh gave me a good price. I'm beholden to him, and you, for suggestin' the sale. Hold on there, Corinna. The ruts up ahead are real deep."

Pain ripped behind Jane's eyes as the wagon dropped heavily into the ruts on their seldom-traveled track down the hill. She began to feel sick to her stomach. Dizziness quickly swept her mind clean of all coherent thought. She grabbed Ed's sleeve and hung on, forgetting why she was moving, lurching, swaying, spinning.

Corinna was saying, ". . . as soon as I get to the first station—oh, Ed, look at her. Her face is gray!"

Ed maneuvered over the last bump and rolled more gently along West Creek Fork's dusty main street. As yet, there was no sign of the stage at the depot.

"If you're worried about your ma takin' on while you're gone doin' whatever you think you can do about a Comanche-bred sister, then don't go, Corinna. That ranger is doing whatever he thinks is right."

Jane pulled on Ed's sleeve as if dragging herself up from a pit of quicksand. She saw Corinna's set jaw and thought, She looks just like Hugh.

"Don't scold her," Jane whispered. "She wants to get Mandie for me."

Corinna's glance was sharp.

Ed parked the buckboard between the depot and the watchmaker's shop. He helped Jane and Corinna down. They all stood silently waiting until a muffled thunder of hooves could be heard to the north.

Corinna clutched her carpetbag. "Ma, you might as well know I'm not going to New Mexico Territory to prove that . . . that *person* is my sister. I'm going to prove she isn't. If she was Mandie, that ranger would've brought her home by now. I've been waiting for him to wire for money. Since he hasn't, I think he's upset us for nothing. It's a horrible joke."

Jane wasn't perturbed. In the past weeks, she and Corinna

had had this argument more times than she could remember. Before she could retort, the stage rattled down the street, coming to a teeth-gritting, dust-boiling halt before them.

Corinna's face went white. Jane fell back, coughing. Ed scowled up at the driver.

Two passengers alighted. The driver clambered over the top of the stage, selected two valises and a small trunk, and pitched them to the ground along with two canvas mail packets.

She herself should be going, Jane thought as her head spun. She should have gone twenty years before. She should have died trying.

While Jane tried to find some last words to say, the driver stuffed Corinna into the stage and yelled, "All who's goin' hurry up!"

Ed dragged Jane back. "She'll do all right."

Corinna didn't wave as the stage rattled away down the street.

"That should be me," Jane croaked, sagging against Ed.

She turned into his arms, and then just as quickly as she found comfort there, she jerked free and began beating her fists against his chest.

"That should be me!"

She didn't look up to see if Ed was angry or alarmed or disgusted with her. What did it matter what he thought anyway? Abruptly she lurched away, her mouth open to let the grief of Corinna's parting out. No sound came.

Stepping down from the depot's boardwalk, Jane stumbled to the watchmaker's shop and leaned against the corner of the building. Then, lifting her eyes, she saw a reflection in the shop's front windows. The reflection was of a once-pretty woman warped in the glass, scarred and ugly now.

Jane stared until her eyes went glassy. She stared until she was able to admit the reflection was of her own face. This was the truth she had spent every waking moment for twenty years trying to avoid. All she had to do was think of Mandie to forget, to forget, to forget, not that Mandie was missing but that she, Jane, was this hideous caricature of her former self.

Then a second reflection appeared next to Jane's, that of a seamed and leathery face, a graying shock of hair, sad blue eyes. Ed Keener caught Jane's shoulders and turned her, looking down into the face she thought so horrible.

He kissed her temple where the scar was most visible. "There, there, Janie. It ain't so bad." Slowly, slowly he pulled her to his chest. "And just think. The good Lord kept both your girls alive. They're about to meet. God willin', they'll be back. Meantime, there's this old man who loves you, stoved-in puss and all. Has for a long, long time."

Too startled to push him away, Jane sagged against the warmth of Ed's arms. Could it be true? Oh, how she wanted it to be true.

Had Carter meant to keep from her the fact that she had a sister? Firemaker wondered. Or was this woman called Corinna Tamberlay so unimportant that she stayed in the back of Carter's mind?

A sister. A blood sister. A girl two years younger, with hair like hers, eyes like hers, a face like hers.

"You're very quiet," Mary had said in Firemaker's room that evening after Carter had gone.

Firemaker didn't answer. She was tired of trying to be something she was not.

Mary released the laces of Firemaker's stays and showed her how to put the long white bed dress over her head.

Able to breathe again, Firemaker let out something resembling a belch that left both women giggling nervously. In moments Mary was tucking her into bed.

"Never mind my questions. We have all day tomorrow to talk. You can be very proud of yourself for the way you handled yourself tonight, Firemaker. Livvie behaved terribly. I'll never forgive her."

"Forgive," Firemaker whispered. She couldn't say more. Her head was filled with too many thoughts. She would need the night to sort them through. "Good night," she said.

Mary paused in the doorway. "I suppose you're right. She only did what I provoked her to do. I hope you sleep well. I'm not sure I will."

Alone at last, Firemaker lay on the uncomfortably soft bed, on the big soft thing Mary said was filled with a million little feathers from white geese. With the candlestick snuffed, the room was as dark as a cell.

The quilt had many colors and shapes sewn together with amazingly thin white thread in stitches so small Firemaker was ashamed of the stitches on her moccasins. The quilt wasn't as heavy or warm as a buffalo robe, but it smelled better.

She could hear the murmur of Mary Small Feet and Lieutenant Mattie in the next room. Mary sounded as if she was explaining something. Mattie seemed worried.

Firemaker decided to ignore the matter of having a sister. She would meet the woman if she made it to Texas. Otherwise a sister was of no consequence. If she was anything like She-Who-Weeps, Firemaker didn't want to know her.

It was the fact that Carter had not mentioned this sister until now that disturbed Firemaker. What other matters was he holding back?

And there was the matter of her white father. Firemaker was certain she understood this particular white man. He had not come for her twenty years ago. He was not coming now.

She had only to look into the eyes of every white man at the fort to understand how her white father probably felt. She dismissed him as well.

Autumn Blaze

Most white men wanted to abuse her, she thought angrily. Some feared her. A few were mildly curious. But Carter Machesney's eyes were warm, admiring, and kind. His touch left her weak. This was not good. This was dangerous. He made her want to forget her obligations to the People.

At dawn Mary tapped at the door, waking Firemaker and calling, "We'll be having breakfast soon. Will you join us?"

"Join?" Firemaker whispered, surprised she'd been able to sleep after all. "Breakfast. Eat. I eat. You eat. We eat. They eat. . . ."

After a moment of relishing the comfort of the enveloping feather tick and quilts, Firemaker smelled the white man's coffee and struggled from the big soft bed. She wandered into the kitchen barefoot, wearing only her bed dress.

Mary was at the backdoor, offering the guard a mug of coffee. The man glanced in, caught sight of Firemaker silhouetted in her bedroom doorway, and gawked like a wall-eyed mule.

"Oh, Firemaker, do put on your wrapper!" Mary cried, blushing to the roots of her brown hair. She slammed the door. "Your bed dress looks nearly transparent."

Not knowing the word "wrapper," Firemaker padded into the parlor, hoping to make notes on Mary's piano. Mattie was nowhere to be seen.

Like a child, Firemaker plunked a few keys and then circled the room, examining all the things she suspected Mary wouldn't let her touch if she were there to supervise. It was then Firemaker remembered the mirror.

She crept to the doorway to Mary's bedroom and peeked in. Oh, what Four Toes would think if he could see this wonder, she thought. He had once possessed a mirror fragment and thought it a window to the next world.

The bed covers were mussed. The room smelled as sleep-warm as a cozy tepee, and Firemaker felt at home at once. Inside, she approached the mirror with reverence, distractedly peering at each pot and jar on Mary's dressing table and fingering the clothing hanging on the back of the door.

Before the mirror she stared thoughtfully at herself. By any standards, she was handsome. But she was a stranger in this unfamiliar-looking body. Her hair was not black. Her eyes were not brown.

She looked like a taller version of Mary. Her hair was tousled, her face as strange as her new life. This was how her mother looked. This was probably the way her sister looked, too.

Firemaker couldn't resist raising her bed dress to peek at her feet and legs. "Firemaker Big Feet," she murmured, chuckling. "Long white legs."

In seconds she'd stripped the gown over her head and stood observing the curves of her naked body for the very first time in her life. All she had on was the locket hanging from the thong.

"Firemaker woman," she said, understanding to a point the fire that had sparked Carter's eyes the evening before when he first saw her wearing the blue dress. He desired her.

The skin of her face, neck, and arms was darker than the rest of her, but there was no mistaking that she was a white woman, as pale beneath her clothes as the underside of a trout.

Her shoulders were square and strong, her arms muscular, her waist nipped in, hips flaring, thighs firm and sleek. Her breasts were full and round, her woman place hidden by hair only a bit darker than that on her head. No wonder she'd been stared at most of her life. She was a horse among ponies.

She had never expected to see herself like this. It was not so surprising, now that she could see her own self, to think that Snakehorn had once wanted her, though she had been but a child.

Once she had worshiped Snakehorn, her elder brother, but as she had matured and noticed how he spent too much time eating peyote and dreaming, her respect dimmed. She understood only too well the allure of dreams, but he had sacrificed too much for his.

When he left a horse for her the first time, she ignored it. He had left a second and a third. When she rejected those, too, he came for her in the night, not to take her virginity, but to sell her to the Apaches secretly. He was not a man to be spurned. She-Who-Weeps had accepted his horses then, and earned her name while he was away year after year making war.

Lifting her eyes from the sensual arrangement of swells and curves that was her white woman's body, Firemaker saw Lieutenant Matthew Graham standing behind her in the doorway of his bedroom.

His eyes transfixed, his face aflame, his feet frozen in the middle of a step, he made a small grunt. "Excuse . . . me. Here . . . she is, Mary."

"Where?" came Mary's worried call.

Firemaker met Mattie's eyes, searching for the lust she had seen so clearly in Clay Burdette's sneer. Seeing only the young man's embarrassment, and his inability to look away, she felt oddly reassured that she was at least pleasing to a white man's eye.

Mary's exclamation was small. "Firemaker, what are you doing?" Her face went crimson. "Mattie, turn around!"

"Firemaker white legs . . ."

Taking on the white man's embarrassment over her natural nakedness, Firemaker decided not to explain. She turned away. It was her right to look at herself, she thought angrily.

"Well, I suppose you would be curious. Oh, dear, you are

lovely, but you must keep yourself covered. It's called modesty."

Mattie was turning away just as Mary gave a soft gasp and sagged, unconscious, into his arms.

Firemaker felt awful to see her hostess in another swoon. She half wished she was back in the cell block, where she could at least be her true self. "How do you do?" she blurted, realizing at once her mistake. "Pardon me. . . ."

Her presence in this house was hard on Mary Small Feet, Firemaker realized. The baby might come early.

"This is my house, too, Firemaker," Mattie whispered huskily. "Think of Mary's condition. She shouldn't be . . . upset. Put on your clothes, for God's sake. Don't you understand that much about being a decent woman?"

She understood more than Mattie Graham ever would, Firemaker thought, jerking the bed dress back over her head. She flashed him an angry eye.

Would she ever be happy again? She needed her life back. She needed her self back. She longed for something that she had no white word for and that she feared she would never find. Sanctuary.

Firemaker was seated at the kitchen table, her bed dress covered completely with a "wrapper" when Leota arrived by the backdoor.

"You're early," Mary said, her manner strained, her face pale. "I suppose Livvie had you up till all hours planning another party for tonight." Her tone sounded falsely bright.

Leota noticed Mary's pallor at once, but said nothing. "No'm, Miz Chiswell's done took to her bed. She's about as upset with you as I ever seed a female get."

Mary's face reflected stormy thoughts. "I should be the one furious with her. She ordered me to her party last night, knowing Firemaker needed me here. What was I supposed to have done?"

As assembly sounded with an echo across the parade

ground, Matt rose from the table, his gaze studiously averted from Firemaker's vicinity. "I must say I'm glad to be called away from this discussion of domestic politics." He strapped on his saber. "Have a good morning, dear." He planted an especially tender kiss on Mary's head.

The moment the lieutenant was through the door, Firemaker felt better.

"Piano," Firemaker said, able to follow the conversation enough to conclude that she would not be required to exhibit herself at the Chiswells again that night. "Walking." She pointed to the door. "The People eating, talking. Ride. Big ride to mountains. Hunting rabbit for Mary Small Feet baby." She rocked her arms together, trying to indicate the need for a cradle board.

Mary put a trembling hand to her forehead. "Mary Small Feet?" She gave a shaky laugh. "Have I earned a Comanche name? I'm honored."

Firemaker sensed she had said something right. "Mary Small Feet friend."

"Yes, I am, Firemaker. I hope you forgive me for being cross with you earlier. I'm quite all right now. Really. We'll try a few notes on the piano later. I have a great deal to think about just now. I don't believe you'll be allowed to hunt . . . just yet. As for walking or speaking with your Comanche friends, we'll need the colonel's permission." She called after her husband. "Have you gone out yet, Mattie?"

He appeared so quickly he must've been standing on the other side of the door, listening. "I'll see to it," he said. "We want Firemaker on her way home to Texas as soon as she's ready."

Leota paused in her breakfast preparations, looked pointedly at Mary and then at Matt and his avoidance of Firemaker's gaze. Then she looked at Firemaker as if to say, "What have you been up to?"

Firemaker straightened in her chair, knees together, hands

folded demurely in her lap. Without the stays, she was quite comfortable in this "ladylike" pose. She was the picture of propriety, except that her bare feet were cold. And inside she was seething. She had done nothing wrong.

By noon Firemaker had not only been relaced into her costume of the day before, but she had also learned how to smooth her feather bed, draw up the covers, empty her own chamber pot, dust the furniture, and mop the dust from the bedroom floor. She had, as well, helped with the breakfast dishes and all chores relating to the kitchen.

Afterward they spent time at the piano. At Firemaker's insistence, they lifted the piano's lid and removed the face so Firemaker could observe the workings of the hammers against the wires inside.

Firemaker frowned with delight as she began to play a tune Mary and Leota thought nonsense. But for Firemaker the song had the greatest of meaning. It was her personal medicine song, sung since she could remember to the leaping yellow-and-orange flames of a tepee campfire.

Fire, fire, come to small girl child, lonely and different, stupid and unworthy, lost and angry. . . . Fire, fire, hot and bright. Give me courage, give me strength. Make my heart burn with pride for my father. Make my mind quick. Fire, fire, fire.

The words were too powerful to speak or sing aloud. No one but Four Toes even knew she practiced the singing of medicine songs because it was forbidden to all but warriors and old women. Firemaker hummed along anyway, plunking out random notes from among the black and white keys.

She found no use for Mary's simple rendition of "Turkey in the Straw." Turkeys had no medicine. They were as useless as coyotes.

She was Firemaker! She had been breaking Comanche rules for many years, doing what only boys and medicine men were allowed to do. Now she was breaking white rules.

It was difficult to smother her secret smile. Even if she was to become this Mandie Tamberlay that everyone wanted her to be, she would always be the troublesome Firemaker, daughter to Four Toes, the comanche warrior.

After another meal at one o'clock that afternoon—white people were always eating if they weren't starving in a stockade—Firemaker practiced more table manners as well as polite conversation. The lieutenant joined them, bringing permission for a promenade around the parade ground at two-fifteen.

Mary crowed with delight. The episode before the mirror that morning seemed forgotten.

Clutching a knitted shawl around her shoulders, although she wasn't chilled, wearing her moccasins beneath her skirt and petticoats, cinched within an inch of her ability to draw adequate breath, and wearing a rather shabby brown bonnet for which Mary Small Feet apologized profusely, Firemaker set out with Mary for their walk at the appointed time.

The adobe houses along officers' row had curious faces in every window that afternoon. As Mary and Firemaker passed, soldiers drilling beyond the encampment fell out of step. It appeared that the reinforcements were preparing for a patrol. There, too, the men paused, agape, as a nine-months-pregnant matron and her tall blond companion passed.

Suddenly every person at Fort Bradley found a chore that needed attention out of doors. Eventually the only sound was the post flag snapping enthusiastically from the top of a twenty-foot pine staff. The only movement was two women, one waddling, one gliding, past a hundred pairs of riveted eyes.

"We wouldn't attract more attention if we were walking naked—" Mary cut herself off.

"Naked?" Firemaker repeated for a definition.

"Nothing. I was only grumbling. Oh, here comes Carter. What a welcome sight." Mary's renewed agitation eased.

Welcome, yes, Firemaker thought as Carter strolled forward from the long building to the east. His long legs carried him swiftly toward her with only the hint of the limp that had noticeably plagued him weeks before.

It was exciting to know he had once been a warrior. He was no Comanche, but his body radiated confidence and purpose. In spite of her resolution to control her attraction to him, her heart beat faster. She yearned to curl against him in the ways she had seen in the tepee years before when Four Toes had had wives.

Firemaker forgot the mental map of the fort she had been memorizing during this first walk. She fixed her gaze on Carter Machesney's handsome face. His smile was even more dazzling as his expression lit at the sight of her.

Suddenly she couldn't remember anything but the feel of his hand on her shoulder the evening before. If she was lucky, he might touch the small of her back now as they walked, or offer his elbow. Escape with the People? Leave him behind? What could she be thinking?

"Good . . ." She searched her memory for the correct salutation. ". . . day."

Mary smiled. "Good afternoon, Mr. Machesney. We've been given permission to speak to the Comanche prisoners as soon as McTigue can be located. I suppose Jed still thinks the Comanches are plotting an escape. Would you be so good as to walk with us to the corral?"

"My pleasure, ladies," Carter said, offering both his elbows. Mary took one, Firemaker the other.

"I believe McTigue is . . . having his laundry done just now. He'll be a while yet, I think."

Inwardly Firemaker thrilled to slip her fingers into the crook of Carter's elbow and feel the rough fabric of his coat over the strong warmth of his muscular arm. She felt a noticeable warmth spread through her own body to the place no man had ever filled.

At the corral Carter smiled as if what he saw there

pleased him. "They're doing better," he said, indicating the dozen canvas lean-tos arranged against the fence in the farthest corner of the corral.

The campfires were small, but strips of antelope hung from sticks over the flames. The Comanche children were dressed in cast-off clothing. There was a feeling of orderliness in the air, of relief. Firemaker knew this was Carter's doing.

Looking up into his face, she had to wonder why he was helping the People. Because she was white? Because he wanted something more from her? Because he wanted *her*? Or simply because he was a good man and cared?

She shivered. She could see why in his eyes, in the closeness of his stance, in his hopeful little smile. He was trying to please her. He felt the same warmth as she. Suddenly she wished they could be alone. She wanted to please him.

She lowered her gaze lest he see that which he hoped for, her increasing admiration for him. She couldn't allow these feelings to grow. They would only hamper her.

But the feelings felt so good. She had so little to comfort her now. She had only to close her eyes to remember the horror of murder and destruction only weeks before. To open her eyes, she saw a man capable of turning her life into a complete mystery. He was helping her. For that she was bewilderingly grateful. At least there was hope. If she succeeded in rescuing the People, she and Carter might be more than friends.

"They're going to be all right," he said softly, moving close enough that she could feel the warmth of his words on her forehead. "You can go home to your white mother knowing these women and children will have a good life on the reservation. I'll see to it personally."

"Good life," she murmured.

She knew the white words she was expected to say—"thank you"—but she didn't say them.

Inside she was weeping for joy to think the People weren't starving or cold, but she had made herself a promise. To go back on it now would be very bad medicine. These People who were her Comanche family deserved a good life, but they deserved a life they'd been born to, not the life forced on them by whites. She was bound to free them, and free them she would.

Carter was about to say more when one of the Comanche women straightened from her work beside the lean-to and turned to stare defiantly at Firemaker.

She-Who-Weeps didn't recognize Firemaker at first. Firemaker could see that and felt suddenly ashamed of her disguise, as if she was dishonest or dirty. Then Snakehorn's wife started marching across the corral, her hollow cheeks testament to the hardships she and the others had endured during the weeks Firemaker was in the stockade.

She had recognized Firemaker's face. "You, White Hair, why are you back here?" She-Who-Weeps demanded in Comanche.

"I'm preparing to help you all escape," Firemaker said hastily in Comanche, looking around for fear the scout was near and would betray her words to Carter.

"Escape to where? What do you care what becomes of us? Look at you. Look at us. Soon we will be slaves to the white man. Already they try to make me their whore." She displayed a bruised arm. Firemaker noticed some marks around her mouth.

"What's wrong?" Carter asked, observing the woman's battered appearance and casting a hot eye toward the guards slouching at the corral fence a few yards away. They were smirking. Carter's eyes narrowed. "Is she all right, Firemaker?"

Firemaker shook off his words. She-Who-Weeps was saying, "We have no more use for you, white daughter of Four Toes. Go away."

Carter pulled Firemaker away from the fence. "Have the men hurt her? Why is she angry?"

Firemaker plucked at her skirt. "Big anger, white dress, no thank you, sir," she said, confusing bits of polite conversation with the truth she hoped to conceal.

"Go!" She-Who-Weeps shouted.

Four Toes was roused from his slump beneath a big gray army blanket covering his head and face. He tried to rise but couldn't. Pausing to gather his strength, he finally found his feet and hobbled toward Firemaker as stiffly as if carved of rotted wood.

"You dishonor your father, Four Toes, in those white woman's rags," She-Who-Weeps spat out under her breath as if afraid Four Toes would hear her. "You are a pain in my eye. Our warriors are all dead. Snakehorn, my husband, is dead, and soon will be our son. You live with the enemy and come to flout yourself before us. You will live. We will die."

"I'm doing this to help all of you," Firemaker hissed back, her heart pounding with anguish, her shame over her appearance growing intense. "If you know a better way, tell it to me. Why has no one tried to escape? Are you like sheep? If you're a better thinker than I, help the People as I'm trying to do. Otherwise close your mouth and let me do what I can."

Carter seized Firemaker's arm. "I can't let you talk like this, Firemaker. You must speak English, or the colonel won't let you come here again. What have you been saying?"

"Learn the Comanche words if you want to know what I'm saying," Firemaker wanted to shout.

Instead she turned away her flashing eyes. "Bad white dress. I am Firemaker. I am Comanche!" Too late she remembered herself. "Pardon me, please. . . ." She lowered her gaze and forced her shoulders to drop in a gesture of surrender.

She couldn't risk rousing Carter's suspicions. If She-Who-Weeps didn't understand what she was trying to do on behalf of the People, then the woman was just a foolish, ordinary coyote deserving of her ignorance. Firemaker couldn't concern herself with the woman any further.

Firemaker's way was clear. She allowed herself to appear confused, then contrite and small-spirited. "I am . . . white woman heart crying," she said, using a whining tone she had learned from the colonel's wife. She pointed to She-Who-Weeps. "No more friend. No more sister. No more . . ." She shook her head, at a genuine loss for words, Comanche or white. She couldn't remember the white word for hate. "Big angry. Very big angry. Big fear. Big . . ." She plucked at her skirt.

Carter looked bewildered. "She doesn't like your dress?"

"Bad Firemaker no more sister. Doesn't like," she parroted. "Doesn't like . . . me. Walking away to Mary Small Feet house today." She started away, but not before catching her father's eye as he arrived at the side of She-Who-Weeps.

With a single black look, Four Toes sent Snakehorn's scowling wife away.

She-Who-Weeps stormed off, shaking her fists at her sides and muttering in Comanche, "Old man. Old fool! May Snakehorn's angry spirit give you no rest!"

"There's talk that Snakehorn is near," Firemaker blurted to her father in Comanche.

She used an inflection designed to make Carter think she was greeting her father rather than imparting vital information. She went on with the pretense, sounding as if she was apologizing but saying, "I'm looking for the way to run from the fort in the night."

Carter frowned all the harder. "I'm telling you, Firemaker, you must stop this."

"Are you well?" Firemaker asked her father. She could see plainly that he was not.

"My heart is dead," Four Toes said softly.

"Dead," she said to Carter in English. "Dead father. Big old."

Carter's expression softened. "I can see he's ill. To my knowledge, Colonel Chiswell has no plans to send to Maguey for a doctor. I'm sorry. We have to go, Firemaker. I see the colonel standing in his office doorway. You don't want to go back to the stockade, do you? I don't."

Pulling free of Carter's hold, Firemaker turned on her heel and stomped away from the corral. Her Comanche blood boiled beneath her paling skin.

FIFTEEN

OLIVIA CHISWELL'S MYSTERIOUS illness ended abruptly with a miraculous cure.

She was seen the next day strolling from neighbor to neighbor along officers' row, swishing her skirts and fluttering her hands, steering every conversation toward the one subject she professed to be loath to discuss.

"Don't y'all trouble yourself on the matter," she said to Lieutenant Forbes's wife. "Mary's a simple girl. She can't be expected to understand a lady's sensibilities. She's a good person at heart, but she's been taken in by that little savage. She doesn't care how the rest of us feel.

"Let's assume that when she was growin' up, her father was forced to assist whatever sort of low, common person crossed his church's threshold. Mary's forgotten the way of things out here. We have to keep ourselves civilized in the face of all this hardship.

"I'll forgive Mary, of course, but I can't allow that heathen under my roof again. She has no family, after all, just a mother somewhere. Goodness knows what *that* poor woman must be feelin', knowin' her daughter's been . . . livin' in a *tepee* all her life. Let's just forget the matter entirely."

Olivia repeated herself at each doorway, gathering her allies, carefully ignoring the sergeants' wives who eagerly

Autumn Blaze 201

bid her good day in hopes of another invitation. They were ignored.

By evening Olivia had an exclusive group of followers in her wake. The officers who dutifully followed their wives to the colonel's quarters that evening were oblivious to Olivia's tactics, enjoying instead the first half hour of the colonel's whiskeyed charm, thinking themselves in line for promotions. Later they could not determine why the colonel was so bitterly criticizing them.

Surprisingly Olivia was capable of playing her own piano, though clumsily. No one failed to note the absence of Mary Graham and her husband.

All too soon a smug feeling overtook the chosen few. It never occurred to any of them that those absent were relieved to be excluded. They knew only that Olivia Chiswell favored them for the moment, and the feeling was good.

But by the next afternoon, and even more during the following weekdays, a noticeable rift appeared between the ladies at the fort. When Mary and Firemaker strolled the perimeter of the parade ground each afternoon, only a scant few neighbors bowed in greeting.

The reinforcements mustered a patrol of forty men expected to be gone a week, and rode out. They returned two days later saying if Comanches had been in the foothills, or up the canyon, they had fled.

Those in the corral drooped with lost hope. Firemaker grew dejected and restless. Mary silently suffered the snubs of those ladies who had previously called themselves her friends. Sunday-morning services were poorly attended.

For all the studiously averted glances and outright avoidance of Mary Graham and her charge, it was noted at once when the pair failed to appear for their daily stroll early the following week.

Carter Machesney could be seen going to and from the Graham quarters, staying only a moment in the afternoon instead of his usual hour or two. Olivia watched it all from the edge of her lace-curtained windows and smiled. She concluded that the enemy had surrendered. Mary and Firemaker were surely too dejected and ashamed to appear in public and were now pining for her attentions.

"Several people have asked me if Mary is ill," Jed said to Olivia late that week, crossing to the dining room where Leota was laying the evening table. "What do you know about this, Leota?" he asked.

"I'm sure I don't know nothin' about what's going on hereabouts, Mr. Colonel," Leota muttered, casting a harsh eye in Olivia's direction. "Ain't been many callers at the Grahams' in days. I ain't been asked to cook or clean or nothing like that. I 'spect Miz Firemaker's doin' it all. Miz Mary could be on her deathbed for all some folks calling themselves friends might care."

Olivia threw down her tatting and stormed into the dining room. "Three dozen women of your ilk would kill to have a job that pays as well as this, Leota High-and-Mighty," she cried flame-cheeked. "You *can* be replaced."

"Yes'm. Since comin' out west after the war, my life's been a heap easier than in slave days. Sure has. I don't know what I'd think if'n I didn't have to tend you folks every day."

"So, *is* Mary ill?" Olivia demanded petulantly. "I'm sure she's just busy with that *Miss* Tamberlay, teachin' her to read. It must be wearin' on her."

"Miz Firemaker's learnin' to play the piano when there's nobody about to laugh at her. Played like a child first time she touched them keys. I laughed, I'm 'shamed to say. Last I heard, she's doin' right better. And she's learnin' to 'broider a sampler pretty as anything. Miz Mary's teachin' her to knit for the bab—"

"My Lord in heaven, does Mary actually think that heathen is going to marry and live in a fine house with servants enough that she can sit about sewin' samplers? Even I haven't that much free time."

It was during that same night that Firemaker woke in the small hours, disoriented and frightened. Her room looked as dark as a starless night and felt as stuffy as the stockade had been, but it was the silence that unnerved her.

The bed creaked as she rolled from its enveloping soft warmth and padded barefoot to her door. No bar held it fast. Firemaker found the door heavy but silent as she pushed it open.

The kitchen was dark and eerie, smelling faintly of their supper from hours before, and of wood ash. The fire had gone out in the cook stove. For several minutes Firemaker prowled around it, marveling that the iron-belly stove didn't catch fire or melt when wood was burning within.

Firemaker peeped from the window to see the guard standing some distance from the door as if he had taken a pause in his pacing. She smelled burning tobacco and thought she could hear him sigh.

In the parlor Firemaker stood before Mary's clock, watching the pendulum swinging all by itself, listening to the perfect ticking rhythm. Was there nothing a Comanche could do to best these white people?

At Mary and Matt's bedroom door, Firemaker stood listening to their breathy snores, smelling the warmth of their sleep together in the bed. She felt sad for the time long gone when she had slept beside Four Toes in his tepee crowded with wives and children. She had been very small then. It was before the sickness came, before she understood her differences from the others, before her innocence died.

Her thoughts moved from the curiosities of Mary's house to the formidable task of getting the Comanche women and children, and Four Toes, who could no longer walk, free of the fort without being seen or challenged. Her first desire was simply to melt into the night with them and never be heard from again. Surely the mountains were vast enough to swallow a few People safely forever.

But what of Snakehorn? How soon would their paths cross, if ever? What if he was dead? What if all the warriors were dead? Firemaker couldn't take women and children to winter in the mountains without provisions.

At the front window she saw the guard seated on the rim of Mary's flower-filled half barrel, slumped against the wall, his head leaning on his carbine, which was braced against his boot and the wall.

Taking exquisite care to lift the bar from the brackets on either side of the door, Firemaker wondered how alert white people were to changes in air temperature and smells should she be able to open the door without a sound. Surely Mary would wake, knowing an outside door had been opened. The rush of fresh cold air through the rooms would be unmistakable.

As for the sleeping guard, he might be awakened by the movement of the door. If she was caught, Firemaker assumed she would spend many more nights in the stockade. All would be lost.

To wait, however, was impossible. She'd been to one of their parties, after all. She was scrubbed, dressed, and docile. They were beginning to trust her. The colonel and his men wouldn't expect her to do anything as risky as leave the Grahams' house in the night.

She should have gone the week before, she thought, watching the darkness intently for any sign of movement, because her woman time had finally come. It would have been a perfect opportunity to sneak about, rendering the white man's weapons useless by looking at them, but too many years of keeping herself private during that time had kept her in her room.

She hadn't flowed since the attack and had feared she had somehow been damaged when the whore-dog Burdette sat on her, strangling her. No amount of persuasion had made her willing to see or speak to anyone the week before, especially not Carter. Finally Mary had understood what was wrong and gave Firemaker a supply of rags with a brief, awkward description of how to use and wash them afterward.

Exerting a steady pull on the handle, Firemaker felt the door begin to open. The moment she was able to squeeze through, she pulled it closed again and stood, holding her breath, her heart pounding in her throat while the guard snorted and rumbled inches away.

She could have easily killed him, she thought, slipping around to the safety of the space between the adobe houses. But there was no use in that.

Officers' row was silent and dark. The parade ground was silent, too, with the encampment dim and still, the many campfires burned down to coals, giving only feeble light and slight smoke into the cold night air.

Beneath her thin cotton bed dress, her skin prickled and her nipples stood erect. She scarcely took note of the cold, however. She had been cold before, much colder, in fact. She would be cold again. Much colder.

Silently as a ghost, Firemaker moved across the flagstone walk to the parade ground of sparse grass and sage cover. She saw no movement of guards, although she knew from her weeks in the stockade that there should be four touring the fort on the hour.

No lighted windows relieved the starlit darkness. There was no sign that a single person remained awake to observe her swift crossing to the barracks veranda. Inside was the familiar sound of snoring men.

She thrilled to be fully free again, Comanche, fleet-footed, silent, sneaking to the corrals where the horses scarcely minded her intrusion. All she had to do was mount and flee. But to where? What else was there for her but this place, this time, and this task?

At a peculiar sound, she gave pause, melting into the shadows uncomfortably near the thick stone walls of the stockade. There she noted a dim light burning in the guardhouse window and heard the murmur of voices within.

At length a guard emerged from the latrine across the way. His boots crunched loudly in the gravel as he crossed to the corral where the Comanches were sleeping in their encampment. She saw his warm breath gust in the cold night air when he belched.

Moving with each of his steps, she utilized his noisy progress while he made a simple pass in front of the corral fence. After a moment he returned to the guardhouse, where, as the door opened, weak yellow light spilled across the flagstone walk. From within she heard the soft shuffling of playing cards.

Soundlessly Firemaker crept between the fence rails and darted across the corral. Her approach, however, hadn't gone unnoticed by Four Toes, who was awake, propped on one elbow, waiting for her inside his canvas lean-to.

"I've come to lead us away," she said in Comanche, panting softly, "but you need a litter, and we'll need food. We can't go tonight."

Her father shook his head. "We grow sick. The one called Carter gives much, but we're not well in our hearts. Our medicine has gone bad."

"I won't hear it!" Firemaker hissed. "I've done too much to give up without a single try. I'll find a way."

Now some of the women were stirring, and a few round-eyed children peeped from beneath thick army blankets. She-Who-Weeps stared at Firemaker in obvious disapproval.

Firemaker was momentarily daunted. She wanted to leap to her feet and scream with angry frustration, but she held herself rigid, fighting her doubts.

Did they not know how much easier it would be for her to wear her new dress and go away to Texas? She didn't have to help them. She was risking her freedom and her life for their future safety in the mountains. To go back into the stockade meant, this time, that the whore dog would get her.

Four Toes touched her arm. "Take those who will go," he whispered. "We're all free to decide the new life. You can't force anyone to go back to the mountains if they are too sick to try. I will be staying here, going to the reservation with those who choose that way. I can't walk back to the mountains."

"We'll carry you," she cried almost at the same time as She-Who-Weeps did.

"You'll have to travel too quickly to bother with me."

Firemaker thought of the miles of open valley they would be crossing, exposed and vulnerable to the horse soldiers' rifles. She thought of the canyons and high meadows, and wondered if her efforts so far had been futile. Could she get any of them safely away? "What about dying in the holy mountains?" she asked softly.

Her father's expression went bleak. If he didn't die in the holy mountains, his spirit would wander between this world and the next for a very long time.

"I'll think of a way," she insisted before he could answer. "I can do nothing else."

Angrily she slipped away to scamper a swift circuit of the corrals, gauging her chances of stealing enough horses for all of them. She wondered how she might raid the storehouse for provisions in spite of the fact that the gates were barred each night from whatever sticky-fingered freighters were staying at the fort. Clearly with so many lives at stake she could not proceed without a well-thought-out plan.

She stood some moments contemplating the freight wagons. New ones arrived daily along the Santa Fe Trail. She wondered if she might find a way to hide everyone among the goods. But such a journey with no weapons was dangerous and would take them southward when a direct flight west was their only chance for survival.

Upon approaching Mary's house once again, Firemaker saw that the guard had awakened. He was now pacing a few feet in front of the door.

She shivered. She couldn't go back inside from the rear door. Not only was the gate in the five-foot-high adobe wall enclosing Mary's backyard locked, but the rear door to the house was still barred as well.

Coming to the side of the house by way of the back of the colonel's house, Firemaker pitched several stones as far into the parade ground as possible. She hit two tents. She tried again, with several pebbles that fell short but made soft noises as they hit the ground.

Only a few feet away, the guard halted and crept cautiously forward into the darkness. His stance indicated that he was staring intently into the sleepy encampment where the pebbles had landed.

Crouching, Firemaker found several larger stones at her feet. She threw them far to the south, hearing one thump rather loudly against what sounded like a coffepot over a campfire.

There was a noisy hissing of the fire and a small plume of smoke. As someone there gave out with a sleepy, questioning curse, the guard moved several more feet away from Mary's front door. Firemaker lifted her hem to free her legs and dashed to the door, pressing it open and slipping inside in one swift motion.

She didn't stop to bar the door, but dashed to her room.

When she was certain her movements had gone unnoticed, she returned a half hour later to slip the bar silently back into place.

"You look tired, Firemaker," Carter said, perched stiffly on Mary's chair by the fireplace late the next afternoon. "When you wouldn't see me last week, I worried you were ill."

Firemaker had no intention of explaining why she had accepted no visitors. Men weren't to ask after the woman time, she thought, holding herself rigid and aloof. Surely he would have suspected by now that that was her reason for refusing to see him.

At length she lifted her eyes and smiled a little. "I am learn—learning to play piano. The piano."

She took her seat upon the little stool and played several simple pieces for him. He looked astonished, and she glowed inside.

"I remember listening when my sister learned to play," Carter said. "That was very long ago."

He went on to talk of his home for a time, and then his expression took on a more intimate appeal. "It's been so many days since I've been able to talk with you, Firemaker. Might we go for a walk before it gets dark?"

"Thank you, yes," she said, rising and going for her shawl and bonnet. It didn't occur to her to ask anyone's permission.

All the while Carter watched her, she thrilled to be pleasing him with her white sentences and ladylike behavior. So short would be their association, she thought, that she wanted to spend as much time with him as possible. She must take her pleasure where she could find it, she reminded herself.

When Carter offered his arm, she took it gingerly. She was aware suddenly how she had missed Carter's smiling face, and his questions, in the past several days. She looked briefly up into his eyes, seeing more questions in them, and wondered why he wanted to know so much about her.

"I am reading the book," she said, finding once again that she felt tongue-tied when Carter was near. She had trouble finding the combinations of words she needed just to talk of ordinary things. "Bible. And to sew. Sew, sewed, sewing. Um, I am sewing . . . the letters." She recited the alphabet, and when she was done, she blushed because he had stared at her lips all the while.

"Mary has helped you learn more white words," Carter said. "You're doing very well."

She nodded, having forgotten enough words of one particular sentence that she couldn't repeat it.

"I'm so proud of you, Firemaker," he said softly as they moved away from officers' row in the direction of the quartermaster's store. The sun was almost beyond the western ridge. "I'd like to start for Texas soon, but the colonel . . . thinks it's not yet safe."

"Texas," she murmured. Always it was Texas with him.

"Now that you have more white words, tell me more of your life with the Comanches," Carter said.

She thought only of the feel of Carter's firm forearm beneath her fingertips, the warmth of his body as he walked beside her, the smell of him and the sound of his voice, and his attention rapt on her.

"I am happy small child," she began, remembering deep grassy meadows and warm summer days. She paused to conjugate silently the verb to be. "I *was,*" she corrected, "small happy girl child run—running the grass, riding the horse, helping the father in the summer. Warm the day, sleep in, under . . . yes, under the stars in sky night. The night."

Carter grinned.

"I am . . . I was taking water for me . . . my father," she went on. "Snakehorn having the new wife not liking me. Pouring out my the water. She-Who-Weeps sick think . . . um, worry Snakhorn riding Texas for horses. Big worry." She indicated a swollen belly. "Having the baby child Snakehorn going Texas many the night. Riding to mountains baby son many days coming out She-Who-Weeps . . . big . . ." She made a terrible face of rage.

"Angry?"

Firemaker nodded. "Very big angry Snakehorn taking horses the many days. So more worry. No eating. No the buffalo. Walking Bear not liking me and taking the horses with Snakehorn." She frowned as she tried to remember the words for respect. "The brother very . . ." Finally she shrugged. "I am worry all dead today."

"Firemaker," Carter said after a pause, "do you want to see your white mother?"

Again changing the subject, Firemaker thought, irritated. She nodded, her expression serious. "After father dying in holy mountain. Much big soon, I worry. I to worry big."

"You are worried."

"I am worried," she repeated.

"I wish there was something I could do to help him," Carter said. "He looks like a good man."

"Um, big warrior, many horses." She flashed her fingers many times to indicate hundreds of horses. "Many fighting for horses. Long riding to Texas. Having Firemaker, me, from Texas, many summer gone."

Carter nodded. "He used to be a great warrior."

"Um, great warrior. Old warrior die in holy mountains. Not good die the horse corral. Not horse," she said earnestly. "Father, me. My. My *father*. Father, they. *They* father." She pointed toward the corrals. "Is Carter having the father?"

"My father died while I was away from my home in a war," he said softly.

"Carter great warrior?"

He chuckled, and she noticed some pain in his eyes that she hadn't noticed before. "I wanted to think I was. I got caught by the men I was fighting. They took me prisoner, like your father and She-Who-Weeps are prisoners now."

"Um," she said, cocking her head slightly, seeing Carter in a new light. She understood, finally, why he was inclined to help the People. He knew their shame.

SIXTEEN

SEVEN MILES NORTHWEST of Fort Bradley, the Butterfield Stage careened along the grassy track known to the dusty freight outfits ahead and the mule trains behind them as the Santa Fe Trail.

Corinna had been traveling for so long it was hard for her to maintain her determination. Utterly exhausted, her patience gone, her nerves raw, she sat dull-eyed inside the stagecoach, clutching the pistol hidden in her reticule, wondering how *anything* could have seemed important enough to come five hundred miles.

By the time Fort Bradley was in sight, she wished only for a bed and three days' sleep. As the stage rolled beneath the crossed timbers of the fort's gate and came to a rocking halt at the southern end of the parade ground, Corinna tumbled jelly-legged out the door, feeling as overwhelmed and frightened as ever in her life.

The fort looked nothing like she'd expected. It seemed exposed and scattered, surrounded by nothing but open valley. She had hoped for stout walls and a feeling of safety. Instead she felt more vulnerable than ever. The reality of a Comanche attack was etched in her mind's eye in the form of her mother's ravaged face.

If only she could be home that very instant, Corinna thought raggedly, with her life back the way it had been before that damnable Texas Ranger had shown up. If only she'd never been born, she added to herself sarcastically.

Why, there was Captain Machesney that very moment, strolling along with some officer's blond daughter on his arm as if he had nothing better to do than idle away his time while Corinna and her mother suffered over his lies. It was no wonder he'd made no haste to return to Texas with her "sister," Corinna thought, having half a mind to shoot the man and have done with it. He was obviously enjoying himself far too much here to care what she'd been through.

As Ranger Captain Machesney and his companion made their way closer, Corinna watched the stage driver fling her carpetbag to the ground. Blue-coated troopers lagged nearby to ogle her and grin. Impatiently Corinna swung away, certain her appearance was bedraggled, but that didn't excuse such rude staring.

In a tiny corner of her mind, Corinna suddenly wondered if there might be a beau for her among the troops. Was that why she had come so far? Really? No, she thought, clutching her reticule more tightly to her chest. The pistol inside was as hard as her heart.

As Corinna turned in bewildered circles her stomach rumbled with hunger. She was dead on her feet. At the moment she didn't care if she ever saw the woman claiming to be her sister. She'd make short work of that identification, Corinna thought with grim satisfaction. Given some rest, she might be on her way back home in a few days.

"Corinna? Corinna Tamberlay?"

The ranger was calling to her now, staring at her, dumbfounded.

"What are you doing here? Is your mother all right?"

Corinna felt smugly pleased at Captain Machesney's incredulous tone. "You didn't think I'd come this far just to check on you, did you, Captain Machesney? Well, here I am. My *mother* is as well as can be expected, considering what-all she's been through these past weeks on your account.''

Corinna ignored Carter's outstretched hand and openly refused to acknowledge his pretty companion, who was roasting her with a wide-eyed stare.

"I took it upon myself to see that . . . I don't know *what* I've been thinking," Corinna blurted. "At the moment I scarcely remember my own name, much less why I came so far. I suppose I'm here to show you up as the charlatan you surely are. But I can't think how to do it. I'm so tired my head hurts."

Corinna noticed several bonneted women approaching and was relieved. Surely one of them would help her find a bed and show her around this desolate, godforsaken place. One, dressed rather ostentatiously for such a dusty outpost, eyed her in a most disconcerting manner.

"I find the behavior of people out here very irritating," Corinna snapped under her breath. "Staring at me just because I'm traveling alone . . . You'd think I was an escaped criminal the way they take on."

"Carter, sugar!" the overdressed, pretty matron cried in a thick drawl as she drew near. "Do introduce us to our newly arrived guest. Why, doesn't she *just* look all wrung out, poor creature. She—" The woman's eyes rounded. Her gaze shot to the ranger's companion. "Oh, my Lord, two of them!"

The women beside her looked equally aghast as their eyes riveted first on Corinna and then . . .

Beyond caring if she behaved as badly as the rest of them, Corinna shifted her own scorching attention to the ranger and his companion, a tallish young woman in a rather shabby blue dress.

"Have I dust on my face?" Corinna cried, her composure crumbling. "Surely folks have been known to arrive at this fort looking a bit worse for the wear."

It was the pale whitey-blond color of the companion's hair that constricted Corinna's throat and cut off her ability to speak any further.

That was the color of her mother's hair.

Corinna gaped at the gray-blue eyes, so like her father's, so like her own. The woman's features were like her mother's, too. They were exactly the same height.

"I . . . I . . . suppose you realize . . ." Corinna's voice caught.

She couldn't think. She began to feel faint. "I've come five hundred miles to discredit your . . ."

Corinna's throat closed tightly over welling tears that nevertheless spurted from her eyes like raindrops. Looking at Carter Machesney's companion was like staring at a slightly older version of herself.

It was true. The young woman was Mandie, her older sister, her mother's firstborn, the one her mother loved and craved and obsessed about. There was no identification to dispute, no lies to refute, deny, or protest.

Corinna despaired.

There, hanging around the young woman's neck, was the locket, that damnable engraved locket. Corinna sobbed until her knees went weak. She began to sag to the ground. What was the use in fighting anymore?

Someone stepped quickly behind her, supporting her with wide, warm hands. She let herself go completely limp. She didn't care anymore. She just didn't.

Corinna clamped her eyes closed to avoid seeing all the strangers staring at her. If only she had the strength to pull Ed Keener's pistol from her bag.

"Why didn't you tell us Miss Tamberlay had a *sister*?" came a southern-bred exclamation from the edge of Corinna's consciousness. "If I'd just seen my own heathen flesh and blood for the first—Carter, *is* this the first time they've seen one another?"

"Yes," came a distant murmur. "Firemaker, this is your sister, Corinna."

Corinna sank into oblivion.

Carter had told her not to move, so Firemaker didn't budge from the stool in the corner of the strange square tepee he called the hospital tent. But she craned her neck to see everything that went on.

Her sister! Her sister. An orderly was waving something beneath her sister's nose.

Corinna gave a cry of discomfort and bolted upright, causing everyone huddled around her to rear back with some relief. "Get that stinking stuff away from me!" Her pale hair tumbled from its knot behind her askew bonnet. Her hair was slightly darker than Firemaker's.

A red-haired, freckle-faced trooper Firemaker recognized as one of her guards was staying as close to Corinna's side as if he were her personal guardian. "Stay back, ladies, troopers, if you please," he said authoritatively, patting Corinna's arm. "Give the young lady some good breathing air."

In moments the colonel arrived, glanced ever so briefly at his wife and the other ladies buzzing nearby. Then he stood scowling down at the young woman sprawled on the cot in a corner of the tent.

"Why are you here, uh, Miss Tamberlay?" He looked greatly annoyed. He conveyed that irritation directly to Carter, standing nearby, with an icy glare. He seemed to be holding Carter personally responsible for this interruption.

"I wanted to . . . My mother's not well and . . ."

"Have you been in touch with any lawyers?" Colonel Chiswell asked.

Carter smothered a smirk.

"What? Lawyers? I . . ." Corinna looked about to faint again.

Olivia took charge. "Can't you see this poor creature's

beyond interrogating just now, sugar? She needs food and rest. I say we offer the comfort of our spare room until such time as she can gather her wits about her and tell us why she's come."

Colonel Chiswell looked at his wife with raised brows. He looked as though his eyes hurt.

"If you ask me," Olivia plunged on, "the reason's plain why *this* Miss Tamberlay has come. She has to know for sure. All this lollygaggin' about, teachin' a heathen English, and sewing, and the two-step most likely, while the rest of us quake in our shoes because of Comanches lurkin' about, wantin' her back. It's disgraceful. I think if the Misses Tamberlay are on their way back to Texas as soon as possible, everyone will be better off."

Olivia's compatriots nodded hasty agreement.

Jed rubbed his eyes.

Corinna struggled to sit. She accepted a sip of water in a battered tin cup laced with whiskey, then coughed and downed it all, asking for more. She looked up directly into Firemaker's intent gaze.

It was as startling for Firemaker to look at Corinna as it was for Corinna to find the savage she had expected, walking about the fort freely, wearing civilized clothes.

Firemaker watched her sister's every move and grew ever more convinced that her own efforts to behave like a proper white woman would be forever lacking. Corinna had a way about her, similar to Olivia's, that a Comanche-bred woman of the mountains would never be able to mimic.

And the hostility in Corinna's gaze . . . Firemaker drew herself up stiffly, narrowed her eyes defiantly, and told herself that no sister, white or Comanche, would intimidate her.

If she wasn't welcome back in Texas, she had no further reason to consider going there. If this was her blood sister's reaction to her, Jane White Mother's reaction couldn't be expected to be any better.

"Why is she staring at me like that?" Corinna whispered,

edging back toward the protection of the young freckle-faced corporal. "She looks like she wants to kill me."

Carter replied, "Firemaker hasn't known about you all that long, Corinna. It's taken time to teach her English."

"It doesn't surprise me that you didn't tell her about me," Corinna muttered.

Unable to abide Firemaker's steady glare, Corinna looked away, up at the curiously eager ministrations of the colonel's wife. Firemaker scowled at them both.

"Hello," the corporal said to Corinna. "Feeling better?"

Corinna's face went crimson. A softening came to her hurt-filled eyes.

"There's no point in all this fuss over me," Corinna said, after an awkward silence. "I'm quite all right. I was just surprised to realize . . . Well, I'm tired. I haven't slept in days. I hadn't truly expected to find my sister here, alive after twenty years. I beg everyone's pardon." She looked as if she wished she was anywhere but in the center of attention, and yet she didn't squirm to be free of the corporal's friendly grip.

"Corinna, y'all simply must stay with us," Olivia chirped. "Mary has her hands full lookin' after Firemaker. We have the space. May I call you Corinna?"

Corinna looked at a loss for words. "I don't know what I'm going to do now. Take her home, I guess. Why have you kept Ma waiting, Captain Machesney?"

Everyone looked at Carter and then at the colonel.

"I'm sending another patrol out . . . tomorrow," the colonel said, his excuse sounding lame. "We've had considerable trouble with the Comanches, Miss Tamberlay. You're lucky you got through in one piece."

His exaggeration hung in the air like all his others, unchallenged.

"Mr. Machesney," the colonel spat out, shifting his attention to Carter. "I suggest you brief Miss, uh, Tamberlay, on the particulars of our circumstances here. And then escort her and my wife back to quarters."

With that, he was gone.

Firemaker returned her attention to her sister's obvious discomfiture. There was no use in pretense, she thought, standing. Everyone shrank back.

"Jane White Mother . . . no liking Firemaker?" she asked in a plainly aggressive tone.

Corinna's face drained instantly to a ghastly white. She looked about to faint again. "She's so gruff. I, uh . . . didn't think she'd actually be able to talk." Her own eyes narrowed. "Does she have to look at me like that? I'm the one losing a mother."

That was all Firemaker needed to hear, she thought, tossing her head. *"No Texas."*

She exited into the gathering wind, her heart drumming and her throat aching. She was not wanted. She would not go. Her place was here with the Comanches until she died.

"Firemaker, wait for me," Carter called, loping after her, favoring his gimpy leg. "Corinna's tired, and I have something to confess."

"Confess," Firemaker parroted sharply without slowing.

"There's a reason I didn't tell you about Corinna for a while."

"No the sister. She-Who-Weeps is good better sister. Not liking Firemaker the dress, the white face, the sun hair." She tapped her temple. "I understand. That sister . . ." She flung her arm back toward the hospital tent. "That sister no liking Firemaker Comanche woman." She searched for the white word meaning hate. She couldn't remember it.

"Stop, Firemaker, and try to tell me what you're feeling. I want to help."

"I no thinking why Carter to help–helping Comanche people. Prisoner in white man's war . . . you feel-feeling worry for us. You good man, Carter Machesney, but you helping me, Firemaker, not having good for me. Not good helping." She tugged sharply at her bodice, tearing the sleeve at the armhole. "I not having Olivia dress. Bad dress. Teh!" she spat. "I sleeping the corral nighttime. No feather bed. No washing the dish and the pot for Mary Small Feet. I am Firemaker. I no Corinna Tamberlay sister. Not good. Not good. I am Comanche."

"Firemaker, give Corinna a little time. You can't go back to the corral. You wouldn't be safe there. You can't live the rest of your life on a reservation. Your white mother wants to see you. Look into my eyes, Firemaker. Would I lie to you?"

"Lie?"

"Bad words. Not true words. Your mother is very sick. She's been waiting to see you for twenty years. You *must* go see her, if only for a few days. Corinna's jealous. She's like a small girl fighting for her mother's love. She's afraid Jane White Mother loves you more."

Firemaker glared at him from the sides of her eyes.

"Jane does love you, very much, but not more. She loves you so much because you've been gone. She lost a baby. Her heart was broken. Her head was broken. Another baby didn't take the place of you. Corinna couldn't heal the scars. Corinna only made your mother's heart more sad. Corinna can't understand that."

Carter had taken hold of Firemaker's arms to stop her flight from the hospital tent. He had never held her so tightly before. His hands were strong. Warm.

He stared fixedly into her eyes. "Do you understand what I just said?"

She did, for the most part.

But she also saw the look in Carter's eyes and felt the power of his touch. She thought that if nothing else, she possessed the singular good fortune to know that this white man was her friend, at least for now. She wanted to tell him all that was in her heart, but until she had the words, there was perhaps no way to share this understanding, this deepest part of herself, with him.

Then suddenly Firemaker blushed a brilliant crimson. She felt the heat of her thoughts radiating from her throat and neck. She looked back at Carter and wished somehow they might be alone so she could give him the truth she didn't know how to speak.

"You good man, Carter Machesney," she said huskily, "good horse man, strong heart. Go Texas after father dies in holy mountain."

"What do you mean when you say that?" Carter asked. He looked worried. Suspicious.

She pretended not to understand.

He seemed to know that she wasn't going to explain, for she didn't know herself what she meant, only that she was not leaving the fort without Four Toes.

The party at the Chiswells' that night was in honor of Corinna Tamberlay's arrival from Texas. And although the poor girl begged off politely, then bluntly, and finally insistently, Olivia Chiswell still dragged her into her guest-filled hall at eight.

Carter found the place humming with excitement when he arrived after mess call. He was scrubbed and girded for what he expected would be a most difficult conversation with Corinna.

He found her tottering in the corner with Olivia firmly attached to her elbow. Olivia steered her from one lieutenant to another, chattering as if Corinna's feelings concerned her not at all. Olivia was in her element, and that was all that mattered.

"I'd like to talk to you privately, right now if you could see your way clear, Corinna," Carter interrupted. "I'm sure Mrs. Chiswell would excuse us."

Olivia tossed her curls at him. "I won't, Carter. Leave my houseguest alone. You're just *too* serious, you ol' fuddy-duddy. Do have a sherry and let me finish introducin' Corinna to everyone. She's come such a long way. I simply refuse to give up this unexpected diversion."

Carter stepped in Olivia's way. "Do forgive me, Mrs. Chiswell, but—"

"Now, how many times have I insisted that you call me Livvie as everyone else does? He's such an ol' wet blanket," Olivia confided to Corinna with a simper. "You don't want to bother your head with him. Every single other man in the room is pinin' after your attentions."

The only man truly pining after Corinna's attentions was the poor corporal pulling guard duty at the Grahams' front door that evening, Carter thought, watching Corinna's bewildered glance around the room.

Recalling Corinna's softened expression when she looked at the young corporal earlier in the hospital tent, and remembering her lament that in West Creek Fork she had no beaux, Carter rallied.

"Perhaps Miss Corinna would care for a breath of fresh air," Carter said. "I know you're still not recovered from your trip, Corinna, but I heard Corporal Johnson saying he wished he was standing guard here tonight. He would like to get to know you better. It would be my pleasure to properly introduce you. Too bad Mary and Matt and Firemaker weren't . . . able to come. Then he'd be right outside this door, and you could be talking to him. We could stroll next door and bid him good evening."

Corinna seemed confused. "You mean the young corporal with the . . ."

". . . and the red hair." Carter grinned.

Corinna's cheeks pinked in a surprisingly attractive way. Until then Carter had not thought her particularly pretty, but that was because of her perpetual frown. Congratulating himself on his cleverness, he offered his elbow and succumbed to a certain amount of gloating as he squired Corinna from Olivia's hall.

* * *

Micah Johnson couldn't be considered attractive in the usual sense, but there was something about his warm blue eyes and quick smile that instantly endeared him to Corinna's lonely heart.

"I'm so glad to see you're feeling better, Miss Tamberlay," he said, plainly blushing with delight.

Corinna could do little but stammer.

"You must be some kind of woman to travel all the way from Texas. I have six sisters back home. Not a one would show such gumption."

Corinna worried that he was criticizing her like all the rest, but he seemed sincere. She allowed a small smile and said, "I was awfully afraid sometimes."

"But you're here, and that's something I really admire," Micah said, rocking on his boot heels and gazing at her as if he thought her a wonder. "Ain't you tired? Miz Chiswell's party must be a trial for you."

He seemed to understand her discomfiture at having to be the guest of the commanding officer's wife, too. Micah appeared to be a wonder in himself, Corinna thought.

Noticing Carter Machesney's distance, Corinna suddenly appreciated the ranger far more than she wanted to admit. Not only had he introduced her to this gentle young corporal, he was staying out of earshot. Grudgingly, she decided Carter Machesney was not so odious as she had first believed.

"Perhaps tomorrow we could go walking," Micah suggested, drawing Corinna's attention back to his eager grin, "when I'm off duty. There's a lot to see at a fort like this. I'd be honored to show you around."

Corinna almost burst into tears. A beau. In New Mexico Territory, of all places.

At length, Carter steered Corinna back toward the Chiswells' quarters. "I'd hate for you to take a chill your first night with us, Corinna, but I need to talk with you before you go back inside."

Carter could see that Corinna's attitude had mellowed, but she was still adamant.

"Captain Machesney, my head's in a whirl. I came all this way thinking I was going to expose all this as a lie. Just as I am realizing F-Firemaker *is* my . . . my sister, she goes storming out, saying she won't go to Texas."

"She was just hurt."

"I'm at a loss, Mr. Machesney. I feel as wrung out as Mrs. Chiswell suggests I look. I don't know what to do. Should I go home and tell Ma what I've seen and heard or . . . Why are you staying on with my sister here?"

"There's something you need to know."

"I don't think anything could make me feel worse, so you must be planning to tell me something to make me feel better."

"That talk of Indian trouble is really just that, talk. The colonel's trying to make out like there's a big danger, but he's just trying to cover his own blunder. He attacked a camp of defenseless women and children. Many were killed senselessly. He took the survivors prisoner, and he's kept them in the corral out of pure cussedness. Have you seen them?"

"No, thankfully."

Carter's neck began aching. Corinna and Olivia Chiswell would likely get on very well.

"You seem to view Firemaker as a rival for your mother's affections, Corinna, but Firemaker has only a passing interest in her white mother. For all intents and purposes, your sister is a Comanche. *Those* are her people over there in the corral. They're her family. She wants to help them. Jane longs to see her, but I'm not sure Firemaker will ever go, willingly or otherwise. Can we really risk disappointing your mother this way?"

Corinna sighed raggedly.

"I can't risk losing Firemaker's trust," Carter went on. "She knows where the Comanches lived and camped. She knows about their habits and such like. I've been teaching her to speak English so I can learn what I can from her. She could be very helpful to the army."

"What are you saying?" Corinna whispered, having taken on his hushed tone. Her expression went sly.

"I'm saying if you alienate Firemaker, I might not learn what I need to from her. I'm trying to end a war. Your sister could be the key."

Carter began to worry that he was trusting Corinna too much by telling her that.

"You may not believe this, but I think your mother loves you deeply. Firemaker's return home won't change that. In fact, I believe Firemaker's return might heal the wounds in your mother's soul. If I don't learn what Firemaker knows, she may never be allowed to leave."

"I don't think anything will ever help Ma. Not long ago my pa came to see me, and Ma nearly shot him to death. I'm afraid she's lost what was left of her senses. I don't know what to do. You're all pulling at me. I can't think!"

Carter kept silent.

Corinna's voice came out a strained whisper. "If I can just get a bit of *sleep*. The colonel's wife is good to offer me a bed, but my head's barely touched the pillow."

Carter forced himself to step back. "Forgive me. I've burdened you, and that's not fair. We'll talk again, if you like, when you're rested. But take care with Olivia Chiswell."

Corinna gave him a long look that belied her claimed fatigue. Bidding him good night, she stormed back into the party. After only a few moments she successfully begged off for the night.

Autumn Blaze 227

Carter was just starting for his quarters when Olivia hurried out and caught his arm.

"Your limp seems much improved," she purred, waltzing along with him without so much as a shawl to protect her exposed white throat and shoulders.

"It does seem better lately," he admitted, having nearly forgotten it. "Must be this thin air. Aren't you going to get chilled, Mrs. Chiswell?"

"Won't you call me Livvie? No? Well, you hurt me, you truly do, Carter. You've avoided me. You're forever arrivin' at my house to march away half my guests. I suppose I do owe you a belated thank-you for takin' that heathen Firemaker away last time before I . . . Oh, but I do keep forgettin' how taken you are with her. There are such rumors goin' around the fort concernin' the two of you. Have your ears felt warm lately?" She giggled.

"Is there something you want of me?"

She circled in front of him, letting the hem of her skirt brush provocatively against his pant legs. Then she moved in close enough for him to smell her perfume.

"I want to get away from this damnable fort, Mr. Carter Machesney of Virginia and Texas. What do you think of that?"

"Nearly everyone here feels the same." The perfume smell was coming from her mouth.

"Hmmm, but I'm not bound by court-martials and threats of prison. I could ride away anytime I liked."

"Why don't you, then?" he asked.

"I need a protector, someone to show me the way. I have some savings of my own. I'd make the trip well worth your while, Carter. I have no intention of stayin' here where the Comanches can get to me."

"You rather risk yourself out there." He indicated the low mountains east of the valley. "I'm only one man, Mrs. Chiswell."

"How many Comanche warriors can there be east of

here?'' she crooned, breast to chest with him by then. He could feel her perfumed, whiskeyed breath against his chin and lips. "They're west, in the high mountains, or gone, or dead."

"We hope."

"Why, look at their women, sluts and beggars the lot of them. I'm not afraid of Comanches. I'm afraid of the fools here at this fort. I'm afraid of this talk of puttin' the women and children into the powder magazine and blowin' them—and me—up in the event of certain capture."

"Who the hell suggested that?"

"Why, the women, of course. Fools. I'd risk the prairie alone, with a Yankee, or I'd shoot myself in the head as my daddy did, but I shall not hunker down in some dismal, dirty powder magazine with the washerwomen and their bastards, waitin' to be blown to bits."

Carter drew a deep breath. "Your father killed himself?"

"What would you do if the . . . Well, that's a stupid question, isn't it? You're a Confederate. You know how it felt when the fight was lost. There's no shame worse than defeat. I thought marryin' a damn Yankee would in some way—oh, I don't know what I was thinkin' in those days. All my beaux dead. My mother half out of her wits. My father dead on the veranda. I couldn't stay there, Carter. And I can't stay here."

"Why do you want Corinna Tamberlay with you?" Carter asked, moving away from a subject he felt certain would bring Olivia Chiswell to the brink of hysteria if he dared believe her.

"What's the difference so long as I'm gone from here as soon as possible?"

Suddenly she flung herself against his chest and kissed him, tight-lipped, so hard he felt her lips and teeth grinding into his. "Oh, you are such a delicious-lookin' man."

Drawing away as if she had bestowed upon him a rare

and precious gift, Olivia sashayed away, wearing a self-satisfied smirk. "*Think* about it, sugar."

When she was back inside, Carter wiped the back of his hand over his mouth.

"Coyote ugly," he muttered.

SEVENTEEN

THE DAY DAWNED as gloomy as Corinna's thoughts. What was she going to do now? She sat hunched over her morning coffee, hearing Olivia Chiswell's incessant chatter on the edge of her thoughts. She wanted to scream.

Mandie was alive. But Mandie was angry and didn't want to go home to Texas. What was left for Corinna to do but go home and face her mother's disappointment?

"When's the next stage?" Corinna blurted in the middle of something Olivia was saying.

"I beg your pardon? Are you plannin' to take your sister so soon?"

"No, I'm goin' back home alone. Firemaker doesn't want to go. Captain Machesney says she knows where that war chief is—I forget his name. There's no tellin' how long they'll stay on here." Corinna glowered at the breakfast Leota laid before her. "Thank you," she murmured, her mind churning.

Olivia Chiswell's fork hung an inch from her lips. She looked sharply at Corinna for several seconds and then took the first bite of her flapjacks. "Snake something," she said flatly.

"I don't know why Captain Machesney can't just come right out and ask what she knows. Why should she feel any loyalty toward those people? I think it's a damn-fool idea,

230

trying to trick information out of her. It seems dishonest to me."

Olivia looked very casual. "If my husband could find Sheepskin, or whatever his name is, he'd march all those heathens off to the reservation. My, wouldn't that be a feather in Jed's cap. I think that's what he's been plannin' all the while and just didn't want to trouble my head about it."

Corinna frowned at her hostess.

"It would be quite a feather. Yes, indeed. He'd likely be promoted. That would mean a move . . . away from this god-awful place." Her eyes began to sparkle.

"I don't know how you've stood it," Corinna agreed, looking around. "The fort's dismal. What *am* I to tell my mother about all this? I . . . I have half a mind never to go back. I couldn't face her. She'd think I discouraged Mandie. I could stay on awhile here, couldn't I? I wouldn't impose upon your hospitality, Livvie, but I could find work here, couldn't I? I'd make myself useful."

"*Why* in God's name would you want to stay at Fort Bradley?" Olivia cried.

Corinna's cheeks became hot. "Back home everyone knows my ma was attacked. She's never been quite right since. Surely Captain Machesney mentioned *that*."

"Attacked? By Comanches, you mean?" Olivia looked ill.

Corinna couldn't reply. "Folks pity us. I have no beaux, no callers, no hope for a normal life. At least here . . . I had quite a nice conversation with Corporal Johnson last evening. He seemed not to care a whit that my . . . my sister was . . . is . . ."

Olivia brightened. "Now, darlin' Corinna, if it's romance you want, stay as long as you like. You mustn't think to work. It's not seemly. I'll see to it you have all the beaux a girl could want."

"I'd like to spend more time with Corporal Johnson,"

Corinna mused aloud. "Could we invite him to dinner? I'm a good cook. I wouldn't trouble you."

"A corporal, to dinner here? How common. But I suppose it could be arranged," Olivia said, toying with the remainder of her breakfast. "We could invite Carter. Yes, indeed, we could. That would be ever so charming."

"You wouldn't mind?" Corinna asked, her heart lifting. With Micah Johnson smiling at her, the problem of having a half-tamed Comanche sister didn't loom so large.

"I relish a good dinner party," Olivia purred, "though a boy like Corporal Johnson might not know how to behave."

"I don't care if he snorts like a pig," Corinna muttered. "He's the first man who's ever showed an interest in me."

"Well, you mustn't let it go to your head. There are a lot of men at Fort Bradley better than he. I must've introduced you to half a dozen last evening, but don't you fret, sugar. We'll serve up somethin' special."

"I suppose you'll have to invite my sister and the people looking after her," Corinna said, noting Olivia's sudden frown. "Unless you object."

Olivia's expression was very sour. "I would invite Satan himself if I thought a promotion and transfer would result for my husband."

"We can talk about the war chief," Corinna offered, brightening. "Mandie might tell *us* something she wouldn't tell a man."

Olivia's eyes danced. "That would be amusing. Such stories she could tell us about Comanche *bucks* and *sexual practices*."

Corinna choked on her coffee.

Firemaker had had about enough of the corset. And the

Autumn Blaze 233

high-button shoes; they were pure torture. She could scarcely stand in her biting-hard new shoes.

Her hair was twisted into a knot at the back of her neck and held in place with sharp little pins that kept working loose. The shawl made her arms itch. Her hands felt clammy.

She stood in the middle of Mary's parlor because she couldn't sit, and there was nothing left to do but wait. She was going to be forced to eat at Olivia Chiswell's table.

"I still don't believe it," Mary whispered to Matt as she fussed to get her skirt arranged properly over her protruding belly. "I thought I was going to live out our days here being snubbed by everyone. Now this dinner invitation. I *don't* understand her."

Firemaker watched Mary's flushed face, and noted Matt's silence. These people were very bewildering indeed. *She* knew why she didn't want to eat dinner at the Chiswells'; she didn't like Olivia, and Olivia Chiswell didn't like her. She just didn't understand why Mary and Matt didn't want to go unless they were worried she'd forget how to behave.

When Carter arrived, wearing a dark coat that hung past his waist and a fine white shirt, shiny blue vest, and gold watch fob across his taut belly, Firemaker forgot Mary's agitation. Whatever was going on, it didn't matter as long as Carter was there.

"Ready, ladies?" he asked, offering his elbow to Firemaker.

Eagerly she tucked her hand into the warmth of his elbow and allowed herself to be led out into the frigid night. By morning there would be a hard frost.

Thoughts of the People weathering the cold were forgotten as Carter smiled down at her. She felt soothed to the soles of her pinched and miserable feet.

"You look lovely," Carter said softly so that only she could hear.

"Thank you," she said.

She was still smiling to herself as they entered the Chiswells' house. Corinna was seated on the divan, having an animated conversation with Corporal Johnson.

When Firemaker entered on Carter's arm, Corinna appeared to choke on her words. Standing, she glared back at Firemaker, her cheeks flaming. Firemaker knew her own expression strongly resembled a pout.

Looking a bit harried, Olivia entered from the dining room. The colonel was lurking in the background, the inevitable tumbler in his hand.

"Oh, you're all here," Olivia cried without ceremony. "How prompt."

After stilted conversation, Leota announced dinner. They all went in to sit down. Firemaker managed herself perfectly throughout every course, but Olivia and Corinna watched her as if she were a coyote stealing food from their very own plates. If Comanches had been prone to bad language, Firemaker would have thought up a thousand insults for them both.

It was only after the sherries that Olivia's teasing remarks became blatant.

"What do you really think is going to become of our *Firemaker*?" Olivia asked, saying Firemaker's name as if it was laughable. "Who would marry a woman with no connections? No family?"

Firemaker leveled smoldering eyes on the woman. Some of the finest Comanche warriors had offered horses for her. It was not her fault they were all dead now. In any case, she hadn't loved a one of them.

The colonel appeared immensely bored by the proceedings. More than once he rose from the table to refill his tumbler with more bourbon. "Machesney believes she'll be famous. Some Boston journalist will write her biography."

Olivia giggled and gulped the last of her sherry. "Oh, Carter, how you do amuse me. Biography, indeed. Within six months Firemaker will be hawkin' *firewater* in a saloon.

Look at her. She can't even carry on a marginal conversation with us."

Corinna looked alarmed and insulted by turns. "Not a saloon, surely." She glanced worriedly at Micah.

"What then?" Olivia countered. "The Chinee women do laundry. Immigrants work in restaurants. Nigras do housework. Firemaker may read a few words, but most white children can do that. She won't be able to teach."

"Ma didn't learn to read until after—" Corinna cut herself off.

"I wouldn't have her as a maid," Olivia went on while Firemaker watched her with angry, hot eyes. "There's no future for her. None whatsoever."

Firemaker searched her memory for a lesson on how to behave when under attack in a language she scarcely understood. She could see they were all waiting for her to erupt, so she held herself rigid, her sole source of comfort Carter's darkening expression.

"There will be a biography," Carter said quietly. "And speaking tours . . . after she finishes college. Where did you go to college, Mrs. Chiswell? Perhaps you'd give a recommendation?"

Olivia looked at Carter as if he'd lost his mind. "A finishing school, for *her*? What decent place would take her?"

"No, ma'am, I said college."

"Well, how can you expect her to go someplace like that when she can't even talk to us? I'll bet she can scarcely read a primer."

"Talk *to* her, then, Mrs. Chiswell, and find out," Carter remarked.

Olivia poured herself another sherry and gulped it. Her cheeks were flushed, her hands trembling. "Very well, then, Firemaker, dear Firemaker, tell us of your life with the . . . Comanche Indians. Where did you live? What did you do with yourself all day? Were you married?"

"Married?" Firemaker repeated.

Mary explained, "Olivia wants to know if—"

"Let her talk, Mary." Olivia's manner was condescending. "I want to know if she can understand and speak for herself. I don't want to hear the little phrases you've had her memorize in order to impress us. I don't believe she can even think beyond taking advantage of us, eating our food and . . . and doin' whatever else she's likely doin' when we're not lookin'."

Mary was about to stand when Matt's hand stole gently to her arm, cautioning her.

Mary took a deep breath. "Livvie, I don't know about Firemaker, but I've had about enough of this. I think you're being horrid. You're trying to make a fool of Firemaker, and as you can plainly see, Firemaker isn't a fool."

"No? Well, I don't believe she knows a thing about the war chief. What's his name again, Jed? Sheepskin?"

The tumbler against his lower lip, Jed's eyes shot to Olivia's face.

She looked away, fluttering her eyes. "Firemaker wouldn't tell us where he is if we begged on our knees. Horses have more intelligence. Was this war chief your *husband*, Firemaker? Was he your *man*? Comanches don't have marriages as we know them, do they? I mean, they don't have churches. I recall McTigue saying the Comanches have no organized religion. Everyone just sort of . . ." She waved her hand. "Fornicates. I think it's my duty to protect Corinna and her poor mother from this farce. At the first opportunity, Firemaker will maim one of us. She'd kill us if she could. Look at her. *Look* at her!"

Jed set his tumbler loudly on the nearest table. "Livvie, by God, shut up."

"I won't. I just won't. We're all makin' a fuss over this heathen creature who is dirtyin' my house with her presence, and she doesn't know anything. Do you, Firemaker? See? She doesn't even know what I'm sayin' to her. How much longer can you hold her for information she'll never give or doesn't even have?"

Refusing to take her eyes from Olivia Chiswell's face, Firemaker turned over the woman's words in her mind, sifting through the obvious insults and biting provocations to find the root of her meaning. They were after her knowledge of Snakehorn! Of course.

She wanted to see Carter's expression, read his eyes, but she wouldn't unlock her gaze from Olivia Chiswell's now-trembling lips.

"I-I believe if she could be killin' me with a look, she'd be doin' it this very minute," Olivia said, her voice shaking. "Jed . . ."

"You started it, you little fool. Is that what this dinner party was really for, to humiliate her? Well, you've succeeded in that. You've probably also robbed us of all hope of learning anything further from her. If I thought it would do any good, I'd thrash you."

Appalled at his public insult, Olivia reared up from her chair. "Would you, indeed? *Is* that why you kept her in the stockade so long? Was that why you released her and let her stay next door so that I'd lie awake terrified for my safety every night, and Mary's? Or is there more, sugar?"

Matt stood, drawing Mary to her feet. "Mary doesn't look well. I'm taking her home."

Firemaker watched the Grahams cross to the door, Matt determinedly, Mary reluctantly. They went out, whispering angrily to one another.

Returning her gaze to Olivia, Firemaker noted the colonel's reckless stance in the corner opposite his wife. Only then did she think to look at her sister, whose face had gone white.

But Corinna wasn't looking at her. She was looking at the freckle-faced corporal. He seemed bewildered, understanding about as much of the emotional undercurrents in the room as Firemaker. Corinna cared nothing about what was being said about her, Firemaker concluded. She cared only about the corporal.

Her mind working as quickly as possible, Firemaker stood. Searching for something to say in her inadequate white words, she softened her expression. "Thank you, Mrs. Chiswell, for a most lovely dinner." Yes, that was the exact phrase Mary had helped her memorize. Every word.

"Mary's little puppet looks mighty temptin' in my castoffs, doesn't she, Jed?" Olivia snapped, glowering at her husband. "Just why do you keep Firemaker around, forbiddin' Carter from takin' her off to Texas? Can't you *bear* to see her go?"

"Stop it!" Corinna cried, leaping to her feet. "*I* can't bear this. I—I don't know what you're trying to do, but . . . I won't stay here another day if this doesn't stop."

Olivia cocked her head and smiled. "Just tryin' to show everyone what you and I already know, Corinna, that a Comanche is a Comanche no matter the color of her skin. Firemaker's a heathen. I wouldn't take her home to *my* mother, I can tell you. We've all been taken in by Jed's hope of gettin' information from this Comanche slut, and it's plain she knows nothin'. I think my husband's keepin' her around, hopin' . . ."

Carter stood. He put his hand on the small of Firemaker's back. Strangely, she didn't want to be touched, by him or any of them. Firemaker couldn't stop herself from taking a step toward Olivia.

The woman gave out with a whimper. "Don't you lay a hand on me. I'll tear out your hair!"

"Snakehorn my *brother*," Firemaker said. "Great warrior. Many horses. Sell you to Apaches for one muleskin. Bad medicine, you whore-dog woman." She cast her eye toward the colonel and made the vulgar hand motion she'd learned in the stockade. "Bur-dette soldier. Bad you woman. Having big stick." She made several hitting motions in Olivia's direction. "No more . . ." She knew the bad white word but decided against saying it.

She heard Carter chuckling softly under his breath. "You'd better stop, Firemaker. You've slandered her reputation. We may never get away from here now. Or we might find ourselves on the road to Texas before midnight, afoot."

"She's not leaving," the colonel hissed, "until I have what I want from her."

Olivia was about to shriek out something when Jed whirled to silence her.

Weeping loudly, Corinna escaped to her room.

The corporal found himself standing with the colonel glaring at him.

Firemaker marched into the colonel's face. "Firemaker not leaving when . . . after . . ."

"Until," Carter put in for her.

"Until father die in holy mountain. You no great warrior. You having bad wife woman. Not man."

And then she was flouncing out of the Chiswells' house, out into the night, fighting the intense desire to throw aside all pretense and run.

Carter was quickly behind her, reaching for her arm, breaking into a run to come around in front of her to make her stop. "Firemaker, where are you going?"

"Holy mountain, make big medicine, find medicine dream, kill colonel, cut tongue bad woman. Slapping white sister."

They had not taught her the white word for stupid.

She made an exasperated cry and threw herself suddenly into Carter's arms. "Hurting," she shouted against his shirtfront. "Very big hurting." She thumped her chest. "Hurting here."

His hands cupped her face, lifting it so he could look down into her eyes. "Are you crying, Firemaker?"

"No," she snapped softly. "White men making Firemaker water eyes. No crying water."

"Tears," he said. "Are we breaking your heart?"

"Heart?" she whispered. "Bro-ken heart."

He was looking at her so tenderly. If the hurting in her spirit was called the breaking of a heart, then, yes, her heart was breaking. They were killing her, stripping her of all that she was, replacing it with a shabby kind of bark. She felt like a hollow dead tree.

"No more Firemaker," she whispered, feeling the pain of her spirit and breaking heart climbing back into her throat. Her eyes began to burn. "No more fire. Black . . . fire. Cold wood."

"No," he whispered, leaning down, his lips looking soft in the darkness, his intense eyes deep in shadows, glinting with what was perhaps tears of his own. "No, Firemaker. You'll always be Firemaker, bright and beautiful."

And his lips closed gently over her mouth, warm, soft, and slightly trembling.

What was he doing? she wondered, holding herself perfectly still lest he stop.

He lifted his lips then and looked down at her wide-eyed stare. "You are so precious. You can't know. I've been wrong to teach you some things but not tell you everything. So wrong."

His lips touched hers again, more urgently this time. His arms drew her against him, so that she felt his chest against her breasts and his torso against her belly. His hard, sharp belt buckle pressed against the crushing bite of her stays. His hips molded against hers, and then she knew. She knew.

She tilted her head up, instinctively surrendering to a joining of the mouths that was but a promise of a deeper joining that her breaking heart and quivering body craved.

She pressed her mouth against his, returning his kiss, feeling herself enfolded by him. This was what she sought, not foolish white words, not release from the guilt of being different from her Comanche family and apart from her ailing father, not honor, not the unknown future as a white woman made famous by a Boston journalist.

This enfolding, this joining, this sanctuary with Carter's arms around her, her hands clutching his lapels, her neck arched as her lips tasted his, this was the yearning in her dream of unnamable things. This was love.

EIGHTEEN

WHAT *WAS* GOING to become of her? Firemaker wondered, alone in her room that night.

She was still wondering that at dawn when she rose to hurriedly dress and take her chamber pot out back. As he always did at that time, the guard looked away.

The sky was pale, the morning air icy and crisp. Firemaker thought about all the mornings she had gone for her father's water and how she missed that simple task.

At the backdoor, the guard stepped aside, glancing at her, and then slumped back against the adobe wall, obviously bored with his duty.

She was just going back inside when she noticed the trash barrel beside the doorway. Inside was her brown skirt, red overblouse, and tattered moccasins. A cold realization went through Firemaker. She was going to die.

That was what was going to become of her.

She was going to free the People, take her father to the holy place where he would walk into the next world . . . and she would go with him. The kiss Carter had given her could mean nothing. She had to force it from her mind. She was going to die.

"What're you gawkin' at?" the guard grumbled, turning to watch her stare into the trash barrel.

"Laundry," she said, "washing the clothes."

Without a shred of forethought, she scooped her old

clothes from the barrel and started back across the yard toward the gate in the rear of the adobe wall. As she hoped, the guard thought nothing of it. For all he knew or cared, she was simply performing a new chore. When she wore the blue dress, her wildness was forgotten.

Firemaker moved along behind the houses on officers' row, heading around the warehouses where the teamsters and freighters were just stirring. Few soldiers were moving about. For all anyone could tell, Firemaker was just another white woman taking laundry down to Suds Alley.

She reached the creek without a single person hailing her. None of the washerwomen was awake. Their dogs sniffed at her as she passed, but none barked. She wasn't thinking, only moving, away from the people who would soon kill her. They had thrown away her clothes, but she would need them in the afterlife.

She was going to die. She felt sad. So very sad.

Seeing a horse tied near one of the shacks, she recognized it as belonging to the scout McTigue. Without hesitation, she loosened his tether and guided him quietly toward the creek. She led him into the icy water and then coaxed him upstream, where the rocks along the bank hid their departure.

Five hundred yards away, Firemaker climbed to a boulder and threw herself onto the horse's back. Still following the creek, she made for the foothills, moving faster and faster as her escape went unnoticed. To be riding again reminded her of how her life had changed since the summer.

Within the hour Firemaker was in the canyon, galloping as fast as the horse would carry her, galloping with her fingers laced tightly into his mane, her knees hugging his sides. She felt strong and powerful once more. If she wanted, she could have disappeared forever.

Several miles up the canyon, Firemaker halted the horse and slid to the ground. She threw her Comanche clothes down and tore open the buttons of her bodice. She tore at the laces of her corset until it opened far enough that she could wiggle it down over her hips. Then off came the petticoat and pantalets. And of course the shoes.

Wearing only the skirt, she stood a long moment breathing deeply, feeling the biting touch of the mountain air on her bare breasts. Then she pulled the bodice back on, buttoned a few of the buttons, and jerked on her knee-high moccasins. How good they felt, how soft and comforting.

Scrambling over some boulders, Firemaker began to climb. She thought of the morning she climbed the rocky escarpment to shake the dream from her mind, and saw the first horse soldiers thundering into the valley to change her life forever. Her heart began aching.

She never stopped to look back. If they were following now, if they were about to shoot her, she didn't care. She had to be free for this one last day. Then she could take what she needed and die when the time came.

At the top of the canyon wall, Firemaker dragged herself to her feet, threw up her arms, and screamed. "Hear me, spirit of the fire. I am lost. Find me! Bring me peace."

She faced east, then west. Then north, then south. She called as loudly as possible, tempting all the fates. As she suspected, this was not her morning to die.

At length she sank down on the rocks where she could see so far, and laid her head upon her arms. Staring sightlessly, she prayed for guidance, and then she wept.

"Where the hell's my horse?" McTigue was bellowing by the time Carter reined in at Suds Alley.

"Must've wandered off," Carter offered, the taste of his morning coffee still strong on his tongue.

They prowled about the creek bank for several minutes, looking for signs. McTigue was fit to be tied. "Don't look like no Comanches were here in the night, but Jockins ain't one to wander off like that."

"I'll bring him back," Carter said, turning back to get Lonesome. "I was going out anyway."

McTigue frowned after Carter and then went back inside the shack where he'd been having his laundry done lately, every night.

Carter was thundering up the creek without a passing remark to anyone before most folks were awake. Behind him came the echoing call to assembly. If Leota hadn't seen Firemaker leave the Grahams' house earlier and hurried to warn him, no one would have likely known she was gone for several hours.

Carter tried not to speculate on why Firemaker had run away. He couldn't fail to marvel at how easily she had. He hoped his kiss hadn't frightened her.

Well into the canyon, he found McTigue's horse grazing. Firemaker's Comanche clothes were lying in a heap in the middle of the trail alongside her shoes, petticoat, and corset stays. Carter gave pause, wondering if someone had waylaid her.

Seeing no sign of a struggle, or any other horse, or any sign that she'd gone farther up the canyon afoot, Carter noticed almost at once her careless path up between the boulders of the canyon wall. He saw the blue of her skirt at the top, and his heart stopped. If anything had happened to her . . .

When he reached the top of the steep escarpment, Carter dropped down beside Firemaker. He took off his hat to wipe his forehead.

"You had me worried," he said, noticing the voluptuous way her bodice was buttoned.

She was sitting like a doll, with her feet sticking straight out in front of her as if she'd been studying the tattered toes of her moccasins. Sighing, she flopped back, threw her arms out to her sides, and stared at the sky.

"Slut," she said flatly. "What is slut?"

"A bad woman," Carter answered, understanding at last

that Olivia Chiswell had managed to hurt Firemaker. "You understood more than you let on last night, didn't you?"

Firemaker sniffed in disgust. "Colonel wife woman slut bad woman. I am big angry."

Carter plucked open the buttons of his coat and pulled it off, laying it across Firemaker's torso.

She flung it off. "No cold. Many cold winter in mountains. Firemaker no child."

He had intended more to cover her breasts, which were scarcely concealed beneath the thin bodice fabric, than warm her. Her nipples were erect, her breasts softly outlined and squashed by the fabric. His hands ached to touch her.

Her gaze shifted to him and she saw the direction of his look. With breathtaking speed, she tore open the buttons and spread the bodice wide, leaving her breasts bare for his feasting eyes. Her expression was fierce, challenging.

Before he could think what to do, she was on her feet, scrambling back down the canyon wall, slipping, sliding recklessly to the canyon floor. He followed immediately.

By the time he reached the horses, Firemaker was several hundred yards ahead, having flung her bodice to the ground. "No having whore-dog woman dress," she grumbled.

Her back was pale and bare, muscled and slim. She was running her hands through her hair, loosening the last of the pins from it, and letting the pale blond waves fall to her narrow waist.

Carter realized he'd left his coat on the boulder above and decided it was prudent to go back up for it rather than stand like a fool, watching Firemaker shed her skirt. He plunged back up the canyon wall as she splashed into the creek.

The creek water was numbing. Firemaker felt the aching cold spread up her feet to her legs as she sought the deepest part of the creek. Soon she was stumbling on the slippery rocks, her feet so cold she couldn't feel enough to find good footing.

Carter wasn't following. Stooping, she splashed herself all over, and when she could stand the cold, she scooped up handfuls of sand from along the bank and scrubbed herself. She scrubbed hard, wanting to change herself back.

She was shivering, and her teeth were chattering when she rinsed off and stepped from the water. Carter had stayed by the horses and was holding out his coat.

Holding her fists stiffly at her sides, she marched back to him, into the welcoming folds of his coat and his arms. He pulled her close and held her tightly until she relaxed against his chest, her heart spilling out words she couldn't have said even if she had dared.

"Carter . . ." she murmured against his chest.

"Shhh," he said, gathering her even more tightly to him. "I think I understand how you're feeling."

He held her such a long time she almost thought she might go to sleep. She felt safe and content suddenly. Then she lifted her face and looked into Carter's eyes.

Never had she seen such a look of gentleness and warmth. The brown of his eyes seemed to glisten with admiration. His brows were tilted with a hint of sadness. It was as if he knew her pain, her confusion, her soon-to-be fate.

He looked at her mouth and then looked back at her eyes with such care and tenderness that she felt a welling of emotion overpower her. Straining upward, she kissed his soft mouth, trying to tell him how very much he meant to her.

Then his mouth was closing over hers, warm and moist and urgent, his tongue plunging between her lips to meld her even more deeply into his arms. She felt lost to the sensations he awakened in her. She hung there against him, wanting the closeness to last forever.

With a dizzying sweep, he released her, gathered up her clothes, and guided her away up the bank toward an overhang of rock where they spread her skirt and sank down together.

He held her close, still wrapped in his coat, as his palms grazed her nipples. Her skin was fiery warm, silken and smooth. His skin was rough with hair and firm to her eager touch.

"Oh, Firemaker," he said, sighing and pulling back to look into her face. "What are we going to do?"

She eased back and held out her arms to him. Smiling then, she caught his face with her hands and drew him to her for another deep kiss.

This was her gift, she told him with her eyes. This was something no other would ever have of her, no other could ever take from her. This was neither a Comanche part nor a white part, but her woman part, her love, her desire and respect for her only true friend.

He was warm over her, kissing her face, looming large and strong and tender. His hands explored her skin as if he had never before touched a woman. When his hands reached her thighs, she was trembling but certain she had never wanted anything more than to be one with him.

His touch was electrifying. She felt as if time had stopped. She believed, for a moment, that they would never have to face those fools at the fort again.

They were free together, safe together. When she found her way past the buttons of his shirt to the hair swirling across the muscles of his chest, she forgot everything but the beauty of this man's body. Her man.

She wanted to touch every part of him, to feel the thick mat of hair on his forearms to the hard rounded strength of his shoulders. She trailed her hands down over the tight waves of muscles along his belly to the coarse dark curls at the waistband of his denims.

Then she was smoothing her hands into those denims, around the tight swells of his buttocks, lightly furred and warm. Soon, he, too, was naked alongside her, his thighs resting against hers as firm and solid as tree trunks.

His manhood was startling, thick and strong against her

belly, the skin as delicate as eyelids, as firm as her resolve to be part of this man if only once.

She couldn't breathe, couldn't think for wanting to share herself with him. And yet still he waited, seemingly content only to kiss her and stroke her body.

When at last she guided him into her possession, and lay still and aware of how he fit and filled her with such joy, she opened her eyes and saw an intensity in his eyes that made her grip his arms almost hurtfully.

"Carter," she whispered urgently, finding her body undulating against his in a motion going back to the dawn of time. "Carter, Car-ter . . ." She moaned, unsure now what her body was telling her.

She was beginning to spin, sink, and plunge, deeper and deeper into herself until all she knew was darkness and the feeling of her body pulsing.

She was an eagle soaring, swirling, swooping, diving, wings spread wide, her mind filled with love for the one, the only man she would ever trust.

She gave of herself all that she had, finding now the flight of her body's heat climbing and climbing, higher and hotter, until there was nothing but a point of light very far away, a point so small and tight and sharp she almost couldn't bear to look at it in the darkness.

And then, like a great waterfall, the light spilled into the darkness, glistening and spreading through her body like sunfire, melting her, charging her until she was gripping his strong muscled back, her mouth locked with his mouth, their bodies tightly bound together with the fury of passion.

He gave one last shuddering thrust and then gave out with a cry so unguarded, so private and pure, Firemaker felt her body convulse again because she was so much a part of him.

Quivering, quickly growing chilled, their bodies drenched in sweat, they sagged together, he in the cradle of her thighs, his mouth pressed to her neck as he fought to fill his lungs.

"Firemaker," Carter whispered, "I love you."

* * *

The guard unlocked Clay Burdette's cell door and stood back. "I don't want to be seeing your ugly mug around here for a long while, son."

Clay swaggered out, brushing sharply against the guard's shoulder. "Yours neither," he muttered.

Emerging into the sunlight, Clay blinked. No more hauling garbage. No more grading roads. No more fear of growing hair on his palms.

Mosie loped up from the direction of the corrals. "Had enough?" he called, grinning, his pimply cheeks flaming.

"Shut up," Clay snapped. "I got latrine maintenance for the next two weeks. Where's my whiskey?"

Mosie handed over Clay's battered flask. Clay drained it in three gulps. They headed back toward the corrals, where the twelve-holer waited his attentions.

"The colonel ain't gettin' me in that stockade again," Clay hissed, pausing in the shade out of the wind where he and Mosie built a smoke. "Leastwise not till he's got good reason. I ain't spendin' no more six weeks rememberin' nothin'."

Mosie frowned. "What do ya mean?"

"What the hell do you think? I got unfinished business with Mrs. Colonel Chiswell, that's what. I got a few questions to ask of her, among other things. And there's the matter of the wildcat white Comanche bitch. I got unfinished business with her, too."

"She's all civilized now. Takin' supper with the colonel and everything. It's blame amazin'. Ain't you had enough trouble with females?"

"I ain't had no comfort in six weeks. Longer, actually. And I ain't got no money, so I can't buy no comfort. What I do got is an uncollected debt. The matter of one locket and the promise that went with it."

"You're beggin' for a hangin'," Mosie warned.

Clay feinted a lunge toward Mosie. "Shut your flappin'

yap 'fore I vent myself on you. Tell me every little thing Mrs. Colonel's been doin' lately. You been watchin', haven't you?''

"Sure I have, just like I promised. She's been poorly, stayin' inside a lot, sulkin'. . . ."

Carter's head was reeling. How could he take Firemaker to Texas now after this, and go away from her then? Tilting up her face, Carter searched her clear blue eyes, wondering what this meant to her. Her pupils were huge, her expression open and vulnerable. "Firemaker," he whispered. "I love you."

"Love," she said in her usual flat tone that meant she needed an explanation of the word.

He couldn't begin to explain his feelings. He was overwhelmed by surprise. Never had he expected to make love with Firemaker. Certainly he had not expected such a thing to happen today. He hoped his eyes conveyed the words he couldn't find to say.

When Firemaker laid her hand against his chest, his heart swelled. He loved her. He actually, truly loved her!

"You've become a part of my life, Firemaker," he said in an awkward attempt to clarify, if only for himself, this confounded development. "You've become a part of me. I want to forget everything now and take you away somewhere safe."

"Safe," she said.

"I want to take you to a place where we can be together always, where there are no bad men or bad women, and no prisoners of any kind."

He sensed a stillness settling over her. She curled tightly against him, listening, scarcely breathing, understanding the depth of what he was saying.

"What're we going to do?" he whispered. "I have a duty here. You feel you have one, too. We're both honorable people. We can't run away. We have to go back to the fort soon, or they'll come for us. I want this day, and all the days to come, to belong only to us. No soldiers and no Indians should have the right to come between us." He hugged her. "I'll take you to see your mother, but after that . . ."

Shaking her head, she drew away. "Father die holy mountains." She pointed west. "Riding two days. Three a little."

A chill went up his spine. She had more honor than he, apparently. "Then we must go soon."

She nodded and pressed herself back against him in a way he couldn't ignore. Her skin was so sleek and warm, her breasts beautifully rounded, her hands eager to explore him. He was immediately lost to her, drowning his doubts and fears about the future in the depths of her mouth and her body.

By noon they were trembling with spent passion, lying on the ground beneath the protective brow of the rocks and rugged canyon walls, watching clouds gathering overhead.

"I am fourteen summers," Firemaker was saying, chuckling softly. "I *was*. Standing high-tall over young Comanche boys, riding the horse very fast." She pointed to her forehead. "Words in head coming very fast. Comanche boys no fast, try hitting Firemaker off horse. They fall. Very laughing."

"Funny," Carter corrected.

"Funny, um, Firemaker laughing." She pulled free of Carter's arms then and stood, making a face to indicate she was dizzy. For a moment she looked down at him most tenderly, almost sadly, and smiled. She blinked. "What is it called?" She touched her lips.

"Kissing," he said.

She smoothed her hands from her breasts to her belly. "Lovemaking."

Grinning, she questioned, "Lovemaker? Firemaker?"

He grinned back at her. "You make a fire in my heart,"

he said, taking on her amused tone, but meaning every word.

"Um, Tall Horse Man Lovemaker." She giggled. "Happy."

She went on smiling.

Carter couldn't remember when he'd actually seen Firemaker smile for so long. There had been moments, fleeting at best, when she showed amusement or pleasure, but never this beaming expression of joy he knew their lovemaking and her play with the white words brought.

He watched her pull on her skirt and fumble with the buttons of her bodice. She cast him coy glances that fired his heart anew, but he, too, knew it was time to go. Their time together was done.

At length Firemaker straightened and looked to the east as if to see the fort waiting for them. "Going back fort," she said with a tone of resignation.

Carter climbed resolutely to his feet. He relished her open appraisal of his naked body. She looked longingly into his eyes then, as if to say she knew their time together was over, too.

"We must find a way to get on to Texas," he said. "I meant what I said, Firemaker. I want you with me always."

He saw that she did indeed understand, but she was moving away from him now, back to the horses grazing nearby, back to the helpless women, children, and dying old man back in Fort Bradley's corral. He wanted to forget them. He wanted to forget all that might be going on across Texas with the Comanches and now the Apaches spreading their rage and terror.

"My name . . . what my white name?" Firemaker asked, absently stroking McTigue's horse.

"Mandie," Carter said, feeling her so close and yet so far that he wondered if he would ever truly know her or possess her.

"What Mandie?" At his frown, she elaborated. "Tree? Bird? Horse? Fish?"

"Oh, you want to know what your name means? It's an old name. It means beloved. Amanda Jane Tamberlay."

"A-manda," she said, apparently judging the sound of it. "Be-lov-ed. Love." Finally she nodded and sighed. "Firemaker . . ." She waved her hand as if to erase herself. "No more making fire in spirit. Comanche Firemaker going . . ." Words failed her. "A-manda."

"You want to be called Amanda now?" Carter asked in astonishment. "Not Firemaker. Not Mandie?"

She nodded. She looked troubled, but she held her head high. She smiled at him with sad eyes. "You—me, Car-ter, A-manda. This day, to-day, very good. You good man, Carter Machesney."

"*Will* you think about a future with me? Amanda? Many happy days at my ranch in Texas, visiting your mother in West Creek Fork, visiting my sister and her husband in Virginia. You would be my woman, my wife?"

The words drifted into the silence of the afternoon. Carter felt awestruck. He had never expected to say those words. "My wife."

He watched for a reaction from her—surprise, reluctance, hope—but saw nothing he understood. Why did she look so sad? So resigned?

Moving toward her and pulling her close, he held her tightly. He felt her strong arms steal around him and grab on suddenly as if she were clutching at their last moments together as desperately as he.

Carter knew he had found the center of his universe. From the moment he had first seen her pacing in the stockade like a caged lioness, nothing else had mattered so much as knowing her. He had never wanted to tame her as much as gain her trust, her respect.

Holding her, he knew that she loved him, too, but she wasn't forgetting those who needed her. They were faces, names, relatives to her. He was protecting strangers. He had a ranch to go back to, a place in society where he would always fit. What did Firemaker—Amanda Tamberlay—have but herself?

"Oh, Lord," he said into her hair. "If only there was something I could do to help you. . . ."

As he released her he saw tears on her lashes. They were the first tears he had seen her shed. Her first smile . . . now her first tears. Carter felt his heart breaking with love for her. She looked as tortured as he, and with that he deliberately softened the pain surely visible in his eyes. He caused himself to smile with some confidence. She looked soothed.

"It's all right," he said softly, his voice deep and thick. "We'll do what we must. Then we'll be free."

NINETEEN

LEAVING MCTIGUE'S HORSE where she'd found it beside the shack along Suds Alley, Firemaker ran at a crouch up the incline. She slipped in behind the adobe walls along the rear yards of officers' row. She found no guard standing at the Grahams' backdoor.

Growing uneasy, she crept across the yard, noting the kettle of boiling water standing over a carelessly tended fire just outside the kitchen door. Was Leota warming bathwater?

Once inside, Firemaker saw no sign of breakfast or lunch dishes awaiting her. It looked as if there had been no cooking that day. Was everyone searching for her?

From the front bedroom came a long groan.

The hair on Firemaker's neck prickled. Of course, Mary Small Feet. She was having her baby!

Throwing off her damp, sandy clothes and hiding them beneath her bed, Firemaker donned her bed dress and wraper. She found Matt pacing in the parlor, his face a mask of anguish.

Hurrying to Mary's bedside, Firemaker wondered if anyone had even noticed her long absence from the house. It seemed impossible, but . . .

Leota straightened from tying a harness to the foot posts of Mary's bed. Mary was lying on her back, swathed in her twisted, sweat-soaked bed dress, her face pale, her eyes wide with fear.

"Oh, Firemaker," Mary whispered. "Where have you been?"

"Sleep late, did you, girl?" Leota interrupted, attempting a lie to cover her absence.

"I am calling me A-manda today," Firemaker said, unsure if she should explain herself. "No Firemaker."

Mary arched her back against her pillows, gasping until she was dizzy. "Hold . . . my hand . . . Amanda!"

Firemaker let Mary seize her fingers and squeeze until there was no feeling or blood left in them. As the contraction ebbed, Mary made an attempt to sound brave.

"I'm told it'll take hours for someone to reach the doctor in Santa Fe, and hours more to bring him here. I was sure I wouldn't need him, but . . . Oh, mercy, what possessed me to stay here? Mattie doesn't need me. Help me, Firemaker—Amanda. You have so much courage. Help me be brave."

"Brave . . ." Firemaker said, needing an explanation for the word.

"I don't want to cry . . . or scream, but this . . . this hurts!"

Mary arched up again to fight another contraction. She gasped and clutched Firemaker's hand. Firemaker could only think of Comanche words. "You are woman," she said in a low, soothing voice. "You were made for this."

She said the Comanche words over and over until the long minute had passed, and Mary was whimpering with relief.

"I'll be all right," Mary panted. "I can do this. I have to do this, for Mattie's sake. Tell me I can do this."

"Mercy, Jesus," Leota grumbled. "I sent for Miz Chiswell 'bout lunchtime, but she ain't come, and she's the only one got laudanum. Ain't nobody else to help. I've birthed many a baby in my time, but it's always frightful."

Ignoring the woman's lament, Firemaker plucked at Mary's soiled bed dress. "Off dress," she ordered.

With Leota's help, they undressed Mary, paused for another contraction, and then got her into one of Matt's old shirts. Mary lay exposed from the waist down, but at least she wasn't tangled any longer.

She writhed and called out words and names Firemaker didn't trouble herself to translate. Firemaker was too busy trying to get Mary to the edge of the bed. One peek told her the birth was imminent. She could see a patch of dark wet hair at the opening of Mary's stretched birth canal.

"Standing," Firemaker ordered. "Feet. Feet!"

"Oh, Firemaker, I can't! No! What are you trying to do to me? I'm having the baby right . . . now!"

Firemaker virtually lifted Mary to her feet, and trembling together, they crouched alongside the bed. Leota, frantic beyond words, hastened to hold an open towel beneath Mary's swollen body.

Firemaker caught Mary's face in one hand and made her look into her eyes. She breathed deeply and slowly until Mary was imitating her. When the next contraction began to build, Firemaker took in a deep breath and held it.

Mary did the same until her eyes were popping and her cheeks aflame. As the contraction waned Mary expelled her breath loudly and gasped in more air. "It's almost out," she said, half laughing, half weeping.

Almost at once another contraction began.

"If only I could rest," Mary gasped.

Firemaker and Mary held their breath again. The tension swelled between them. Mary began bearing down.

"Here it comes!" Leota cried, stooping closer to guide the reddened head as it emerged. "Oh, mercy. Oh, mercy Lord!"

Mary sucked in another deep breath and held it, letting gravity assist the little body, so large inside, so tiny once outside, squirming slickly into the towel's folds.

Mary looked down at the infant, worry beginning to pinch her eyes. "Dear God, no . . ."

As the silence lengthened, Firemaker felt her powerful fire spirit swelling inside her heart. Releasing Mary, leaving her tottering in her awkward squatting position and clutching for the nearest handhold, Firemaker snatched the silent newborn girl child to her breast.

"Spirit in child!" she commanded. "Back! Back!" She was speaking in English, calling upon Mary's God.

Firemaker had seen too many Comanche babies die to release this one without a fight. Sucking the mucus from the baby's tiny mouth, and then breathing her own spirit into the tiny form, Firemaker shook the tiny body until the arms were flopping.

"Come to me!" she shouted, breathing again into the little mouth. "Not die."

At once she felt a rush of life flood the small chest. A sudden, startled squall filled the bedroom. The infant girl opened her unfocused slate-gray eyes to the world and gave a fierce frown.

"Ah!" Firemaker laughed as tears burst from her eyes. "Good baby." And she threw her head back to give thanks to the fire spirit that saved little girls.

Matt rushed in, looking as if he hadn't breathed since the baby emerged. Openly sobbing, he sank to Mary's side and drew her into his arms. "I love you, Mary," he wept. "I love you!"

Jed stood at the front window of his quarters, watching the dancing campfires of the encampment in the middle of his parade ground. It was night, and Lieutenant Graham had been a father since early afternoon.

"I don't understand you, Livvie. I thought you wanted to supervise the birth."

Livvie went on brushing her hair. From the bedroom she muttered, "After the way Mary and her silly little lieutenant of a husband walked out on us the other night? I hope she had a perfectly hideous time. High and Mighty Goody-Two-Shoes. I've never liked her.''

"You were drunk," Jed said, turning, observing her through burning but sober eyes. "You behaved like white trash. No wonder they walked out."

Livvie flung her hairbrush into the mirror, cracking it. "I won't take that from you, Jed. Not after all I've been through with you. For the past six months you've been soused by the time you came to bed."

"That's true," Jed mused.

He couldn't remember the last time he'd been this sober, this cold, this empty. He couldn't remember what he'd been hiding from in that bottle. Perhaps it was everything.

Jed didn't know why he didn't want a drink now. Perhaps it was the look in Firemaker's eyes that had shamed him so deeply he finally looked himself in the eye.

He, a United States Cavalry colonel, graduate of West Point . . . and decorated Union war veteran, had less honor than a scrap of a girl raised by heathens in the mountains of New Mexico Territory.

The thought was staggering. It was staggering because if that was true, it could only mean that for all their murdering ways, Comanches might perhaps possess something he didn't. That could not be tolerated. Jed could not abide being wrong for fighting them.

Crossing to the bedroom abruptly, Jed swept his wife into his arms and planted what he supposed was a breathtaking kiss upon her hard little mouth.

"*What* are you doing?" Olivia snarled against his lips. She twisted away, her face mirroring contempt. "You can't treat me like this. Have a drink. It'll relax you."

"You'd like that, wouldn't you?" he said, jerking her toward the bed. "You don't really want me. You just want to complain."

"*What* are you doing now?" she cried.

Jed flung her onto the counterpane and tore open her wrapper. Her wide startled eyes gave him pause.

He was still a gentleman, he reminded himself, not a rapist. He hadn't done his duty with Livvie in so long the deed was but a dim memory. To his consternation, he found no interest for her warming in his loins.

"If you dare . . ." Livvie quailed, "I'll scream. Is that what you want our houseguest to hear? At least close the door."

Closing his eyes instead, Jed threw out his arm and almost laughed. "I don't care what Corinna Tamberlay thinks. You're only using her, in any case, the same as you have used me and every other man, woman, and child who has ever had the misfortune to cross your path."

"Whatever is wrong with you tonight, sugar? I seem to remember you going to some lengths to win my affections."

"Pity I am incompetent at so many things but successful in that regard. Why did you marry me, pet? I'm curious."

Olivia looked alarmed.

"No matter," he said, opening the door and realizing he had nothing whatever to do but drink, sleep, or bumble along with his command. And that, surely, was in a shambles.

He was holding a passel of useless Comanche women and children who would die, given the first opportunity, further tarnishing his ridiculous efforts to capture the infamous Snakehorn. And Firemaker . . .

Yes, Firemaker. There was life in his loins for her, Jed thought ruefully, but that would not do. No, indeed not.

He started away.

"Where are you going?" Olivia's voice was like an infection in his ear.

Jed turned, considered the question, and then ambled back toward her. He caught her hand and jerked her to her feet. "I'm going to try, one last time, to capture the fierce and elusive enemy. You, my dear, can go to hell in a hand basket. I need some sleep, and tonight I intend to sleep alone. Try not to disturb me whilst you dally about with the low and callow lads beneath my command. If this nightmare I have created ever ends, I intend to divorce you."

Olivia stormed in a circle, turning from the parlor window to the bedroom doorway until she couldn't decide what to break first. She had to flee to think.

Divorce her, would he? She'd just see about that.

Outside, clutching her shawl around her shoulders against a thirty-degree temperature, Olivia stifled a hysterical giggle. The fool. He'd never have the courage to divorce her.

As she hurried along the flagstone walk she noted the guard at the Grahams' door, watching her.

"Get back to your post!" she snapped.

"Oh, it's you, Mrs. Chiswell. Excuse me. Are you all right? Is there anything I can do for you?"

She wanted to slap him. Or perhaps she should be kissing him, she thought, pausing. What was the use? She didn't even like kissing. She liked sexual intercourse even less. The entire business was merely a means to an end.

"Get out of my way," she snapped. "What are you doin', still guardin' that savage? Don't you know she owns this fort by now, body and soul? Someone should be guardin' me and my husband from her."

Olivia plunged on, her anger fueled all the more by the thought of that heathen bitch getting all the attention. She was beginning to shiver, more from fear than from the cold.

Her mind spun with horrifying possibilities. She had no family to go back to, no money sufficient to carry her for more than a few months on her own. How could Jed even *think* to humiliate her in such a way? She would've indulged him tonight, sober and violent, or drunk and impotent, but . . . he hadn't wanted her.

From behind, Olivia heard scuffling footsteps. Whirling, she glared into the darkness.

"Who dares to follow me?"

There was only silence and shadows behind her. Was it Comanches? She nearly screamed. If she was killed now, that would show Jed what a wretch of a husband he'd turned out to be.

Clay Burdette emerged from the shadows at the end of officers' row.

Olivia clutched at her hair. "Oh, it's only you. What are you doin' out here, followin' me?"

Clay moved closer. Rubbing the angry scar along his cheek, he looked her up and down. "I don't know which hurt more, gettin' the stitches put in, or gettin' them jerked out, one by one by one, *Miz* Chiswell."

Olivia's patience felt ready to snap. "If you're goin' to be difficult—"

Clay blocked her flight back to her house. His voice was a hiss. "You never once came to visit me while I was in the stockade."

"Y'all can't be serious. I'm a married woman. Y'all caused me untold grief, revealin' you knew me. I thought you smarter than that, but obviously I misjudged you."

"I thought you'd put in a good word for me with your husband. You and me was friends. We were goin' to be a lot more. I lost my stripes on account of you."

"What did you expect, givin' me a token of your so-called affection which you stole off that white Comanche slut? I'm glad Jed kept you in that cell six weeks. Y'all made me look like a fool." She tried to stalk past him. "Get out of my way. I have business—"

"Business with another trooper? Is he goin' to forfeit his stripes for a kiss?"

"I *never* kissed you!" Olivia cried. "I never would."

"No?" Clay moved close enough that Olivia could smell how long he'd been in the stockade. "Are you tellin' me you did all that sashayin' around me as a tease? We got names for that."

Olivia tried to slap his scarred cheek.

Clay caught her wrist and twisted it to her side. She began whimpering.

"Just hush up, Livvie. You and me had an understandin'. I was goin' to take you away from here. You were goin' to pay me, in cash money and kisses."

"I never—"

"I said hush! You came twitchin' around me, and I took the bait. I gave you the locket"— he jerked her to keep her silent—"and now I'm callin' in the debt."

Yanking Olivia close, Clay smeared his whiskeyed mouth over her tightly closed lips. She twisted away and spat at him.

Instantly Clay had his hand over her mouth and was wrestling her to the ground. Before she could fully comprehend the seriousness of her predicament, Clay was groping her legs through the layers of her skirts and petticoats.

"Wait, wait!" she said against his grimy palm. "Wait, damn you, and listen to me. I—I have a plan."

"No more twitchin', bitch. You're payin' up and you're payin' up tonight."

"A-all right, but you must listen. I—I have the money I promised you. We can go away together, west, to California. I—I tried to visit you in the stockade, but there was all that fuss over Firemaker. Carter was always there . . . Oh, do stop! You're hurtin' me!"

Shudders of terror were going through Olivia. Clay was swiftly finding his way beneath her skirts. He was no bumbling fool with a woman's body. His aim was deadly.

She wrenched herself free only to scramble a few yards deeper into the darkness, where she wouldn't be seen by a passing guard.

Clay was upon her again, crushing her with the weight of his body, tearing at her clothes, bruising her thighs.

"Please," she choked out. "Listen! You can . . . do that in a minute. Just don't hurt me. I want you to . . ."

Clay let up long enough for her to draw in a ragged breath that was very nearly a scream. "What do you want?"

"I want you to . . . kill my husband."

Clay went still.

Coughing and gasping, Olivia squirmed from beneath his hold. Scrambling backward several more feet, she thought about what she'd just said. Of course. It was the only way.

"What?" he hissed.

"Find a way, soon, and kill him. There'll be a campaign soon. In the confusion surely y'all can find a way for him to fall from his horse. If there's a battle, you could just shoot him. Who would be the wiser?"

"And if there isn't a campaign or a battle?" Clay whispered.

"You—you could make it look like *she* did it. Yes, you must do it like that. Kill him and leave her knife. She'll hang!"

Clay's voice came out soft. "Slit his throat?"

Olivia's blood ran cold. Divorce her, would he? Not in a pig's eye. "Yes . . . and then we'll . . ." She couldn't go on. She'd go away a respectable widow. Clay be damned. "I'll give you some money . . . tomorrow."

Clay caught Olivia's ankle. He slid his hand up her stockinged calf all the way to her warm, soft thigh, and beyond. "You'll give me more than that."

"Yes, yes, later, when we're away, safe."

He seized her hair. "Now."

TWENTY

SHAKING MATT'S HAND and accepting a thick Havana cigar tied with a scrap of pink knitting wool, Carter offered his congratulations.

"Thanks, Carter," Matt said, looking exhausted. "I hope everything's going to be all right. We've had several visitors already. Mary's scarcely had any rest."

"I'll only stay a moment. I promise not to tire her."

"It's not that," Matt said in a low tone. "It's the stories the women are telling her. About childbed fever. Two ladies were just here discussing whether the fever sets in after two days or three—right in front of Mary, as if she had no terrors of her own to battle. 'Don't touch the baby until you're sure you're going to live,' they said. 'Otherwise she'll die, too.' I sent them home."

"Is Mary ill?" Carter asked, his heart suddenly in his throat. "Leota told me she was fine, delivered it 'Injun style.'"

Nervously Matt chuckled. "Yes, she did, bless her heart. She seems to be all right. If anything happens to her, I'll never forgive myself. Why did I ever come here and bring her, too? I'm no soldier. I never was any good at it. I'm not staying on, Carter, I can tell you that much. When the life of the one you love is threatened, everything gets very clear very quickly. If I'd ever heard of childbed fever before today, I never would have—"

To halt the spiral of the man's panicked thinking, Carter clapped his hand onto Matt's shoulder. "No more visitors today, then. I can see the baby another day. Get some rest."

Looking as if he was battling his emotions with all his strength, Matt shook his head. "Please don't go just yet. I could use the company."

Closing the front door, Carter allowed himself to be drawn toward the chairs before the fire. Taking a seat, Carter watched Matt drop into his wife's usual chair. With reverence, Matt picked up her needlework for the baby and stared at it.

"I love the baby," Matt said in a near whisper. "How could I help but love something that is part of my wife, but the baby's so new, a stranger. Mary is all I've ever cared about."

"Seems natural to feel that way," Carter said. He was no longer surprised by Matt Graham's sensitivity.

"The moment I heard she was in labor this morning, I left my post. Colonel Chiswell will have me bucked and gagged, I'm sure."

"Would you like a drink?" Carter offered.

A small grin softened Matt's strained features. "Mary would never allow spirits in the house."

From the bedroom came a small cry. Carter couldn't help but smile. He heard soft voices within the room, and then Firemaker emerged, wearing her wrapper, holding in her arms a tiny infant swaddled in white.

Matt sprang to his feet. "Mary's not . . ."

Firemaker hastily shook her head. The moment she saw Carter, she began beaming. "Baby!" she said, coming to Matt to show him the tiny wailing face. Then she said in mock sternness, "Making . . ." She drew an imaginary cradle board around the bundle in her arms. "Rabbit pelt, very warm." She looked to Carter for assistance.

"Cradle board," Carter explained to Matt. "She thinks

you should be making your daughter a cradle board. You have a powerful godmother for your child, Matthew."

Matt looked down at Firemaker, his eyes glistening. "And quite a friend to my wife. Thank you, Firemaker, for helping Mary. She told me she couldn't have done it without you."

"Amanda," Firemaker corrected. "Firemaker Comanche woman gone."

Carter gave a confirming nod. "She's given up her Comanche name."

"Well, then," Matt said. "I suppose you'll soon be on your way home to Texas. Mary will be sorry to see you go. So will I. Forgive me for my doubts about you."

Appearing not to notice Matt's apology, Firemaker looked tenderly at the infant in her arms. Her brows began to knit over troubled eyes.

"May I see her?" Carter said, turning aside a corner of the blanket to reveal the quieting child.

How lovely Firemaker looked with her hair tied back and with a babe in her arms, Carter thought. Matt was too absorbed to notice the look that passed between Carter and Firemaker, a look warmed by the memory of their morning together.

"I'll speak to the colonel on your behalf, Matt. No man would blame you for leaving your post today. Jed may have been short with you because he doesn't understand. He has no children."

Matt lifted his eyes. "I've never seen him like this. He's rock sober and worse than ever." After a pause Matt's brow lowered. His shoulders straightened. "What does it matter? I'm resigning the moment Mary and the baby can travel. I've had enough of the west."

Through the open bedroom doorway, Carter could see Mary propped in her bed, her eyes springing wide. She'd been listening.

Autumn Blaze

"Go talk to your wife," Carter told Matt. "Fire—Amanda and I will tend the little one."

"Little one," Firemaker repeated, looking deeply into Carter's eyes, setting him on fire. "Baby."

Down the road from the fort, the First National Saloon sat like a squat shadow in the evening gloom. Its single filmy window was lit with pale yellow light. A faint curl of smoke rose from the stove stack jutting up through the roof.

Inside sat a half-dozen off-duty troopers. The bartender was behind the bar, writing something in a ledger. A lone civilian sat at the far end of the bar, slowly loading and unloading a revolver.

Periodically filling and draining a shot glass, the man appeared to be having an argument with himself. When he finished his first bottle, he ordered another. By midnight, half the bullets from his gun had rolled onto the dirt floor. The others were slippery with spilled whiskey. The man seemed to be losing the argument with his inner demons. He could no longer get the bullets into the chambers.

He could scarcely see the bottles along the mirrored shelf on the far side of the plank bar. The bartender's face had become a blur with a single dark brow over hollow eyes.

The whiskey tasted as bland as water.

There was movement near the door. Blue-belly troopers were coming in from the darkness outside, filling the place with noise. Hugh Tamberlay could hear them, but they were little more than dark ghosts moving across his consciousness. He downed the rest of the second bottle and called for more, unsure if he had actually spoken.

"More," he managed to grunt. "More!"

When the bartender declined, Hugh found himself leaning over the bar, holding the man's throat with numb fingers. He didn't remember moving.

Suddenly he was falling backward, scrambling for handholds and losing his footing, smashing to the dirt floor like a felled tree. Two shadows loomed over him.

A voice with a Yankee twang echoed. "Who's this dandified jackass?"

". . . pickled skunk . . ."

"Texas trash."

Moments later—perhaps hours—Hugh opened his eyes to darkness, to the press of cold, hard gravel against his cheek. He was outside the saloon, but couldn't remember how he'd gotten there. His hat lay beneath the hitching rail nearby. Had he fallen or had he been thrown? He didn't know. He didn't care. He couldn't move. If he was blind drunk, he wouldn't have to look at her. If he was dead drunk, he wouldn't have to kill her.

But he was still remembering her. *She* was less than a mile away now. He had to decide what to do about her, once and for all. Mandie had to be erased, or he would never sleep.

Hugh had tried to forget her. He'd managed quite well all these years, but there she was to haunt him again, to shame and scorn him. Mandie. Mandie! Goddamned Mandie!

Why wasn't she dead? Why wasn't she in Mexico? Why wasn't she . . .

Hugh wanted to reach for his pistol and empty the chambers into his own brain to silence the expanding madness there, or into hers, whichever, it didn't matter. But his hand and arm were caught beneath the deadweight of his sodden body. He couldn't move except to open and close his burning eyes, and remember, remember, remember . . .

. . . Jane's blood-bathed face. Her matted, sticky, whitey-blond hair—what was left of it. Hugh relived the horror of seeing her like that and knowing that if he'd come home just an hour earlier . . .

Hugh closed his eyes. It was done. The past couldn't be changed, but it could be killed. Shame and dishonor could be avenged and buried. He had wished Jane dead, but she

Autumn Blaze

hadn't died. He'd assumed Mandie was dead, but here she was, alive after twenty years.

Where was the bottle? He needed more whiskey. He was still thinking.

What more could he have done? How could he have brought back that savage ten-year-old, filthy beyond words, tainted and debauched? What would folks think if Mandie walked into West Creek Fork now, a Comanche slut heathen whore? They'd shoot her in the street.

Hugh's belly heaved.

The entire matter was a pounding mass of confusion in his brain and stomach. He couldn't find the right of it. No matter how he turned, it came back to stare at him. Jane was his wife. Mandie was his daughter. He should have . . . He should have been home to . . .

To die? The Comanches would've tortured him. He'd been right to wait.

Somewhere, close by in the darkness, he heard the troopers laughing again. Then someone was standing over him, prodding his churning belly with a boot toe.

"Where'd you come from? What're you doin' here?"

"Leave him be, Clay. He's drunk."

"I got me somethin' for dirty rebs what can't mind their own business. Eh, what the hell you mumblin' about, reb? Who'd you say you're goin' to kill? You think you're man enough to kill me? Look at you, your nose in the dirt. I got me half a mind to teach you a lesson."

Seconds later Hugh was vomiting into the dirt, pain radiating from a well-placed kick in his ribs.

"Clay, don't!"

Hugh's mind was reeling. He wasn't in New Mexico Territory anymore. He was back in Texas, drinking and drinking and drinking, trying to blot out the truth.

He'd done nothing out of the ordinary that summer day but what came naturally to a man like Hugh Tamberlay. He'd sidetracked to town after finding that stray.

Coward.

The word erupted from his gut, spilling bile from his mouth.

Dirty, lying coward.

The trooper was beating him now, just for the hell of it. Hugh took each kick and punch as penance. He couldn't lift a hand to defend himself. He didn't want to. He was the one who deserved to die.

In moments—perhaps hours—it was over. Hugh Tamberlay lay throbbing, dragged to the side of the saloon where troopers often paused for relief. He had no intention of telling anyone why he'd ridden so far into New Mexico Territory from Texas.

He shouldn't have spared Jane. Hard as it would've been, he should've killed her. He should've shot ten-year-old Mandie when he had the chance, his own hide be damned.

He could still do it. He could still silence the voices in his conscience. In forgetting, forevermore, he could have back the manhood he lost the afternoon he watched from the grassy rise while nine Comanches raped his wife and then rode away with his horses, his pups, and his baby.

Later, when he swung down to stand jelly-legged beside the ravaged body of the nineteen-year-old woman who had adored him, Hugh had known for himself what he truly was. A coward. He'd been running from that truth ever since. He feared he would go on running until he died. Or she did.

The morning sky was white. Frost lay sparkling on the scrubby grass cover and along each hitching rail. The air felt sharp and exhilarating in Carter's lungs as he crossed the frosty parade ground to the colonel's office.

Two troopers in greatcoats, gusting clouds of white breath into the cold morning air, dropped a tarp-covered body near the commander's door. A bloodied hand flopped into Carter's path.

Without glancing at Carter's curious face, the grumbling troopers shuffled away. Crouching, Carter lifted a corner of the tarp and gazed sadly into a battered, unrecognizable face. What a way to die, he thought, his breakfast congealing into a greasy knot in his stomach.

Bracing himself for yet another battle with his adversary, Colonel Jed Chiswell, Carter straightened and stepped inside the overwarm office. Jed was stoking his own heating stove.

"Morning, Colonel. Who's the dead man outside?"

"No one knows. He was found out on the road this morning. Robbed. I say it's a warning. The Comanches are so close we don't even see them. It'll be my guards next."

Carter rubbed his eyes. "That's a good ol'-fashioned American-style beating, Colonel. Comanches don't kill that way. If I were you, I'd be looking for a trooper with a hangover and bleeding knuckles."

Jed shot Carter a silencing glance.

Carter shrugged.

Taking his place behind the desk, Jed said, "I'm told the man rode in early yesterday and drank until the bartender threw him out. They found him like that this morning. Even his horse is gone. I'll file a report. I'll send a telegraph message to Fort Kirby. He'll be buried. It happens that way sometimes."

Carter gazed into the colonel's red-rimmed, weary-looking eyes. "I see. Well, I'm here on behalf of a friend. I'm hoping you're not going to punish Matt Graham for going to Mary's bedside yesterday."

"Whatever gave you the idea I would? Never mind. I don't have time for this. My concerns go well beyond childbirth, downy-cheeked lieutenants, and unidentified corpses."

As Carter moved to leave, Jed motioned for him to wait.

"My efforts to draw Snakehorn into the open have failed," Jed said with surprising candor. "I'm left with a passel of sickly Comanche women and children no one really cares about or wants except you and Firemaker. Any day now that old man, the one you call Four Toes, is going to breathe his last. Where am I supposed to bury him? Beside that John Doe out there? Beside the Comanche baby?"

Carter straightened. "Let Firemaker and me take him to the mountains to die. She's talked of nothing else since she learned English."

Rising, the colonel went to the stove and poured himself a cup of coffee that smelled as strong as tar. After he'd sipped at it, he fixed Carter with a disconcerting eye. "Interesting you should suggest that. It would seem, for once, we're in agreement. The three of you can leave tomorrow morning, on one condition."

Holding back his surprise, Carter braced himself. "Sir?"

"Traveling into the mountains with a sick old man will be slow. I doubt the trail will be easy to follow, dragging a travois. You're sure to be noticed."

Carter digested the implications. "You think Snakehorn will show himself if he sees we have the old man?"

"Yes, and in case he doesn't see you, Firemaker or the old man will likely take you right to Snakehorn's camp."

Carter measured his words. "You're asking the worm if he wants to bait the hook?"

"I'm not asking, Machesney. I'm giving you a direct order. These matters go beyond the wants and needs of an individual. A commander learns that all too quickly."

Carter knew the man was right.

"A full company will be following you. This is my last hope for redemption, Machesney. Thanks to your efforts,

Snakehorn and his warriors could yet be brought in. They'll all go off to the reservation. You and the famous Miss Tamberlay—and her sister—can go away to Texas. And good riddance."

"If Firemaker knows we're being followed, she'll never—"

Jed's patience was short. "You're not going to tell her."

"She'll never trust me again."

Jed's face reddened. "Would you like to see the reports of what is found after an attack on a Texas homestead? Firemaker's mother got off easy."

Carter didn't like it. Firemaker might be injured. She might decide to rejoin the Comanche war chief. He didn't want to lose her.

"If you're captured, Machesney, and if the company following you can't effect your rescue, I'll release the Comanche prisoners in exchange for you. They'll all go into the mountains. Snakehorn will appear to guide them . . . wherever, and we'll take him then. There's danger, but I believe the risk worth the try."

"Would you think so if you were the worm, Colonel?"

Carter's first stop was the corral to instruct the troopers working there to use the horses he'd had brought in from his ranch in the event the Comanche prisoners were released. He checked on Lonesome and ordered Dolores, who had arrived a few days earlier, readied for the trip into the mountains. He knew Dolores would be the perfect horse for Firemaker. He had been planning for this eventuality from the first.

The moment he walked away, he knew, too, that the grapevine would soon begin humming. By noon every person at the fort would know something was afoot. Speculation would run rampant.

His next stop was the sutler's store, where he made out a

list of provisions, paying for all with one good bay mare for the sutler's personal use. Everything was to be delivered to his quarters that night.

He was about to burst into the Grahams' quarters and tell Firemaker the news but decided at the door he'd best think the plan through.

Circling the perimeter of the parade ground, Carter tried to determine if there was any hope for their budding love should Snakehorn be captured. His victory over Jed Chiswell went quickly sour in his mouth.

Carter realized that in shattering Firemaker's trust in him, he'd be going home to Texas alone. She would never forgive him. And yet there was no getting around the necessity of making this trip into the mountains.

Snakehorn had to be stopped. The Indian wars had to come to an end. Once again, Carter had to set aside his personal needs for a larger goal. He wished, just for once, he could do exactly what he wanted.

When he found himself standing at the corral fence, gazing at the Comanche women grouped at the far corner, he found himself torn by the desire to see them set free to live out their lives in the mountains and not at the reservation. It was the same conflict that had haunted him during the war. He'd fought on the Confederate side, which espoused slavery, while coming to believe that slavery was wrong.

Once again he was at cross purposes with himself but could see no way out. This war over who had the right to the western lands had started before Carter entered into it. It would likely go on after he was gone. It was just possible that no matter what he did, his efforts would have little effect on the fate of the west.

With that, Carter started directly across the parade ground for the Grahams' quarters. He might sacrifice his life and love for nothing, he thought, but he felt bound to honor his commitment. To abandon it now selfishly, and run off with Firemaker, would leave too much on his conscience.

How bitter was the taste of honor as he tapped at the door. To save countless strangers a savage death, he must kill the thing he valued most, his lover's trust. At least for this one night, he decided, they would be happy. He would reveal none of his ambivalence over the events to unfold the next morning.

TWENTY-ONE

FIREMAKER SCARCELY KNEW what to think. In the parlor before the fire, Carter was studying his map of New Mexico Territory. Mary was rocking the baby nearby. Matt had come in for the noon meal, and they all talked excitedly of the coming trip into the mountains.

Later in the afternoon Firemaker and Carter went to give Four Toes the news of his release. Still, Firemaker could not determine how to feel. To be freed was a triumph. To take her Comanche father into the mountains to die filled her with silent misery.

It would not be so difficult to send her father into the next world with honor, she thought, but there was so much more at stake. She was almost certain Carter would be sacrificed by Snakehorn.

"As soon as we've seen your father properly . . ." Carter looked at a loss for words and couldn't go on.

As they neared the corral Carter turned to Firemaker, his expression intimate. Then he sighed and made an attempt to smile. She could see he was troubled. She knew he wasn't happy about this trip any more than she was. His disquiet was not from fear, however. He was worried about something.

He likely suspected he would meet up with Snakehorn, too, but he made no reference to the war chief. Firemaker said nothing, either. An unspoken bond seemed to make them play out this game to break the deadlock.

Carter went on " . . . afterward we'll come back here. By then Corinna will know if she wants to come with us back to Texas. Do you want to tell Corinna you're leaving?"

Firemaker shook her head no.

When Firemaker explained to Four Toes that at last he was going to the holy mountains to die, he looked scarcely able to understand. She-Who-Weeps gave no protest. She just stared at Firemaker with wide, puzzled eyes.

"You will make him ready," Firemaker said to her sister-in-law when she was satisfied Four Toes understood the plan. "You will look after the People for him now, and guide them to the mountains. You will ask for supplies if I'm not here to ask for you. You will tell everyone to go on living."

She-Who-Weeps looked overwhelmed by the responsibilities Firemaker was thrusting upon her.

"But *you* have chosen the white man's way," She-Who-Weeps pointed out.

"Surely you have known all along what I've been trying to do," Firemaker said. "I expect to . . ."

Firemaker couldn't let herself admit her fear of impending death. For the first time she doubted the rightness of sending her Comanche family back to the mountains where they would be free to freeze and starve.

In the past weeks she'd glimpsed the scope and power of the conquering race. Would it not be wiser for the People to adapt now and avoid suffering? Or was the true honor in fighting to the bitter end? Did the white man have the right to erase the People from the face of an earth peopled by so many other races? Shouldn't the family of man be as varied as the animals?

"But if we're not released?" She-Who-Weeps asked.

"Then you must carry the mountain alone wherever you

are forced to go," Firemaker said flatly. "For if you aren't released, we three will be dead. And Snakehorn. And any warriors we once had. You'll have to protect the young boys and teach them as best you can because you are the daughter-in-law of Chief Four Toes and the wife of Snakehorn."

Unable to determine She-Who-Weeps's reaction, Firemaker turned away. She had nothing more to say. She-Who-Weeps had been known since her acceptance of Snakehorn as husband to whine and complain about everything. To entrust the People to her gave Firemaker little peace of mind.

Firemaker forced herself to march away from the corral, to avoid good-byes. She had no choice. It was time to ready herself for a journey with no end.

That night while Mary watched, misty-eyed, from her rocker, Matt played "Lorena" on his violin. Firemaker picked out the tune on the piano.

Supper was strained. Carter talked animatedly of their journey to Texas. Firemaker found his chatter suspicious. He likely found her silence equally disturbing.

"Your mother's going to be so happy to see you, Amanda," Mary said as the hour grew late and her strength ebbed. "I cannot imagine losing this precious bundle and not seeing her again for twenty years. I can certainly understand how your mother could yearn for you all this time. The power of her love kept you alive and brought you here. It'll bear you home again. You must be excited to be soon on your way to such a strong woman."

Firemaker tried not to think of all that would be lost to her should Snakehorn appear in the mountains—not just her white mother, but her love, and her life.

Firemaker feared she would not be able to protect Carter from Snakehorn's peyote-induced wrath against any and all white men. Snakehorn would surely take Carter prisoner.

Carter would be murdered. Jane White Mother's feelings were but a small concern compared with that.

"You know," Mary went on, unaware of the emotional undercurrents in the room, "of all the things you've learned in the past weeks, Amanda, you haven't learned to dance. Wouldn't you like to dance with Carter tonight? It would mean so much to me to watch you both together."

Carter proceeded to show Firemaker the two-step. For a time the mood lifted. Carter grinned. Firemaker stumbled over her feet but enjoyed turning about in Carter's arms. His hand was warm on hers, his body strong and solid and close. There were times when being white was most enjoyable, she thought.

Then it was time for Mary and the baby to retire. "You'll wake me in the morning before you go, won't you? Promise," Mary said, moving toward the bedroom on Matt's arm.

"Not if you've had a long night with the baby," Carter put in.

Awkwardly Mary gathered Firemaker close and patted her back. Drawing away, her eyes tearful, she could not begin to disguise her sadness. "Take care . . . and we'll see you again in a few days. This is a good thing you're doing for your father, Amanda. By the time you get back," she added, brightening, "I'll have decided on a name for our little treasure."

Firemaker found her heart too full to speak.

At six-thirty the next morning, Firemaker pulled herself atop Carter's horse Dolores. The white man's saddle felt broad and cold between her thighs. Twisting, she couldn't see Four Toes swaddled on the travois lashed behind the horse.

The morning was frosty, with a low gray sky promising snow. It was a bad time to set out, she thought, but Carter wasn't hesitating. He had two pack mules loaded. He was wearing a greatcoat and was loaded down with saddlebags and a rifle. He looked determined to leave, the weather be damned. She wanted the journey over with, too.

Firemaker was wearing her blue dress over a gray union suit and trousers to keep her legs warm. Mary had given her a sweater and a shawl for her head. Firemaker had lined her moccasins to keep her feet warm because she refused to wear army boots. When she refused to wear a blue-belly coat over the sweater, Mary insisted she wear one of Matt's old civilian coats. It was a huge brown wool, bulky but warm.

At the corral fence, all the Comanche women and children looked on, as forlorn an assortment, huddled in their army blankets, as Firemaker had ever seen. Glancing sidelong at the colonel pacing nearby, Firemaker wondered if he knew what must surely result from this trip into the mountains. Was he as stupid as she hoped, or did he have plans of his own she must guess at?

Carter's cheeks and nose were red as he swung onto his horse and signaled the start of their journey. As they passed the graveyard where two troopers were setting a wooden marker over a newly turned grave, Firemaker wondered if she shouldn't take Little Cloud's body along to the holy mountains. She hesitated, feeling a strange attraction for the place. Finally she decided against disturbing the child; he was surely in the next world by now.

At the gate, Carter paused. Behind them, the bugler was calling assembly. As they did every morning, the troopers fell into formation. There seemed to be considerable activity among the reinforcements; supposedly they were starting back for Fort Kirby that afternoon.

The colonel, who had been about to approach and bid Carter and Firemaker good-bye, stopped to review his troops. It became obvious even to Firemaker that something was unexpectedly awry. Looking as if he was questioning several of the troopers, Colonel Chiswell seemed to forget about Carter, Firemaker, and the old Comanche chief.

"Go," Firemaker hissed. "Going. Colonel not stopping us."

Carter's expression showed agreement with her anxiety. There was no use waiting. They struck out, following the road down past the sutler's. Firemaker concentrated on guiding her mount between the ruts so her father's ride would be smooth. Four Toes had done little more than mumble since they woke him at dawn to get him fed and settled on the travois. She was afraid he might die before they even reached the canyon.

They were well on their way before Firemaker gave up listening for her sister's footsteps behind. Corinna was not going to see them off.

Their progress was as slow as the colonel had predicted. Pausing at noon, scarcely ten miles from the fort, Carter roused the old Comanche while Firemaker built a hasty fire to warm them all. They were on their way again within an hour.

By dusk they had begun the steady climb into the mountains. Firemaker took the lead, finding a deer trail that snaked deep into the pine forests. Carter marveled at her knowledge of the terrain. He spent most of the afternoon watching for bears and mountain cats.

By Carter's compass, Firemaker was bearing steadily west by northwest. After making camp the first night, he attempted to make a rough map while Firemaker and Four Toes talked quietly beneath the lean-to she had erected for him. The map was more to ensure Carter's retreat from the tangled forests than to record a way for the troopers to follow. In any case, Carter couldn't imagine the men finding this route an easy one.

The night was long and numbingly cold. Carter had little to say. Firemaker was equally somber. She sat apart, staring into the campfire's flames. Carter kept his pistol or rifle close. Firemaker turned to scowl at the slightest changes in the shadows surrounding their camp.

As Carter twisted and turned in his bedroll all night, scorching first one side of himself while freezing his other side, and then reversing, he cataloged a thousand sounds. Every night cry was a Comanche warrior giving a signal. Every rustle was a Comanche footfall. He wondered what it would feel like to loose his scalp.

In the morning his bones ached with cold. He sat sucking scalding day-old coffee at dawn, trying not to ask himself for the thousandth time why he was here.

When he heard someone approaching from the trail behind, he was on his feet in seconds, pistol in hand. Dragging a pine bough to disguise their trail of the evening before, Firemaker emerged from the dense cover of pines. Every few steps she stopped to examine needle cover disturbed by the travois and rearranged it to her satisfaction. Carter had thought she still lay curled against Four Toes, warming him.

Seeing Carter, Firemaker kept her expression focused and blank. Her desire to throw off any followers was intense. Carter's heart swelled with love for her. He smiled and offered coffee, but his heart was heavy.

"Did your father sleep well?" Carter asked.

Ignoring him, Firemaker lashed the pine bough to the end of the travois. Then she gathered up the blankets covering Four Toes and shook them out.

"He is died," she said matter-of-factly. "In the sleeping. Coming now, Carter Machesney. We are going today. Many more riding."

As Carter digested the disturbing fact that Four Toes hadn't even survived the first night, he watched Firemaker erase every trace of their campsite. Making an alarming amount of smoke, she smothered the fire. It was then he noticed she had hacked off a foot of her hair on one side, and one of her forearms was bleeding. She was in mourning. His heart felt sore for her.

Loading Four Toes' stiff, cold form onto the travois, Carter paused to look down on the weathered old copper-colored face. This was the man who had smashed Jane Tamberlay in the head and stolen her baby. This was a Comanche warrior who had likely murdered hundreds of Texas settlers. Lying still like that, he looked about as frightening as a stone carving. Carter could hardly believe he was bearing such a man away to his grave.

In moments, they started up the trail again. Firemaker had nothing more to say. Within the hour fat white snowflakes began falling from a leaden sky. Firemaker indicated she had no need to stop at noon. Carter offered the canteen; she declined. Munching on biscuits and beef jerky from his saddlebags, Carter kept his thoughts to himself and followed her.

As long as the snow fell, Firemaker made no effort to go back to cover their tracks. At four that afternoon, they were so high in the mountains that the snow left off, and the wind began to blow. Firemaker found a protective overhang where she erected an amazing lean-to–style tepee out of the blankets and tarps Carter had brought along on the pack mules.

Carter saw to the horses while she got a campfire started inside the makeshift tepee. Four Toes' body remained undisturbed on the travois, covered by a pristine three inches of glistening snow.

With the horses tethered in a wind-protected hollow for the night, Carter started for the shelter. Within, he heard the low, sad keening of Firemaker's voice. He stood for some moments, affording her privacy. Then, stooping through the flap opening, he found her staring into a low, crackling fire, rocking slowly.

His fingers were stiff, his toes numb, but it was his heart that suddenly turned to ice. This might be their last night together, he thought. And for the first time since weeks before when he saw Firemaker in the stockade, he realized she was, in fact, Comanche.

She looked up, her gray-blue eyes fathomless. She watched him bring in armloads of dry pine twigs and branches gathered from nearby. If she disapproved of him visibly disturbing the area so they might be warm during the night, she gave no indication. For this last night, they would have each other in peace and solitude.

With the wind moaning outside and a few snowflakes sifting in through the overlapping edges of the blankets and tarps, Firemaker relished their haven, snug and warm.

Curled beside Carter's warm body, she stared at the licking flames of the fire and watched the showers of sparks climb the draft of smoke that was sucked up through the opening she had left at the top between the rocks and the uppermost blanket.

She wanted to talk to Carter, but the effort to find the white words was too great. Besides, what was left to discuss? She was leading him into certain death, and she suspected the horse soldiers were following, which meant certain war. She had never thought she would face the end of her life so reluctantly.

Carter's hands felt warm as he stroked her arms beneath the thick cover of blankets. When she turned her face toward him, his mouth came to hers quickly. His cheeks were hot from the fire, his lips soft and moist.

She tasted his mouth, savoring the explosion of desire that erupted in her belly and spread to her legs. This was the joining of souls she had sought all her life. She must know this man tonight, every part of him. She must offer herself up, heart and mind, and join with him in unforgettable passion. Each moment was more precious than a lifetime.

"Firemaker, I love you," Carter whispered against her lips.

Autumn Blaze

"Love," she said. "Love Carter Machesney good man."

She shivered with delight as his hands moved over her breasts.

She had purposely selected a shelter large enough for them to sleep together without the worry of disturbing the fire. Already the enclosure was warm enough for them to throw off their covers and remove their clothes.

This time they had the luxury of time and warmth to complement their lovemaking. She spread herself willingly before Carter's adoring gaze, and let his eyes and hands savor her every curve and swell.

She savored him as well, from the full breadth of his shoulders to the fascinating swirls of hair across his chest. The hair on his thick, strong forearms felt sensuous to her palms. The hair on his head was silky when he dipped his head to kiss her breasts. She tangled her fingers in it. He smelled of the crisp mountain air.

When his hands and lips followed her contours to her hips and thighs, she lost her ability to think. Her hands smoothed over his back and strained to reach his thighs, muscled and furred almost as heavily as his arms. Her body called for him, but he took what seemed like hours to explore her.

His palm felt warm and firm, pressing against the mound of her womanhood. Squirming for more, she reached to find his strength eager to penetrate. When she could no longer wait, but urged him to mount her, he settled comfortably between her legs, but made no move to enter.

She opened her eyes to see him looking down at her. He was smiling, and not sadly. She had made him forget the wind outside and the dangers awaiting them. He knew only her. His eyes were only for her. His lips found hers, and she forgot, too.

They were warm and safe. That was how it should be for them, she thought, opening her eyes again, watching him. He was there for her then, scarcely moving, just smiling blissfully, briefly closing his eyes to concentrate on the pleasure their joining brought him.

Then he moved ever so slightly, causing in her a swelling sensation of pleasure that made her swirl into herself with delight. He moved like that for what seemed like the entire night.

Even when the fires within them were raging, he moved with exquisite slowness, lifting to tantalize her and then plunging so far she was driven to gasp with delight.

In time she could think of nothing but the pleasure he gave her. Her mind was a universe of blackness, her body spinning into focus, all sensations pinpointing to a white-hot place deep within her where she was unprotected, innocent, and totally aware.

She felt the darkness expanding to blot out everything but the gathering need he stoked with such loving expertise. When the spilling sensation of the waterfall of light washed into the darkness of her consciousness, Firemaker cried out, her hands gripping Carter's arms, her body convulsing uncontrollably. He plunged again and again, diving into her pleasure until he was experiencing it himself, filling her with everything she had ever lacked.

He smothered his face in her neck, panting, whispering her name, promising her his life. She held him with her arms around his shoulders, her legs twined about his hips, her womanhood in a grip that wilted to heartbreak. They deserved so much more than war. They deserved life. They deserved love. She couldn't let go without a fight.

A long while later Carter rolled away. They huddled together, emotions stampeding, hearts slowing. He held her fiercely, protectively, his muscles trembling. Part of her felt like weeping angrily for the responsibilities she must again take up in the morning. She felt a sadness for the body lying in the snow outside. But also there was joy, deep and clean, to have and to know this man.

Carter kissed the back of her neck. She tucked herself tightly against him. An hour later they made love again.

And then again.

At dawn, Carter laid more branches on the coals. Stepping outside to survey what snow the night had left, he found everything covered in white—the travois, the surrounding pines, the mountains visible in the distance.

Four Comanches on scrawny ponies were standing at the head of the trail as well. They looked startled, as if they hadn't expected a white man to emerge from the snowy side of the mountain.

Wondering how long the men had been there, watching, swathed in buffalo robes, Carter tugged his blanket more tightly about his shoulders. He was glad he'd put on his boots, but underneath the blanket he was naked.

When the Comanches made no move against him, Carter stepped some distance from the lean-to, relieved himself into the snow, and went back inside to wake Firemaker.

Part of him wanted to burst into hysterical laughter. I just pissed in front of four Comanche warriors, he thought, fighting a reckless grin. Part of him was crying, for he loved Firemaker with all his heart. He was afraid he would soon shame her. He had no idea of the depth of his courage. It hadn't served him terribly well during the war, and that, he realized with a warm rush of surprise, was why he had felt so ashamed all these years.

It wasn't that his father would have thought his capture during the war shameful. It wasn't that the women at the hospital thought he was careless, stupid, or both. It wasn't his sister's opinion, or Sarajane's, that cut to the bone. It was his own disappointment in the very simple fact that he was a man with limitations.

It was gone, the claustrophobic feeling of being inside an enclosed space. Carter hadn't felt it in days, perhaps weeks, so long in fact that he'd forgotten about it. All that was left was understanding and forgiveness. He was human.

Smiling, he shook Firemaker's shoulders. She opened unfocused gray-blue eyes, so beautiful, so beguiling. "Good morning," he whispered, kissing her.

She smiled. Instantly she saw sad thoughts moving into his eyes. It was miraculous to have another person read him so well, Carter thought, his grief that their time was over beginning to sting his eyes.

"Snakehorn," she whispered.

"I don't know who they are. There are four of them. Why didn't they wake us?"

"More coming," she said, her brows knitting.

Already she was planning what to do. Carter bowed to her better judgment.

Quickly they dressed, the night tucked away in their hearts. Firemaker emerged to find four Comanches she didn't recognize keeping watch over their camp. By the time she had torn down the lean-to, more Comanche men had arrived, summoned by Kills Otters. Those men she knew from childhood. They looked hollow and haggard.

"I remember you from the day you were born," she said to Kills Otters, the lad of seventeen summers. "Where is Snakehorn? Walking Bear? Who are these?" She pointed to the strange Comanches watching her. "They are not of the Tall Horse band."

"I am Kills Otters, and I speak for Walking Bear, who now leads us. These men have joined us to fight the white man at the fort. We have seen you coming. We have seen those who follow. Why do you come? Why do soldiers come? Are the women and children all dead now?"

Firemaker found herself shivering and hungry. Hearing Carter behind her, saddling their horses and tending to the packs on the mules, she stepped forward. The time to use the ways of women was past. The time to use the fire of her spirit was upon her.

Autumn Blaze 291

"Why do you leave the rescue of the People to a woman?" she demanded. "Where is Snakehorn? His wife weeps for him. His son is shamed to be the white man's prisoner. I am having to do what is a warrior's place to do," she said in Comanche, her tone insulting.

Carter paused to listen, having no idea what she was saying. His face gave no clue to his galloping heart.

"What have you been waiting for so long that our father Four Toes must die in the snow?" Firemaker snapped, tearing away the tarp covering her father's frozen body. "This is no way for a Comanche warrior to die."

The Comanches looked down at the body with blank expressions.

"There has always been much talk of you, white sister," Kills Otters said, his tone diplomatic, immediately flooding Firemaker with increased confidence. "You were always apart. You didn't try to behave as a woman. You thought yourself a warrior. If you were left with the responsibility of the People at the fort, and for your father, it was an honor you earned and deserved. Or perhaps not, if you take this responsibility in anger."

"Where is Snakehorn?" she asked, her tone deeper, holding a note of warning.

"He is dying. He may already be dead. They tell me I am too young to be the new war chief, but I take the responsibility on Walking Bear's advice, and I take it with pride. Walking Bear is a good man, but he cannot think in times of war."

"If Snakehorn still lives, I must speak to him," Firemaker said, chin high, emotions under a surprising amount of control.

"Who is this white man with you?" one of the strangers cut in.

She kept her eyes on Kills Otters.

"I am thinking you show much respect for Four Toes if you bring him to the mountains to die," Kills Otters said when Firemaker refused to answer. "I'll take your part when we speak with Snakehorn. He waits at the pit. He seeks renewed medicine. You come with us now, and bring your white man and your father. We'll talk."

"I will talk when the People are free of the fort. If you give me your word that no harm will come to this man, I'll go back for the People. I can promise supplies to last the winter, too, but if you allow Snakehorn to kill this man who has helped us, the People will be killed. And the horse soldiers will find you."

After thinking over the offer, Kills Otters said, "Go, then," gesturing to the trail down the mountain. "We'll take Four Toes for you. You will bring the People to the pit."

This was not how Firemaker had expected the events to go, she thought, battling her fears. She had assumed she would be dealing with Snakehorn and his peyote-muddled mind, but Kills Otters was young and bold. She knew not how far or how long she could trust him.

She couldn't betray a single doubt about his integrity. To question it would be to kill Carter instantly. She dared not threaten Kills Otters. She had too little power. If he was the new chief, she must offer her respect unhesitatingly.

Her thoughts settling, Firemaker nodded. "I will bring them back," she said. "You will show this man who helped the People with food, blankets, clothing his due respect. He is our friend, our only friend."

Looking to Carter to gauge his reaction, Firemaker saw calm acceptance. He looked ready to do whatever she asked. Her heart filled with love for him.

She dared give Carter no instructions on how to behave among the Comanches. He must stand on his own as a warrior among warriors.

But she was afraid. So terribly afraid. She hated to turn away. How long and empty life might be without him. How short would be her death if the following soldiers caught her. How futile her efforts if she failed to get back to the fort.

Giving no outward sign of her tumultuous feelings, Firemaker went to Carter and, giving him only a glance, took the reins of his horse. She took the reins of hers, too. Then she waited, her drumming heart growing still at the prospect of an angry response, or confusion, or even refusal.

"Go," she said in English.

Absorbing the fact that he was expected to walk now, Carter gave a questioning nod toward the pack mules. One of the Comanches stepped forward to take charge of them.

Another man attached the travois bearing Four Toes' body to his horse. With Carter sandwiched in the middle of the grim procession, they all started up the trail, moving quickly out of sight beyond a tumble of boulders.

Carter never looked back.

Firemaker felt the white silence of the mountain enfold her in its unforgiving cold.

TWENTY-TWO

OLIVIA CHISWELL LAY rigid beside her husband, listening to him snore. How could he sleep when her world was in pieces?

The word "divorce" rang in her head like a funeral bell. Then the scene with Clay Burdette sprang full-blown and ugly into her mind. As her heart raced and her head spun she relived every painful, disgusting detail of his attack on her. What if she was now pregnant with that cracker's bastard? She'd have to kill herself.

What had she been thinking, asking him to kill Jed? Her behavior went beyond explanation. She'd only wanted a little attention, and now because of the first meaningless flirtation with that arrogant piece of white trash, she faced utter ruination. Jed had driven her to it.

Hearing the creak of a door, Olivia wondered briefly if Corinna was having trouble sleeping. She didn't trust the girl wandering around her house in the dark. Perhaps she should get up and chat with her awhile.

Firemaker hadn't had the chance to kiss Carter good-bye, she thought, crouched low over Lonesome's neck. She could feel the horse tiring as he galloped into the night. "Not dying," she whispered. "Not dying now. Fast. Fast!"

She had reerected the lean-to–style tepee against the mountainside with the tarps and blankets Carter hadn't had time to reload onto the pack mules. Inside she'd built a fire designed to burn long and slow.

She hoped the smoke curling from the opening in the top of the lean-to tepee had bought her several precious hours. She hoped an army scout had been watching the mountainside, thinking the smoke meant they decided to stay the day in camp.

Firemaker had left the campsite with as confusing a mass of signs and tracks as possible. Then she started down the mountain with the two horses by a treacherous route no white man could follow. She made the canyon by midafternoon.

There she had found the trail of the soldiers following them into the mountains. They'd gone by more than a day before. She'd been right. The colonel had arranged for them to follow. It was just possible, she thought, that Carter had known about it all along.

Regardless, Firemaker forgave Carter. She knew only too well the press of duty. It mattered little now in any case if he had deliberately tried to deceive her or not. She had done so to him. They were even.

By now the following soldiers were at the abandoned camp, realizing Carter had gone on ahead with several riders on unshod ponies while she doubled back alone.

When Dolores had been about to give out, Firemaker had left her and mounted Lonesome for the final sprint to the fort. Nearly there now, Firemaker prayed the exhausted horse would make it a few more miles.

It was dark now, several hours past sundown. Firemaker was worn-out, thirsty, and hungry, but she remained low over the horse, galloping ever more slowly back up the road.

She was sure Carter and the Comanches had long since reached the pit where Snakehorn had earned his name as a boy of thirteen seeking his first vision. It was a lonely, isolated, terrible place, suitable for visions and death. She prayed there was no medicine left there for her brother.

* * *

Olivia smelled the cold bite of the outside air swirl through the darkened quarters into her bedroom. What was Corinna doing, sneaking outside at this time of night? Olivia wondered in anger. Was she going to meet that corporal of hers?

The thought twisted in Olivia's jealous mind. Slipping ever so carefully from the bed, she tiptoed barefoot from the room. The rear door in the kitchen was open; there was no mistaking the cold night air flooding the rooms.

In the doorway stood a trooper. Olivia first noted his snowy boots tracking spots across the floor and was about to reprimand him when she noticed his blue uniform coat was unbuttoned to the waist. That seemed odd.

It was odd, in fact, that one of the guards should be so bold as to enter the colonel's quarters at such an hour, and from the rear. . . .

Olivia's hand stole to her mouth. That was no guard. It was Clay!

She ran to him, pushing at him with both hands. "What are you doing here? Get out! You can't do anything now. She's gone. You have to wait until she—"

Clay seized Olivia's wrist, twisted it behind her, and wrenched her close. "I ain't pinnin' no throat slittin' on that white Comanche bitch. I'm pinnin' it on you, bitch, after I get done with you."

Was he crazy? "Why? Why?" she hissed. "Didn't you get what you wanted from me the other night?"

"That little poke? Wasn't worth the wear and tear on my knees." He started forcing her to hers.

Panic seized her. "No!" she growled, trying to tear free.

His mouth slammed against hers, cruel and revolting. He smelled of whiskey and sweat. Olivia twisted to be free, but he only bent her arm more sharply up her back.

"All right, all right, down on the floor," he said against her mouth. "Hike up that bed dress."

"If you must rape me again, take me outside. And be quiet about it."

He snickered. "Shit. You don't know the half, bitch. I'm goin' to kill me a colonel, and you're goin' to watch me do it. Then I'm goin' to kill me a slutty colonel's *wife* easy as I pinch lice outta my hair."

"Oh—" Shuddering, she wrenched herself so violently from Clay's grip that she felt her shoulder tear.

But at least she was free. She came at him all teeth and claws, raking his already-scarred cheeks with both her hands. "Dirty cracker," she said louder, wishing Jed would awaken and save her.

Knocking her backward so that she sprawled at his feet, Clay threw himself on top of her. Olivia felt the floor cut hard against her shoulder blades. He was crushing her hips, too. She couldn't breathe. She couldn't make a sound. He had her by the throat.

The muzzle of a pistol dug here and there into her thighs, cutting little bruises as it jabbed. Finally Olivia opened for him in the desperate hope he would release his hold on her long enough for her to catch her breath. He jabbed hard enough that the pain caused her to scramble backward, kicking and biting like a wild animal.

"I won't let you! I won't!" she cried.

From the kitchen came Corinna Tamberlay's gasp as she saw the two grappling on the parlor floor.

Firemaker felt Lonesome stagger and then stumble. He'd put his heart into the ride down the canyon. She wanted to push the horse on until he dropped, but she had a mile to go. She allowed Lonesome to slow, to stagger again, and then to plod on as if knowing Carter's life depended on his strength.

Making the gate, Firemaker urged Lonesome not to stop even though the guard was shouting, "Hey, you!"

Heaving and foaming, Lonesome dragged across the parade ground and started to fall just as they reached the colonel's quarters. The parade ground was dark and virtually deserted. The only lighted window Firemaker could see was at the Grahams' next door. It was later than she had realized.

Just as Lonesome went down Firemaker slid to the ground. She ran to the colonel's door and was about to beat it down when a shot rang out inside. Someone screamed.

Firemaker sprang away. Instinctively she dropped to a crouch, listening, trying to comprehend what was happening.

The guards converging to Firemaker's left stumbled, baffled and confused by the sound of the shot.

"She got a gun?" one whispered.

"I don't see none. The shot sounded like it came from inside," the other said.

Hearing nothing more, Firemaker threw herself at the door and began pounding it with cold-numbed fists. "Colonel!" she gasped, afraid she would be unable to remember the white words to say what she needed of the man.

Another shot split the night.

Jerking back, seeing that no bullet had penetrated the door, Firemaker edged close once again and laid her cheek against the wood, listening. Inside someone was crying hysterically, in the rear of the house. It sounded like Corinna.

A volley of pistol shots sent several troopers arriving from the barracks around to the rear of officers' row. There was the sound of a horse and rider galloping away. Shouts and running feet faded into the distance.

"What're you doin' back here?" one of the guards demanded, grabbing Firemaker's arm and jerking her back from the door.

Another trooper beat on the colonel's door. "Colonel? Colonel?"

Firemaker was trying to twist free when the colonel's door fell open. Corinna stood in the doorway in her bed dress, a smoking pistol clutched at her side in her right hand. She looked wild. "They've shot each other!" she wailed, looking as frightened as a child.

Two guards pushed past her into the dark quarters.

From the direction of the barracks, Micah Johnson was running, calling Corinna's name while trying to get his trousers and suspenders up. The moment Corinna saw him, she flew to his arms. "They've shot each other!" was all she could say before dissolving into sobs.

Nearby the sound of a wailing newborn grew louder as Matt Graham appeared in his open front doorway, revolver drawn.

"Firemaker?" he said, staring at her incredulously. "What are you do—" Almost instantly Matt drew the necessary conclusion. "They've got Carter, haven't they? They've sent you to . . ."

Nodding her head emphatically yes, Firemaker grabbed Matt's arm to make the night stop spinning wildly out of control around her. She was so tired she could scarcely stand. It was impossible to think. She pulled Matt toward the colonel's open doorway.

"Has he . . ."

Matt didn't seem to know what to ask. He saw Corinna in Micah's arms, shrieking in what appeared to be a combination of angry hysterics and terror, and began to look a bit overwhelmed himself.

"Fast! Fast!" Firemaker cried, tugging more sharply at Matt's sleeve. "The People going to the mountains. Snakehorn is—"

"They've shot each other!" Corinna shrieked savagely up at Matt and Firemaker. "Don't you understand? Now there's no one to free your goddamned savages. We're all doomed."

One of the men who had gone inside the colonel's quarters appeared in the doorway. Within, the other was lighting a lamp. "Lieutenant, the colonel's been shot. Mrs. Chiswell, too."

Inside, Olivia's ragged voice sliced into the stunned silence. "He's not dead?"

The trooper who had been inside came to the door and shook his head. "He's unconscious, sir, but it don't look good. I can't figure what the hell happened. Miss Tamberlay insists someone broke in and was attacking Miz Chiswell when the colonel came out of the bedroom and shot into the darkened room."

"He went out the back!" Corinna insisted, pointing. "I tried to hit him, but . . ." Micah tried to quiet her. Corinna glared at Firemaker as if to say everything was her fault.

She glared so long and intently that Firemaker wondered if her sister was going to shoot her. Those standing around began to wonder the same thing.

Corinna's face twisted. She shook her head and folded against Micah's chest. "I don't know anymore. I just don't know."

All Firemaker cared about was that the colonel lay on his back on the parlor floor in his own blood. There was no white man's surgeon at the fort, not for birthing babies, and not for filling bullet holes in men.

"I can't think," Matt Graham snapped, clutching his hair with his fists. "The colonel's half-dead. The major's out with the patrol. I'm the ranking lieutenant."

Mary's eyes were huge with anguish. She nuzzled her baby's downy head. "Do as your conscience dictates, darling."

Straightening, Matt scowled down at Firemaker, who stood in his parlor with imploring eyes. "Very well. I hereby authorize the release of any and all Comanche prisoners who want to return to the mountains. It's a pointless journey, for they'll just be captured again in a year or two. But for now let them go. Let the record show I saw

Carter Machesney's horse shot dead a moment ago after a killing run back from the mountains, testament that the man is Snakehorn's prisoner. In hopes of sparing his life, I take this action."

Not one half-dressed trooper standing in the crowded parlor disagreed.

"Carter left horses for them Comanches, sir," one of the troopers put in.

"They'll need supplies, too, Mattie," Mary added.

Matt turned to Micah. "Find out how many want to go and how many want to stay, to move onto the reservation. Firemaker, tell them it'll be a hard winter in the mountains. If they go, they'll be hunted down later—don't tell them that. We'll never get Carter back. Did they . . . did he . . ."

Firemaker didn't stop to explain how easily Carter had been taken prisoner. "Thank you," she said, darting out the door. She had too much to do. "Thank you."

Matt waved Micah after her. "Carter's got a lot of horses here, Johnson. Load all the supplies you can find onto them. I don't think a wagon can make it where they're going. And I don't think the colonel would appreciate me giving one away." He turned to another trooper. "Keep me posted as to the colonel's condition." He pinned another with clear eyes. "Send word to Fort Kirby of what's happened. Get a doctor here right away. And a replacement for the colonel. I want to be relieved of this responsibility as soon as possible."

Mary hugged his arm. Matt's mouth curved slightly upward. For the first time in his life, he felt like a man.

Carter knew Snakehorn the moment he saw the man. Even though Snakehorn was confined to a pallet in a lean-to far less comfortable than the one Firemaker had made for them the night before, the dying war chief still looked like a formidable foe. His snakeskin headdress sported an openmouthed, fanged rattler's skull between crossed snake rattles resembling horns. Even dull-eyed and listless, he looked savage, as deadly as any snake.

Many years before Snakehorn's face had been ravaged by smallpox. His copper-colored cheeks were badly pitted. Though he wasn't a particularly tall man, his frame was bulky, his arms and legs that of a once-powerful horseman.

But his cheeks now bore the hollow mark of near starvation. His hair was matted. He couldn't find the strength to utter a word. Even his great malice toward the conquering white man was hooded and dimmed.

Carter found it difficult to determine just where Snakehorn's wound was located. The man's lower body looked swollen almost beyond belief, and the stench was terrific. It was only a matter of minutes now before he died. Surely no man could go on living with so much gangrenous poison saturating his system.

Around Carter stood the warriors, not so fierce without war paint. They looked hungry, tired, and disheartened. Some of them were already tearing into his pack mules' food stores. One had brought down a deer while they marched toward the pit. The smell of roasting venison was making everyone glance more toward the raging campfire now than at Snakehorn, the dying war chief.

Snakehorn himself looked as if he cared little who Carter was, or for what reason he'd been brought to their isolated camp. Getting the Comanche women and children back was a mere formality now, but Carter worried Firemaker would never find her way here. He had never seen a mountain hideaway more remote.

Any number of accidents might have already befallen her, too, he thought, maddened to be such a small player in this game of life and death. Carter's only comforting thought was the fact that one of the warriors had argued long and hard with the fierce young leader to go back, presumably to make sure that the Comanche women and children actually were freed as promised. What would happen after they left the fort, Carter could only guess.

Carter had no doubt that Firemaker would effect their release. He could picture her tearing Jed Chiswell to pieces to extract the order. He just hoped she'd be able to come back for him.

He was smiling, imagining Firemaker doing battle with Jed, when he realized Snakehorn was watching him with those black, half-dead eyes. Carter's expression was apparently insulting, for all at once the Comanche warriors were hollering at him, prodding him toward the leaping flames of the campfire, gesturing with violence.

This was not so very different from being captured by Yankees, Carter reminded himself, keeping that infuriating smirk on his lips. If he was going to die, he thought, he was going to go honoring Firemaker with his courage.

He was but a man, but he was a man in love now. That love gave him courage he had never before possessed. He faced the Comanches unafraid. Even if he never saw Firemaker again, there was always that next world she talked about. Carter was certain Firemaker would have ridden Lonesome to death to get back to the fort. He'd have his horse in the next life. His father and brothers would be waiting. . . . And his mother. Perhaps one day Firemaker would join him.

The Comanches were dancing all around him, shouting, prodding, getting no response. Carter felt apart from himself, safe from the pain he expected would soon be inflicted on his body. He would die with Firemaker's name on his lips.

When they pushed him backward, he fell almost as slowly as a feather, down, down, down into a pit as dark as anything he had ever known during the war. Landing hard on his back, with his wind knocked out, Carter was able to hear a soft, ominous rattle not two feet from his head.

* * *

Preparations for the people's journey back to the mountains and freedom were well under way by three that morning. Firemaker spared no time to visit with Mary. She gave no thought to Corinna, whimpering on the fringes of her concern. She took the colonel's own pacer from the stables, mounted him bareback, and galloped out of the fort into the frigid darkness.

The animal was fresh and strong and thundered into the waning light with gratifying speed. Firemaker was just rounding the curve near the darkened First National Saloon when a shadowy figure sprang from the side of the road, causing the pacer to rear and paw the air.

Firemaker was thrown and landed hard on the road on her right shoulder. Pain exploded where a rock cut into her muscles, but her thoughts went immediately to the sound of the horse galloping into the night without her.

Giving out with a savage shriek of impatience, Firemaker found herself battling a broad-shouldered, sandy-haired whore dog she knew only too well by feel and by smell. Where had he come from?

"By damn," Clay Burdette hissed, bashing his face into hers in lieu of a kiss. "I thought that might be you. . . . I got somethin' for you, bitch."

She didn't have to think. She didn't think to hesitate. She went limp for only a fraction of a second, enough time to catch Clay off guard. He settled against her, pressing her into the cold, hard road with all his weight. He started to chuckle.

But Clay Burdette, drunk and shot once in the back of his left thigh a while ago at the colonel's backdoor, was no match for Firemaker bent on returning to the mountains. She appeared to curl to the side in a kind of defensive posture. She offered no resistance as Clay's hands began to roam her body.

"This is better than I hoped for," he murmured.

Autumn Blaze

In less time than it took to draw a deep, strength-giving breath, Firemaker had Carter's jackknife drawn from her moccasin. With precision known only to a huntress, she jabbed, feeling the knife blade sink deep into the chest of the man squirming atop her like a giggling schoolboy.

Clay's eyes widened. Looking puzzled and disbelieving, he made a small grunt. Twisting her wrist, she shoved her fist deeper, harder, finally slamming the knife handle with her palm. "I . . . am . . . *Comanche,*" she seethed through her teeth, feeling a gush of warm blood wash her hand in a life-draining cascade.

Clay was dying even as she pushed him aside and scrambled up from beneath his twitching body.

The pacer had started back toward her. Shedding her blood-soaked woolen coat, wiping her hand on the lining so as not to alarm the horse with the smell, she gathered up his halter and shinnied onto his back.

"Run," she whispered, heeling the horse to a full gallop. This horse would not slow again until he could breathe no more.

TWENTY-THREE

FIREMAKER WOKE TO silence. Her back was cold. Every muscle in her body burned. Her throat was parched and raw. She stared mindlessly into the glowing red-gold embers of a small, smoky campfire, wondering where she was.

Unsure if she had abandoned the colonel's pacer to exhaustion somewhere in the mountains or fallen from him, she realized she'd found her way back to the camp and the lean-to-style tepee.

She was alive, but barely. Her arm felt trembly and weak as she dragged a slim branch onto the fire and blew softly until tiny yellow flames leaped to life. For a long moment she hummed to the uncertain flames, drawing what strength she could from them.

Her stomach cramped with hunger, but they'd left no food within the lean-to or outside. Taking stock of herself, Firemaker wondered if she had enough strength remaining to find Snakehorn's pit, where the rattlers lived. In snow, it might be impossible to find.

Momentarily a sense of defeat swept over her. She was only one woman, she thought. She'd done all she could to free the People. She'd even been forced to kill, and for that the horse soldiers might eventually hang her.

But for the moment she was free to face her future as a white woman with a Comanche heart. The uncertainty of that future left her feeling more afraid than ever in her life. The hereafter held more familiar perils.

Then she thought of Carter. She thought of how he had looked, calmly joining the haggard, short-tempered Comanche warriors, facing a fate neither he nor she could imagine. He had done it for the future safety of the homesteaders in Texas, but Firemaker also knew he'd done it for her as atonement for leading the soldiers to Snakehorn's hiding place. And he'd done it because he loved her.

The wind snaking in between the gaps suddenly seemed less biting. She felt less tired. Fixing her thoughts on Carter's smile, on his warm, giving hands, on his kind, gentle brown eyes, she found she was able to get to her feet and stand without falling.

The padding in her moccasins had served well to protect her feet and toes from the freezing snow. The layers of clothing Mary had insisted she wear had saved her in the night.

Momentarily she stared at her right hand and the dried blood in every tiny crevice of her skin. She had no remorse for taking the whore dog's life, but she would not kill again. There had to be a better way to survive.

She longed for a world where death was not her companion, where the white men and red could live on the same lands without war. She longed for harmony, love, family, and singing. She would walk now toward that dream until her heart stopped.

She found the strength to step out into the cold. She was free, free to find Carter. He was her North Star.

Taking down part of the lean-to, she wrapped herself in one of the blankets and started out. The day had dawned clear. The sun glinted blindingly off a half foot of snow. She could see that the soldiers had passed that way, perhaps the evening before, missing the lean-to completely.

Following their tracks, she soon came to the clearing where they had spent the night. She found and devoured scorched biscuits that had been thrown into the snow. It was her first meal in more than twenty-four hours.

Strengthened, she pressed on until, three hours later she saw the soldiers plodding wearily up the trail ahead of her, five hundred feet up, picking their way higher and higher toward the timberline.

Looking back to the east, Firemaker could see across the entire valley. The fort was but a gray smudge in the newly fallen snow. The road leading past it was a fragile crooked line like those drawn on Carter's maps in faded ink. For the first time Firemaker visualized the world, vast and bewildering, and herself as an insignificant speck. Surely there was some small place for her in it.

At that moment there was no way for her to know if the People had successfully left the fort the night before. If they had, they were well into the canyon by now, possibly even joined by one of the warriors sent to watch for them.

She realized she might never know how any of them fared, for if they were wise, they would disappear into the depths of the Sangre de Cristo Mountains, where even she would never find them.

Feeling a strange kind of sadness, Firemaker realized she was also filled with relief. Sometime during her desperate ride through the night, the Great Spirit had lifted the black mountain of responsibility from her shoulders. Once again the Tall Horse Comanches belonged to themselves, to live or die as they chose.

She straightened, breathing in great gasps of icy mountain air. Even if she must go on alone, even if she never found her love again, she thought, she was richer for having known Carter Machesney. And the People.

Having sighted Firemaker on the trail behind them, the soldiers ahead paused while she hobbled closer. Upon reaching the major, she explained all that had happened since she had left the fort with Carter and her father three days before. "Go back now," she said. "Making no more war."

"Sorry, miss, but I got my orders to bring back Snakehorn. Dead or alive," the major said. "I'm not leaving these mountains till I do just that."

If she'd had a weapon left, and strength, she would have killed him, too. Then she remembered her promise to herself. She looked up at the man, trying to convey the uselessness of this fighting between the children of the Great Spirit and God's world. She appealed silently to his inner spirit.

He began to squirm. "I guess I could leave most of the men behind to rest while a detachment went on with you as our guide," he said.

Nodding, she started out. One of the men offered his horse to her, and she stopped a moment to frown up at him in puzzled gratitude. She concluded not all horse soldiers were whore dogs, only those found in stockades, perhaps.

By dusk, Firemaker and the major and six volunteers had ridden to the summit. The weary horses were wading through foot-deep snow, past craggy granite outcroppings to a place where it was clear the Comanches had camped for some time.

Firemaker climbed down from her horse, her heart in her throat. Where was Carter?

The place was deserted, undisguised, desolate.

Firemaker saw evidence of a once-large campfire that had burned itself out over many hours, leaving a great snowless black circle in the midst of the clearing. Nothing remained but ashes.

Footprints indicated hours of dancing. Bare patches of ground showed where the shelters had stood around the perimeter. Smashed tins and torn packs lying about indicated Carter's mules had given up all provisions.

"Look up there, Major," one of the men called, pointing

to a rock formation where a snow-covered body lay facing the sky.

Firemaker's arms prickled. "Four Toes," she whispered, able now to feel the first pangs of grief for her Comanche father. Now she must speak to her father only in her heart. She found him there, lending her courage and comfort, but she was sad just the same.

Where was Carter?

Another trooper pointed to a table rock where a large snow-dusted buffalo robe covered what was unmistakably a body. The major tried to hold Firemaker back.

She flung off his hand and threw herself across the body, tearing back the long-furred hide. Her heart leaped as she stared into the fangs of a rattler-skull headdress. The death stench made her stomach heave as she reared back.

But it was not Carter.

Giving a cry of relief mixed with anguish, she fell away and threw her arms around herself to keep from flying to the four winds.

Where was he?

"Is that Snakehorn?" the major asked, staring balefully down at the sunken, pox-scarred cheeks.

The wind teased the long, tangled black hair. The stench of the poisoned body drove the curious soldiers back. The major recovered him and hurried away to confer with the others.

Giving only half her attention and a brief nod, Firemaker returned to examining the signs around the snowy camp. Someone had come into it from the back route, the spotter perhaps, who had been watching for the freed women and children leaving the fort. There was evidence of a sudden, hurried departure. They'd taken the mules and thirteen horses and gone around to a trail she was certain led down to the canyon.

"Where'd they go?" the major asked, watching Firemaker grow more and more anxious.

"Gone," she said flatly. "Gone. No more."

She went on searching. Carter's body could be anywhere. She saw no stakes, no sharpened sticks, no blood in the snow. Wanting to shriek with frustration, she suddenly remembered. The pit. Snakehorn had said it was hidden but easily accessible.

Scowling ferociously at the rocks jutting all around like angry walls, she noted that the only boot prints she'd seen had nearly been covered by the prints of circling moccasins. Carter had not left the camp . . . at least not with his boots on.

On all fours, Firemaker crept toward a narrow crevice banked by rocks. Peering down into the darkness, she heard a strange sound, but not the rattling of snakes' tails. At this time of the year, snakes were no danger. It was too cold for them to be moving about.

She heard snoring.

EPILOGUE

Texas

FOREVERMORE THE SOUND of Carter's snoring would bring Firemaker comfort and peace. As the Texas countryside rolled by outside the window, and the stagecoach rocked in all directions at once, Firemaker smiled.

Carter was beside her, snoring. He was alive and well. And he had asked her to marry him. She had said yes.

Instead of facing a frightening unknown, she felt the future opening before her, exciting and filled with possibilities.

Spreading her hands over her skirt, her smile became thoughtful. Corinna had been unwilling to return home with her. "You and Ma . . . you get to know each other without me. I'll be along later."

But Corinna had presented Firemaker with one of her traveling dresses. They had sat for a time together at Mary Graham's, talking.

"I don't know if I'll ever get used to you," Corinna had said. "You're not anything like I imagined you'd be. I have to admit you seem to be a good person. I'm sorry if I've . . . All I can say is, if you go to Ma, you've got to stay with her awhile. Don't go off to college or something, leaving her alone. I want a life of my own now. Micah's asked for my hand. It's too soon to know for sure if I should marry him, but I think I might. If I do, I've got to know there's somebody looking after Ma."

"Ma," Firemaker had said, testing the name of Jane White Mother. "Mama."

She and Corinna had parted more friends than enemies. Firemaker was certain she would see her sister again someday, if for no other reason than to see her goddaughter, Amanda Corinna Graham.

After digging the bullet out of the colonel's shoulder, the fort barber had said around his chaw of tobacco. "If this damn fool lives, I'll ask for a transfer."

But after regaining consciousness, Jed left Matt Graham in command. Though most attributed his thoughtful, mellowed mood to his injury, everyone agreed Jed Chiswell seemed different. For one thing, he asked for no more bourbon. For another, he seemed glad to hear his Comanche prisoners had been freed.

An informal inquiry determined Firemaker had killed Clay Burdette in self-defense. Since no one doubted Clay's murderous intentions in shooting Jed and Olivia Chiswell that terrible night, Matt Graham had no difficulty closing the case.

Olivia Chiswell could now be found at her husband's side, showing a devotion—and an ostentatious arm sling—that bordered on convincing.

The Comanche women and children had vanished. Though weak and sick, none had chosen to remain behind and take up a new life on the reservation in the Oklahoma Territory. With them they'd taken enough supplies to last several months. And all Carter Machesney's Texas horses.

Four Toes' body still lay on the outcropping over the snake pit in the mountains, but Snakehorn's body had been packed in snow and returned to the fort as proof of the colonel and major's success. After the making of photographs of his body, the news of his death was telegraphed across the southwestern theater. There was celebration at two dozen forts across the land.

Except for bruises and thirst, Carter had been no worse for the wear after spending a night in the snake pit with a thousand sleeping rattlers. Once he was pulled up, he wanted to forget the ordeal and move on. He was intent on telling Firemaker of his plans for the trip to Texas that he'd made while lying there.

"I think the Comanches were too tired to kill me," he told everyone, snatching Firemaker to his chest and hugging her. "Thank you for coming for me. I got mighty hungry. I've had my fill of falling in holes, I can tell you that." He seemed a little different, too.

Firemaker had kissed him in front of a half-dozen gawking troopers and laughed as she cried for joy. "You good man, Carter Machesney. I am loving you very big much."

He'd tangled his fingers in her flowing whitey-blond hair. "I feel like the luckiest man alive to have you."

Now they were an hour out of West Creek Fork. Her corset wasn't too tight; Corinna's dresses weren't stitched as small as Olivia's, but Firemaker was certain she would never tolerate the wearing of shoes. The pins holding her hat on were pulling her hair. Her fingers felt stiff, encased in snug kid gloves. Even her skin felt tight with anticipation.

The ride across Texas had been wearisome, yet fascinating. Firemaker could scarcely wait to see all of this place called the United States. Already she'd seen a few towns, and they were overwhelming. Carter had told her of tall ships that sailed for weeks across a vast water, and not so very far away was the iron-horse railroad he was sure she would want to see.

With a snort, Carter woke and blinked at her. He lifted his head from her jostling shoulder. "I dreamed I was an eagle, soaring. When did our fellow passenger get out?" he asked, speaking of a traveler they'd bumped knees with for two hundred miles. He rubbed his face and stretched, thrilling her with a glance that said he would be making love with her again very soon.

With great ceremony, Firemaker pulled Carter's pocket watch from her reticule. He'd given it to her to study. She frowned at the tiny numerals, shook the watch, and then put it to her ear. "Three hours," she said, still convinced there was a tiny spirit inside the case, ticking.

Carter grinned. "Very good."

Carter didn't know that inside her reticule was also a piece of flint, a wooden figurine of a bear, and the paws of a bobcat. She missed the jackknife, but Matt had refused to return it to her. She intended to get another.

She was Amanda Tamberlay now, but always the Firemaker would live inside her, smoldering with the spirit of the Tall Horse Comanches and the once-great Four Toes.

Around her neck hung the locket, too, still tied to a thong. She wrapped trembling fingers around it. Now was the time to face her white mother, the woman whose spirit had lived in her even before Four Toes changed her life from white to red.

"Are you getting nervous?" Carter asked softly.

Firemaker nodded. "Big nervous."

"Very nervous," he corrected.

"Very big nervous," she agreed, cocking her brow at him, letting him know she understood quite well what she'd said.

He laughed. "I love you . . . Amanda. We're almost there."

Carter had asked the driver to stop at the place where the Tamberlay ranch had once been. A few moments later the coach rolled past a vast sea of buffalo grass and came to a stop. Carter got out and pointed. In the distance was a bit of corral fence showing above the grass, and the remains of a shack.

Firemaker pictured her mother there, holding a baby wearing that long white dress. She imagined Four Toes a young warrior, his brother who had died that day, and eight others, topping the western ridge.

Moments later they were on their way again. When they rolled into West Creek Fork and debarked at the depot, few people were on the streets. It was a brisk, windy day, with a partly cloudy sky.

Carter took Firemaker to Ed Keener's livery, and there they saw the leathery-faced man inside, currying a horse. When Ed looked up and saw them standing in the doorway, silhouetted by the sunlight outside, he squinted. "Corinna?" he called out. "You back so soon?"

He started toward them. Two feet from the door, Ed Keener stopped. It was Corinna's dress Firemaker was wearing. Her hair and build were similar to her sister's, he seemed to be thinking, studying the strange young woman before him. Then Ed's head tilted down and forward. He squinted and scratched his hair.

"I'll be damned," he said.

Firemaker found her heart pounding. Was this her . . .

"This man used to work with your father," Carter quickly said, seeing Firemaker's confusion. "And he's your mother's friend."

"I'm more than a friend," Ed put in, a grin spreading across his face. "I'll be marrying Janie if she'll just have me. Well, now, Mandie, I don't hardly know what to say to you. Welcome home." His face nearly glowed. He thrust his hand toward her. "Welcome home."

Feeling light-headed, Firemaker shook his hand like a man. "Ma?" she asked. "Mama?"

"Lemme get us a rig, and I'll drive us up."

Since early morning Jane had had an intense desire to rock on the porch. She'd intended to wait for Ed to come up for supper and take the rocker out for her, but the urge now overtook her.

By herself she struggled to get the parlor rocker out the front door. The wind was brisk and turning cold. She could almost hear Corinna in her imagination, scolding her for risking her health. If she couldn't risk her health, watching for Mandie's return, Jane thought, why have her health at all?

And, Jane realized with a pang of sadness, she missed Corinna. She'd done wrong by the girl and wanted to make up for it. She wondered if she ever could.

Bringing a shawl and a lap robe, Jane settled onto the rocker and stared toward the west. She remembered so many days and nights in the past when she'd rocked and watched and waited.

She hadn't heard from Carter Machesney in weeks now. She'd received not a word from Corinna since her departure. She had a feeling she would never see Hugh again, but didn't know why.

It was odd, she thought, rocking slowly, to have her own aging ma back in Kentucky come to mind at a time like this. In more than twenty years she hadn't gone home to see her. She didn't want her ma to know just how badly she'd been hurt by those Comanches.

But suddenly the prospect of going home didn't seem so impossible. If Corinna could accept her scars, and if Ed could love her, perhaps . . .

Though it was early for Ed to be coming up the road, Jane saw his buckboard wagon turning in from town. She felt so happy to see him, tears sprang to her eyes. He loved her. She could still scarcely believe it.

Two people were on the seat with him.

Jane's fingertips began to tingle. Her breath went out. She squinted with her good eye, trying not to get her hopes up. Folks had started calling since Corinna's departure. It might be only more of them, eager to show her a kindness now that she was willing to accept it.

Something told Jane they weren't callers.

Jane would've gotten to her feet, but her body went limp. Her head began whirling. The sound of an urgent, rushing wind filled her ears, whispering thoughts too jumbled to make sense. Her hands opened and closed as if by themselves.

Her eyes riveted on the woman sitting between the two men on the buckboard's seat. In moments they were stopped outside the gate. Ed jumped down and opened the gate. The other man, whom Jane recognized as the young Texas Ranger, jumped down on the far side and handed down the girl who was wearing Corinna's traveling dress.

Jane's heart shivered. It was Corinna, she thought, watching the young woman round the buckboard and start through the gate. She was back and Mandie wasn't . . .

But then Jane saw that the woman walked with an unfamiliar, catlike grace. The woman was frowning as Corinna was often wont to do, but it was a frown of concentration rather than bitterness. Like a wildcat stalking prey, the woman came forward with her pale eyes fixed unblinkingly on Jane.

It was not Corinna, Jane thought, her heart shivering to a stop. Jane's hands flexed, opened, closed. She couldn't catch her breath. She felt cold all over. The memory of Comanche warriors whooping all around gave her the feeling that she was in a living dream.

At the bottom step, the young woman looked up at her, her pale, gray-blue eyes quick all over Jane's face, on her hairpiece, on her shawl-covered shoulders, on her blanket-covered lap, back to the face so hauntingly faded inside the locket.

She started up the steps, closer and closer, until Jane

could see the pale whitey blond of her hair. It was the same color as what was left of her own.

Though she still couldn't move, Jane devoured her firstborn daughter's grown face with starving eyes. There was clearly a shadow of Hugh's features in the shape of her cheekbones and jaw. She had the color of Hugh's eyes, but her mouth was Jane's. And the hair . . . the hair was Jane's, lovely and escaping in glistening sunlit tendrils from around the edges of an old traveling hat.

"Mama?" The young woman's husky voice was soft, almost childlike. She pulled her hat off, releasing a cascade of pale hair across her shoulders.

A shudder of fulfillment rippled through Jane's body like quicksilver. Her child's voice . . . Her child's silky hair.

A warm hand slipped into one of Jane's flexing hands. Another warm hand closed around them both, lending comfort, lending strength. Jane felt a delicious sense of relaxation spread through her body. The wait was over. The wait was over. The wait was . . .

But Mandie was so much like Corinna, nothing like that plump not-yet-walking infant Jane had lost so long ago. There was a sudden stab of sadness in realizing nothing would bring back those years forever lost. All that she might have gained by paying attention to Corinna during her childhood had been lost, too.

Jane's throat hurt with unshed remorse. If only . . .

The young woman, who looked so much like Corinna, was studying her reaction. "Mmm," she said thoughtfully. "You great warrior, Jane White Mother."

Jane forgot the lost years and focused on the strong, handsome young woman before her. And her strange words. The sadness began to fade.

"Many coups with the Comanche man, Mama. You great warrior. My father, Four Toes, cutting on . . ." She made a slashing mark across her chest in the very direction Jane recalled slicing the Comanche warrior who had seized her twenty years before. "Strong woman, you. Great warrior."

Jane almost wanted to laugh hysterically. Her daughter sounded like . . . She was a Comanche!

Then the young woman smoothed her hand along Jane's scarred temple. Her touch felt like a soothing salve, penetrating to ease the confusing whirl of thoughts in Jane's mind. The trembling fingertips gently probed the hairless scalp. Never had Jane allowed anyone to touch her there.

Nodding, the young woman stood, still holding Jane's cold, shaking hands in her own warm ones. She drew Jane to her feet.

Then, embracing her mother, Amanda Jane Tamberlay returned the love to her mother that had sustained her for twenty years. Firemaker felt the power of her mother's heart beating against her own.

Within her lived the spirit of this courageous white woman, Firemaker thought, and with it the spirit of a proud, old Comanche warrior. Firemaker knew in that moment she didn't have to choose between the shattered parts of herself, casting away one half for another. She could be her whole self, a blend of two powerful races.

Standing back to look into her mother's wide eyes, Firemaker pulled the thong, hanging around her neck, over her head. She showed the locket hanging from it to her mother and whispered, "Ma."

Jane Tamberlay began to laugh. Tears flowed from eyes that had been dry twenty years.

Mandie-Firemaker-Amanda Tamberlay reached back to draw Carter closer. Ed Keener moved in close, too. Jane Tamberlay closed weary eyes.

The flame of Jane's anger, burning in the darkness, had lived long enough to change to the living fire of love, burning in the light. And Mandie Tamberlay was home again.

NATIONAL BESTSELLING AUTHOR

Katherine Sutcliffe
MY ONLY LOVE

"Romantic, exciting...memorable characters and delightful surprises."—Linda Lael Miller, *New York Times* bestselling author of *Daniel's Bride*

Her passionate nature and secretive past made Olivia Devonshire one of the most notorious women in England. Miles Warwick was a disreputable rogue, the black sheep of his family. But he never gambled on losing his heart to the woman he married for money...

__0-515-11074-4/$5.99 *(On sale April 1993)*

For Visa, MasterCard and American Express ($15 minimum) orders call: **1-800-631-8571**

FOR MAIL ORDERS: CHECK BOOK(S). FILL OUT COUPON. SEND TO:

BERKLEY PUBLISHING GROUP
390 Murray Hill Pkwy., Dept. B
East Rutherford, NJ 07073

NAME_____
ADDRESS_____
CITY_____
STATE_____ ZIP_____

PLEASE ALLOW 6 WEEKS FOR DELIVERY.
PRICES ARE SUBJECT TO CHANGE WITHOUT NOTICE.

POSTAGE AND HANDLING:
$1.75 for one book, 75¢ for each additional. Do not exceed $5.50.

BOOK TOTAL	$ ____
POSTAGE & HANDLING	$ ____
APPLICABLE SALES TAX (CA, NJ, NY, PA)	$ ____
TOTAL AMOUNT DUE	$ ____

PAYABLE IN US FUNDS.
(No cash orders accepted.)

434

If you enjoyed this book, take advantage of this special offer. Subscribe now and...

Get a Historical

No Obligation

If you enjoy reading the very best in historical romantic fiction...romances that set back the hands of time to those bygone days with strong virile heros and passionate heroines ...then you'll want to subscribe to the True Value Historical Romance Home Subscription Service. Now that you have read one of the best historical romances around today, we're sure you'll want more of the same fiery passion, intimate romance and historical settings that set these books apart from all others.

Each month the editors of True Value select the four *very best* novels from America's leading publishers of romantic fiction. We have made arrangements for you to preview them in your home *Free* for 10 days. And with the first four books you receive, we'll send you a FREE book as our introductory gift. No Obligation!

FREE HOME DELIVERY

We will send you the four best and newest historical romances as soon as they are published to preview FREE for 10 days (in many cases you may even get them before they arrive in the book stores). If for any reason you decide not to keep them, just return them and owe nothing. But if you like them as much as we think you will, you'll pay just $4.00 each and save at *least* $.50 each off the cover price. (Your savings are *guaranteed* to be at least $2.00 each month.) There is NO postage and handling—or other hidden charges. There are no minimum number of books to buy and you may cancel at any time.

FREE Romance

(a $4.50 value)

Send in the Coupon Below

To get your FREE historical romance and start saving, fill out the coupon below and mail it today. As soon as we receive it we'll send you your FREE Book along with your first month's selections.

Mail To: **True Value Home Subscription Services, Inc. P.O. Box 5235
120 Brighton Road, Clifton, New Jersey 07015-5235**

YES! I want to start previewing the very best historical romances being published today. Send me my FREE book along with the first month's selections. I understand that I may look them over FREE for 10 days. If I'm not absolutely delighted I may return them and owe nothing. Otherwise I will pay the low price of just $4.00 each: a total $16.00 (at *least* an $18.00 value) and save at least $2.00. Then each month I will receive four brand new novels to preview as soon as they are published for the same low price. I can always return a shipment and I may cancel this subscription at any time with no obligation to buy even a single book. In any event the FREE book is mine to keep regardless.

Name		
Street Address		Apt. No.
City	State	Zip Code
Telephone		
Signature		

(if under 18 parent or guardian must sign)

Terms and prices subject to change. Orders subject to acceptance by True Value Home Subscription Services, Inc.

853

*NO MAN AND WOMAN HAD EVER HATED SO
FIERCELY... AND LOVED SO RECKLESSLY...*

RECKLESS

Anna Jennet

As wild and beautiful as her fiery Scottish heritage, Ailis faced the torment of marriage to a man she despised. Then without warning, she was kidnapped by her worst enemy...

As strong and brutally handsome as he was arrogant, Alexander plotted against her beloved family. Now Ailis was his to use for revenge...

__1-55773-865-3/$4.99 (March 1993)

For Visa, MasterCard and American Express ($15 minimum) orders call: 1-800-631-8571

FOR MAIL ORDERS: CHECK BOOK(S). FILL OUT COUPON. SEND TO:	POSTAGE AND HANDLING: $1.75 for one book, 75¢ for each additional. Do not exceed $5.50.
BERKLEY PUBLISHING GROUP 390 Murray Hill Pkwy., Dept. B East Rutherford, NJ 07073	BOOK TOTAL $ ____
NAME_____	POSTAGE & HANDLING $ ____
ADDRESS_____	APPLICABLE SALES TAX $ ____ (CA, NJ, NY, PA)
CITY_____	TOTAL AMOUNT DUE $ ____
STATE_____ ZIP_____	PAYABLE IN US FUNDS.
PLEASE ALLOW 6 WEEKS FOR DELIVERY. PRICES ARE SUBJECT TO CHANGE WITHOUT NOTICE.	(No cash orders accepted.)